THE DOCTO

ISBN 978-1-64456-553-7 [Hardcover]
ISBN 978-1-64456-554-4 [Paperback]
ISBN 978-1-64456-555-1 [Mobi]
ISBN 978-1-64456-556-8 [ePub]

Library of Congress Control Number: 2022948083

INDIES UNITED PUBLISHING HOUSE, LLC
P.O. BOX 3071
QUINCY, IL 62305-3071
indiesuited.net

Stroud, your strength and love keep me going.
This is for you.

THE DOCTOR'S WIFE

MYRA HARGRAVE McILVAIN

INDIES UNITED PUBLISHING HOUSE, LLC

Chapter One

Dear Papa and Helga, doors open and close...

November 5, 1845

The ship's gangplank slid into the fog obscuring the Galveston dock. Amelia Anton scooped Frau Regina von Ewald up in her arms, practically carrying the grieving woman as they made their way down the narrow wood walkway onto the pier. Herr von Ewald ignored them both, shoving ahead to the waiting carriage. The hood of Amelia's cape protected her blonde braids from the chill and offered a hidden place from which to stare at black men who appeared and disappeared into the mist, heaving bales of cotton off a nearby freight wagon. The heavy air muted their slow work song and sweat drenched their ragged clothing, even in the bone-aching cold. Southern slavery—as described in the immigrant guidebooks—had been one of her first lessons for her pupil, young Otto.

The boy's papa, Amelia's turnip-shaped employer, clambered into the enclosed carriage without turning back to look for his wife, the dear lady responsible for Amelia being hired. Her reason for being in this strange land—as the boy's private tutor—had died along with her student. Amelia, shuddering at the thought that she may have made a huge mistake, pulled her cape tight against her body and glanced through the back window of the carriage toward the mournful sound of slaves, invisible in the white haze.

The three of them rode in silence, squeezed into the lurching coach, its wheels making slushing sounds in the rutted street. Freight wagons clanked past and coarse voices shouted commands in English. From under her hood, Amelia watched Herr von Ewald, aspiring merchant prince, staring sullenly at the faded, low-slung buildings, so different from his family's sprawling estate. Was he hating his older brother for inheriting the family fortune? For sending him to seek his own way in Texas? He leaned forward expectantly when the Tremont House, a broad white expanse hugging the mud street, loomed out of the fog. Black men dressed in spotless white uniforms stood on each side of double doors. Herr von Ewald, who had ignored Amelia throughout the three-month ocean voyage, turned toward her, "If they can't speak German, you'll have to get us registered." He bolted into the hotel, ignoring his wife.

Dear Papa and Helga, all the months speaking English may be about to pay off. Amelia clenched her jaw and stepped from the carriage without waiting for von Ewald's instructions. She laid her hand on Frau von Ewald's shoulder as the doormen gently lifted the trembling woman from the carriage.

"Amelia, come talk to these people," von Ewald shouted.

"Please move madam into the hotel," she kept her voice low as she spoke to the doormen who averted their eyes as though they were not aware von Ewald was stomping up and down on the hotel's broad wood porch.

She lowered her head to avoid gazing like a peasant at the sprawling lobby circled by thick white columns. Candles lit a large chandelier hanging from the high ceiling. She nodded to the doormen who settled Frau von Ewald on a long red sofa.

"There you are, Stein," von Ewald bellowed. "Tell these people who I am."

Amelia turned to see Dr. Joseph Stein, the ship physician who had cared for Otto and for his mama, rush through the hotel's broad front doors.

"I asked you not to leave the ship until I could join you." The doctor kept his voice low; his wiry black hair tousled as usual, his disheveled jacket hanging loose as he bent almost double to glare—eye level—at Herr von Ewald.

Amelia watched a thin man with slick black hair and a pencil-wide mustache rushing across the lobby, clasping his hands at his chest, and nodding at the two men. "Pardon me, gentlemen. I'm Oscar Wilhite, manager of the Tremont House."

Dr. Stein turned quickly and surprised Amelia by switching into perfect English, "We want to get Frau von Ewald settled very quickly."

Oscar Wilhite looked around like a man hoping something would happen to call him away from his difficult task. "Please explain to her husband that when a foreign ship comes in, we seclude our guests who are ill until we are sure they aren't carrying a contagious disease. You understand? It's just a precaution."

Amelia was torn between feeling sorry for the manager and wanting to laugh, as his eyes darted toward von Ewald, pacing the lobby like an over-heated bull.

"An isolated room will be fine. Please place her husband in separate quarters." Dr. Stein's brows rose, commanding the hotel manager's understanding. "She needs rest. And send for a local doctor. I want to arrange for her care before my ship sails in the morning for Indian Point."

Oscar Wilhite nodded, glancing toward von Ewald. Then, holding his head high—eyes avoiding the little German's angry gaze —he fled toward a door leading off the lobby.

Frau von Ewald's room was small, at the end of the hallway and on the backside of the hotel. The only window looked out on a narrow alley. A single straight-back chair sat next to a matching dark oak table supporting a porcelain bowl and pitcher. The dark bed frame towered above the frail woman.

Dr. Stein turned to Amelia. "Will you stay with her? You'll be in quarantine."

Quarantine? I thought the poor woman was dying of grief. Papa and Helga would be frantic. I don't know the first thing about caring for sick people. She sucked in a breath to compose herself. "Do you have to leave? She became so attached to you on the ship."

"I'm employed by the *Adelsverein* to travel with the immigrants all the way to Indian Point on Matagorda Bay. The noblemen who

3

organize these immigrant groups assure them that a physician will accompany each vessel. I'll stay with you as long as possible."

She turned to answer a soft knock at the door. A young black woman wearing a fluffy white cap and a white apron over a black dress nodded solemnly. "I'm Fannie, your chambermaid. I'll get what you need and bring you food." She stepped into the room, a tiny body with strong, over-sized hands folded at her waist, waiting for instructions.

Dr. Stein smiled at the chambermaid, the look in the giant man's eyes as gentle as when he had spoken to young Otto during his illness. "Please bring enough hot water for a mustard plaster." He nodded toward Amelia, "and hot tea for Fraulein Anton."

Just as Dr. Stein finished showing Amelia how to apply the mustard plaster to draw out toxins, a diminutive man with receding black hair, swept into the room. "I'm Dr. Ashbel Smith." He shook Dr. Stein's hand, peering all the while with piercing bead-eyes at Frau von Ewald. He bowed slightly to the chambermaid. "Good morning, Fannie. I'm glad you're here."

He appeared not to notice her curtsy as if she were greeting royalty. "I hear the patient came in on the brig *Johann Dethardt* from Bremen."

"She was our only sick passenger when we arrived early this morning," Dr. Stein said.

Dr. Smith gazed at Frau von Ewald's flushed face, murmuring softly, comforting the listless form. He turned abruptly, looked up at the towering doctor. "It's rare that we have an arrival from Germany with yellow fever. Did you come into another southern port?"

"A brief stop in New Orleans. Not even overnight."

"If it's yellow fever, we'll know soon enough. She's already very weak."

"She lost her only child at sea," Dr. Stein said.

Dr. Smith glanced sharply at Amelia, then turning to Dr. Stein, raised his chin like he was ready for an argument. "I'm convinced yellow fever's not contagious. Quarantining her is useless. I ate some of the black vomit several years ago. Didn't harm me in the least. Most people think I'm crazy. Many of them work at this hotel."

Dr. Stein clasped his hands behind his back, bending slightly at his waist, appearing unmoved by the doctor's revelation. "In

Germany, we've had no experience with yellow fever. What treatment, in addition to quinine and mustard plasters, do you recommend?"

"Quinine. Plenty of quinine to lower the fever, keep down the muscle aches. No sense bleeding her. She's too weak." Dr. Smith suddenly smiled. "I understand you're going on to Indian Point. Give my regards to Dr. Reuss and his bride. They married here last month. Made quite a stir in this hotel." He placed his hand on Frau von Ewald's head in a farewell gesture or maybe a blessing. Then, he strode from the room saying, "I'll check on the patient each day."

Fannie stared at the door through which the doctor had passed.

"You have great respect for Dr. Smith?" Amelia asked.

"He's the best doctor in the world. He saved me from yellow fever." Fannie's black eyes flashed with pride. "That's why I'm called to help. I'm immune."

Dr. Stein spent the afternoon pacing in long strides across the floor and smiling reassuringly at Amelia as she tried to follow his instructions. When he spoke, which was rare, his voice remained so low that she had to draw near. He had been the same nearly silent presence after little Otto died. Day after day he had stood beside Amelia and Frau von Ewald as she gripped the ship's railing where the boy's body had been lowered into the sea. For brief periods, as the ship's only doctor, he slipped away to care for other passengers. But he always returned to stand vigil with the grieving woman.

The evening grew late, and he motioned for Amelia to follow him into the hall. "I'm sorry to leave you alone. May I write to you?" He ducked his head and then stammered, "To inquire after your mistress."

"I'm happy to keep you informed."

"I hope to see you again," he backed away, then turning to leave, banged his black case into the wall as if the passageway had shrunk.

The hotel fell silent except for an occasional drunk stumbling down the alley. The first time one of them knocked a greeting on the shuttered window, Amelia had jumped, and Fannie rolled her eyes. "They won't hurt you. They'd like for you to return their knock, but if you do, they'll make it a game of tempting you to open the window and give them enough money for another bottle."

Amelia laughed. "The drunks in our village loved a good time."

I can never tell Papa and Helga that continuing to teach in our village's little school offered no better choice for a husband than Helga found in Max—a drunk who loves to have a good time, but can't hold a job—or one of the local peasants who will toil forever in the von Ewald's extensive fields.

Fannie had placed both candles near the bed offering plenty of light for Amelia to apply the mustard plasters and bathe Frau von Ewald's feverish body with cool rags. When Fannie returned with a fresh pitcher of water, she whispered, "I remember where it hurts to be touched. I'll lift her real easy, and you slip the spoon of quinine between her lips."

This is the closest I've ever been to black flesh. The skin on her face looks soft as warm chocolate. Amelia nodded and watched Fannie's calloused hands move with the gentleness of a feather around the whiteness of Frau's body.

"Fannie promises this quinine will help," her voice soothed like powder.

"Otto, where's Otto?" Frau's blue eyes, paled to a dull gray, searched a far off place.

"He's right here. Next to you." Amelia caressed the trembling fingers, then blew out one candle and watched the other fade to a flicker. She and Fannie worked in silence, applying cool rags without ever slowing the raging fever cooking its victim from the inside.

Light had crept through the shutters, casting a frame around the drawn face of their patient, and sending Fannie for a fresh pitcher of water. Herr von Ewald stuck his head in the door and quickly backed away. Amelia hurried into the hallway and called, "She needs to see you, sir."

He stopped and raised an eyebrow toward Amelia.

"She's calling for Otto. She needs you."

"I'll handle my affairs without your comments." He turned, and his bulk almost knocked Dr. Smith to the floor. *"Dummkopf,"* he snorted and rushed into the lobby.

"That fat man called me a blockhead," Dr. Smith announced, as he brushed past Amelia and stood in the center of the room, staring at his patient. "Continue making her as comfortable as possible."

"Is there nothing else I can do?"

"Expect the black vomit. Pray it doesn't last long."

"Fannie said you cured her of yellow fever."

"Fannie's different. She's young, and she's got mule strength. This lady started from a position of weakness. Probably why she was the only one on the ship to get sick." He walked to the bedside, bent over Frau von Ewald and murmured, "You are in good hands, madam."

"Otto? Is that Otto?"

Amelia clasped Frau von Ewald's hands. "Otto's right here. He's next to you."

She held these soft palms together as though offering a prayer to her husband, pleading with him to employ me. She said I was the village's best teacher, that I spoke English, that Pastor Anton had taught Helga and me to love the classics and religion. She said I would be a blessing. Amelia bent to kiss the fevered fingers. "Thank you, my lady."

Late that afternoon, just as a welcome streak of sunlight moved along the alley painting the room—for a moment—in its rosy glow, Frau von Ewald roused toward the light, her eyes searching, "Dr. Stein...." The gurgle began like a low moan that grew into convulsive retching. Amelia anchored the woman in her arms, steadying her as Fannie held the basin. The slimy black bile spilled from her lips in acrid gushes.

Father in Heaven, take this woman. Amelia cradled her lady and watched the room grow dark. She did not know when Fannie lit a candle and eased onto the other side of the bed to take the convulsing woman into her arms. The noises from deep inside had stopped, and her breath came in shallow, slowing gasps. Then, she heard Fannie's hoarse whisper, "Bless her soul; it's over."

Fannie came around the bed, clutching Amelia against hard little breasts, patting her like a baby as they both cried from exhaustion and relief.

"No reason that poor woman had to die with only you and me. Where's that good-for-nothing man?"

"Hiding somewhere. Afraid he'll get sick."

"If he does, I ain't taking care of him."

Amelia laughed, pulled away to sop at her tears and blow her nose on some of the clean rags. "Neither am I." *But what if I do have to care for him? I have no choice.*

She had assumed the tiny space on the backside of the hotel's first floor was hers, and that she would remain there after she and Fannie washed Frau von Ewald's skeletal body and dressed it for burial. Instead, before the graveside service, von Ewald sent one of the hotel slaves to announce that she would be moving across the alley to the servants' quarters.

The knock at the door that night was sharp, insistent, and well past the decent hour for an unannounced caller. Amelia held her candle high as she peered into the narrow hallway. The yellow light from Herr von Ewald's lantern made his smirk look almost menacing. His eyebrows rose sharply toward the smooth spot where hair had once grown. His pink jowls shook when he spoke.

"My dear Fraulein Anton, I've borne the expense of your passage from Germany. With the loss of my son Otto, I no longer need your tutoring services. The passing of my wife has freed me of all my obligations to you. I've secured passage on a riverboat at daybreak for Houston. From there I'm destined for my new mercantile business in the village of Industry."

Amelia leaned her slender frame against the door for support and stared down at the pudgy little man, trying to grasp what she was hearing.

He held up one finger, indicating that he had not finished. "Do not give in to self-pity, my dear, for I have spoken to the manager of this fine hotel. You are young and strong and will be well received as a chambermaid." Sucking in his breath, which caused his nostrils to flair like bellows, von Ewald waved the lantern toward a black man, more than a head taller than the German, standing in the shadows at rigid attention. She recognized the uniform of the Tremont House slaves. Light from the lantern made the man's black skin glow against his white linen jacket encrusted with gold epaulettes.

"This gentleman was kind enough to deliver my wife's travel trunk. You're a good fit for her clothing, even her slippers. Von Ewald stroked the goatee darkening his chin. I've left a token of my appreciation for your service."

"A token?" Amelia was disgusted to hear the tremble in her voice. She cleared her throat, and in a rush of fury over being cheated out of what she was due, she held up *her* finger. "Sir, you hired me to tutor your son. You said 100 Prussian Thalers a month and my keep."

I didn't listen when Papa reminded me that my teacher's pay was 400 Thalers. I was willing to accept anything to avoid living like Helga. Besides, the articles in all the newspapers quoted settlers raving about success in Texas. "I did not claim my pay on shipboard or after we reached Galveston. I thought you were too burdened over Otto's death and—"

"Report to the kitchen in the morning at 4:30. Good evening, Fraulein Amelia Anton. Do well in your new position." Wheeling away from her, Herr Gustav von Ewald practically bounced down the hall—a man freed of his last burden.

"Ma'am?" The uniformed slave bowed toward the glimmer of Amelia's candle. He slid Frau von Ewald's travel trunk into the room. His voice was a deep baritone. "I'll come in the morning to move your trunk to our chambermaids' quarters."

Amelia nodded. Was she supposed to curtsy?

The slave bowed again, his face a blank slate, as he backed into the darkness.

Amelia knelt beside the barrel-top trunk. Her fingers stroked the painted cluster of Alpine roses that Frau von Ewald had painted along the top and sides of her trunk, explaining that they would help her remember the beauty of her homeland. On shipboard, after Otto died, Amelia had had to look away when his mama retrieved something from the trunk and remained kneeling, caressing the image of the spring flowers.

Placing the dwindling candle high on the windowsill, she gently unpacked the little trunk. Frau von Ewald had followed the advice of the Adelsverein, the trip managers, and brought mostly practical clothing for the Texas heat—cotton dresses, white stockings, and work shoes for long days in her husband's new mercantile store. In the very bottom of the trunk lay the cotton suits selected for Otto, clothing he had never worn.

Her fingers curled around *Galopp*, Otto's horsehair pony that he slept with every night, tucked between them in their narrow upper berth. She clutched the stiff little horse to her lips.

She remembered that first day when Frau von Ewald brought Otto to meet her. He had stepped from the von Ewald's fine carriage, removed his narrow-brimmed hat, and bowed formally from his waist, a gesture that Amelia discovered his papa demanded Otto perform for every adult. "Good day, Fraulein Anton."

"Good day, Herr von Ewald." Amelia bent to one knee to offer Otto her greeting. "Your English is very good."

The boy smiled broadly and asked in German if that little house was where she lived.

"It is my *vater's* home. I live there with him."

"And where is your *mutter*?" Otto's brown eyes occupied most of his slender, white face.

"She has gone to live with our Heavenly Father."

"When?" Otto leaned close.

"She took ill last spring and died very quickly."

"Did you cry?"

"Yes. I still miss her very much."

Otto nodded, and with Amelia still facing him at eye level, he laid his hand on her shoulder. "I'll try not to make you cry. I'll be a good student."

She wanted to throw her arms around the serious little boy, but she sensed that affection would have to grow slowly with this child. "I am confident you will be an excellent student."

Chapter Two

You will never believe what chambermaids do…

The slave from last night, who said his name was James, knocked softly on her door. She was dressed for work as a chambermaid, although she had no idea what a chambermaid was expected to do.

"You go to the kitchen. I'll take your trunk to your new quarters." James smiled, and one gold tooth sparkled.

She stepped into the alley to find thousands of fiddler crabs making the mud look like it boiled. Shaking her skirt to knock away the grasping claws, she scurried through the sea of ugly little creatures and into the intense heat of the hotel's kitchen.

"You must be the new girl?" A large black woman smiled broadly, sweat beading her upper lip. "I'm Mary Van Dunn. Mr. Wilhite made me in charge of the kitchen because I'm experienced. Been cooking for white folks all my life."

"I'll be glad to help as best I can." Amelia held out her hand and pulled it back to her chest as Mary Van Dunn quickly turned her back.

"I ain't your boss. You be a chambermaid. Frau Beatrice is your boss."

She recognized Frau Beatrice the instant she stepped in the door. She was a wiry little German wearing the same uniform as Fannie— a black dress covered with a spotless white bib apron and a white cotton hat that bloused over her hair. But Frau Beatrice's hat was edged with a fringe of tatting.

"You're on time. *Gut.* We start early." She looked up at Mary Van Dunn and spoke in a commanding voice, "Mary Van Dunn will have breakfast ready. We go upstairs by five every morning."

"Yes, ma'am." Mary Van Dunn turned toward the giant iron stove and dipped into a black pot, filling a cup with something that looked like gruel.

After she served Frau Beatrice, the cook winked at Amelia. "It's grits. Tastes better than it looks, sweet girl. Old Mary will not let you go hungry."

"Thank you, Mary." Grateful for the kindness, Amelia lowered herself on to an unpainted bench next to a sweating wood wall.

Frau Beatrice stood, holding her cup close to her chin as she ate, eyeing each chambermaid—two black and two white—enter the kitchen in different states of sleepiness. "This is the new girl. Name is Amelia," Frau Beatrice told each new arrival.

"Amelia," Fannie squealed. "You're the new girl?" She threw her arm around Amelia's shoulder. "We've been working together. Her lady just had the yellow fever."

"I hope she stays longer than the last German girl," Frau Beatrice snapped. "Harriet barely got Anna broke in before she was off with that doctor to Indian Point."

Fannie accepted her bowl of grits. "She'll be a good one. She stayed with that sick woman. Never complained, not one time."

Amelia wanted to hug Fannie. From the admiring looks on the faces of the other chambermaids, it was obvious that Fannie had paved the way for her acceptance.

After finishing the grits and their mugs of steaming coffee, they filed into the adjacent room where five black dresses and five white aprons hung against the wall on wood pegs. The white hair caps lacked the distinctive tatting of Frau Beatrice's.

"You clean the hotel rooms, and keep yourself clean. You always stay tidy so the guests will think the place is tidy. When your day ends, you hang your uniform, so it's ready the next morning." Beatrice handed Amelia a dress that almost touched the floor and black hose that were held up with garters. "When you get your dress dirty, you wash and iron it before time for work. We keep irons heating on the kitchen stove." While Frau Beatrice issued instructions, the other girls stripped to their undergarments and quickly dressed in their uniforms.

Amelia had undressed in front of her sister, Helga, but never in a room full of women. She turned her back, faced the unpainted wooden hook where she was to hang her own clothing and quickly changed into the stiff dress. She tied the apron and was startled when Frau Beatrice yanked the bow loose. "We make our bows large and very precise. Nothing will be wrinkled." Frau's hands moved roughly against Amelia's back as she quickly retied the bow. When Amelia turned to face the others, they all smiled wickedly, obviously familiar with the reprimand.

Frau Beatrice directed Amelia up the narrow back stairs that rose as steep as a ladder to the second floor. The hall spread wide, and a thick rug woven in designs of swirling leaves and naked elves ran its full length. Large mirrors with gold frames reflected light from clusters of candles in the overhead lamps—a much grander scene than the first floor. She wondered if this was where Herr von Ewald took his room. It must be for the wealthiest travelers; it was more beautiful than Amelia had ever seen, even on the few occasions when she had gone with her papa to pray with the von Ewalds' sickly mama at their fine house with its glittery, cavern-like rooms.

"You and Harriet will work together up here. As each guest leaves or goes down to breakfast, you will clean the room. You will have mostly businessmen up here. We have couples and a few ladies on the first floor near the lobby. Keeps them safe." Frau Beatrice nodded toward Harriet, transferring Amelia to the senior maid's authority, and disappeared down the back stairs.

"Safe?" Amelia had not thought about dangers.

When Harriet smiled, her lips looked pink against her creamy white skin. Her black hair, which had slipped out of the white bonnet in perfect little curls, framed her face. "Plenty of drunks come in off the ships. Mr. Wilhite manages a proper place. He sees that traveling ladies are welcome here."

A door at the end of the hall opened, and a gentleman wearing a handsome brown suit with a silk vest, stepped into the hall. "Good morning, ladies." He rushed past and hurried down the wide front staircase toward the lobby.

"Here we go again," Harriet heaved a sigh and headed toward the gentleman's door. "This will get you broken in first thing."

Amelia could smell the vomit before Harriet opened the door.

"He does this several nights a week. I'm always glad when he finishes buying furniture for his store in Austin and goes back home."

"What's wrong with him?" Amelia whispered. They began scooping the mounds of food mixed with vomit into the soiled chamber pot.

"He's a drunk. The night staff have to carry him back from the fancy Gothic Saloon and put him in bed." She shook her head. "I don't know how he manages to vomit all over the room if he's too drunk to walk back to the hotel."

Harriet opened the window and the door, which led to a wide gallery extending across the front of the hotel. "Let's air out the room and get this mess cleaned up."

"Are all the rooms this awful?" Amelia hated the smell of vomit, but the odors of rotten fish and horse dung coming up from the street were little better.

"Every room has a chamber pot that we empty into a big bucket. We carry it downstairs to the privy. It's a rare guest that bothers to go to the privy. When I get rich, I'll never soil a chamber pot."

"Good for you." Amelia couldn't stop the throat constrictions that made her gag as she carried the receptacle to the large bucket waiting discretely at the end of the hall.

"Breathe through your mouth. You don't smell so much." Harriet called.

Amelia nodded and took gulping breaths, keeping her head up to avoid looking into the stinking mass.

"We don't stop for lunch," Harriet said. "We finish our work about four in the afternoon. Mary Van Dunn gives us a big sample of what she'll serve the guests at supper time."

"I couldn't eat a bite and then come back upstairs to this."

Harriet cackled like a little hen and tossed sheets into a mound on the floor. "Your English is so good, much better than Anna's, the last German girl who worked here."

"When people in our village began reading articles and notices posted at the town hall about the opportunities to join groups immigrating to Texas, my students' parents asked me to start teaching English. My sister Helga and I started speaking English at home, completely stopped speaking German. Her children picked it up quickly."

"Are they planning on immigrating?"

"The Adelsverein, which is the Society for the Protection of German Immigrants in Texas, charges $240 for each family. That's way more than Helga and her husband Max can pay. We had dreamed they would come for a visit...before Herr von Ewald left me here." She turned away, grabbed a chamber pot and rushed down the hall, breathing deeply and blinking her eyes to stop the sudden rush of tears.

When she returned, Harriet reached for her shoulder. "Sorry, I didn't intend to open a painful wound."

Amelia nodded.

She learned to fill the bucket only half full before maneuvering the narrow stairs after she had splashed the contents on the hem of her dress. Fearing the odor might linger, she scrubbed her uniform at the end of the day. While it dried beside the big iron stove, she ate the delicious supper that Mary Van Dunn called shrimp gumbo and rice.

"You Germans don't know what you've been missing 'til you taste some of my Creole cooking," Mary Van Dunn said. "Don't let nobody tell you I cook Cajun. Cajun is country cooking. I make Creole for city folk."

She crossed the alley to the chambermaids' quarters where narrow beds, spaced with barely enough room to step between, backed up to a wall of dresses hung on wood hooks. Trunks sat at the foot of each bed. A sheet and cotton blanket covered each cornshuck mattress.

The girls were already stretched across their beds, listening to muffled sobbing coming from the bed at the far end of the narrow little room. "Sorry I didn't wait on you to finish ironing," Harriet whispered from the next bed. "Angela just got word that her father died. He left her here and promised to come get her when he brought in his cotton crop. She's been waiting and watching every day since October. We knew something must be wrong. Never dreamed he might be dead."

"She's not used to working alongside slaves." It was Fannie on the other side of Amelia, holding her hands over her ears to shut out the sound of Angela's crying, and speaking to anyone who would listen. "I guess she's gonna have to get used to us. No more high and mighty white girl ways."

This white girl doesn't feel high and mighty. I feel ashamed for encouraging Helga's children to speak English, for filling their heads with visions of visiting their tante Amelia in Texas. A chambermaid will never fulfill those promises. She sank into the crunch of her cornshuck mattress.

"You hear what your boss man did now that his woman is dead?" Fannie sat up cross-legged in her bed. Without giving Amelia a chance to answer, she said, "He bought himself a real young slave girl. Took her on that riverboat this morning. You best count yourself lucky that he left you here, girl. When white men buy young slave girls, they have one thing in mind." Fannie grinned like she knew all the secrets.

Harriet rose on her elbow. "I'm surprised he bought a slave. Germans usually think slavery is wrong and look down on American slave owners."

"We don't have slavery. But gentry like von Ewald have peasants who work the land for them. They don't own peasants, but they pay so little that peasants rarely get a chance for a better life. That's why so many are coming here. The Society for the Protection of German Immigrants in Texas has offered cheap land, and peasants are grabbing the opportunity."

"Americans like slavery. Just like in this hotel. You're not going to see many white folks like Harriet working here because they don't hang around. Slaves can't help themselves. We're stuck here."

Harriet glared at Fannie. "You're right. Angela and I would both leave if we had some place to go. That's why Angela's crying. She's stuck here just like me."

And I am too. Amelia stared at Frau von Ewald's trunk at the foot of her bed.

Harriet shook her head and heaved a sigh, "Did Fannie tell you that she was free for a year? Then, she asked Samuel May Williams to buy her. Let her work here at the Tremont House."

"You were free?" Amelia gasped, "What made you do such a thing?"

"Free blacks aren't safe. After I had the yellow fever, I couldn't work much. I knew it wouldn't be no time before they'd decide I was a burden on the town. Sell me to the first planter to come in here. Miss Fannie would find herself picking cotton on some god-forsaken plantation."

"How'd you get that man to buy you?"

"Dr. Ashbel Smith arranged it for me. He was proud of me for getting over the yellow fever so fast. He's friends with Mr. Samuel May Williams, who happens to be the rich owner of the Tremont House. I started in the washhouse and got promoted to being a chambermaid. Next, I'll be a server in the dining room. That's a top job."

Harriet rolled her eyes, "She'll make it, too."

Sarah, whose bed was next to Angela's, raised her voice over Angela's sobs. "You be the second German girl we had with us. Anna, that last one, got her a doctor husband and left here last month."

Fannie, still holding both hands over her ears, dramatically shutting out Angela's crying, laughed deep in her throat. "Yep, that doctor stayed here in one of those plain downstairs rooms. He courted Anna for a month. But don't get all teary imagining how some doctor man will come take you away." Fannie lay on her back, staring at the ceiling. "She was already a grand German lady."

"It was still a miracle," Harriet snapped. "Anna's ship was in such a bad storm that they threw everything overboard to lighten the load. When she got here, all she had were the rain-soaked clothes she was wearing. She was lucky to be alive."

"And double lucky that German doctor came here looking for a wife." Fannie fell back on her bed, laughing and covered her ears.

It was time to get up, and Amelia realized that Angela had finally stopped crying.

As they hurried to dress in the damp chill, Fannie said, "Why'd you come here with those people?"

"I wanted more opportunities. I planned to tutor for a while and then find a school where I could teach. Maybe open my own school."

I didn't want a husband like Max—a handsome drunk that sings and plays beautiful music—that lives like a peasant. She pushed open the door and stepped into a fog that turned the early morning darkness into a ghostly white.

As they climbed the stairs to begin work, Harriet said, "Don't let Fannie upset you. You'll never hear a word about her past, but she'll ask all about yours. She's very ambitious—plans to work in Mr. Samuel May William's big house."

"So becoming a chambermaid was a step up for her?"

"We have clean uniforms. We don't bend over tubs of scalding hot water scrubbing lye soap into filthy sheets and greasy napkins that must be spotless white before we quit. And we don't iron linens all day long." Harriet tossed sheets on the floor. "Believe me; this is better."

Harriet's face was blazing red, already wet with sweat despite the chilly December temperatures.

It's time I learned from Harriet's example and start noticing how much better my life is than if I'd stayed in von Ewald's employ. She grabbed a nasty chamber pot and hauled it to the receptacle at the end of the hall.

Chapter Three

A new day is here...

Amelia's spirits lifted in late December when she realized Christmas would not be forgotten at the Tremont House. The upstairs hall smelled of cedar, and swags of fresh-cut boughs tied with red ribbons hung from the gallery railings. At the end of each day, Mary Van Dunn added to the festive spirit with bread pudding heady with the rich taste of rum.

When all five chambermaids crossed the alley toward their Spartan room, Harriet called out, "They've put up the biggest tree I've ever seen right in the middle of the lobby. Real candles are burning on almost every branch and colored glass balls hang on every limb. Prettiest place in this world."

Fannie rushed ahead, shoved the door open, and tumbled onto her bed as the rest of the crew filed into the room. "Last year I was working in the laundry room. Mr. Samuel May Williams himself came in and gave every one of us a bag of sweets and oranges. Best Christmas I ever had. I knew right then I'd been smart to sell myself to him."

Sarah, who never spoke above a whisper and kept her eyes lowered as if she thought that even the chambermaids were her masters, coiled herself on her bed and mumbled, "We baked all the sweets. We had watery mouths all the time we cooked. Then we got to eat some." Her voice trailed off, and she stared into space like she could still see all those goodies.

It would be boastful for me to share my memories—the rich cinnamon and spice aroma of mama's pfeffernüsse, my doll with a china head, and the cradle that Papa carved for me. Amelia curled into a ball on her bed and willed herself back home. Papa would be sitting next to the light of the hearth, reading the Advent scriptures, and planning his sermon for Holy Christmas Eve. Helga would be coming up from their little cabin at the back of the property to bake the spice cookies in Mama's hearth oven. The children would be in the forest gathering hazelnuts for their old *grossvater* to string for hanging on the *Christbaum.*

The bold knock on the door jolted everyone to attention. James stood outside the door, his epaulets shining in the light of the full moon. "Fraulein Anton, you have a visitor in the lobby."

"Who?" Amelia clutched at the neck of her nightgown.

"You best dress up, fraulein. It's a gentleman."

"There's a mistake, James. I don't know any gentlemen."

"He knows you. He came in here asking about Fraulein Amelia Anton." James grinned, obviously enjoying his messenger role. "He appears in a powerful rush."

All four girls were already digging through Amelia's trunk, holding the candle high to carefully examine every item. "You've got mighty fine dresses."

"They were my pay."

"This blue one will be perfect with your eyes. I'll iron it while you wash yourself." Harriet hurried out the door.

Fannie pulled a washtub into the corner. "I'll get a kettle of water."

As Amelia stepped in the tub, Fannie whispered, "you got the whitest body and the yellowest hair I ever saw."

"I feel like a princess getting ready for the ball." Amelia giggled. "You're going to be disappointed when we discover the visitor wasn't looking for me."

"When I finished ironing your dress, I peeked in the lobby. I saw a giant man in a black suit, kind of rumpled. He was pacing up and down. Then, he circled the Christmas tree. I think that's him," Harriet helped button the back of the dress that had belonged to Frau von Ewald. It lay softly against Amelia's skin.

Amelia decided, since her hair was still wet, to braid it in one long rope and smooth it back enough to keep curls from popping out around her face.

When she stepped into the lobby, surprise caused her knees to almost buckle. "Dr. Stein? I thought you went to Indian Point."

The huge man stood awkwardly in the middle of the lobby leaning toward her like he wanted to speak and could not form the words. "I came back for medicine. So many are sick. And ... and I was hoping the German had not left for his mercantile store in Industry."

"You've missed him. He left right after we buried his wife."

"The staff told me. I heard left you behind. I heard you're working as a chambermaid."

"He arranged it."

"Well..." Dr. Joseph Stein moved like a wooden marionette as he turned toward the red horsehair sofa. "Will you sit with me?"

Amelia nodded and sat lightly on one end of the stiff seat. "Did you hear that Frau von Ewald died?" She stopped, feeling a slight twitch in one eye as she realized she was repeating herself. Her mouth had gone dry. "I didn't get a chance to thank you for asking Dr. Smith to look in on her. He was very kind. But she kept asking for you. She was too sick to understand that you had gone on with the settlers to Indian Point."

"I worried about leaving you alone. I knew it wouldn't be long before she passed." He shook his head. "I wouldn't have left if I'd dreamed von Ewald would abandon you."

Amelia felt as if she might cry. "You're so gentle with your patients. And you're gentle with me." She felt her neck blazing against the high collar. She knew her face was beginning to flame. Had she sounded too forward?

"Fraulein Amelia..." Dr. Stein had also turned a deep crimson. He sucked in his breath, like a man about to plunge into deep water. "I had planned to court you. I started my first letter as soon as we sailed from here." His fingers, which looked too slender to fit his massive frame, spread across his chest, patting the rumpled breast of his black coat. "Circumstances have changed for both of us." Dr. Stein hunched forward, his hand still pressing the pocket holding his letter. "When the hotel staff told me Frau von Ewald had died, I feared her husband had already taken you to Industry."

I'm not sure what he's saying. Would it be rude to ask him to repeat it?

22

"I don't mean to offend you, Fraulein Anton. I planned to start by telling you how lovely you look. That blue dress makes your eyes shine. I know I'm shocking you." He shook his head like a man trying to get his wits about him. "I've practiced this. Now, I can't remember how I planned to ask if you will marry me."

"Marry?" It was Amelia's turn to feel awkward.

"Amelia. May I call you Amelia?"

She could only nod.

"Amelia." He said her name like he was practicing. "I saw you every day on that ship. I watched you with little Otto. I watched you struggle to compose yourself as the child was dying. You gave him so much love and such good schooling. I first noticed you when we reached the North Sea. Your stories for Otto were delightful about the North Capes, about how they were a kind of whale. And you guided him past every landmark as we came through the English Channel. You kept him thinking all the time, encouraging his eagerness to learn."

"My goodness, Dr. Stein, I was telling Otto things I'd read in a book for immigrants. I didn't know you were…" She didn't want to say eavesdropping. Dr. Stein looked so pained that she added, "I was admiring of you, of course. I never. I mean, I never thought of you as a suitor."

"Please call me Joseph or Joe. University friends decided I was tall, so I needed a short name."

Amelia nodded. "I don't think I can."

He cleared his throat and took another huge breath. "Don't let me frighten you. I'm asking you to return with me to Indian Point. For you to be my wife."

"Leave now?"

"In the morning. Dr. Reuss and I are the only physicians caring for hundreds of immigrants stranded on that coast. Many of them are dying from the cold and lack of shelter. This afternoon, as soon as the ship arrived, I bought all the medicine the apothecary would sell. Then, I came to the Tremont House to find you."

"You planned this?"

"Absolutely. On the ship, I kept watching you. I kept thinking what a good wife you'd be. All that day I stayed with you in Frau von Ewald's room, I wanted to tell you how much I admired you.

23

But I thought I should court you for a while. I thought I should ask von Ewald's permission to court you." Dr. Stein had been leaning toward Amelia, speaking first in English and then switching midway into German. Then, he stopped and his face twisted in a flash of anger. "He was a pompous little man. He made a show of the cabin he had for his family when the other passengers were huddled below, cramped in the middle deck. Now he's abandoned you in this place. I can't leave you here."

Amelia looked around the lobby at the tree sparkling so beautifully and people walking past the front door. "This is so fast. I'm not even sure it's really happening."

"It's real, Amelia." He reached for her hand. "I must be honest with you. We'll live in a one-room cabin. They'll build it as soon as the lumber is shipped in. It's a desolate place. I plan to stay there with Dr. Reuss and a few others. We aren't going to follow the Adelsverein when wagons finally arrive to move the settlers to New Braunfels. We're planning to develop a German port, away from the false promises of the group of greedy noblemen who organized the Verein. We believe that many of the newly arrived Germans will decide to make our village of Indian Point their new home."

"My papa always said I was too impetuous. Even my decision to come to Texas seemed rash to him."

"I'm glad you did." Dr. Stein's laugh was almost a giggle. "I'd have never seen those smooth blonde braids and watched you laugh with Otto when the salty spray splashed over the rails and drenched both of you."

"You saw all that?"

"I couldn't help it, Amelia. You captured my heart."

She closed her eyes and imagined her papa sitting by the fire still reading his Advent scripture. "Papa, your impetuous daughter is about to do it again. I'm going to marry Dr. Joseph Stein." Before she opened her eyes, she felt Dr. Stein fold both her hands gently between his big palms.

"I will care for you, but I'm not a romantic man." His black eyes looked steadily at her and then he looked away as he added, "I need you to understand that about me. I am almost thirty. I've always been devoted to my work. It's been my whole life. I know a doctor is more respected if he has a wife. A good wife." He stopped and appeared to be waiting for her response.

"I understand," she nodded, without understanding at all.

If he's worried about me being a good wife, I'll show him. She leaned forward and kissed his very warm lips. "I must tell Mr. Wilhite I'm leaving."

Dr. Stein did not move or even blink. "I'll tell him for you. Our ship sails at dawn. We'll ask the captain to marry us as soon as we get out of the channel." He smiled, "Thank you, Fraulein Amelia Anton for not turning me down."

When she stepped from the lobby into the back hallway, she was startled to see all four chambermaids clustered beyond the door.

"You kissed him. Right on the mouth," Harriet squealed. "We could hardly keep from shouting."

"I'm going to marry him. Tomorrow on the ship as we sail to Indian Point."

"We were betting on that. We could tell by the way he looked at you that he was captured."

"I'll be with Anna. Her husband and Dr. Stein are going to make Indian Point a German port. Maybe Mr. Samuel May Williams will open a hotel, and you can all come to work there."

Fannie smirked, looked sideways from under her lowered black lashes. "That's a good dream, Amelia. A white-girl dream."

After they helped her pack, no one could settle down to sleep. "This is too much like a fairy tale," Angela said. "My mama used to tell me fairy tales about the beautiful blonde girl who got picked to marry the handsome prince and live in his castle."

"You German girls know how to find husbands," Fannie rolled her eyes and covered her mouth, giggling suggestively.

"Don't scare me. I'm already frightened enough. I don't think it could be any worse than staying here and emptying chamber pots every day."

"You would be crazy not to jump at this chance. Every one of us would do the same." Harriet put one arm around Amelia and looked at the faces smiling at them. "And every one of us is jealous."

Chapter Four

Your impetuous daughter...

Amelia had barely finished dressing when James knocked on the door. "Dr. Stein sent me for your trunk. He asks you to join him in the dining room for breakfast."

"Dining room? I thought I'd eat in the kitchen."

James shook his head. "Fraulein, you're no longer a chambermaid."

"We'll be peeping," Harriet said. "Make us proud."

Amelia clutched her in a fierce embrace. "It should be your turn getting out of here."

Harriet's eyes brightened with tears, "If you find an extra doctor who is looking for a wife, send him my way."

"I will, dear friend."

Fannie grabbed both Amelia's shoulders. "Your hair looks mighty fancy with those braids circling like a halo round your face."

Amelia threw herself against the little body that felt like a bundle of hard muscle. "Someday you'll be in charge here."

Fannie's lips puckered, then she slapped Amelia's bottom. "Get out of here, fancy lady."

Not to be outdone, Angela and Sarah took turns hugging and blessing her before she turned quickly and headed out the door. Her breath coming in short gasps.

I know, Papa, I am your unpredictable daughter. I pray this decision won't break your heart. She picked her way carefully across the alley and entered the steaming kitchen.

"I heard. You're going to be a grand lady." Mary Van Dunn

placed her knuckles on each broad hip and looked slowly from Amelia's head to Frau von Ewald's nice leather slippers. "You look prettier than most fine ladies I've known. Now get yourself into that dining room with your man."

Amelia threw her arms around the sweating woman. "Thank you for feeding me so well. Every morsel of your Creole cooking is perfect."

"That's enough. Get on out of here." Mary Van Dunn used the back of her hand to wipe at her eye and turned back to the stove.

The dining room's white walls gleamed under candle-lit chandeliers, and the tables were draped in white cloths, reminding Amelia of how long they had been scrubbed to make them spotless.

Dr. Stein rose, kicked the leg of the chair at the next table, and lumbered toward her. "You look pretty at this early hour."

"You, too... I mean...you look rested."

He pulled out her chair. She clutched the seat as he lifted the chair off the floor to ease it closer to the table. All the servers wore starched white aprons and black dresses just like the chambermaids. They murmured "madam," each time they poured her coffee or set a plate before her.

No one has mentioned that at this hour yesterday I was upstairs emptying chamber pots. She lowered her voice, "I've never been treated so royally."

He frowned. "I fear this will be the last time for a while. I'm taking you to a very primitive place. I hope you won't be sorry."

I can see Papa's round, pink face fighting back tears as I hug him goodbye. "When I left home, I told Papa that I wanted adventure."

Dr. Stein leaned toward her, "It won't be an adventure, Amelia. The Adelsverein has failed our people. When I reached Indian Point, I discovered that we had been too trusting. The noblemen who arranged this grand immigration scheme know nothing about this land or about settling people in a wilderness."

"The advertising and articles about Texas convinced so many in our village to begin saving money, dreaming of a new life. What happened?"

"Greed. Twenty-one noblemen purchased cheap Texas land planning to sell it to German immigrants. Last year at this time when the first four ships landed on the coast of Matagorda Bay, they found nothing except Samuel White's house. There were no trees for building shelters. There was no water. And no food."

Amelia stared at Dr. Stein, "What happened to them?"

"Prince Carl of Solms-Braunfels, the inept manager, discovered that the land grant the Verein had bought is in the middle of Comanche Territory—too dangerous and too far from civilization." Dr. Stein's voice got lower and deeper until he was almost whispering, anger making his black eyes flash the way Amelia remembered when he had ordered Herr von Ewald out of his own cabin. Otto had been sick and whimpering. His papa accused the child of behaving like a baby. In a flash, Dr. Stein had whirled toward the German and looked as if he might hit the man if he didn't get out of his sight.

She reached for Dr. Stein's clenched fist. "Remember all the excitement on our ship? People felt so blessed to be getting 320 acres of their own land."

"They won't get it. The first group last year got a town lot and ten acres outside town." He shook his head, staring at the ceiling in frustration. "Yet they named their settlement *Neu Braunsfels* in honor of Prince Carl's home."

"What's happened to all those people on our ship?"

"They're stranded on the coast. Living in tents and waiting for wagons to take them inland. They're dying from disease and exposure. The rains have turned the prairie to mud and wagons can't get through."

"Do you really believe Germans will stay at Indian Point, decide not to move to New Braunfels with the Verein?"

"Absolutely. As word spreads, people will settle where there's evidence of a little prosperity."

Sitting across the table, she could look directly into his face— wide-spaced gentle eyes, a strong Roman nose—and she realized that despite his rumpled appearance, he was a handsome man.

His face became as animated as a young boy's as he talked about the construction of their cabin and his dreams for having a good medical practice. "I've thought of building a pier, so passengers don't have to be put in little boats and lightered to shore. Maybe open a mercantile store at the foot of the pier."

It may be a terrible place now, but this man will not embarrass me by becoming a peasant. When they started out of the dining room, she noticed Fannie's little black face grinning through an open crack in the kitchen door.

"He stayed on the first floor last night. And he left a spotless chamber pot. He didn't even wrinkle his bed." She giggled, covering her mouth, "He had a full tub of water. He's really scrubbed himself."

Amelia stuck her hand in the opening of the door, patted Fannie's cap-covered head, and turned away quickly to keep from laughing out loud.

I'm leaving my only friends in all of Texas. Her hand clutched at a fluttering surge of emptiness that swept through her belly.

Their carriage rumbled through the pre-dawn; the wheels stirred the slush covering the shell street. Shadows of men lurked in alleyways and the occasional squeal of a loose pig cut through the thickening fog as the coach neared the docks.

"We'll be on an American steamship. The Verein's Galveston director has crowded three shiploads of immigrants—about 400 passengers—onto this one vessel for the trip to Indian Point. You'll hear it called *Carlshafen* when we get there. Despite his lack of organization, Prince Carl renamed Indian Point for himself. He should have been ashamed."

"The immigrants aren't warned in advance of what they're going to encounter?"

"No, they sail with blind hope to Indian Point. You'll feel the disappointment and anger the minute we step ashore."

"It sounds like Herr von Ewald was wise not to sign up with the Verein."

"He didn't need to. He has plenty of financial backing to come to Texas on his own."

"Do you think he can run a mercantile business in the village of Industry?"

"I doubt it. He's too arrogant to get along with ordinary folk— the sort that'll be coming to his store."

I don't think I'll tell him about von Ewald's slave girl. Perhaps I'll tell him later. She tucked her hands into the folds of her cape and stared ahead at the steamboat looming out of the fog at the end of the dock. A few dim lights, hazy—like they were draped in gauze—burned through the fog, giving an ominous look to the giant vessel. He lifted her from the carriage, almost pulled her up the steep gangplank.

"Good morning, Dr. Stein. This must be Fraulein Anton. I'm Captain William Whipple." The captain bowed, his white beard glowing in the dim light. "We're pleased to have you aboard." He shook Dr. Stein's hand. "Your packages from the apothecary arrived last night." He leaned close to Dr. Stein. "We'll perform the ceremony when we reach open waters." He cleared his throat, "it will be my pleasure to offer my cabin." Without giving Dr. Stein time to respond, the captain turned away and began giving orders to men who were heaving trunks up the gangplank.

"Let's find a place to watch the sun rise. We probably won't be back this way for a while." Dr. Stein squeezed them next to the railing between families who were chattering in anticipation of the final leg of their three-month journey.

As the sun rose, light bathed a treeless landscape of small wood houses raised on poles several feet above the earth. Seagulls squawked; their white shapes took form against shadows on the dock. Black men moved up a nearby gangplank, bent, balancing barrels on their backs. Wagons inched along piers under the weight of cotton, its whiteness glowing in contrast to the mud-caked dock.

The ship's horn blew, the gangplank rumbled as it was drawn in and sailors, their arms bulging under chest-tight shirts, hauled in ropes. Water churned into foam against the pilings along the dock. The railing shuddered under Amelia's hand, and the journey began. Finally, the narrow channel opened, and the green waters of the Gulf of Mexico began lifting and rocking the ship in undulating waves.

"Here you are," Captain Whipple came across the deck smiling. He raised his voice, "People, I have the privilege of performing the ceremony to unite Dr. Joseph Stein and Fraulein Amelia Anton in wedlock. You will be our witnesses." Amid a scattering of timid applause, Captain Whipple pulled a worn black book from his breast pocket and began to read the marriage vows. The passengers pressed in close, creating a warming cocoon of unwashed bodies and smiling faces. Amelia felt the heave of the ship cutting through the waves. She could not follow Captain Whipple's words until he said, "Your answer Fraulein Anton is, I do."

"Oh, yes, Captain. I do." She thought Dr. Stein must have said the same, but she wasn't sure.

"By the authority vested in me as captain of this vessel, I pronounce you husband and wife."

While the passengers—setting their shyness aside—clapped and cheered, the captain shook Dr. Stein's hand, then kissed Amelia on both cheeks. He raised his voice, "Let's allow the bride and groom to retire to my quarters. Dr. Stein will be very busy when we reach Indian Point."

She felt Dr. Stein's hand pulling her through the parting throng. Strangers slapped him on the back and gently touched her shoulder with warm wishes.

By the time they had climbed to the captain's cabin, she was feeling light-headed. She had gotten too hot with the crowd pressed so close. The cool breeze off the Gulf made her suddenly cold.

The captain made a gallant show of unlocking the door to his cabin. The thick, cloying smell of cigars burst into her face. "Excuse the noise in the wheelhouse. It's next to my cabin."

Dr. Stein kept thanking the captain until he moved toward the bow and entered the wheelhouse.

Dr. Stein closed the door and pulled the latch down securely. "Are you okay? You're so pale."

She could not stop trembling. "I need to get warm."

He grabbed a cover off the bed and wrapped it around her shoulders. "Lie down. I'll get you some tea."

"Nothing, please. Let's be still. Maybe we could look out the porthole. I heard someone say we'd stay near the coast all the way."

"I'll pull the captain's chair up to the window for you."

"Please stand with me. Let's watch the shore together."

He stood very close, but he made no further move to touch her. Finally, as the sun burned through the fog and the flat, treeless shore stretched as far as she could see, she leaned close to him, let her head rest against his shoulder.

"I won't force myself on you, Amelia. Don't be fearful of me."

"I don't think I'm afraid."

"Why don't we rest? I did not sleep last night. I fear you didn't either."

"We should feel better after a nap." She crawled up on the captain's high bed that was tucked into an alcove of wood.

Dr. Stein lay down very gently, smiled at his bride, and was asleep almost instantly.

She watched her husband breathe, and she made up her mind that she would be a satisfactory wife when he awakened. They both slept until late afternoon when the blast of the ship's horn greeting a passing vessel jolted them awake.

He got up immediately. "It's almost time for supper. The captain invited us to join him."

She sat on the bed watching him brush his hair that seemed to fight back with each stroke of the bristles. He poured fresh water into the basin for her. *He doesn't seem eager to touch me. The grooms in our village were always touching and trying to kiss the brides before they left the church.* She slipped off the bed and brushed the stubborn blonde curls that made her look like a school girl away from her face and back into the braids wrapped around her head.

Captain Whipple had removed his jacket and wore a knitted blue shirt that captured the intense blueness of his eyes. When he lifted his arm to offer a toast, the elbow of his undershirt poked through a hole the size of a saucer. "I hope you like roast duck. We always enjoy our first night out of Galveston because the cook finds the tastiest dishes for our supper. After that, we're back to dried beef and potatoes."

"Do the passengers get the same feast?" She nibbled carefully at her first duck, a food she had never imagined since her papa did not hunt.

Captain Whipple shook his graying shock of hair. "I'm sorry to admit that they have only what they brought on board. The Verein's shipping agent in Galveston is very stingy. He claims the trip is only eighteen hours—hardly enough time to need food service. He hires this steamship because it has enough space below for all the luggage.

The passengers remain on deck. Some come prepared with ample food and warm clothing. Others huddle together on the deck."

Dr. Stein spoke through clenched teeth, "If it rains like it did when I made this trip last month, we'll have a shipload of sick people."

"Exactly why this is my last trip. I can't fix the Adelsverein's problems, but I won't contribute to the misery of people who came with so much hope."

"Where are you going?" *Maybe I can change the subject, get Dr. Stein calmed down a bit.* She laid her hand over her husband's cold fist.

"I'll captain a ship for the Morgan Lines between New Orleans and Galveston.."

Dr. Stein nodded at her like he understood her concern and then pulled his hand away.

The captain poured more wine. "Last year the prince rode on ahead of the wagons and purchased the *Neu Braunfels* site a week before they arrived."

"I hear he abandoned them within a month. Before von Meusebach arrived to replace him."

Except for the wine, this doesn't resemble any wedding party I've ever attended. She laid her hand on the stiffness of her husband's jacket sleeve.

"Did Reuss tell you that when Meusebach arrived last April and saw the financial mess, he rushed to Galveston to catch Prince Carl? Creditors were holding the prince, refusing to let him sail until they got their money." The captain began to laugh and as he talked his laughter became infectious, pulling Dr. Stein and Amelia into his story of the pompous prince.

"Meusebach refused to pay off the prince's $10,000 debt until his Majesty agreed to convince all twenty-one noblemen to double Meusebach's credit with the New Orleans bank."

She did not release Dr. Stein's sleeve. "Did the Prince keep his word?"

Dr. Stein shook his head. "Last October Meusebach got a letter informing him that 4,000 more immigrants were on the way. Only $24,000 had been placed with the New Orleans bank to cover expenses."

"Our ship must have been part of that number."

Captain Whipple smiled at Amelia. "They're grateful to your husband and Dr. Reuss for all the medicine they're providing."

"We can't let them die during their first Texas winter. We believe many will help us make Indian Point a German port town."

"You'll be surprised at how quickly your little village will grow. Those who go inland will need your port to bring in their equipment and supplies. In a few years, they'll be ready to ship out their produce."

"The passengers on this ship don't realize that the money they deposited for safekeeping in Bremen, won't be available. Several of us are celebrating that we weren't so trusting."

"Those who trusted and turned their savings over to the Verein can't afford to strike out on their own. They're at the mercy of whatever transportation von Meusebach can arrange." The captain hurried to answer a loud knock on the door. A sailor, panting hard from his race to the upper deck, gasped, "Can the doctor come? A woman's having a bad time having a baby."

"Of course," Dr. Stein rose immediately. "I'll get back as soon as I can."

"May I come? I've been with my mama to births in our village."

"I'd like that, Amelia."

A crowd of women held a curtain of quilts, the only privacy for the woman who lay in a pool of sweat on a pallet stretched on the deck. Dr. Stein knelt beside her. His few softly spoken words must have assured her, for she allowed him to reach under her modest covering. The glow from a ship's lantern cast shadows over the stone-faced women holding the quilt shield.

They remind me of the midwives at home. They'll stand here as long as it takes, never abandon one of their own. Amelia stood quietly outside the circle.

"I need to turn your baby." The doctor spoke to the woman in a low, gentling voice.

She gasped a weak guttural monotone. Crouched on his knees, Dr. Stein reached into his bag and withdrew forceps that flashed cold steel in the light of the lantern. "I'll tell you when to push, Frau Deutz. We can work together to get this baby born."

Her deep groans were the only sound as everyone on the deck

listened, waiting for the doctor to help. Then, as if charged with a last burst of energy, she arched her body in a final push. Once again, she arched forward, and the cry from under the cover was distinct.

Dr. Stein worked quickly, tied off the cord, wrapped the wailing boy in a bundle of rags that had been stacked on the pallet where the woman lay. He placed the blood smeared bundle on his mother's breast. Her hand trembled as she grasped the squirming blob of bloody flesh. Dr. Stein wiped his instrument, placed it back in his bag, and folded the afterbirth into a mound of rags.

A few women moved in like a hive of honey bees, tending mother and baby. The new father materialized out of the crowd, reached for Dr. Stein's bloody hand. "Thank you, Herr Doctor. This is her fourth child. She's never had trouble before."

"The boy needed a little help. I've told the women to keep packing her with rags to stop the bleeding. If it doesn't stop soon, call me to check on her."

Dr. Stein wiped his hands on his handkerchief as they pushed back through the clapping crowd.

"Mighty kind of you to leave your *hochzeitsbett*."

"We'll leave you alone for the rest of the night."

Laughter followed them as they climbed the narrow stairs to the captain's cabin.

Dr. Stein washed his hands and sat down on the edge of the bed. "I'm sorry if the comments and laughter embarrassed you."

She shook her head. "I felt proud. It's a terrible place to have a baby. You knew how to end her misery."

"Can you relax after all the excitement? The captain will drop anchor soon. The waves should rock you to sleep."

I'm not sure what he's asking, what I should say. "I think I'm ready for bed."

He helped her unbutton the back of her dress and then turned his back while she pulled her gown over her head. She crawled between the captain's coarse sheets and waited; her heart pounding.

He blew out the lantern, eased into bed like he feared waking her, lifted her hand to his lips and kissed it. "Sleep well, my dear wife."

I think I should lie still and wait for his next move. I can't see or feel a thing in this darkness. I hope he can't hear my heart pounding. He's breathing so deep. He's asleep. She rolled toward the wall, her chest aching with disappointment.

If only I could write to Helga, ask her if this is the way marriage begins? She told me about bulls leaping on a cow's back and roosters pecking a hen's head. She was silent about husbands.

36

Chapter Five

My husband is very kind...

The roar of the boiler firing the ship's engine woke Amelia with a start. Her body was pressed against the wall, the top of the bedchamber so low that she thought for an instant she was in a casket. Dr. Stein was standing with his back to her, pulling up his trousers. Their wedding night had passed. Scalding tears welled up. She turned back toward the wall, holding the coarse sheet against her face.

I need to ask Helga how it was with Max. She felt Dr. Stein's hand press her shoulder.

"The captain's table will be ready. Will you join us for breakfast?"

"I'd like that."

"I'll step outside while you dress."

She nodded, thought of telling him to stay. Would that be too forward?

I can't write home to ask Helga what is appropriate. Papa will share every letter. She dressed quickly and braided her hair. Why had she imagined Dr. Stein would like it hanging loose?

Captain Whipple was jubilant. "We've been fortunate. Despite the rain, we made it through the night without a single problem. Didn't have to call on the good doctor to deliver another baby or prescribe something for a toothache."

Dr. Stein was also in great spirits, a man as happy as any that Amelia could remember. "I expect that's our last full night's sleep for a while. Since I was in medical school, every holiday, especially

Christmas, has brought a rash of births."

Amelia dared not complain about the bone-chilling wind. The passengers had spent the night on the deck huddled together, circling their children with their bodies to keep them warm. All eyes searched the horizon looking for the first sign of Pass Cavallo, the opening between the barrier islands along the coast that would usher them into the calm waters of Matagorda Bay. When someone spotted patches of yellow flowers or blankets of green grass, they called out in amazement over how those signs of life had survived the piercing winter cold.

Dr. Stein had warned her to be prepared for a rough ride through the shallow, treacherous opening of Pass Cavallo. She wondered if the Verein's director had told the immigrants to expect a rough passage. In mid-afternoon, a tiny settlement of a few houses dotted the near shore. Sitting on poles to keep them above the storm tides, they looked more like long-legged birds than homes where families lived. "Decrow's Point," became the whispered chorus as the passengers stared at the bleak, flat scene. A few cattle clustered together, their backs turned against the steady wind. Seagulls swooped toward the ship and then caught air currents and drifted away like dancing, springtime kites.

The ship moved easily into the pass; low stretches of land fanned out on each side of the vessel. Dr. Stein pointed to the flag the captain had raised, the signal asking for a pilot from Decrow's Point to guide them through the turbulent water.

The captain's voice came over a horn, directing the women and children down into the narrow space of the middle deck where luggage was stacked in great solid walls. "The waters here are rough. Women and children must remain below until we make it through the pass."

"We should go back to the captain's quarters." Dr. Stein slipped his arm around Amelia's waist and almost lifted her up the steep ladder.

"Is it that dangerous?"

"The captain wouldn't move passengers into such tight quarters if he weren't expecting some rough water."

Amelia was very aware of how close together they stood looking out the captain's narrow window into the wheelhouse. Dr. Stein's body felt warm against her, but it didn't feel like he was snuggling or offering affection.

His behavior was so different from Blaney Evers at last year's Octoberfest. She had agreed to dance with Blaney, and before she knew it, he danced her into a corner of the hall and was all over her, groping and pulling at her blouse. He kept saying that he couldn't help himself, that her skin was so soft he had to touch her. She had finally shoved him away and told him she could help herself and to leave her alone. Max was always pulling at Helga when he was drunk. Maybe it was that way with peasants. Dr. Stein was educated, certainly not a peasant.

A small boat pulled alongside the ship, and a quick little man, with a beard spreading down the front and hair hanging down the back of a slick coat, boarded and began maneuvering their ship into the churning, crashing waters of Pass Cavallo. Waves came in solid sheets over the bridge. The ship rolled violently to one side and then heaved to the other, bumping what Dr. Stein said was a sandbar. Then it surged toward land, pounding hard against the side of the shallow channel then ricocheting back against the opposite bank.

Fearing the ship would break to pieces, Amelia clung to both the brass railing attached to the cabin wall and to the body of the stranger she had just married. Over the roar of the crashing waves, cries of passengers made a most piteous sound. And then she realized Dr. Stein was talking to her, soothing her with his words. "It's going to be all right. These men know how to get through here. They do it every day."

She felt his breath against the top of her head and she relaxed against him. If it took this awful experience to find a way into his arms, she would accept it.

"Look, the pilot's signaling we're through the pass." Dr. Stein's voice stayed calm, and he patted Amelia's back. "We're picking up speed, moving into the protected waters of Matagorda Bay. The captain will take us as near Indian Point as the ship's draught allows." He squeezed her shoulder and then reached for the door. "Let's go back on deck so you can see Indian Point as we approach."

Amelia nodded, sorry the time of closeness had passed.

The setting sun spread a red glow across the horizon, lighting the distant landscape of white tents and green cabins sprawling as far as Amelia could see. "It looks like a village," she whispered.

"It isn't. It offers the merest existence. I hope we draw near enough to get ashore tonight. I need to get this medicine unloaded." He sucked in his breath. "I must stop fretting. Whipple understands the importance of this medicine."

Almost immediately the ship surged against a sandbar and reversed course to avoid damage.

"That's as far as we go." Dr. Stein gazed out at the people who were gathering along the shore. "If the captain is able to lighter luggage on the ship's flat boat, he'll get me in with the medicine."

"Let me go with you." Amelia pushed tight against his body. "Don't make me stay here."

"I'll do my best."

They moved down to the main deck. Passengers chattered, assuring children they were almost there. They would land soon. The long journey would be over.

Dr. Stein whispered, "How I wish it were true. They'll be marooned here until the weather clears. Tents and lean-to frames are the only protection they'll find. I was hoping von Meusebach had gotten some wagons in here, but it doesn't look like it. That house sitting back away from shore belongs to Samuel White and his wife. He owns the land. He's the one who allowed Prince Carl to start landing immigrants here last year. He's tried to help, but it's more than any one person could do to care for these masses. It's a sin the Verein continues sending ship after ship."

A few of the people on shore returned the waves of the eager passengers. Others turned their backs and huddled around fires burning outside tents and frame lean-tos.

"They don't look very friendly," Amelia whispered.

"You can't blame them. They see another 400 souls who'll crowd into the already miserable hovels. It's enough to make you sick to see what greed has done to our people."

"Herr Doctor, my wife isn't gaining strength. Will you see to her before we land?" Herr Deutz removed his hat, revealing scales on his face and spreading over the top of his bald head, the price of several serious burns in three months at sea.

Dr. Stein followed the husband through the crowd. Amelia tried to follow, but the throng stood so close together that she couldn't see where the men had gone. She turned back to watch the efforts to maneuver the ship into position to anchor and unload.

Dr. Stein's voice rose loudly above the chatter, insisting on a passage for his patient. "We must get her ashore immediately." His face was ashen as he guided a litter holding the body of the woman over the side of the ship toward the little boat sloshing below. Almost as an afterthought, he called up to Amelia. "I'll tell them to bring you ashore as soon as possible."

The crew lowered the cartons of medicine and Amelia's trunk to a second lighter bobbing precariously at the foot of a narrow ladder. Determined not to be left behind, Amelia threw her billowing skirt over her arm, slipped through the opening in the rail, and scooted down the ladder without allowing herself to think about her drawers showing or how far it was to the water or how violently the little boat heaved against the ship.

Nearing shore, the crew leaped into the waist-deep surf and pulled the boat onto a shell beach. Dr. Stein and the woman had disappeared into the crowd. Suddenly, a man lifted Amelia onto dry land. "I'm Dr. Reuss." Without waiting for her reply, he began unloading the bundles of medicine.

"I'm Anna Reuss." A young woman with thick black hair pulled into a tight bun that made her face look like a piece of delicately carved ivory, took both Amelia's hands. "You must be with Joe."

Amelia stammered, "Joe? Yes... I'm Dr. Stein's wife." Feeling foolish, she continued, "we married yesterday."

"Dr. Reuss and I are too. I mean. . . just married." She burst into laughter. "It's wonderful having you here. Someone who plans to stay." She kept smiling and rubbing her arms against the cold. "Come to our cabin. Joe's taking that sick woman to a tent."

Making their way through the crowd, she felt strange each time Anna presented her as Dr. Stein's wife.

A woman clutched Amelia's arm, "You were on the ship with us from Bremen. I remember you cared for Herr von Ewald's little boy. That von Ewald was a nasty man."

Amelia only had time to nod before Anna introduced someone

else. She shook hands and tried to remember each name and where each person was from, but as she moved to the next, she had already forgotten the name of the last. She didn't know how to respond to the desperate looks on their faces. Finally, she understood that she was with the man who had brought the medicine, the only hope that many of them had for getting well or for healing one of their children.

Moving away from the shore, Anna placed her arm around Amelia's waist and whispered, "Most of them don't speak English. They're very friendly but terribly upset over conditions here. The few days that Joe was here, he made a wonderful impression. He's very caring."

"He told me about the illnesses and that the Verein hasn't fulfilled its promises."

Anna stopped suddenly and pointed to a tiny, unpainted hut raised on wood blocks about a foot above the gravel earth. "That's our cabin. Yours should be finished tomorrow. If it doesn't rain." She clasped Amelia's hand. "Stay with us tonight. The doctors will be late after going through the tents with the medicine."

"Shouldn't I be helping?"

"There'll be plenty of time to help. Come meet Sarah White. This is their land. We've organized the women for preparing huge kettles of soup or stew every day. Sarah's teaching us about the odd foods they have here."

Sarah White looked thin and tired, but strands of brown hair framed a face that glowed with such a welcoming smile that Amelia liked her immediately. "Welcome to Indian Point. Joe mentioned you almost every day. We knew when he volunteered to go to Galveston for the medicine that he had more than medicine on his mind. Let's get you broken in. We've got a huge kettle ready with thick beef stew."

The White's faded wooden house looked like it had seen years of constant wind and rain. A raised garden stretched back toward several small huts. Large stones surrounded a fire and supported a huge black kettle steaming with a delicious aroma. Smoke rose through an opening in the roof of a frame that extended from the cooking area to cover about twenty rows of bare wood benches. People began lining up, pushing their children forward, or sending them to save space on one of the benches. Each person held a bowl and a spoon.

"You pass out the bread. Tomorrow, when you get your work clothes on, you can dip the soup." Sarah handed Amelia a tray of generous cuts of a thick, white bread. "It's cornbread," Sarah said. "Your stomach will get used to it. In a few days."

"You're Dr. Stein's new wife? He nursed my baby back from death's door."

"He listens to our worries. We're glad he's back."

"You're lucky to find a man of his kindness."

The comments continued as Amelia served the cornbread. Even those who had something angry to say about the Verein or Prince Carl or von Meusebach, had nothing but kind words for the doctors who provided free medicine. Amelia grew eager to meet Henry Huck whom they praised for bringing all the lumber for the shelters and for furnishing free wood for the coffins. It was painfully clear that coffins were in constant demand.

By the time they had served all the stew and washed the kettle, blackness surrounded them. Not even a star glimmered in the night sky. Anna clasped Amelia's hand guiding her along a path to the Reuss' cabin. She kept cautioning Amelia to watch the sharp thorns of prickly pear cactus and the weeds pulling at their skirts.

"You can sleep with me tonight and let the men sleep on the floor." Anna giggled like a schoolgirl. "Unless you don't want to miss a night with your groom."

Amelia smiled and dropped her eyes in a deliberate attempt to look as though sleeping with Dr. Stein was something she didn't want to miss.

"That settles it." Anna whispered conspiratorially, "Your cabin's framed, and it has a roof. There's no reason you can't take enough blankets to sleep there tonight. Joe will have to keep you warm." When Anna giggled again, Amelia was convinced that her wedding night had not been like Anna's.

They heard the low murmur of their voices before the men entered the cabin still talking. Anna leaped to her feet and threw her arms around Dr. Reuss' waist.

Overcome by a feeling of emptiness, Amelia turned her head away from the couple. "How's Frau Deutz?"

"Deutz waited too long to call me. She's lost too much blood."

Anna continued cuddling, her arms around her husband's waist, her face pressed against his chest. "I've told Amelia they're welcome here, but I know they want to have the second night of their marriage in their own cabin."

Dr. Reuss stroked his wife's head, his hand resting on her cheek. "You're both welcome."

"Our cabin's already more comfortable than what those poor wretches are enduring in those tents." Dr. Stein reached for Amelia's hand. "We'll see you in the morning."

Anna grinned mischievously. "Sleep well."

Low black clouds opened, sending gauze-like streaks across a sliver of moon. Dr. Stein held Amelia's hand, guiding her farther down the beach away from the tents. Pointing to clumps of green pods lining the path he warned, "Be careful not to touch the cactus. The thorns are vicious. Reuss says by March, when the prairie's in full bloom, they produce beautiful flowers. Meantime, the Germans are chopping them down as quickly as they can. Samuel White says during drought, ranchers burn the thorns off and feed the pods to the cattle."

"They look like a larger variety of the cactus we grow in pots at home."

"The people in the camp don't see any resemblance. When I first arrived, I saw groups of men stalking across the prairie in a mad fury, chopping down clumps of cactus that grew higher than their heads. They looked like they were raging against a vicious enemy."

"Don Quixote and the windmills?"

"Exactly," Dr. Stein bellowed in a full-throated laugh.

"It's so different from home," Amelia whispered into the steady roar of waves washing against the beach. The wind beat a mist of rain against her face, wetting her hair, and sending a chill through her body.

Out of the darkness, the skeleton of their cabin took shape—bare wood forming an open frame under a wood shingle roof. Dr. Stein scraped his boots on the plank step and then guided her through the space where the door would be. "Henry Huck assured me tonight that his men will get the walls enclosed first thing tomorrow."

"We'll be in our own home for Christmas."

"It's only one room, little larger than a good chicken coop." He spread his arms, which extended almost halfway across the cabin. "When the iron stove arrives, we'll run a pipe through the roof. Huck says there's no stone anywhere near here for building a hearth."

Amelia copied Anna by wrapping her arms around Dr. Stein's waist.

He patted her back and then pulled away, pointing to the windows already set in the frame on each side of the cabin. "Huck said windows on these opposite walls will give us better ventilation. It's hard to imagine needing any more wind, but I've heard summer gets pretty warm."

"With our bed under a window, it should be nice."

"I'll mix medicine on top of my trunk until we get a table. When von Meusebach moves some of the immigrants on to New Braunfels, we can eat here by ourselves." He shrugged and spread his arms again. "Welcome, Mrs. Stein. I shall work hard to make a better home for you than this primitive place."

She reached again for his waist. "I'll make a good home for you right here in this cabin."

He stroked her head, and she pressed against him, ignoring the icy rivulets of moisture from her hair running down her neck. She closed her eyes, feeling the hardness of his chest, the steady thump of his heart.

"The ship's crew set our trunks in here. I brought a good supply of goose down quilts. We can make a pallet for one night." Gently releasing her arms, he reached for his trunk and fumbled for the quilts. "Sleep in your clothes tonight. Undressing in this damp breeze may give you a chill."

She nodded and lifted her skirt to unbutton her petticoats.

He's turning his back. Am I being immodest? She stretched out on the soft quilt and lay still. Dr. Stein tucked the edges of the cover around her. Air coming up between the floorboards smelled like fresh sawed wood.

"Scoot close to me if you get cold." He pulled the quilt over her shoulder.

When he lay down, she pressed against his side and then lifted her head to his shoulder. He patted her back for a few seconds before his breaths began coming in a deep, constant pattern.

Her last awareness, before sleep brought relief from gnawing doubt, was the steady pounding of waves against the shore and the breathing of the man beside her.

Chapter Six

I am teaching again...

He didn't make a sound as he eased off the floor and slipped out of the cabin. Is he being thoughtful or avoiding me? Crawling from the warmth of the quilts, the wind hit like sheets of ice whipping through the open frame, making her teeth chatter. She stripped out of the clothing she'd worn since they left Galveston—the dress she had imagined as her wedding gown—and quickly wrapped her body in a wool dress she had brought from home. Huddling in her shawl, she had started re-braiding her hair when Dr. Stein returned with a candle, a bucket of water, and a basin.

"I got all this from Joseph and Anna. We'll build a cistern and a privy as soon as we can." He set the candle on the floor, lit it behind the trunks away from the wind, then poured water into the basin. He rummaged in the top of his trunk and handed Amelia a pencil and paper. "I brought only one cup and plate. Make a list for Captain Whipple to take back to Galveston. He'll send what you need on the next ship. I'm going to check on Frau Deutz and another woman who is about to have a baby much too early."

Amelia hunched on the floor watching Dr. Stein's long, loping strides toward the tents that were emerging like ghosts in the first rays of morning light.

She scooted behind their trunks into the candle light to begin listing items that a wife would need to make the cabin into a home. A tub for washing clothing and bodies would have to sit in the middle of the floor.

Will he allow me to see him bathe, look at me when I bathe?

How does Helga's family manage baths in their little cabin? Helga would laugh, say that Dr. Stein's a doctor. He knows about bodies, even women's bodies. Amelia pulled her shawl up over her head and bent over her shopping list.

Just beyond the tents, down near the bay, men were pounding three spindly trees into the shell earth. Children scurried about dressing the crooked branches of each *Christbaum* with painted shells and tiny glass ornaments, probably brought from home. Tears stung Amelia's eyes. They were not going to miss this evening's Holy Christmas.

Several women were bent over black pots, cooking on makeshift campfires beside the round tents. At the pavilion, a line of people huddling under shawls and quilts waited as a small group of women served from huge pots of coffee and pans of cornbread.

Anna called to Amelia, "The Verein delivery wagons brought those little cedar trees in from the prairie last night with our weekly rations."

"Rations?"

"From the storehouse up the bay. The Verein sends each of us a half-pound of coffee a week. Four ox-carts bring supplies of vegetables, peas, and other greens. Usually we get cracked beans, pot-barley, rice, and lentils. Sauerkraut comes regularly too, but they deliver beef every two days. We feast on the first morning after the supply train arrives."

"Everyone shares their rations?" Amelia looked back at the women working next to the tents. A few were grinding corn as others spooned cornbread into iron skillets.

"The Verein provides every family with a grinder for the corn, but they don't all share," a round-faced, giant-sized woman muttered. "Some eat up their rations. At the end of the week, they send their children over to our supply." She looked through squinty little eyes. "Did you come with the Verein?"

"My husband did."

"Then you won't be eating with us?"

"Yes. Frau Stein will be eating. Dr. Stein paid for her food."

Looking up at the woman towering over her, Anna stood firm, almost glaring.

"You're Dr. Stein's new wife?" The woman's face softened. Her cheeks stretched into a toothless grin. "He's earned his keep and yours too. He mixes up the best herbs for a toothache." She pulled her bonnet tight under her chin and walked away.

Amelia lowered her voice, "Did Dr. Stein pay for me?"

"I don't know. But the good woman's right. He has more than earned his keep and yours too."

"I remember you. You speak English. You were teaching that little boy who died on our ship." A very young woman, whose round, childlike face Amelia remembered from the *Neptune,* held an infant greedily suckling under a woolen shawl. A boy of about three clung to her free hand.

Amelia nodded.

"Will you teach us? We need English if we're going to prosper. My name's Rachel Swartz. My husband is Conrad. This here baby girl is Hulda and my boy is Peter."

"You want me to teach English?"

"Oh, yes." Rachel Swartz dropped Peter's hand and crushed Amelia into an embrace of soured milk and suckling baby. "Can we start right away?"

"After breakfast?" Amelia stammered.

Rachel Swartz whirled away, grabbed her son by the hand, and rushed toward the cluster of tents calling, "I'll see you after breakfast."

Anna laughed, "You'll have a lot of students when word gets out. They won't be asking if you've paid your way for very long."

"I planned to teach again, someday. I guess that day has arrived."

"The women and children will be interested. I doubt you'll be able to stir the men," Anna muttered and turned to serve another cup of coffee.

As soon as they finished clearing away breakfast, Rachel Swartz arrived with her brood and husband Conrad in tow. He looked as young as Rachel, his sandy hair hung straight to his shoulders and swung across his eyes as he peeked at Amelia. Rachel began immediately by saying "good morning" in English. She turned first to Conrad and then to little Peter, who both said, "good morning" on cue.

Amelia burst into laughter. "That's wonderful. You've made a good start."

They sat on benches at the back of the pavilion. As they began naming objects and items of clothing, several women who had helped with breakfast cleanup settled nearby and recited the words and phrases with them. Peter found the process a wonderful game, jumping and shouting his response with each new word.

The air exploded with the crack of nearby rifle fire. Amelia jumped, clasping her ears as several more volleys ripped through the air.

The women broke into peals of laughter. "That's our Sunday *Schuetzenverein*. With no church services to distract them, our men spend every Sunday using the good-for-nothing plants on the prairie for target practice. We try to ignore them."

Billows of black smoke rose like angry clouds just beyond the tents. "Do they shoot all day?"

"Depends on how much black powder they have. We keep hoping they'll run out, but the Verein ox-cart drivers are glad to sell more powder each time they come."

"Here you are, Frau Stein," a man whose face had turned a bright pink from too much sun, rushed into the pavilion. "Dr. Stein said for you to come see the cabin. We've closed all the walls."

"Will you hold a lesson after lunch?" Rachel reached for Amelia's hand.

"May we bring our children?" asked a woman who had been watching.

"We have room for everyone," Amelia called as she hurried after the carpenter.

The cabin looked even smaller with wood covering all the walls.

"The stove should be here in a few days," the carpenter said. "We'll come back with your bed. Dr. Stein said he didn't want to sleep on the floor again tonight." The carpenter grinned, and Amelia pretended she didn't know what he was implying.

"Did you make the bed extra long? Dr. Stein's so tall."

"Of course. He asked for a rope bed."

"A rope bed?"

"You sleep on ropes instead of wood. It's a lot cooler, and it's softer. My wife sewed the ticking for the corn shuck mattresses. They don't mildew in this dampness like feathers."

"I'll be eager to see it. Do you build cisterns and privies?"

"Dr. Stein asked us to build everything you need."

He's trying to be a good husband. I need to be more patient. She hugged her arms around herself, "If you'll leave some boards, I'll start a garden."

Amelia walked up the beach toward the rows of white tents and wooden lean-tos that had been smeared with a green stain and offered little more than a windbreak and limited shelter from the rains. Drawing near, she realized the tents were much larger than she had thought. Several families had made private huts out in the prairie with stacks of twisted limbs from thorny bushes. They had overlaid the limbs with weeds and brush and daubed it all with mud. Farther back on the prairie, a lone wagon sat with a white ship's sail stretching over its bed, creating a private tent.

Across the bare, windswept landscape, cattle grazed. Two black men on horses drove some calves toward the White's house.

"They're the White's slaves." A rail thin woman wrapped in a wool shawl and close-fitting wool cap spoke in German from behind her hand as though she were sharing secret information. "They have four. Samuel White makes good use of them."

Amelia nodded, and the woman went on. "Never saw a man do less work. He's got a lot of cattle, hogs, and milk cows, but he does nothing to care for them. The cows come in before dark to nurse their calves. His slaves get enough milk for the family and then turn them loose." She shook her head again. "The slaves till his tiny garden. Even with all the Germans dumped here for the past year, he's not enlarged his plot. Americans are a lazy lot if you ask me." She turned and walked away without offering her name.

Amelia found Dr. Reuss in his apothecary tent, explaining to a woman the way to administer Ayer's Cherry Pectoral for a persistent cough.

Stepping to the next tent, she introduced herself to Henry Runge, who had opened a small general store in the tent beside the Reuss Apothecary. Amelia had not understood what Dr. Stein meant when he told her that Henry was called "Short Runge" and his younger brother was known as "Long Runge" until Henry waved to her. He was so short he could barely see over the counter. He, too, was busy with a customer. Dr. Stein had said Henry's store doubled as a bank. Perhaps he was making a loan. A shelf at the back of his tent held a few plain white pitchers and bowls and some cups they could use until the supplies came from Galveston.

Amelia started home with her purchases. Rachel Swartz, still nursing Hulda and holding Peter's hand, called, "Good morning, Frau Stein."

Amelia pointed to the sun that was high overhead. "It's good afternoon, Frau Swartz."

Rachel laughed and repeated the English words. Amelia asked, first in English and then in German, if she could see their living quarters.

"It's so crowded," Rachel apologized. "We sleep fourteen in this tent. Some tents hold sixteen. We lie down in a ring with our feet touching in the center. All our possessions sit outside in the rain."

Rachel ducked under the drooping edge of the canvas and motioned for Amelia to follow. The tent stank of unwashed bodies. Conrad and several men, sprawled on feather mattresses that fanned in a circle around the tent, stopped talking and nodded, only after Rachel introduced her guest. The feathers had molded, creating a sour odor that stayed with her even after she hurried back outside.

Rachel appeared unconcerned that they had interrupted the men's conversation. "If we could get our money back from the Verein, we'd leave here. Go where Conrad can begin his furniture business."

"Conrad makes furniture?"

"It was his family business. For generations, the Swartzes made beautiful wood pieces. They say walnut's plentiful in New Braunfels. If it'd stop raining, von Meusebach could get wagons down here." She smiled, her little-girl eyes brightening with hope. "That's why we need to learn English. Conrad plans to have many customers as soon as they see his work."

Amelia laid her hand on the chattering girl's arm. "My husband needs a table, and we need two chairs. I'd like to hire Conrad."

"Rachel's eyes bulged like she'd seen a ghost. "Conrad! Conrad!" She ran toward the tent shouting.

Immediately the sandy head appeared, his boyish smile animating his face. "I'll ask Henry Huck if he has wood that'll do." Conrad rushed off down the bay calling over his shoulder. "I'll make you the best table and chairs."

Rachel swiped at a tear. "You see how they are?"

"The men?" Amelia wasn't sure what Rachel was talking about.

"They've given up. And they influence Conrad." She stopped, pressed the fingertips of her free hand to her forehead, her eyes closed. "I'm praying this minute that Henry Huck has some wood. He's been giving it away for coffins. I'm praying he has enough for a table and chairs."

"Dr. Stein said Henry Huck's bringing lumber from New Orleans."

"He's built a lumberyard down the coast." Rachel stared after her husband who was almost running.

When Amelia returned to their cabin with her purchases, the carpenter, and another man were angling the long bed through the door.

"I've never used a rope bed. That lattice work of ropes looks stiff. Will we slip through those open spaces?"

"Spread a good quilt over the ropes. My wife will bring you an extra thick corn-shuck mattress. With Dr. Stein being such a big man, the ropes will stretch out." He picked up a wood mallet hanging on the foot of the bed, slipped it into the rope laced through the bed's footboard. "Use this bed key to twist the ropes to tighten them."

Amelia thanked the men and stared at the giant bed dwarfing the cabin.

She was serving sauerkraut when Conrad Swartz pulled a cart

loaded with large pieces of wood to the rear of the pavilion.

"It's pine," Conrad called. "No one knows how long it'll take to get walnut from New Braunfels. I can make a nice table and chairs with this pine. You won't have to wait."

"A pine table and chairs will be perfect," Amelia said.

As soon as lunch was cleared away, several more families stayed behind and asked to be included in the English lessons. While the growing group of Germans practiced English, Conrad sawed and sanded and mouthed the English words like a man set on fire.

The evening sky was black, offering not a single star to guide the settlers' Holy Christmas. A rich tenor voice began quietly, then a chorus of male voices joined in, filling the air with *Stille Nacht.* Adults and children began pouring out of the tents holding flickering candles. Voices rose, drawing throngs onto the shore to join the heavenly sound. Candles, glowing on the faces of smiling children and tear-streaked adults, shut out the sight of the dingy tents and the cactus-plagued prairie. Only the music and the voices mattered. They were home again.

Then, like the crescendo of an organ in a great cathedral, thunder crashed, and a streak of lightning lit the prairie, igniting a clump of cactus. The skies opened with a deluge of rain that snuffed out the candles and drove the shrieking sojourners to their only protection—the stinking, crowded tents.

Amelia and Dr. Stein reached the cabin at the same time and slammed the door shut against the pouring rain. They had started pulling off wet coats and shoes when the loud knock startled Amelia. Dr. Stein fumbled in the dark to light the candle.

A woman that Amelia recognized as one of the older passengers on the *Neptune* who had been kind to Frau von Ewald after Otto died, stood on the step with rain drenching her wool shawl. Mud clung to her shoulder. "I fell as I ran along the trail."

Amelia pulled her into the cabin and helped remove her mud-smeared shawl.

Dr. Stein introduced Frau Fischer and wrapped the cover from their bed around the shivering woman.

"I'm sorry to bother you. I don't know where to turn. My son Hans has been listening to Augustus Buchel talk about forming a military unit. He's saying the Victoria newspaper predicts war with Mexico as soon as Texas joins the United States. My Hans says he's going with Herr Captain Buchel." Tears rolled, unchecked, down Frau Fischer's cheeks.

Dr. Stein motioned for Frau Fischer to sit with Amelia on the new bed. He pulled his trunk around and sat on it facing the two women. "Buchel's had a lot of military training in Hesse and in Paris. He's been a mercenary in Spain. I'm not at all surprised that he's talking war to the young men."

"Dr. Stein, Hans is all I have left. I lost four precious babies before the Lord blessed me with that child. I sold everything and left Germany to keep him from serving in the army. The Hessians killed his papa. I didn't want that for my Hans." When she reached for Dr. Stein's hand, rings sparkled on all her fingers. Several fingers were bulked with more than one large stone. "You're respected among our young men. Tell them to remain here. With their families."

Dr. Stein leaned toward Frau Fischer. "I'm sorry Buchel is frightening everyone with this war talk. He's taking advantage of the paper being printed in English, making it sound like war's about to happen. The newspaper report says it'll take a while." Dr. Stein smiled. "Meantime, maybe we can get a *Saengerbund* organized. I heard Hans' tenor tonight. He has a beautiful voice. I'll speak to him about getting something going." Dr. Stein's face lit with a broad smile. "If we keep our young men occupied, military service won't look like the only option. When the roads dry up, and the Verein gets wagons in here and moves you up to New Braunfels, Hans will see more hope for his future."

By the time Frau Fischer left, she had stopped crying. The rain had stopped as well.

"You're a kind man, dear husband. No wonder they love you."

"Our numbers have reached over 2,200. Word came today that another 800 are waiting in Galveston. Hopelessness is sweeping like a plague through here. The men hate the place so much; they won't work to improve it. I felt encouraged tonight when everyone was singing with such enthusiasm. Then, the damn rain spoiled it all." He stretched out wearily on their new bed. "This feels heavenly. The carpenters said you instructed them to make it extra long to fit my height."

Amelia lay down beside him. "I want you to be comfortable when you come home."

He fished in his trouser pockets. "I have a Christmas gift for you." He held up a plain gold band. I didn't have time in Galveston to buy you a ring. A man gave this to me. His wife passed away when we first landed at Indian Point. He told me, today, that he had carried the ring too long in his pocket. He decided it should be worn by my new wife."

Amelia took the ring, which was worn of all design, and pressed it to her lips. She stretched her arm across his chest. "Please place it on my finger, Husband." When it slipped on easily, she raised up and kissed his lips. Not feeling a response, she lifted her head and looked at him.

"I'll buy you another, finer ring, when we prosper."

"Don't ever replace this one." She kissed him again, this time letting her lips linger. She tried to feel something in his body, to get a sense that he was wanting more, to feel him stir and stroke her head like Dr. Reuss touched Anna. Drawing back, she said, "Why don't you respond to me? I know from all the winks and nods I keep receiving, it's expected that you respond to me."

His face clouded, and he turned his head toward the wall.

"Don't turn away. I need to know. Am I doing something wrong?"

He winced like she had slapped him and turned toward her. "Oh no, Amelia. You've been wonderful." He smoothed back the fuzz of curls, which had slipped out of her braid. "I fear there's something wrong with me."

"Can I help you?"

He shook his head and looked toward the wall. "I thought marriage would make it different. I thought it would rouse me like it does other men." His eyes were pleading. "I've grown to love you. You're a fine wife." He began wiping tears. "I can't find desire for you." The sob came in a rush of air. "I feel selfish to find pleasure in your nearness and yet not desire your body." With both hands covering his face, his body shook, and he rolled away from her.

She lay her head on his heaving shoulder, her hand stroking his tear-streaked cheek. "It's going to be better," she kept saying and wondered why she was saying something she did not believe.

Chapter Seven

1846 brings new challenges...

Amelia awoke to the New Year and to the sound of Dr. Stein quietly closing the door—the early morning pattern he had established over the past week.

He had poured a cup of coffee and started toward the tents with a piece of bread in his hand when Amelia arrived and reached to caress his shoulder, to feel some intimacy.

"I tried not to wake you. I need to check on my patients."

What is it that makes him unaware that I just stroked his shoulder? When he touches me, even brushes against me, I feel it. Is there something wrong with me that makes me so hungry for him? She turned back toward the makeshift community hearth just as the sun peeked above the horizon, casting light on white cranes rising from the brush like an undulating cloud. Each pair croaking in duets shattered the morning hush. A few women standing nearby lifted their heads to stare at the display, then turned back to the task of seating children. Others, inched forward in the serving line, eyes hollowed from sickness, bodies wrapped in shawls and quilts hunched against the cold.

The breakfast crowd had thinned when Dr. Stein hurried toward the tables clutching a faded woolen bundle against his chest. His face held such pain that Amelia started toward him as he raised his voice above the conversations. "Frau Deutz has passed. She left four children. This baby boy is in need of a wet nurse."

Rachel Swartz, sitting with her two children toward the rear of the pavilion, raised her hand. Ignoring Amelia's stammered introduction to Dr. Stein, Rachel reached for the baby.

"Herr Deutz will come after he buries his wife. He can pay a little for your help."

Rachel lifted her thick rosy shawl, moved her baby Hulda over enough to guide the shriveled face to her other swollen white breast. "Frau Deutz would have done the same for one of mine." She smiled, her face a picture of contentment. "What's his name?"

"Joseph." Dr. Stein laid his hand on Rachel's shoulder. "Thank you, dear woman." He gripped Amelia's arm and led her away from the cluster of women and children gathered around Rachel and the new baby. His face contorted into a mask of pain. "He named that baby Joseph Stein Deutz." He turned abruptly, his shoulders stooped and disappeared between the tents.

Must I stand here and watch when all I want to do is throw my arms around him, comfort him? She turned back to watch Rachel Swartz rocking two suckling babies.

Amelia had spent the afternoon looking forward to Dr. Stein coming home to see the new table and chairs, hoping it would lift his spirits. He stood in the darkened doorway, staring at the beautifully finished table, its rich luster gleaming in the candlelight.

"How lovely." His fingers slipped lightly over the wood surface.

"It's my late Christmas gift. Maybe it's my late New Year's present." Amelia leaned her face against the damp chill of his coat sleeve.

"It's beautiful. How did you pay?"

"Conrad accepted my Thaler banknote from von Ewald, and I had ten silver dollars from my earnings at Tremont House." Amelia laughed. "I must admit to being penniless, not another *pfennig* in my pocket."

"You're my treasure." He smiled faintly and moved toward the bed. "I must sleep for a few hours. I expect a call before morning. Herr Thiele's little girl is almost gone."

Amelia jerked awake thinking that one of her papa's milk cows was bawling. Then, she realized Dr. Stein was bounding from the bed, jerking on his trousers and grabbing his coat and bag. "I'm coming Herr Thiele." The sound came again as he opened the door to a man, his arms extended holding out a tiny body like an offering.

Dr. Stein reached for the limp child, carried her to the new table. Amelia pulled the quilt off the bed and wrapped it around the man's bare arms, pulling him into the cabin.

Candlelight flickered across the child's very still face as Dr. Stein worked on her rag doll body alternately pressing her chest and then blowing into her mouth. Finally, Herr Thiele moved Dr. Stein away and knelt beside the table, his face buried into the body of his lifeless child.

Dr. Stein bent down next to him, and Amelia lowered herself to the other side, holding the man between them as he shook like a wind was ripping him apart. When the storm passed, he lifted his head and reached a calloused hand to smooth the strands of blonde hair from the still face. "She's my last. I've lost them all."

He stood and reached for Dr. Stein's hand. "My thanks, Herr Doctor." He turned, nodded toward Amelia and felt for the walls like a blind man walking out the door.

Amelia had laid out a clean sheet and started washing the frail child when the explosion ripped through the night air. Dr. Stein bolted for the door. "Stay inside, Amelia."

Dear God, don't let it be. She leaned her face against the door.

Dr. Stein returned for a quilt. "I don't want you to see this. Take care of his baby girl."

A crowd gathered; the voices were hushed, shocked, disbelieving.

Anna came to the door, her face ashen. "I tried not to look."

"I don't even know her name," Amelia choked back tears as they washed the little body and wrapped her in a clean sheet.

When daylight finally made it possible to pick their way through the mounds of graves, a long, silent procession followed the coffin bearing the body of Herr Thiele and his little girl. No one knew where to find the graves of her mother or the other children. At the open hole that had been quickly dug, Dr. Stein lifted his voice so that it carried into the blowing north wind. "We all knew Herr Thiele was frantic with worry over Pearl's illness." He raised his hand as though offering an oath, "I hope that as a community you will join me in a pledge to be more sensitive." His voice broke, and he hurried away, cutting through the rows of crosses toward their cabin.

People rushed forward, circling Amelia and clutching her hands, touching her shoulders, offering warm wishes for Herr doctor and promises to do a better job of watching out for each other.

Dr. Stein was stretched out on their bed, both arms raised across his face. "He took his rifle from his trunk and came away from the families to blow his head away."

She lay down beside him, wrapped her arms around his body, and held him in the same tight embrace she would have offered a suffering friend. She listened to his breathing grow deep as he slipped into sleep. When the chatter coming from those who were lined up for breakfast began fading, she eased off the bed and returned to lead the morning English class. Near the end of the exercises, Dr. Stein came for coffee and bread. He raised his cup to her and disappeared among the tents.

More and more adults fell ill, leaving children to wander about the settlement. Amelia encouraged them to come to the English lessons while Anna and Sarah kept bread baking to lure them away from their sick parents. Rachel, with two babies nursing under her bulky wool shawl, was the most faithful student in the class, insisting on speaking English exclusively to Conrad and to all three of the Deutz children who clustered around her chattering like magpies. Peter's three-year-old enthusiasm attracted the younger children and helped Amelia divert their attention away from the rise behind the camp where crude crosses stretched across the horizon. Two or three men spent most days stooped over the soil, digging one grave and then another. Somber treks to the cemetery became so frequent that formal services were rare. Usually, the dead were quickly buried, sometimes as entire families. Survivors mourned in silent—or sometimes—angry acceptance.

Henry Huck's carpenters tried to keep up with the construction of coffins, but before the end of January, most of the dead went to their grave wrapped only in the quilt on which they had died.

Despite the construction of cisterns and the use of tubs and buckets to catch the rain, there was never enough water. Most people relied on coffee that Sarah and Anna kept available all day. In early February, Amelia had finished the English class and started back to the cabin when she saw one of the women who helped serve meals, slap a young woman with waist-length blonde hair. The blow made such a noise that it halted the conversation around the tables. "You never share a grain of your coffee and you come here several times a day to drink ours."

Women rose from the benches and moved forward; their faces clouded in angry scowls. Their children gathered round, wide-eyed at the spectacle.

"Wait a minute," Anna stepped between the two women. "We need to resolve this right now. Without violence."

The young woman stroked her red cheek, her eyes darting around the crowd circling her. "I'm not stealing. As soon as the next delivery arrives, I'll ask my husband to share some of our coffee."

"Perhaps you could donate your week's supply. Then you could feel free to continue coming every day." Anna's smile was genuine.

One of the women in the group spoke loud enough to be heard throughout the pavilion, "You can't sit in that tent brushing your hair all day. Come help us cook and share your supplies like the rest of us. We've watched you sneak in here for weeks."

"Good," Anna perked up like the conductor of a band. "We're all agreed. We share, and we do not hit."

The girl's eyes were red with tears as she brushed past Amelia saying, "Why did I ever let that man talk me into marrying him and coming to this hell hole?"

I imagine there are a lot of us who feel that way. We don't have the courage to say it. Amelia headed on to the cabin instead of remaining in the pavilion listening to the anger that still simmered just beneath the surface.

Late that night Dr. Stein brought in a bucket of water from their cistern and set it bedside the table. "I'd like a bath, but I hate to waste this precious liquid. Rain's a mixed blessing. We're desperate for the water, but if the roads don't dry up, wagons will never get in here to take the families out of this wretched camp."

Amelia poured heated water in the basin and handed her husband a warm cloth for washing his face. "This should feel good. And you won't have to undress in front of me."

Dr. Stein looked at her over the top of the rag and then began scrubbing his face. "Please don't badger me tonight, Amelia. I've spent the last three hours arguing with men who should know better than to dig wells in this shell-covered soil. The water's salty, and they're getting dysentery. It's killing those who are already weak from chest congestion." He sank to the bed. "I'm glad for an excuse not to bathe. I'm too tired to go through the motions."

He may feel terrific pressure, but he sleeps as sound as a house cat. Amelia blew out the candle and crawled into bed with the man who had brought her to this hell hole.

Chapter Eight

At the end of February, the clouds are lifting...

Rachel hurried along the path, lifting her chin over the bulk of both nursing babies and called out, "We're building a house. Runge's giving Conrad a loan."

"That's the best news I've heard in a month." Amelia picked up Peter and swung him in a circle. "Have some tea and tell me about it."

"Don't tell Conrad that I'm taking credit for some of his success."

Amelia laughed. "That'll be our secret."

"It started when you hired Conrad. I insisted that he make your table and chairs at the back of the pavilion. I knew he'd get more orders if people saw his beautiful work."

"Anna and Sarah were the first to place an order."

"And he's been busy ever since. Some of the rich families asked for special coffins for their children. He's creating angel and shepherd boy images. Now, he's carving wreaths of vines and roses for the adults."

They will finally have privacy. What will that be like for them? Amelia leaned against the door, watching Rachel hustle back down the trail. She breathed in the crisp, almost springtime air, grateful for Rachel's cheerful presence.

During the weeks that followed, each time Amelia stepped

outside, her eyes were drawn down the coast toward Rachel and Conrad's new home. A large work shed extended off the back. Conrad was always there, bent over his bench. At night, he worked by the light of a ship captain's lantern.

In mid-March, the rumble of 100 wagons pulling into the settlement turned the camp into joyous chaos. When the cheers had died down, those who had been on the coast the longest were instructed to pack their belongings and be ready to load the waiting wagons by early morning. Like a fresh wind blowing, spirits lifted. Tents full of dirty, exhausted families, folded moldy feather beds into tight bundles, gathered laundry stretched between the canvas flaps, and packed sea trunks faded and decaying from sitting for months in the weather. Families who had argued over space in the tent or the distribution of food mellowed as they turned to those who were being left behind offering promises of future reunions, of continued friendship, or memories that would last a lifetime.

Von Meusebach became the hero as word spread that he had arranged a contract with the Torrey Brothers, a freighting company out of Houston, to haul the desperate Germans to New Braunfels. The wagons would continue returning for settlers until all the immigrants at Indian Point had been moved inland.

After a day of frenzied activity and a late night of singing and saying goodbye, Dr. Stein and Amelia rose the next morning to watch the sure-footed oxen inch forward, pulling the wagons mounded high with trunks and bundles and giddy children sprawled on top. A few women perched on the narrow sides of the wagons, but most started the journey walking beside their husbands.

Dr. Stein leaned close to Amelia's shoulder, "Let's pray the prairie has dried enough for those heavy wagons to get through."

Nodding, she entwined her fingers between his long slender ones and made her own prayer. *And may springtime warm our hearts and thaw what is frozen inside both of us.*

That night, Dr. Stein came to the cabin soon after Amelia returned from serving supper. In the light of the candle, dark circles under his eyes disappeared behind a jubilant smile as he curled himself onto his chair. "Remember what I told you about wanting to build a pier out into the bay?"

I heard your grand plans. I also heard how I captured your heart. She nodded.

"Runge says Prince Carl boasted of building a loading pier over a year ago. Since it hasn't happened, and the Verein keeps dumping shiploads of immigrants in here, Runge agreed to loan me the money to build it myself." He spread his fingers across the table like the lines in an account book. "I'm not making any money with my medical practice. If they offer to pay at all, it's with some family treasure that I can't bring myself to accept." He looked across the table at Amelia and whispered like he was sharing a secret. "The pier will make it easier for everyone to get to shore. I'll charge the Verein for the service, and we'll have a business that will bring in some money."

Amelia leaned forward, swept into this new feeling of intimacy, of sharing a secret. She whispered, "When will you build it?"

"As soon as Huck's carpenters can get to it."

A week later, Huck's men had started driving the cypress pilings for the pier deep into the bay waters. Dr. Stein had just started eating his supper when hard knocking sent Amelia scurrying to open the door. Three men, their faces stern in the dim candle light, stood shoulder to shoulder.

Dr. Stein rose from his chair. "Come in, Herr Sneed."

"We're here to talk about that pier," Herr Sneed nodded to include the men standing on each side. "We don't see a benefit to making it easier for the Verein to crowd more immigrants in here. We're already half starved. Having to ration water. Watching our families suffer."

Dr. Stein motioned for the men to sit on the bed, for Amelia to take her chair, and he sat lightly on the edge of his chair, his knees almost touching Herr Sneed's. The man sitting directly across from Amelia leaned forward, elbows on his knees. The stench of rancid clothing was so strong that Amelia formed her lips into a small opening to breathe through her mouth the way she had done when she carried chamber pots at the Tremont.

Dr. Stein took a slow breath and stared into the hardened eyes that never left his. "The Verein doesn't care a whit about that pier.

They will keep sending people as long as they are willing to pay."

The man sitting in the middle slapped his palms on each knee, "But we've got to stop them. They're sending Germans to their death."

Dr. Stein's body did not move. His eyes did not blink. "The only way you're going to stop the Verein from sending hoards of settlers in here is to write home. Tell your friends not to come. Tell them not to trust the Verein. All that pier will do is make it easier for trusting souls—like you and your families when you arrived —to get off those ships without climbing down twenty-foot rope ladders into those unsteady little boats."

Herr Sneed looked at the men slumped beside him. "Several have already sent letters and articles to the papers warning about what to expect."

The other two nodded.

Dr. Stein did not lean back in his chair. He sat still, his focus on the men staring at him.

The men sat in silence for what seemed like a long time. Finally, as though Dr. Stein's words had soaked in, all three stood at once. "Sorry, Herr doctor, for interrupting your supper." Herr Sneed glanced at both men. "We can write letters. That's something we can do."

Dr. Stein patted each man reassuringly on the shoulder. "Come to Saengerbund practice. We can use a lot more voices."

Amelia closed the door and whispered, "You've kept down a riot."

Dr. Stein dumped his soup back in the pot to heat it up and dipped out another serving. "That pier could have been the symbol of all that's wrong at Indian Point. I hope we caught it before they stirred up a lot of trouble."

After the last plank was nailed, the pier became a new walkway stretching out over the waves. Amelia and Dr. Stein sat at their table watching out the window as all ages lined up to promenade along the boardwalk. *It feels like we're in our little nest, looking out together on the world.* "You convinced Herr Sneed and his friends that the pier wasn't a bad addition to our shore."

"I never dreamed it would be such an attraction." Dr. Stein leaned against the table running his fingers through his hair. "It's roused the men out of the tents. By daylight they're out there fishing, and they're back out there again at sunset."

"We've cooked red fish and trout every day. It took the pier to make them realize that the bay isn't an enemy."

Dr. Stein laughed. "Now I've got mothers complaining about their boys leaping off the end into the cold water. They want me to tell their sons it's too dangerous."

She reached for his hand, pulled it to her cheek, "You're much more important than you realize."

"I'm not going to supervise the children." He rose and moved to the bed. "It feels good to see all this activity. The place has been still as a graveyard for so long."

Amelia and Dr. Stein stood among the throng that swarmed out of the tents watching the first ship dock at the new pier.

Frau Fischer spoke in a loud voice. "It's hard to celebrate the pier when it invites another 300 or 400 to crowd in." Several people nodded in agreement. Amelia and Dr. Stein exchanged glances.

"The Verein freight drivers are pulling in," a voice shouted over the buzz of the crowd. In mass, the settlers turned and headed toward the ox wagons delivering the latest supplies.

Before they reached the supply wagons, they met Dr. Reuss, his usually serene face had changed to a mask of anger. "The drivers heard that the Torrey brothers' wagons sank in mud to the axles. It took back-breaking effort to cover every inch of the way to New Braunfels."

The eager new arrivals rushed down the pier chattering about the blanket of flowers covering the prairie and how wonderful it was to finally be on dry land. Without complaint, they followed directions to the tents being erected to accommodate them.

I'm trying to see the prairie with the immigrants' fresh eyes. Blackberry vines in full bloom cover the ground, and flowers of every color make the land look like a patchwork quilt. Cactus clumped together like shrubs are poking lush blossoms from thorn-covered pads. Her eyes lifted to the wide bank of clouds rising off the horizon, and she imagined that tree-covered hills hid behind the thick mist.

On the first day of April, the Torrey brothers returned with their line of wagons to transport a second load of settlers to New Braunfels. Two days after the wagons pulled away with their excited cargo, the heavens opened, and word came back that rain turned the trip into a four-week trek through hell.

When Frau Fischer realized that she and Hans would not be included in the second group to move inland, she had come for another fretful visit. "Hans is determined. He says with Texas joining the Union, the war with Mexico is inevitable." She pulled out a fine linen handkerchief. With arthritis-twisted and bejeweled fingers, she dabbed at her eyes. "Hans knows nothing of American politics. He quotes Captain Buchel."

Dr. Stein seated her in Amelia's chair and sat on the bed facing her. "I'm encouraging Hans to lead the Saengerbund. His tenor is beautiful, and the Saturday night fests are good for the men and even better for the settlers."

Frau Fischer stomped her fine, mud-encrusted slipper. "And there's your problem. Hans is encouraging those young men to join him in the fight. They're so disillusioned with their lot . ...." She rubbed her swollen hands together. "Several refused to go to New Braunfels with their families. They're waiting to go to war."

"Let me give you more willow bark for your hands. When your body feels better, your spirits will be brighter." Dr. Stein rummaged in his bag and drew out a vial of a crushed woody substance. He poured carefully into the widow's opened handkerchief. "Chew on it and get some sleep. Morning will look better."

They watched her rounded shoulders disappear into the dark. "She's right," He sighed heavily. "The ships keep arriving, and this place gets more like a cesspool every day. You can't blame the boys for being swept into the excitement of going to war."

Amelia had already used some of the compost from the White's giant pile to enrich the soil in her raised garden when Sarah White offered to share squash and cucumber seeds and potatoes she had saved from last year.

Patting the earth into mounds, I can imagine I'm helping Mama plant the garden. The pounding of the surf and the shouts of children brought her back to the present. She soothed the ache, the sense of something lost that gnawed at her belly, by reminding herself that good things were happening. The children and many of the adults were speaking English on a regular basis. The warming weather and the departure of the two wagon trains had changed the environment. Most everyone had a new sense of hope, renewed belief that they would soon be leaving the desolate life at Indian Point.

Chapter Nine

Our young men go to war...

Each time a German ship arrived, the tent dwellers gathered to watch for a mail bag tossed onto the pier. The captains who had made previous trips always had the mail bags packed on top of the luggage so that messages from home were the first things unloaded after the passengers disembarked.

Clutching the letter scrawled with Helga's big bold handwriting, Amelia waved it excitedly at Anna, who also held a message from home. Amelia hurried to the cabin choking back sobs of relief and longing.

> *Dearest Amelia,*
> *Papa is well. Spring has brought a riot of the rose-colored Paul's Scarlet cascading down the side of the manse and along the fence. It's been so warm that geraniums are forming lush red borders around Papa's garden. The von Ewald's cows love the fields of saatwicke waving on spindly green stems.*
> *Hermie is proud to be seven. He's learning to read English. Paul continues to look for his tante Amelia under Papa's kitchen table, expecting her to surprise him. Gretchen wants her hair braided like her tante's.*

Amelia kept drying her eyes on the hem of her apron and then returning to the pages where the ink was splotched from Helga's tears.

> *Max is working again at the tavern. He serves*

71

*the customers and plays his violin or harmonica
upon request.*
We continue to dream of a visit.

She folded the letter and held it against her wet cheek. As always Helga had remained silent about how Max managed to get home after a night entertaining customers and himself. Amelia smiled at the irony: she had not married a drunken peasant like Max, who was scorned by the neighbors. Instead, Dr. Stein was admired by everyone but was not a husband. *Why do Helga and I put up with such unsatisfactory husbands?* She tucked the fat letter into her apron pocket and made up her mind that someday Helga's dream of coming for a visit would come true.

Captain Augustus Buchel had recruited most of the young men in the camp to cordon off a parade ground down the coast. Each morning, he assembled his company of volunteers—young men standing tall, heads held high—in uniforms of shabby, ill-fitting clothing they had lived and slept in for months. Following a regime of calisthenics and marching, sharp blasts from marksmanship practice jolted the silence. Throughout the spring, despite the departure of the two wagon trains moving settlers inland, the boys had become more and more invigorated by war preparations. Parents watched the military activity in anger and frustration.

A woman stared at the rigorous training, tears streaming unchecked onto her heavy breasts. "Herr Buchel makes war sound like a game."

"They'll find out soon enough. I served under Buchel in Spain. I thought when I brought my son to Texas that I was getting him away from the grime of war." The man's face was pocked with scars; his watery eyes never left a tall boy whose muscled arms bulged under a shirt he had outgrown long ago.

"That Fischer boy keeps agitating for war at Saengerbund. The good doctor might have some influence on the other boys if he weren't so eager to please Hans." The man kept his voice low. "You should see him; he never challenges a word that erupts from Hans. He's totally taken in by that tenor voice."

When Dr. Stein came home for supper, Amelia asked him what the man had meant about Hans. "You rarely mention him, yet it sounded like he's the only one you're interested in at Saengerbund."

He flushed and shrugged, then he raised a finger to his lips like he had a sudden insight. "They want me to stop their sons from going to war. You remember, they wanted me to keep the children from jumping off the pier into the bay?"

"Is Hans voice so good that he's getting all your attention?"

He waved his hand dismissively. "His voice is terrific, but I work with every one of the men and boys at practice."

She sighed heavily and turned to the stove to serve the plates. "I suppose we must accept that they think you can fix anything."

Despite the parents' despair, the exercises drew them like magnets, compelled to stare helplessly at the spectacle transforming their boys into soldiers.

At the end of April, Captain Buchel's company joined Albert Sidney Johnson's First Texas Rifle Volunteers, and despite Frau Fischer's pleadings, her handsome Hans marched with the other young men to the cadence of a single drum onto the deck of a transport headed for the Rio Grande.

What is it about the rattling rhythm of a drum beat and the act of marching that fills both marchers and observers with giddy patriotic pride? Amelia stuffed her fists into her apron pockets, grinding her nails into her palms to keep from crying at the sight of parents clutching their sons until the young men awkwardly pulled themselves away.

"When they have uniforms, they'll be so handsome." A small girl of about sixteen with ebony colored hair and dancing blue eyes stepped next to Amelia, gazing at the departing ship. "Aren't you friends with Hans Fischer?"

Amelia nodded, surprised at the question from a girl she had not seen.

"He's the handsomest of them all." She giggled into her cupped fingers. "Frau Stein, will you introduce us when he returns?"

"I'd love to. You know my name, but I don't know yours."

"Everyone knows your name. Next to Hans Fischer, Dr. Stein is the handsomest and kindest man here." She giggled again and cut her eyes around toward Dr. Stein, who was deep in a soothing conversation with a very distraught Frau Fischer. "I am Maria Christina Vogel, named after the Spanish queen. My mama is a proud Spaniard."

"And your papa is a proud German?" Amelia suppressed a laugh.

"How ever did you know? They fight like the Carlists and Cristinos." She grinned, "Papa fought with the mercenaries under Captain Buchel. He wanted me named for his regent, the queen."

"Unless the war ends quickly, you'll be in New Braunfels or all the way up to Fredericksburg by the time the boys return."

"Oh no, Papa plans to stay here. When we first arrived, he had Herr Huck build our house way down the coast." She pointed to an indigo-colored house in the distance.

"Papa doesn't want me infected with all the diseases in camp. I have to sneak away to get up here. Papa says he'll build houses for all the people who aren't leaving with the Verein."

Amelia watched the sassy girl dance off through the crowd, following the ship as it eased away from the pier and sailed down the coast. She waved like she knew every young man on the ship and they all waved at her.

The parents trailed the departing vessel until it moved away from the coast and then they stood like sentinels, the wind off the bay whipping at their tattered clothing.

Frau Fischer clutched Dr. Stein's hand and whispered, "I can't watch." She planted a wet kiss on Amelia's cheek and tottered away through the crowd.

Dr. Stein and Amelia stared after the ship until it became a dot on the horizon. Turning, he muttered, "You can't blame them for leaving. Reuss told me that thirty-six ships have landed here since October."

"How many are still in the camp?"

"More than 2,000 and the desire to get away is like a fever racing through the tents." Dr. Stein stared at the bay rippling peacefully against the shore. "They left Germany to avoid the draft. Now, they're signing up for war by the hundreds."

In the midst of all the war talk, the new state of Texas drew up boundaries and created Calhoun County—the area along Matagorda and Lavaca bays—with Lavaca, twelve miles up the coast, named as the seat of government. So many of the Germans at Indian Point, including Henry Huck, were elected to county offices that Indian Point began to feel like an organized community.

The first of May, the children were playing English word games under the shade of the pavilion when a group of people began to congregate around the ox carts that had just arrived with the weekly supplies. The voices kept rising until it was clear that the drivers brought disturbing news. Amelia dismissed the children who had become too distracted to continue.

The first words she heard were curses. Dr. Stein and Dr. Reuss approached from the cluster of tents to investigate the clamor.

"It's the god's truth," a bearded oxcart driver said. "General Zachary Taylor's army has sucked up all the wagons. The Torrey brothers sent von Meusebach a letter ending their contract."

"Did General Taylor pay more than the Verein?" Dr. Stein kept his voice low, which forced the loud chatter to stop so that he could be heard.

"Yep. The U.S. Army pays in gold—way more than the Verein. Can't blame freighters. We got to make a living, and this here's our chance. Even the farmers are using their wagons to haul army supplies to the Rio Grande."

When Dr. Stein returned late that night, he paced the floor, raking fingers through his hair. "The heat of summer is closing in. This place will be alive with bugs." He stopped and looked at Amelia like he'd just noticed she was in the cabin. "We've ordered as much mosquito netting as we can get. I want to cover our windows and door. We'll give away all that's left. Even with the sides raised, those tents already holding the afternoon heat until late at night. There's no way they can endure mosquito nets around the sides, blocking the air circulation. They'll have to sleep out in the open to keep from sweltering."

As the days warmed, the humidity lay against Amelia's skin like a smothering, wet blanket. Mosquitoes and green stinging flies descended in black swarms, filling the air with a constant buzz, piercing exposed flesh, and leaving welts that were scratched into open sores. Activity in the camp slowed to a languid pace—one day dragged into the next. The steaming, stench-filled tents offered the only shade from the sky faded almost white by a relentless sun. Late afternoon rains, greeted by upturned faces enjoying its soothing goodness, left behind nights of restless sweat-soaked heat.

Hopelessness pervaded the community, and sanitation was forgotten. Both doctors preached the need to dig trenches deep enough to cover waste, but their words fell on deaf ears. Flies settled on every bite of food and clustered around the eyes and lips of small children. Only an occasional fisherman ventured onto the dock's hot surface. A few children—desperate to escape the relentless bugs—leaped like grasshoppers over the pier's oven surface to dive into tepid bay water.

Late one night in June, Dr. Stein slipped into the cabin through the mosquito net draping their front door. He stood very still for a long while, his eyes gaunt in the candlelight. "Amelia, if you want to leave, I won't blame you. You could go to Galveston. Sickness is bad there, but Ashbel Smith would help you find a safe, clean place. You could take an upstairs room at the Tremont."

Amelia had been writing a letter to her papa and Helga. She lifted the candle to get a clear vision of Dr. Stein's face. "Do you want me to go?"

He stared at her, leaning forward, his mouth forming a silent O. "Why, no, Amelia. I thought you might be afraid. Welcome a chance to get away. We have our first case of typhoid. I expect it'll race through Indian Point."

He's as unsure of me as I am of him. I must show him that I'm committed to him. She stood, wrapped her arms around his waist, pressed her face against his sweat-soaked chest. "I wasn't sure you wanted me to stay."

Her heart sank as he loosened her arms and sank onto his chair. "If we could get this place cleaned up, it might not stop the sickness, but we'd all feel better. At least we'd not smell like a sewer. I never expected Germans to be so...." He stopped and looked away. "Lazy."

I'm a fool. He doesn't know I'm here. Why do I keep trying? "Not everyone's lazy. They're learning English, buying lots from Samuel White, building houses, and trying to make this a real town." She watched for an instant as he lifted his head, a look of total confusion in his eyes. "Even my words can't touch you." In disgust, she pushed through the mosquito net and rushed into the still, night air. The bay lay smooth, an endless expanse glowing under a great round moon already high, casting deep shadows on mounds that looked like graves sprawled along the beach. As the bulges moved, she realized they were settlers—desperate to escape the heat inside the tents— huddled under mosquito nets. *They have found their hidden place, a chance to be alone.* She looked away, the ache of loneliness crushing her middle. Fanning her arms to ward off the buzzing insects hovering and tangling in her hair, she turned back to the dark cabin and her sleeping husband.

Chapter Ten

Typhoid spreads...

A barrel-chested man Amelia had not seen around the camp accepted a cup of coffee. "This is the first I've taken from you, good women. My family's been managing for itself." He took a sip of the steaming brew. "I couldn't sell my wagon for a decent price in Bremen, so I brought it along. It's made a good shelter. Now, I'm going on my own. I've bought two longhorn steers to pull us."

Amelia offered her most encouraging smile, "I wish you a safe trip."

He didn't seem eager to leave. "You know in Prussia I wore a stiff, white collar, a silk stovepipe hat, a swallow-tailed broadcloth coat, and kid gloves. My cane had a gold head." He held out his arms. "Look at me. I'm reduced to a wrinkled jacket, a cap, and this crooked stick." He grimaced, "My family suffers equally. We must leave here."

Anna had approached as the man spoke. "Take this loaf of bread for your first day."

The man's face, which had been a pasty white, grew crimson. "Thank you, Frau Reuss. That's very generous."

"My pleasure, sir. We wish you well on your travels."

He walked away swinging his stick like it still had a gold head.

Anna whispered, "Latin farmer—one of those intellectuals who assumes that farming is easy. They expect to stick seeds in the ground and walk away. Let's hope he can drive those longhorns."

Typhoid and cholera and something the doctors called cerebro-spinal meningitis had been coursing through the tents like a mad angel of death. Early one afternoon, as they watched the arrival of another ship, Frau Fischer whispered. "Should we warn them about the dangers here? Warn them of what might happen to their babies? If I had been warned, I might have turned back."

"I came with so much hope. I don't think any warning would have stopped me." Anna's voice trembled. "Now, I don't know…."

Frau Fischer ran her spider-like fingers along Dr. Stein's sleeve. "With all your medical training, would you have brought a child into this?"

Dr. Stein gazed into mid-space, "When that soft spot in the top of a newborn's head starts to bulge, I know it's meningitis. At least, with such crowded conditions, not as many babies are being made." He turned abruptly and rushed away.

Could it be his fear of disease that's making him turn away from me? Fear isn't keeping Anna and Dr. Reuss from touching. Amelia watched her husband towering above the new arrivals streaming toward the maze of tents.

"I should have known better than to upset that dear man with such talk." Frau Fischer whispered as she followed Amelia and Anna to the pavilion to serve lunch. Afterward, she trailed Amelia back to her cabin, sat on the front step and swatted flies while Amelia worked the garden and cleaned out the privy, which was being used by more and more of the tent dwellers.

When Amelia returned to help with supper, Anna tilted her head toward Frau Fisher. "Have you grown an appendage?"

"She's lonely. She hates sharing that tent with so many farmers she feels are beneath her."

Anna rolled her eyes and muttered. "Get Herr Vogel to build her a house. She flashes her rings. Tell her to offer Vogel some jewelry for a house."

"I'll suggest that to Dr. Stein. She hangs on his every word."

"I've noticed," Anna smirked. "If she were thirty years younger, she'd need to murder you."

79

She might be sorry she got him after their wedding night. "Aw," Amelia muttered and continued shooing flies and serving the supper plates.

She woke the next morning with a headache and headed toward the breakfast line hoping to find someone who would lead the children in the word games. *I don't want to smell the food, and I certainly don't want to spend the morning listening to Frau Fischer extol the merits of her son.*

"You aren't looking well." It was Frau Fischer dressed in one of her beaded morning gowns.

"I'm a little tired. I'll rest for a while after the class."

"Are you with child?" Frau Fishers' bushy eyebrows arched as her eyes scanned Amelia's middle hidden under her broad apron.

She couldn't suppress the laugh. "I'm afraid not, Frau Fischer." *Helga and Papa would be as shocked as Frau Fischer and the rest of the world to know how sure I am that I am not with child.*

She was surprised at how much energy it took to walk the few hundred yards back to their cabin. She lay down, but cramps roused her from sleep. Voices drifting in the window signaled that it was already time for lunch. She started to the privy to relieve the stomach pains and realized she could not make it. Reluctantly, she used the chamber pot, ashamed to leave it for Dr. Stein.

She was asleep when Dr. Stein burst through the mosquito net, covering the door. "Amelia, are you sick? Anna and Frau Fischer are worried about you."

She felt him ease onto the side of the bed, his long, cool fingers moved across her face, opened the front of her dress and moved across her chest. She wanted to say he had never touched her there. She must remember to tell him later.

His voice was a soothing balm as he buttoned her dress. "You have a fever and a rash on your chest. Have you been eating?"

She wanted to respond, but it felt like rocks banged around in her head. The cough jangled her brain with a fierce pain. Dr. Stein spoke to someone standing next to her head. She didn't want to open her eyes. She'd speak later when the cough stopped.

Days must have passed. She knew Dr. Stein touched her. She heard his soft words telling her that he needed her, telling her that he loved her. Or did she dream his words? She knew she did not dream his touch. The others who talked to her and helped her move and cleaned her had a different touch—not rough, but not the feel of Dr. Stein.

She heard his voice against her ear, whispering that she was better, that her fever was not as high. She tried to nod, to let him know she heard, but she couldn't make her head move. She felt cool water slip between her lips; her tongue searched for more. The cloth stroking her body opened her eyes into the smiling face of Dr. Stein.

"My god, Amelia, you see me. You know I'm here."

She would tell him later that she knew he had been there all the time, that she heard him telling her that he needed her and loved her. She was sure it was not a dream. Maybe she would call him Joe. Would he like to hear it from her?

She felt him against her in bed. The blur of stars shone through the mosquito net. He held her against him as he slept, his breath came in deep healing waves.

She woke with a start as his warmth moved away. He lit a candle and poured water into the bowl.

"I see you, Joe." She heard her voice and smiled as he fell to his knees beside the bed and buried his face in her breast.

"I thought I'd lost you." He sobbed, pulled her into his arms, and rocked her.

She stroked his head and realized he had a beard, prickly against her hand. "How long has it been?"

"Seven weeks of hell." He murmured, his face still against her chest, stroking her back and arms. He kissed her forehead and lifted her up. "Let me wash you. Frau Fischer will be here soon. She and Anna and Sarah have helped care for you."

"Seven weeks?" She loved the feel of his hand moving the cloth across her body.

"Typhoid. You must rest. It can roar back."

She pulled his hand to her lips. "I heard your words of love."

81

"I thought I was too late. I let you feel unloved all these months."
"I know better now."

Chapter Eleven

I'm stronger every day...

Is it a continued disappointment that's slowing my healing, or is it taking more strength than I expected to walk to the dock? Amelia gripped the firmness of Dr. Stein's arm and welcomed the sturdy support at her elbow of Frau Fischer.

"Look what's happened in the past two months." Frau Fisher spread her arms, her rings flashing in the sunlight. "Indian Point's an official town. Herr Thielepape has laid out eighty-two blocks." She squeezed Amelia's arm. "See that little house down the bay—the white one beyond the Swartz's? The one facing the water? Herr Vogel built it for me. I bought three lots across the street to assure my view of the bay."

"It looks like a real village." Amelia gazed at the shoreline dotted with mostly one-story brightly painted buildings, some fronting the bay and others sitting back into the prairie. "They look like Easter Rabbit eggs."

Frau Fischer pursed her lips, "There're no *Osternesters* tucked around them."

"There will be. Look at the oleanders and trees around our cabin." She felt Dr. Stein squeeze her arm.

I had thought there would be more than pats and squeezes. Did he touch me when I was ill because he knew I couldn't respond, couldn't ask for more? Like a ghost drifting in and out of a dream, he touches me and smiles, and disappears as I draw near.

"When Hans sees how Indian Point..." Frau Fischer's voice trembled. "I'm counting on Hans returning from this dreadful war, and Dr. Stein helping him get work in Indian Point."

Dr. Stein smiled and looked off down the coast like a man seeing an image that no one else could see. "Now that we have an official town, Samuel White's selling lots from $10 to $100 to those who refuse to go inland with the Verein."

Frau Fisher glared at Dr. Stein. "He's also selling to Americans. They're swarming in here with their slaves and plans to get rich in our new town."

He nodded, his eyes crinkling into an amused smile.

He disagrees completely with her view of Americans. Just last night, he said they would bring fresh investment into our economy. He said Indian Point wouldn't prosper if it remains only a village for Germans. Amelia looked at her husband's relaxed face. *Why is he so careful with Frau Fischer?*

"I'll check on patients before it gets dark." He kissed Amelia's forehead, patted Frau Fischer's stooped shoulder, and strode quickly back toward the coughs echoing among the tents.

Amelia walked back toward the cabin listening to the sounds of the growing village—hammers barking against resistant wood, mingling with shouts of children in the camp always playing, even as the sick lay nearby in sweltering tents.

Frau Fischer leaned close. "You're so fortunate. He loves you dearly. He went for days without sleep. Anna and Sarah and I helped all we could, but he hovered over you." She laughed low in her throat. "You remember that day you got sick? I thought you were with child."

"I remember." She found herself liking the aristocratic little lady, even if she had no idea of what she was saying.

"I need a housekeeper." Frau Fischer pulled her shawl tighter around her shoulders. "It's too far to the pavilion for every meal. I'll sacrifice my food deposit with the Verein if I can get someone to come in every day." She touched Amelia's arm. "Do you suppose someone would move into my upstairs room? Be with me when I need something?"

Amelia almost laughed at the absurdity of a full-time housekeeper in the tiny cottage until the serious look on Frau Fischer's face stopped her. "One of the unmarried girls, perhaps?"

"Will you ask for me? I have trouble communicating with those people. They're so...coarse."

She stopped, held Frau Fischer with a steady gaze. "You want to live with one of them?"

"Oh, my dear. I would train her."

"I'll see what I can do." She lied, knowing she had no intention of asking someone to submit to Frau Fischer's training.

Amelia waved to Micah, who was approaching, his cart loaded with dried dung.

"Master White was glad for me to scoop up this manure for your garden."

"Thanks, Micah," Amelia called.

Frau Fischer whispered loud enough for Micah to hear, "Do you mind if I hire Micah to plant around my house? Dr. Stein keeps him busy, but I thought you'd soon be back to your garden. Then, Micah might have time for me."

"Of course."

During her illness, she had heard someone chopping in the garden and thought it was Papa getting the soil ready for Mama to plant. As she roused, she saw through the mosquito netting the fuzzy image of a black man. He kept a steady pace with the hoe, moving in and out of the window frame, his head always down, a red bandana tied around his forehead. When she could form words, she had asked about the vision.

Dr. Stein had sat on the side of the bed and looked out the window. "That's Micah, one of Samuel White's slaves. White offered to rent him to work in the garden. I couldn't rent a man. Then, I heard he was working extra jobs to buy his freedom."

Amelia had been stunned, remembering Fannie wanting to give up her freedom. "Did he get free?"

"Almost. White agreed to Micah hiring out after he completes the chores on White's place. Before daylight, he works at White's. He's here by the time the sun gets a quarter way up. He does whatever needs doing around here and then goes to the dock and spends the day unloading ships or making repairs. When he's done with what we need, he helps Vogel build houses. I've never seen a man work so hard."

"When can he buy his freedom?"

"He needs a little over $200 to pay the $1,000 that White's

asking."

"$1,000. For his own freedom?"

"White says a good worker like Micah goes for $1,200."

"Did he expect you to think he was being generous—only charging Micah $1,000?"

"Well, I don't. I'm paying Micah as much as I can without appearing to buy it for him. He's a proud man."

"I'm proud of you." Amelia had raised herself up in the bed, reached for Dr. Stein's hand and pulled it to her lips.

He had squeezed her hand and stood. "I'll get back as soon as I can."

She remembered the searing pain in her belly as he pulled away. She had tried to act as though she hadn't noticed by saying, "I haven't been aware of anything except voices and people bending over the bed. Are they still dying in the tents?"

"Yes, typhoid's killing them by the dozens."

She had watched him pick up his bag like its weight was almost more than he could bear and disappear through the mosquito netting. She had drifted into a restless sleep listening to the rhythmic chopping of Micah's hoe.

Despite Amelia's impatience, her strength returned slowly, forcing her to spend part of each day in bed and to continue depending on food Anna and Sarah brought from the pavilion.

Dr. Stein came in late one night with a big grin masking the deep circles of fatigue around his eyes. "Since I've almost paid off Runge's loan for the pier, he'll put up the money to build a store."

"Are there enough settlers, enough customers with money?"

"The United States transport ships have started using our pier. Soldiers would be good customers. Unlike the majority of camp dwellers, the soldiers have money." He leaned back in his chair and laughed. "A few of them look old enough to need razor strops and shaving mugs. A lot of the others would buy razors hoping to need them by the time they reach their post out west."

"You really think boys who don't shave will buy razors?" Amelia laughed at the idea.

"I remember shaving a full year before I had any beard at all. It's built in. Boys want to make those facial hairs grow."

Amelia smiled. "I guess it's the same for girls. We look for the first sign of bosoms." Dr. Stein looked at the floor. *I've spoiled it again with too much intimacy.*

"The soldiers are sick of ship food when they get here. If they could buy something to eat, they wouldn't wait for the supply wagons to be unloaded."

"Do we have money to stock a store?"

"Runge's loan will cover merchandise. We'll have to decide what and how much to buy." He grinned, his eyes creasing into teasing slits. "I'm hoping you'll be strong enough to run the store until we find someone who wants to work full time."

She leaped from the bed and threw her arms around him. "You trust me to run the store?"

"You're tough and smart. What else could I want in a business partner?" He unclasped her arms and reached for the fried redfish that Anna had left on the stove.

Business partner. I'm already a partner in this pretend marriage, not a wife. She slumped back on the bed and watched him settle at the table over the mound of food on his plate.

Chapter Twelve

A Business Partner...

Sitting together at their table, the candlelight made a warm glow on their faces and on the paper as Amelia listed merchandise to be ordered.

"You're not going to like my suggestion," he said.

"What?"

"Several barrels of black powder and lead. I'm sure you've noticed fewer men firing with the Sunday club. Most of them are out of powder and lead. The Verein has run out of its supply."

"I'd hoped, with the boys off to war, they'd gotten the shooting out of their systems."

"German men don't stop loving their guns and their *scheibenschiessen*. It's born in them."

"Not in you?"

"I have other things to occupy me. I feel the same way about gambling. I don't want to spend money on something I can't recoup.

"You're on your way to being prosperous."

A weary smile flickered, "that's my hope. Being successful in business brings respect, which brings patients. More patients increases respect. One feeds on the other, offers a cushion against a failure you don't expect."

He is so fearful, unaware of the love that surrounds him. "You don't need to worry about gaining respect in this community."

He waved his hand, warding off invisible interference. "Add to your order several reams of paper and plenty of pens and ink. More people are listening to Herr Sneed and sending letters and articles to

German newspapers warning against signing up with the Verein."

"Do you think the number of arrivals will drop off?"

"That's all that'll save this place. Get them to settle at Indian Point or get out of the camp. Then, stop the ships."

"Is it wise to build a store when we're hoping Germans stop immigrating?"

"Locals will be our paying customers. Vogel can't keep up with the demand for new houses. American investors see that the U.S. military vessels are landing at Indian Point. If we don't build a mercantile store, Americans are going to beat us to it."

"Settlers complain that Americans like Samuel White are lazy. On the other hand, they love Sarah."

"White's been in this part of the country a long time with connections all over the region. He'll be attracting more investors, and they will not be Germans."

She dipped her pen in ink, "I need to remind some of the folks who are complaining about Americans that they're learning English so they can be a part of America. That means living with the Americans."

"Exactly. In the beginning, I think we'll need a large inventory of supplies for the colonists to take inland. Most will barter rings and bowls and family treasures in exchange for supplies. Locals will pay in silver, and they'll buy those treasures you take in as trade."

Even after they went to bed, her excitement grew as they lay in the dark talking about the store. Finally, his words became slurred, and his breaths became long and slow. *The store is going to make us closer.* Drifting in half wakefulness, she sensed a difference in his body; his breathing picked up; he seemed to be experiencing a restless dream.

She lifted her head to his shoulder and stretched her arm across his waist. The bulge in the sheet surprised her. She let her hand move down where the hardness caused his drawers to bulge. She folded her hand over him, her heart pounding as she added a little pressure.

There was a thrust against her palm and then he gasped, "What are you doing?" He dodged away, pushing at her, his hand clasping over himself as he pulled his legs up, his knees making a wall between them.

"I thought you needed me."

"No. It must have been a *nachtmahr*." He rolled over, still guarding himself with his hand.

He said I captured his heart. Was he lying? I'm certain I heard him telling me he loved me. She rolled over, curled into a ball, her knees against her chest to press out the pain and the shame of touching a man on his privates when he didn't want her.

Amelia sat at their table working on the merchandise list, which grew longer as she thought of needs for settlers to run a household and necessities for the trip to New Braunfels.

"May I come in?" Maria Christina, the young woman who planned to capture Hans' attention as soon as he returned from the war, pushed the netting aside and stepped into the cabin. She held a loaf of bread wrapped in a cloth. "I made it especially for you."

"It smells so good." Amelia pulled the warmth against her face.

"I've come to see you every day. You didn't recognize anyone, and you grew so thin."

"I heard a jumble of voices."

"You almost died. I've never seen a man so upset as Dr. Stein." Maria Christina accepted a chair and carefully arranged her gingham dress that clung tightly, emphasizing her waist. Leaning forward, she whispered, "I hope Hans Fischer will love me with such ardor."

Ardor—only his patients inflame his passion. Was that it? I was sick, and it roused his emotions? "I didn't think you and Hans were sweethearts."

Maria Christina wriggled her tiny shoulders. "Not yet. I'm being very kind to Frau Fischer. I insisted my papa build her house the minute she asked." Maria Christina rolled her eyes that were as blue as the bay. "Hans is very close to his mama. If I can be friends with Frau Fischer, I imagine I'll be invited to supper soon after he returns."

"You have planned it so carefully."

The confident young woman rearranged her skirt and placed her hands on each knee, leaning so close that Amelia could see the dusting of powder on her nose. "I have a nice voice, and I'm inviting several ladies to join a *Frauenverein*. We can visit and sew and sing together once or twice a week. By the time Hans returns, we'll surprise him with a *saengerfest*. The women will sing just as beautifully as the men. And" she took a deep breath, "if I'm the leader, and he hears my soprano, he'll naturally want to get to know me."

Amelia couldn't hold back her laughter. "Maria Christina, I think you'll be very successful."

She wriggled her shoulders again. "I'll tell you a secret. I thought it would help if I became friends with you and Dr. Stein. It's obvious Hans adores Dr. Stein."

Amelia watched Maria Christina—her shoulder-length curls catching the luster from the sun—hurry down the shore toward their new indigo-colored house. *Perhaps I should take lessons from Maria Christina.* She went back inside, loosened her braids, and began brushing her hair.

When Amelia announced one evening that she felt strong enough to return to helping in the pavilion, Dr. Stein grasped both her hands and looked at her with an intensity she had not seen before. "You must not go into the tent area. Limit your contact with the camp people to the food line and the store."

"What about you? Are you immune?"

He sank to the bed as if the question had sucked all his strength. Staring at the candle flickering on their table, he finally said, "So many innocents have passed. I wonder at a God who spares the likes of me." A flicker of a smile curled his lips, "Maybe it's my punishment for being half a man. I don't die."

She caught her breath, reached for his shoulder and could not think of a comforting response. *Half a man? Does he feel as barren as I do?* She turned away to hide tears that she shed for both of them.

On the morning that Amelia returned to help with breakfast, Anna seemed near weeping, and Sarah had clearly been crying. As soon as the lines were no longer pushing forward, Amelia tucked her arm around Sarah's waist. "What's upset you two?"

"Samuel sold our house. Just like that. We've lived on this head right for three years. He didn't even ask me."

"Surely you won't be leaving." Amelia felt a hole opening in her chest.

"He wants to move me back to my home in Victoria. He'll come down here often to watch his land interests, but I'll be stuck in Victoria." Sarah made no effort to stop the tears. "My family was among the first Irish settlers welcomed into the De Leon Colony. Samuel wants me to get involved in the social life, open doors for his law practice. At Indian Point, I've found a calling. I can't imagine socializing every day."

Rachel Swartz shooed the children away that had moved close to watch Sarah cry. Rachel had taken over the English class during Amelia's illness. Now, with two babies nursing, the three Deutz children, and her own Peter trailing after her, Rachel looked like a mama cat moving all the children to the class at the back of the pavilion.

Sarah sagged on the bench, "He'll run for political office right away."

Anna scooted close to Sarah. "You can help him be a success."

"What if I don't want to work for Samuel's success? What if *I* want to feel some success? Like Amelia. Dr. Stein's building that store for her...."

I can't tell them that the store is compensation for his lack of interest in me. I am capable. Not desirable.

That night Dr. Stein came in late, and as was his custom, went immediately to the washbasin. "Did you hear about White selling his place? Two weeks after Thielepape finished surveying the town, White up and sold his house and garden for $800. One of his Victoria business partners is planning on staying in the house until he moves his family down here."

"What happens to Micah?"

"It seemed less complicated if I bought Micah. I paid White the balance of what Micah owed. We walked down to Henry Huck's lumberyard. I figured with Huck being the new probate judge...he could sign my paper stating that I was on this day freeing Micah. Felt really peculiar. Never thought I'd own a slave, even for a five-minute walk down the beach. He's a free man who has a debt of less than $100 to me. Won't take him long to pay it off."

"Where's Micah?"

"He'll stay at White's, work mornings for hire. When White leaves, Micah can move into the store's extra back room. We won't need it for a while." Dr. Stein lowered his bulk to the bed, began unbuckling his wet boots, dropping pieces of encrusted shell on the floor. "I'm going to buy some lots that back up to the bay for future warehouses and stores. The new market square should be another good place to own property."

"Anna's upset. She doesn't want to leave, not with all these new arrivals needing so much help."

"Don't suppose she had much say in the matter."

Amelia sat on her chair, looking at the man on the bed, announcing his plans for buying land, "Wives don't have much to say about how investments are bought and sold, do they?"

"Not usually." He pulled a soiled rag from his pocket and wiped wearily at his face.

Anger flashed like lightning through Amelia. "I'd like to ask you to remove your dirty boots before coming in this cabin."

He lifted his head in surprise, then gazed at his boots. "Looks like I've been wading in a hog wallow." He seized one in each hand, padded across the floor in socks faded orange by wet leather. He set the boots on the step outside the door. "I'll try to remember that ladies like a clean house."

When Amelia crawled into bed, Dr. Stein was already taking the deep, relaxed breaths of someone perfectly at peace.

Everyone says he's a good man, but he's a man, and he expects to be in charge.

The next morning, Micah was pouring cistern water on the garden as Amelia returned from helping with breakfast.

"Congratulations, I hear you're a free man."

"Yes, ma'am. I'm free as them gulls flying over the bay. Not as noisy, but just as happy."

"I'm sure you'll miss the Whites when they leave."

"No, ma'am, won't miss them a little bit. A man don't miss his master. He's just glad to be shut of him."

"I thought I'd bake you a cake for a celebration."

Micah lifted his nappy head and for the first time his eyes, with whites as yellowed as parchment, looked directly into Amelia's. "I thank you. I ain't never had a cake baked for me."

"That makes it even better. I'll get busy right now."

I pray Micah will never feel, like Fannie, that he is safer from white men if he's protected by a benevolent slave owner.

Chapter Thirteen

I've become a merchant!

Carl Vogel's house construction business had flourished by employing men from the camp eager to find work and settle at Indian Point. But when he went through the tents announcing the need for more craftsmen to help build Dr. Stein's mercantile store with his office on the second floor, men, happy to have a way to help Herr doctor, worked like inmates released from their prison of boredom.

"The store needs to back up to a wharf at the base of the pier," Dr. Stein had insisted. "We'll have wide sliding doors opening onto the wharf for hauling in merchandise. With the front door facing the new Main Street, we'll be perfectly located for wagons from the interior traveling the old road through the camp. Someday, the wharf will extend down the coast, and other businesses will back up to it."

Amelia was writing to her family when Dr. Stein burst in the door with his latest idea. "I bought the White's three milk cows and their chickens. Having fresh milk and eggs in the store will attract regular customers."

Building the store has given him a new liveliness. "I'll gather the eggs. Let's hire Micah to do the milking and turn the cows out every morning." She dipped her pen in ink and let her sister know that she had managed to get out of milking, the old task they both hated.

Micah's freedom sent an added burst of energy that drove his wiry body from task to task, reminding Amelia of the beavers she watched as a girl. They scurried along the riverbank, not slowing for a minute as they felled logs that looked far too large to be handled by such small creatures. Yet, they always maneuvered the logs to their lodges. Each day, as Micah finished his work at their cabin and started to one of his other jobs, whether in the rain or in the blistering hot sun, he grinned his almost toothless smile and said, "It bes another fine day, don't it, Missy?"

And despite how many had been buried the day before or how late Dr. Stein had stayed out with those who were dying, Amelia felt buoyed, and she responded, "It certainly is a fine day."

One evening as Dr. Stein and Amelia climbed through the tangle of wood beams forming the store's skeleton; he said, "We need to decide what we're going to do about selling spirits. Several tent-dwellers, including a few of the women, have asked me to stock some good brandy. I'd like a little brandy myself. But too many of the men are lying around with nothing better to do than drink. If it were as handy as the store, we might develop an even bigger problem."

Amelia looked toward the tents where the flaps had been lowered against the chilly evening breeze stirring off the bay. Only a few children were still outside. Candlelight created silhouettes of adults moving around inside, laying out quilts for the night; some appeared to be sitting in clusters to visit. "I'd say it looks peaceful if I'd never been inside one of those tents. They remind me of holding pens for cattle, and they don't smell much better. They're not places for adding alcohol."

Dr. Stein stood beside her, looking out toward the camp. "They've reminded me that ship captains offered brandy to soothe disgruntled passengers. And last winter when the weather was especially cruel, the Verein oxcart driver brought a barrel from the warehouse at Lavaca."

I still hear Max loudly singing his way home from a night of drinking and Helga pretending not to notice. Amelia lifted her skirt and stepped carefully across boards lining the wood floor to the opening that would be the store's front door. Without looking back, she said, "A barrel of brandy is fine for special occasions. I don't want to run a tavern."

Stein's Mercantile was completed in early November, just as the first cold front blew in with piercing rain and driving wind. The windows rattled until Amelia feared they might break. She was sweeping up the scraps of wood left scattered by the workmen when Dr. Stein hurried in the front door and clapped his hands together for warmth. "It's as cold in here as it is outside." He hurried to the black cast iron stove he'd ordered back when the heat and humidity made Amelia's clothing stick to her body like wet rags. At the time, he'd said that keeping the store comfortable would attract more customers, especially the poor souls trying to stay warm in those God-forsaken tents. Standing beside the cold stove, he said, "Why don't you light a fire?"

"I'm waiting for the order of firewood."

"That farmer up the Lavaca River assured me he'd get it here by now. Until it arrives, use all that scrap wood."

"I don't want to waste it before the store opens." She kept sweeping, ignoring him beating his hands along his arms for warmth.

The ship from Galveston brought the first of their merchandise and Micah hauled the barrels through the wide doorway into the store. The mingled aromas of coffee, brown sugar, tobacco, and soap transformed the sprawling room into the cozy feel of a village store. Dr. Stein had ordered a bell for the front porch, insisting that Amelia could go home when there were no customers and listen for the bell to call her back. As an added treat, he had ordered a barrel of New Orleans pralines, strictly on the advice of Henry Huck, who claimed the sugary morsels were the best candy he had ever tasted, even better than the Christmas candy he remembered as a child. Dr. Stein had muttered as he added the candy to the supply order that only rich children in Germany received candy at Christmas.

Amelia made mental notes of the ragged condition of the clothing being worn to the pavilion and let that be a guide for ordering items that the Germans were lacking or had already used—bolts of calico to replace dresses that were worn thin, white linen to patch and bolts of wool to repair jackets, needles, thread, mother-of-pearl shirt buttons, cotton suspenders, and cotton socks. She added extras to help with personal care such as shaving mugs, combs, good bristle hair brushes, and one and two-blade knives, cigars, and plugs of tobacco—the list stretched to several pages. For those planning the 140-mile walk to New Braunfels, she ordered kettles, blankets, sturdy boots, and shovels for digging campfire trenches.

Before they finished stocking the shelves with socks, warm hose, shirts, and new mosquito netting, word spread that Dr. Stein had ordered the new weekly paper from Victoria. Families, eager to hear news of the war in Mexico, crowded into the store to get the latest news from the *Texian Advocate.*

Frau Fischer was the first to arrive, trailing the driver gripping a bundle of papers in each powerful hand. She tossed a quarter on the counter and grabbed a paper the instant Amelia cut the twine holding the first bundle. Planting her glasses firmly across her nose, she struggled to read the account in English of John Coffee Hays' Mounted Rifles. Pulling her glasses off her nose, she wiped a tear with the back of her hand. "I'm sure my Hans is in that group. He's a marvelous shot. His papa started training him as a boy to handle his hunting rifle. My husband wanted Hans to be a fighter—one of the rowdies. It wasn't to be. Shooting was the only interest they shared. Hans liked music, piano, books." Her voice trailed off as she stared out the window into the bay as if she were watching a scene from Hans' childhood.

"Against my wishes, he gave Hans a rifle for his tenth birthday." She clutched the paper against her face and shut her eyes, hiding from the vision. "Hans polished that thing. My, he was proud. I never knew if it was because it was from his papa or because he actually loved shooting." She tossed the paper aside and stared at Amelia. "When his papa was killed, he put that gun in our carriage barn. Never touched it again. I expected he'd bring it with us, but he gave it to our gardener."

She pulled her shawl around her shoulders and turned away. "I've read enough. Give my paper to the next customer." She nodded at a twisted little man who had removed his cap when he entered the store and wrapped his hands in its wooly warmth.

"Looks like you have a free paper." Amelia extended the *Texian Advocate* as the man backed away.

"Frau, I hoped you'd read it for me."

"Of course, I'll read as soon as I help the others who've lined up."

He pointed a thumb over his shoulder. "Most can't read a word of English."

The grim-faced Germans nodded, their eyes pleading for any word of their sons.

"We'll start right now." She read that a large group of volunteers, including Texans under Col. John Coffee Hays' Texas Mounted Rifles had stormed Monterrey's defenses in September and declared an armistice with the Mexican General Arista. President Polk had refused the armistice, sending the army south to Saltillo and east to Victoria.

"So, the United States president doesn't want to stop fighting? He wants our boys to take more Mexican land?" The man stared at the group huddled in a tight circle around Amelia. "We came here to get our sons away from war. While we wait for the Promised Land, we're burying our wives and little ones, and praying our sons come back from that greedy man's war."

A burly man with bright pink cheeks who wore no coat said, "Come on, Peter. We don't want to get something going in here." He smiled until his bushy eyebrows came down on his cheeks. "We thank you, Frau Stein, for reading the news."

They turned in a body to leave. Each man nodded and bowed in appreciation.

As soon as the door shut, Micah raised his head from a barrel he was unloading. "Looks like them papers aren't going to be selling like Dr. Stein expected."

"I can't blame them if they get a riot going." Amelia slammed shaving mugs, razor strops, and combs on the bare wood shelves.

Amelia had been so busy getting the store shelves stocked, waiting on customers from town, and making trades with people from the camp that she had grown accustomed to the hammering and thumping noises coming from the construction in Dr. Stein's upstairs office.

Dr. Stein suddenly leaned in the front door. "Didn't you hear me knocking?"

"When?"

"For at least ten minutes. I've been knocking on the floor to get you to come see my office." His sleeves were rolled above his elbows. Sweat made the front of his shirt stick to the muscles of his chest.

"I didn't know you were upstairs." She didn't say that she had tuned out the upstairs hammering and banging in the same way she tuned out the thumping of his feet on their cabin's wood floor.

"Conrad's finished every detail. I have my first medical office." He kept running his fingers through his hair. Then, he realized what he was doing and used both hands to smooth it down, which made him look more like a disheveled field hand than a medical doctor.

She followed him onto the front porch, shaded by the second floor extending overhead. He spread his arms triumphantly under the sign, *Stein's Mercantile,* printed in bold black letters. A smaller sign —*Joseph Stein, Medical Doctor*—swung from the corner of the building at the foot of the outside stairs.

He led the way and flung open the door into the patients' waiting room. "Allow me, madam." Wood benches, stained a dark brown, lined plain white walls. He hustled to the next door and with a dramatic bow opened it into the office where deep shelves stretched to the ceiling between all the windows. A shiny oak examining table that had a thin leather cover over the end that raised the patient's head, occupied the center of the room. A broad oak desk topped with rows of drawers sat next to a window offering plenty of light and giving Dr. Stein a view of the pier stretching out into the bay. A wood chair for patients sat at the opposite end of the desk.

She threw her arms around the waist of her excited husband and leaned into the tightness of his arms squeezing her against him. Then, it was over, and he pulled away to turn in slow, awkward circles around the room. "Now, my practice is really beginning."

When she turned to leave, Dr. Stein said, "You can knock on the ceiling with the broom handle if you need me. Why don't you try? See if I hear you?"

Laughing, she hurried downstairs; glad no one was in the store to see her beating on the ceiling with the broom.

"I can hear it," he shouted. Then he stomped on the floor.

"I hear you," she yelled just as one of the settlers from the camp came in the door.

Each morning, Frau Fischer hurried to the store as soon as Micah returned with the milk and waited for him to finish churning. "I love the butter, but it's the buttermilk I can't resist. It keeps me healthy," she said each time she filled her pitcher and tossed her money on the counter.

Pralines had proved so popular that Dr. Stein suggested they order two extra barrels to give the children after the Christmas Eve carols. Very few men remained who were willing to practice every week. All through December, Dr. Stein posted notices of their singing schedule on the pavilion poles and on tents throughout the camp. The day before Christmas, the Verein ox carts rolled in with a huge cedar tree thrown atop the weekly rations. A barrel of red wine occupied one wagon seat.

From the store window, Amelia watched the children dressing the tree in ribbons, painted shells, and ornaments dug from sea chests. Several adults, encouraged by the merriment, hurried to the store to purchase more ribbons.

The children aren't noticing that the Christbaum is scrawny, not lush and full like the firs at home. It's a tree, and that's all the children need to pitch their spirits high. The wine is doing the same for the adults. She hugged her arms tight across her breast to ease the yearning for her family.

The sun, moving low over the bay, cast a golden glow on the dingy white tents and the colorful *Christbaum*. Dr. Stein led six men into the space around the tree singing an a cappella *Stille Nacht.* His clear baritone held the voices together until their shyness dissolved into sweet, four-part harmony. The crowd burst into robust song, warming the evening chill. Families pulled from the tents by the sounds of home, joined the roaring chorus. When a soprano voice rose above the crowd, Amelia knew that Maria Christina Vogel was making her presence known. The singing spread like a tonic, invigorating the crowd that refused to let the evening end as carol after carol soared into the moonless sky.

That night Dr. Stein stretched out on the bed, his face in the glow of the candle looked more relaxed than Amelia had seen in months. "I'm not going to let the Saengerbund dissolve. Their music did so much for the morale tonight."

Amelia sat on the bed beside her husband. "You have a beautiful voice."

He grinned, staring at the ceiling, "Was that your soprano I kept hearing?"

She laughed. "That was Maria Christina Vogel, who plans to marry Hans Fischer."

Dr. Stein frowned. "Are you serious?"

"As soon as he hears her voice, he's sure to fall in love with her."

"That'll be an interesting chase to watch." Dr. Stein rolled over.

Is he already asleep or avoiding me? She uncoiled her braids that she had styled for the special evening, crawled between the cold sheets, and moved her body against her husband's back. *Why can't I set aside this desire to touch him when he clearly has no desire for me?* She rolled away, bouncing the ropes on the bed. Dr. Stein did not appear to notice.

Chapter Fourteen

1847—Stein Mercantile becomes a gathering place...

Each week when copies of the *Texian Advocate* arrived, the numbers increased of those who trailed the man delivering the bundle of papers. Amelia made room among the display tables and shelves for the growing crowd to gather round while she read the latest news from the war.

The doctors had been correct in their assessment of the effect of letters being sent back to Germany warning friends and family not to trust the noblemen who organized the Society for the Protection of Germans in Texas. Weeks passed between the arrival of ships, and those that came carried better-informed passengers. They brought more supplies and many brought small wagons for their trip inland. The majority continued on their journey to New Braunfels and beyond, but a growing number decided that Indian Point offered potential for a new life.

On an especially warm March morning, Amelia finished at the pavilion and instead of going directly to the store, walked onto the prairie stretching down the coast away from the cross-strewn burial sites, toward the newly laid out streets lined with houses in all stages of construction. Primrose spread a broad pink blanket under clusters of leafy stalks edged with bunches of tiny blueberries. Drawing near massive prickly pear cactus, which the settlers had not chopped to the ground, she shuddered on seeing that they were pocked with holes from vicious target practice. The survivors stubbornly bore fresh buds fanned along the edges of their flat pods in wild patterns of reds, oranges, and purples. Some were already bursting with white and pink blossoms. She stepped carefully around gnarly vines edged with button-sized leaves, delicate red flowers, and clawing thorns. Occasionally a flutter of birds scattered from the brush. Egrets, clothed in frilly white feathers, waded in shallow ponds that wound into a narrow waterway where ducks paddled serenely unaware of her intrusion.

Spring in this foreign land is so different from home. It's time I write of all the beauty, instead of listing complaints about the Verein. She turned back toward the store and saw a man and woman huddled in the slip of shade created by the second-floor overhang. The man removed his hat when Amelia approached.

"I'm sorry to make you wait. I didn't hear the bell."

"We didn't ring the bell. We've been watching you." He gestured toward the woman, "Frau Bickel and I wondered how you kept from ripping your skirt to shreds among those devil plants. We've heard prairie snakes can strike in a flash, get you in the neck before you know what got you."

"I walked carefully. Everything's blooming like spring is finally here."

"This isn't spring. It's barren desert. A hell hole." A streak of yellow tobacco juice creased the corners of Herr Bickel's mouth; his black eyes pinched almost shut with an anger that felt like he could attack with more venom than any prairie snake.

Slipping the heavy key from her apron pocket, Amelia turned the lock. Herr Bickel reached for the door. "We heard you trade for supplies?"

Amelia nodded and followed the man into the store. "We're leaving. May take us two months if the damned rains start again. We're headed to the Fountains."

"*Neu Braunsfels*," Frau Bickel corrected from beneath a woolen shawl that folded over most of her face. "It's not called Fountains anymore."

"Should be. Never should have honored that scoundrel with the name of his family home."

"Have you decided what you'll need?" Amelia moved behind the counter, a safe distance from the fist that gripped white around his flimsy felt hat.

"Everything," Frau Bickel said, as she laid a thin, cautionary hand on her husband's shirtsleeve. "We've tried to save back some of the Verein's pitiful provisions. We need to know how much you'll give us for my mama's *Biedermeier* wardrobe." Her voice broke as she lifted blue, red-rimmed eyes.

"It's been wrapped in canvas since we sailed from Bremen. Better protected than either one of us. Never saw a drop of the damned rain."

"Will you come look? It's too heavy to be carried here for speculation. You understand, your husband being a Jew, might drive too hard a bargain."

Amelia caught her breath at hearing this stranger's accusation delivered in such a hateful tone. *Jew? Why would she think he's a Jew?* A flash of red fury blazed her face. "Dr. Stein is an honest man, Frau Bickel. You'll find no one who'll claim otherwise."

"Now see there, Mama. You raised the frau's ire. We'll never get enough supplies to get out of here."

"I'll look at your wardrobe. You'll find I'm as honest as my husband." She stomped to the door and did not slow as she headed toward the tents. *Back home, the merchant Klein was the only Jew in our village. Papa dismissed Klein's peculiar habit of leaving his carriage at home on Saturdays by explaining that Klein walked to his store to observe the Sabbath.* She turned and waited for the couple to catch up.

The wardrobe was indeed well wrapped and was as fine as Frau Bickel claimed. It was six feet of elegantly carved wood resting on short curved legs. "I carried the key in my pocket." Frau Bickel stroked the curved facing on the door and slipped the key easily into its brass lock.

"It is a fine piece. I see how well you've cared for it." Amelia tried to calculate the value of furniture grander than any she had ever imagined owning. "I must ask someone to help me. I want to offer you a good price."

"Your husband?" Herr Bickel stretched his head toward Amelia.

"My husband is not a furniture expert. I think Frau Fischer would offer good advice. May I ask her to come have a look?"

"She's that old lady that wears all the rings?"

"Yes. Where else would she keep her jewelry?" *Temper your tongue. This is business.*

"How soon will she come?" Frau Bickel looked near tears. "I've got to do this quickly, or I'll never get through it."

"I'll go to her house right now."

Frau Fischer was sitting on her front step watching Micah till her new garden. "He's the best gardener I've ever had. Look at all the oleanders and tamarisk he's made flourish. This garden will be bursting by May." She lowered her chin, looked accusingly at Amelia. "Now, all I need is a housekeeper."

Amelia explained her dilemma as they walked back to the camp. "You're the only person I know who can estimate the value of this lovely wardrobe. I plan to keep it in our cabin until they come to buy it back."

"You'd let them have it?"

"You'll see how painful it is for Frau Bickel to give it up."

Frau Fischer sighed heavily as they approached the tents. "I never intended to get near this place again. Let's get this over with quickly."

Herr Bickel was standing beside the wardrobe with his feet spread apart, and his arms extended straight down to fists—a man prepared to fight the fifty-year-old woman who had come to place a value on his wife's wardrobe.

"My goodness, it's a lovely Biedermeier. And you've kept it beautifully." Frau Fischer surprised Amelia with a glowing smile as she stretched her ring-encrusted hand toward Herr Bickel.

The startled man looked at the hand like it might be one of the prairie snakes. Frau Bickel moved forward, let her shawl slip back revealing hair as red as sunset, and took Frau Fischer's hand. "Thank you for returning to the tents. When I get away from here, I'll not return for the rest of my life."

"I think if Frau Stein gives you two hundred dollars for the wardrobe you'll be well paid."

Herr Bickel looked at his wife. "I can get a yoke of oxen and a small cart for a hundred dollars. That'll give us plenty to get out of here."

Amelia looked at the woman's stricken face gazing at her

family's last treasure. "When you get established, I'll let you have it back for the two hundred dollars."

"No interest? I thought you people would want interest."

"No, Herr Bickel. You're confusing us with the money-changers in the Temple."

"Hansel, say no more. We have a deal, Frau Stein. I'll ask one of the men in our tent to help my husband carry the wardrobe to your cabin. We'll purchase our supplies right after."

"You want the canvas?"

"No, Herr Bickel. I expect you'll need it." Amelia turned, took Frau Fischer by her arm, and the two walked in silence back to Stein Mercantile.

That night Dr. Stein stopped the instant he entered the cabin and stared at the wardrobe dominating the rear wall of the room. "It's elegant. How did you manage that?"

She moved the candle from top to bottom of the wardrobe to show its rich patina, used the key to unlock the heavy oak doors. After she had related the terms of the barter, she set the candle on the table. "Are you Jewish?"

He cocked his head, a questioning look on his face. "My papa was a rabbi, part of the reform movement in Germany that didn't follow orthodoxy. My old *grossvater* was a very strict rabbi. Kicked Papa out of the family for being a free-thinker. Probably made Papa lenient with me. After I was bar mitzvahed, I drifted away. Then I went off to school, and that was the end of my religious observance."

"Didn't your mama insist you attend synagogue?"

"She was Lutheran. When she married Papa, she left her faith and her family."

"She must have loved your papa to change her life so drastically."

He nodded. "It was mutual. Mama went to synagogue every week and never understood a word of it. I don't think she ever thought about it as something I needed to do. She went through her days waiting for Papa to come home."

Something else I didn't know. At least he grew up seeing a happy marriage. She looked at his face and did not see a hint of discomfort. "Why didn't you tell me?"

"I saw no point in it. I'm not part of that world anymore." He ran his fingers through his hair and shook his head like he was forced to say more than he wanted. He blew out his breath and looked at her with eyes as hollow as an old man's. "Amelia, my papa was a poor man and a Jew. I grew up feeling on the outside. Of everything. Family, the town, my school. Despite Papa's liberal friends making regular contributions toward my education, I set the faith aside. I wanted to amount to something more than a free-thinking Jewish scholar. That's the whole story of my life." He reached for his supper waiting on the stove.

"We both wanted to improve our lot. The only time I *didn't* feel like a peasant was when my papa wore his *talar* to preach. What did your papa wear?"

"At synagogue and around his Jewish friends he wore his *kippah.* When he went into Munich or came to university to visit me, he stuffed it in his pocket." He set his bowl on the table and lifted solemn eyes, "Papa being a rabbi did not make me feel less poor."

We may be Germans, but our worlds are miles apart. She served her plate and sat down across from her husband.

Amelia read, to the ever-growing weekly crowd of news-hungry Germans, an article in the *Texian Advocate* that was meant to poke fun at the coastal communities. The editors claimed that Gallinipper, the underwater shell bar that made it dangerous to sail to Lavaca at low tide, got its name because "mosquitos imbibe a gallon of blood with each nip, thus the name 'Gallinipper.'" From then on, when a ship passed Indian Point and sailed on up the bay toward Lavaca, it became common practice for the Germans to gather on the shore and shout, "Watch out for the Gallinipper," which always brought some much-needed laughter.

The editors never knew that their snub offered a few minutes of laughter for the destitute huddled on the shore at Indian Point. Gallinipper Bar also benefitted Indian Point because only the smaller, shallow-draught vessels frequented the Lavaca port; the larger, government-chartered steam-propelled ships discharged their men and arms at Stein Pier. As Dr. Stein predicted, the soldiers became excellent customers.

Amelia chopped cabbage and onions on one side of their table while Dr. Stein mixed herbs on the opposite corner. Without lifting his head from his task Dr. Stein said, "Let's ask Vogel to add a bedroom and extend the kitchen. Hire Conrad Swartz to build you a kitchen cupboard and worktable. This room could be a real parlor to show off the Biedermeier wardrobe."

She squealed, then clamped both hands over her mouth, surprised to hear that long-ago sound she had almost forgotten.

He laughed, "You sounded like a young girl."

"I've tried since von Ewald hired me to behave like a responsible woman. I was a boisterous child."

"I like your lively side. That's the first thing I noticed about you on the ship. You had so much fun playing with Otto."

This feels like a perfect time to embrace. We should reach for each other. She sat still watching him methodically turning the mortar, crushing the pestle into the herbs.

Although the number of immigrants steadily decreased, Amelia continued helping with breakfast before opening the store. Amid the clatter of Rachel's English class, which had grown to many children and about a dozen adults, Anna leaned against Amelia's arm and lowered her voice to a whisper, "Let's visit when we finish here."

"I can tell you've got good news. You've been smiling all morning."

As soon as they stepped into the Stein's front door, Anna squealed, "I'm having a baby."

Amelia stretched Anna at arm's length. "Let me look at you. I don't see a single bulge in that apron."

"It should come near Christmas, a gift under the *Christbaum*."

"Let's celebrate with a cup of tea." Amelia opened the wardrobe and withdrew a mix of cups, teapot, and sugar bowl—all bartered items from Germans eager to secure supplies for the trek inland. When she turned around, Anna was wiping tears spilling down the front of her dress.

"Will you be there with me? Neither my family nor Joseph ever let me go to a birthing. The screams sound like pure agony. I'm scared."

"I'll stay right with you."

"Joseph doesn't think it's a big event. He sees so many babies born."

"If he were having the baby, it would be a big event."

Anna reached across the table, laid her hand over Amelia's. "It'll happen soon for you. Our husbands come in so tired." A devilish grin spread across her face. "I started telling Joseph that he could get to sleep much faster if he noticed me several times a week. It worked."

"If Dr. Stein fell asleep much faster than he does now, he'd be dead." Amelia joined Anna in gales of laughter.

Anna thinks my tears come from laughing so hard. Amelia clutched a handkerchief against her face.

Chapter Fifteen

Two years since its beginning, Indian Point is thriving...

The April first arrival of the *Texian Advocate* attracted an even larger crowd than usual. The first man in the door was laughing and choking back tears that ran into his straggly tobacco-stained beard. "Right here on the cover, it says our dreams are coming true. We're going to the Promised Land."

Amelia grabbed the paper and began reading to the hushed throng the article headlined across the top of the page. "On March 2, 1847, von Meusebach, commissioner-general of the Verein, and forty-five men from Fredericksburg formalized a peace treaty with the Comanches."

The bearded man trembled, rubbing at tears streaking along creases in his face. "At last, the promise of 240 acres will come to pass. Bless von Meusebach."

"You farmers can continue trusting the Verein. Those of us staying here want to know about the war." Frau Fischer nervously fingered a paper searching for an article providing some answers. "Here it is, Amelia. Please read about our children."

"In the Battle of Buena Vista on February 23, U.S. artillery repulsed a much larger Mexican force under the command of Antonio López de Santa Anna, who had just returned from exile."

"What about our boys? How many have died for this folly?" A grim-faced woman who was taller than most of the men, raised her voice above the murmuring about Santa Anna. "We'd all leave here if we weren't waiting for our sons."

"Over 250 were killed; almost 400 wounded, and six are

missing."

"I hope my Wilhem's one of the six who got out of that hell. Maybe he'll show up here. We can take the first ship home."

"Don't speak blasphemy, woman. There're no cowards in this family." A twitchy little man next to the towering woman, bellowed with such force that his face flamed red behind a blonde beard hanging limp as sewing threads off his chin.

"Are there any names listed among the perished?" Frau Fischer's voice shook.

"No names of the dead. It does say that Augustus Buchel has advanced to the rank of major."

"I don't want to hear another word about Buchel." Frau Fischer held both hands over her ears. "He led our boys into this."

The crowd parted to make way for Frau Fischer as she pulled her shawl up over her head and rushed toward the door.

As soon as the door slammed shut, a voice from the back of the store said, "Ain't nothing much sadder than an old hen scratching around looking for her only chick." Several in the crowd followed Frau Fischer out the door. Others began selecting socks, scooping up dried beans and tobacco, talking about what they would need for that long walk to Fredericksburg and the farmland beyond.

The bearded man and his wife kept hanging around the store, picking up first one item and then the next until the last customer paid and closed the front door. The woman approached first, stood looking down at Amelia—a hawk sizing up its prey. "You better do the talking, Rudolph."

Rudolph positioned himself in front of his wife and began carefully withdrawing a tightly wrapped cloth from inside his breast pocket. "It's my papa's Meerschaum." He displayed a dark red tobacco pipe with a bowl carved as the head of a full-bearded ship captain. Holding it with the reverence of a communion chalice, Rudolph extended it toward Amelia, his piercing eyes staring. "It's the finest tobacco pipe made. Years of smoking have turned it this cinnamon red."

"You can tell she doesn't know a thing about a fine pipe, Rudolph. Show her the other one. Let her compare." The woman spoke to her husband as if Amelia weren't present.

"I will, I will, Hannah. I'm supposed to be handling this

business." Rudolph drew a second tightly wrapped object from his opposite pocket. "This here's my young brother's almost brand new Meerschaum. He wanted to be like Papa. Have a special smoke every night. He took consumption, died on the ship before he ever set foot in Texas." Rudolph extended an almost ivory-colored pipe with a bowl that curved up like a hunting horn.

"Let me show her the difference." Hannah took the captain's head pipe and held it toward Amelia. "Spit on your finger and rub it on the pipe."

"Go ahead. You'll see how to test for a genuine Meerschaum." Rudolph resumed his place in front of Hannah. "Put a lot of spit on your hand. Now rub it in."

Amelia felt the smoothness of the material and was surprised the moisture seeped quickly into the delicate creases in the captain's face.

"Now do the same with my brother's." Rudolph shoved the pipe into Amelia's hands. Again, the spittle absorbed into the pipe.

"I don't see the difference," Amelia said as Rudolph and Hannah stared at her in obvious triumph.

"Exactly our point. They're both fine Meerschaums. My papa's is more valuable because it's absorbed all the oils from years of tobacco smoke. Someday, when the proper man smokes my brother's Meerschaum, it'll acquire this beautiful red sheen."

"So. How much will you give us for both pipes?" Hannah took charge.

Amelia felt like she'd just fallen out of a tree and couldn't find her breath. "My goodness. I know nothing about the value of pipes. I can hear my husband upstairs in his office. Let's call him down."

Hannah and Rudolph both crossed their arms, looked at each other as though they had a secret code built into their intense stare. "Call him," Hannah said.

Amelia hurried to the back room, grabbed the broom and tapped hard against the ceiling. Dr. Stein's voice came through the floor. "Do you need me right now?"

"Yes, please come down." Amelia tried to keep her voice steady.

The doctor's feet thumped noisily on the outside stairs, and he entered the front door carrying a mortar and pestle. He nodded at the couple. "I have two patients, Amelia."

Rudolph did not say a word. He extended the red pipe toward Dr. Stein.

Dr. Stein's mouth formed a silent O. He quickly set the mortar and pestle on the counter. "Is that a Meerschaum?"

"Absolutely," Hannah said and stepped up so that her eyes were level with Dr. Stein's. "Your wife doesn't know what to offer us for it. What do you offer?"

Dr. Stein reached for the pipe as he spat a wad of saliva on his fingers and rubbed it in. "Look at that. Soaked right up."

"Now, try this one." Rudolph shoved his brother's pipe toward Dr. Stein.

After the same spittle test, Dr. Stein looked at Amelia. "Meerschaum's are valuable when they turn this dark red. I think you should offer eighty dollars for the red pipe. This newer one is worth about half."

"We'll take it." Hannah spoke quickly as though she expected Dr. Stein to change his mind.

"We want it all in silver," Rudolph said. "When Wilhem gets back from the war, we'll buy passage on the first ship home."

"Good day, sir. I wish your son a safe return and your family Godspeed on your journey home." Dr. Stein grabbed the mortar and pestle. Amelia could hear the thumping of his feet on the steps and his trail across the waiting room to his office.

Amelia was making a list of supplies she needed to replenish the store and trying to forecast the ever-increasing demands of the permanent residents when Rachel Schwartz opened the door. Clutching both good-sized babies against her bulging breasts, she peeked in, her smile as bright as the morning sunshine. "Do you have time to visit?"

"Absolutely." Amelia laid her pencil aside and walked around the counter to embrace Rachel and the squirming lump of nursing babies.

"I want to talk to you before I jump into my latest plan." She pulled Hulda and then Joseph Stein Deutz from her breasts. They toddled off to entertain themselves with cans of peaches that Amelia handed to young Peter, who rolled the cans toward each of the babies.

"The camp people are leaving in droves. Those that are settling here don't want to come to the pavilion for their lessons. Parents are asking if I'll continue with the English classes. And I want to." Rachel's smile had slowly faded into trembling lips. "Conrad says I need to stay home and care for all these children."

"You have a gift with children."

"I know. The children are all speaking English. And..." she covered her face with both hands, "Conrad says I'm immodest when I say I've taught the Deutz children their numbers and reading. They are far advanced of the other children." She lifted her head and looked at Amelia, both brows arched defiantly. "Parents in town are offering to pay me."

"That's wonderful."

"Not to Conrad. He says women shouldn't earn money. I reminded him that you run Dr. Stein's store. He says that's different. It's Dr. Stein's store. He's just letting you do it until Hans comes back from the war. Then you'll stay home. And have babies."

Amelia stared at Rachel. "What makes Conrad think Dr. Stein is waiting for Hans?"

Rachel flushed and looked embarrassed. "Conrad thinks Dr. Stein sort of adopted Hans. Helped him with the Saengerbund. He's kept it going while Hans is away..."

Do townspeople know more about Dr. Stein's plans than I do? Amelia shrugged, "I suppose Hans would be good in the store. But don't allow me to affect your plans."

"I knew you'd say that." Rachel sucked in a deep breath, her bulging breasts stretching the front of her dress. "Conrad may not like it at first. When I make some money, he'll change his mind."

Amelia couldn't suppress her laughter at the image of Rachel bustling out the door toward her dreams—defying her husband—her squirming brood anchored on each hip and Peter clutching her skirt.

All of Indian Point was swept up in boundless motion. American businessmen from the East Coast and all through the South were coming into town to buy property, while down the coast, near Henry Huck's lumberyard, the Runge brothers—Henry and Herman—built their own long pier and warehouse for their new commission and forwarding business. They included a cool cellar for storing wet barrels of brandy, wine, and mustang grapes.

Chapter Sixteen

Many sides of Dr. Stein

Dr. Stein burst into the store one morning, breathless, his hair limp with morning dew. "Guess who just arrived? Almost forty young men from home. They're calling themselves '*Die Vierziger.*'"

"Surely they didn't join the Verein with all the letters warning against it."

"They heard von Meusebach had made the peace agreement with the Comanches, that the land on the old grant is really cheap. They organized a commune and set sail for Texas. Just like that! They've already named their settlement Bettina."

"Bettina?"

"That's Bettina von Arnim, a revolutionary who's been arguing for human and civil rights." Dr. Stein grimaced in frustration. "It's not important who she is. Her writing's influenced these young intellectuals. Mostly from universities at Giessen and Heidelberg. I studied with some of their professors." He stopped, sucked in a deep breath, "Amelia, I'm trying to say I need your help. Reuss and I want to entertain them tonight. My office is the largest private place available."

She had watched his face contort in a flash from a condescending sneer to a look of panic. *He's worried about his image.* "Tell me what you need?"

"Go to Runge's, have them deliver a barrel of brandy and their best mustang grape wine."

"Shall I see if Runge still has pecans? We could hire Micah to roast them this afternoon."

Dr. Stein had been nervously raking his fingers through his hair while clumping back and forth between the aisles. He stopped and gazed at Amelia. "Perfect! Pecans will be a novelty. Nothing like that at home."

Amelia found Micah turning manure and compost into Frau Fischer's garden, while the good woman sat on her front porch and directed every move.

"I'll be happy to haul the barrels of liquid refreshment and the pecans," Micah grinned like a man being offered a paid vacation. "Let me dump the last of this load of manure, and I'll be right along."

"Come back in the morning, Micah," Frau Fischer called.

"Yes, ma'am. I'll be here by sunup."

Micah walked beside Amelia planning the strategy as they headed toward Runges' warehouse. "Soon as we get the pecans shelled, I'll take one of them new iron wash pots from the store. Build me a fire next to Dr. Stein's building. If I stir the pecans real regular, they'll roast mighty fine, and they'll smell so good, the doctors' friends will be asking for more."

Amelia had dressed for bed when Dr. Stein returned, quite drunk, late that evening. He wore the silly smile of a man who was bursting to brag on himself. "This evening was a triumph. They're brilliant young men, and they finally had a favorable impression of Texas. When they reached Galveston, they waited several weeks for their ship to be repaired. Just when they were ready to sail, the United States government took over the vessel, chartered it to transport troops to Vera Cruz. They had to wait for its return. Tonight we showed them genuine hospitality. They'll be heading out west before the week is out." All the time he mumbled his own praises, he was fumbling to get undressed.

Amelia pulled off his boots and helped him out of his pants. *A drunk looses his inhibitions.* She put her arms around him, pressing her breasts against his chest. His hands came up her back, holding her for an instant that made her catch her breath.

"I should have thanked you for making the evening such a

success." He moved her aside and crawled—his drawers sagging like the rear end of an old bull—across the bed.

She blew out the candle and crawled into bed, pushing hard against his shoulder to shove his foul-smelling snores toward the window. *I wonder if Dr. Reuss came home feeling amorous.* She rolled away from Dr. Stein imagining what it must be like to have a man press himself against her in the bed.

When the *Texian Advocate* arrived in August, an article claiming von Meusebach had resigned as commissioner-general of the Verein and that Hermann Spiess would be his replacement stirred such shock and commotion in the store that Amelia was relieved to see Dr. Stein step in the front door.

"Who is this Spiess fellow?" the man's voice was loud and harsh.

He dropped his arms to his side like a man in a casual conversation and looked around the circle of hardened faces staring at him. "Spiess and Prince Carl wrote letters and made speeches touting the opportunities for professional men in Texas."

A burly man stepped forward and glared at Dr. Stein. The man's neck was thick; his upper arm bulged through a long tear in his sleeve. "So he's one of those dreamers? Don't know a practical thing about this damn place."

Dr. Stein did not flinch. He lifted his shoulders, rising several inches taller than the spokesman. "That leaves it up to you, doesn't it? Decide to get work and stay here—strike out walking with your family—or perish in those god-awful tents."

The room grew so silent that Amelia feared everyone could hear the thumping of her heart. The man's lips formed into a tight little pucker, his bushy brows arched, and then he turned on his heel and stared at the group. "Are we going to take this? The Verein took all our money, claimed to keep it safe for us. Von Meusebach's deserting us. And Herr doctor isn't even on our side."

"I have no side. I'm pointing out your choices." Dr. Stein's expression remained stern, his unblinking eyes canvassed the faces.

"Hold on, Herman," a man lifted hollow, watery eyes to the speaker. "Herr doctor has treated most all our families, never taken a pfennig. I ain't gonna cause him no trouble."

Men who had been staring defiantly at Dr. Stein looked away, not at each other, but at the floor or toward a window or into themselves.

Finally, a man near the back of the group raised his voice, "When I look at my holdings, I realize me and my clan will be better off staying here."

Another said, "Vogel still needs help. I'm a farmer, but I expect I could learn to drive nails or tote barrels of cypress shingles."

Amelia realized she had been holding her breath as the ice melted slowly as a snowdrift. The men nodded, shuffled their feet, and began milling about the store.

The speaker, seeing he had lost his support, walked out the door letting it slam behind him.

"I've got patients waiting." Dr. Stein went to the back room and brought the broom to Amelia, who had moved behind the counter to take money for a tobacco sale. "Knock on the ceiling if you need me." He nodded to the men as they opened a passage to the front door.

That night Dr. Stein paced the full length of the house past the iron stove—marking the opening into the new kitchen—and back again. "We've got to get these people moved inland or convince them to make something of themselves right here."

"When the war ends, there'll be wagons to move them."

"Who knows when that'll be?" He grabbed his leather bag that sat on the end of the new visitor's bench. "I've got to check on patients."

"It's late. There's not a sliver of moon."

"I won't be long." His footsteps thumped loudly on the new front porch—a reminder that when he was upset, he could be as clumsy as someone who had forgotten how to work his feet.

Is he testing his safety, roaming among all those darkened tents? She pulled on her gown and lay staring into the night, listening for a sound of trouble, remembering how much her husband needed respect. He had stood up boldly to angry peasants and had melted into near panic at the prospect of entertaining university men.

Chapter Seventeen

Anna has a baby...

Anna Reuss greeted each customer in the store as she made her way to Amelia. "I couldn't wait to visit with you."

"Sit down behind the counter. I'll pour you a cup of tea." Amelia took the hot kettle off the stove.

As soon as the last customer closed the door, Anna's smile faded. "My husband brought the *Texian Advocate* home last night with news of the Verein declaring bankruptcy."

Amelia nodded. "Expecting it hasn't made it easier. It didn't have to happen. The Verein's ignorance about Texas and greed has killed hundreds of our people."

"We'll never know the number." Anna stared out the window at the scattering of tents where a few women were bent over steaming pots balanced atop campfires. Her blue eyes pooled with tears. "At least those coming now are prepared to manage for themselves. I still feel sad about shutting down the pavilion."

Anna grieves for the lost ones, and I'm relieved to see the numbers growing smaller who are living in those tents. I'm sick of constant death and soul-grinding poverty. She looked at the front of Anna's bulging dress and pushed away a tinge of jealousy. "Remember, hundreds made it to New Braunfels and on to Fredericksburg. Most are thriving." *I don't mean to sound like I'm scolding.*

Anna leaned her head on Amelia's shoulder. "That's what my dear husband says when I start looking at all those crooked crosses and mounds of raw earth."

In early December, Amelia grabbed the binoculars to watch the approach of a sleek little steam packet with *Yacht* scrawled across its bow. As soon as it docked, she recognized the bearded Captain Whipple coming down the gangplank. She knocked on the ceiling and yelled. "Look at the pier! Captain Whipple's here."

By the time she opened the wide rear doors, Captain Whipple and Dr. Stein were pounding each other on the back.

"The *Yacht* is the Morgan Line's newest and fastest steamship from Galveston to Matagorda Bay. We'll connect with steamers from New Orleans. Make it here in one day, three days all the way to New Orleans." His grin made his whiskers almost cover his blue eyes. "I'll be stopping every week. As soon as we're unloaded, I'm heading to Lavaca while the tide's still in." Captain Whipple pointed to a darkening sky. "I'm aiming to cross Gallinipper Bar before that north wind cleans off the water covering it."

Amelia kept returning to the window to watch the *Yacht*'s sails glowing white against the ever-darkening sky. When the wind began rattling the north windows, Amelia hurried to check on the little's ship's progress and felt a stabbing pain of disappointment. The *Yacht* had not moved up the coast toward Lavaca.

Dr. Stein came downstairs shaking his head. "He'll be stuck on the bar until the next high tide."

The sun slipped below the horizon, painting an orange sheen on the waves thrashing against the helpless *Yacht* and crashing against the shore. The temperature dropped steadily introducing the season's first fierce cold front.

Rousing from sleep, Amelia thought the wind was beating against the cabin. Then, she realized Dr. Stein was opening the door to a breathless Joseph Reuss.

"Can you come? Anna's having the baby."

"Be right there." Dr. Stein shut the door and snickered. "Reuss raced toward home like a thunderbolt. His boots aren't even buckled."

Amelia tied her shawl around her head. "It's different when it's one of your own."

"I'm sure that's true." It was barely a whisper.

Despite the cold, Anna was sweating. "How am I doing?" She spoke through clenched teeth.

Amelia held both lanterns for Dr. Stein.

He moved Dr. Reuss out of the way and bent to examine Anna. "You're well on your way. This baby will be here soon."

Anna grabbed Amelia's shawl. "Hold my hand."

Amelia handed the lanterns to Dr. Reuss, who had been pacing the length of the room, banging his feet on the floor as noisily as Dr. Stein. She clutched both Anna's hands and said, "Squeeze me when you need to. Yell if it helps."

The next contraction shoved a yell from Anna's lips. When it subsided, a sweaty grin spread across her face. "That takes too much effort."

In short order, Dr. Stein announced that the head was showing. Anna rolled her body into a powerful arch and with one last blow, she pushed August J. Reuss into the world.

"You have a son, as bald as a goose egg, but handsome as his proud papa." Dr. Stein, sweating almost as profusely as Anna, wiped the fat boy, laid him on his mama's stomach, and tied off the cord.

Dr. Reuss knelt beside his wife, buried his face in her shoulder.

Anna's face was rosy with sweat. "That wasn't as horrid as I feared." She stroked her husband's cheek. "But I don't want to do it again for awhile."

Both men laughed with extra gusto. Dr. Stein washed his hands. "Let Amelia clean August. Then we'll leave you with your family."

Dr. Reuss raised hollowed, bloodshot eyes. "I'll clean my son." He grinned sheepishly. "I think I've settled down enough to care for both of them."

Dr. Stein slapped his friend on the back. "We'll see you tomorrow."

He swings the lantern like we're out for a middle-of-the-night stroll. Does he see how different we are? We have just left two people who find pleasure in each other?

Dr. Stein set the lantern on the table. "We have an hour or two before dawn. How about a nap?"

Amelia slipped her arms inside his bulky coat and squeezed her body against him. "I would love to have a baby."

He gently withdrew her arms. "I'm sorry." The words were a hoarse whisper. He moved into the bedroom, carrying the lantern with him. She watched from the darkened parlor as he stripped to his drawers, and crawled into bed.

"Is that all you give me? You're sorry? You need sleep?" She threw her shawl on the floor and followed him to the bed. *I hear myself screaming, and I don't care.* "Do you ever imagine that I need something? I feel absolutely empty."

He sat cross-legged on the bed, his face a twisted shadow in the lamplight. "I need something too. I am an empty sack of a man. The sight of Anna and Joseph—all these families having babies—rips me open. Because I can't do it, Amelia. I can't make a baby with you."

"Why did you marry me? Why didn't you tell me instead of making all those promises to be a good husband?"

"Because I thought I could. I thought having a wife as beautiful and kind as you would make me come alive." He rolled over on his side, pulled the quilt over his head.

God, help me stop fighting the life I've been given. Stop beating a dog when he's down. She built a fire in the stove. Pulled an old quilt from the wardrobe and curled into an aching ball on the kitchen floor.

Chapter Eighteen

New life moves next door...

Morning arrives like it does every day and we go about our parallel lives, wearing our pleasant, false faces. Amelia pulled her shawl over her head, covered her face against the sharp wind, and hurried to open the store. Dr. Stein disappeared into the darkness between the tents.

For two days, Amelia could not keep from returning again and again to the back windows, scanning the bay, watching the *Yacht* being tossed by an unforgiving north wind, clinging like a white skeleton to Gallinipper Bar. *She is trapped as surely as I am.* When the wind lay down, and the high tide began lifting the little ship, she held the binoculars whispering, "Go, get away as fast as you can."

Dr. Stein came downstairs and stood with Amelia watching the captive escape toward Pass Cavallo and the open waters of the Gulf. "A patient just told me that Harrison & McCulloch started a weekly stagecoach service between Lavaca and Victoria. If Whipple can figure out how to successfully cross over Gallinipper and keep the *Yacht* on a weekly schedule that connects with that stagecoach in Lavaca, passengers will skip our port and sail on to Lavaca."

Amelia watched her husband pacing the floor, his hands shoved in his pockets like a man carrying the world on his shoulders. "Our values are so different. You don't want the *Yacht* to cross Gallinipper Bar because we might lose business to Lavaca. I don't want to see the ship stuck, held like a prisoner."

In mid-January, as the sun was sinking across the bay, Amelia locked the front door just as Dr. Stein came down the stairs. A stagecoach pulled by two sweating horses rumbled to a stop in front of the store. The driver, a young American, who looked like a cowboy in his tight-fitting pants, jumped down, removed a dusty felt hat, and bowed in one quick motion. "I'm Charlie Masters. I just completed my first run from Victoria in one day."

"That's forty miles." Dr. Stein, who looked like a ragged German scholar in his rumpled black coat and disheveled hair, leaned against a porch column eyeing the young man.

"I changed horses in relays." Charlie Masters pulled a tow sack from under the high seat and began rubbing down his horses. "With fresh teams, it can be done."

"How often will you make the run?" Dr. Stein stepped off the porch and bent to eye level with the stage driver's clear, steady gaze.

"Every week. I heard the *Yacht*'s making regular runs from Galveston, connecting with ships from New Orleans. I want to meet it. Get those passengers into Victoria in one day."

Dr. Stein motioned for Amelia to unlock the store's front door. "Do you need a depot or a relay stop?"

"That's why I'm here. I'd like to put a stable on your property. I'll be moving my missus from Victoria. She can manage the stable."

"Where will she live?" Amelia lit a lamp and put a log on the dying embers in the stove.

"Above the stable. She knows horses. Been around them all her life."

Dr. Stein pulled a chair close to the stove for Amelia. "She must be awfully young."

Charlie looked puzzled. "We're both twenty. Been married two years. She won't need anything except feed and water for the horses."

Amelia left the two men to work out an agreement while she hurried home to make cornbread, fry bacon, and boil a pot of Swiss chard.

Before Dr. Stein brought his new business partner home to

supper, they had made a deal with Micah to help build the stable. Charlie ate like a man twice his size, while he explained his challenge, "The Mitchels, Lou's parents, have a ranch outside Victoria. They agreed to finance our stage line. It's really a loan. Mr. Mitchel has a half-interest until we pay him back." His eyes cut mischievously first to Amelia and then to Dr. Stein. "We aim to show them we can make it."

Amelia laughed. "I bet you can."

"So do I." Dr. Stein pounded Charlie's shoulder. "We'll get some sleep and let you start first thing tomorrow."

Charlie appeared to be asleep the instant he stretched out on the parlor floor.

Before dawn, Charlie and Micah headed to Huck's for lumber. Amelia kept glancing out the store window, enjoying the sight of the two men working together like well-oiled machinery. Despite the cold, Charlie's shirt was drenched with sweat and stuck to his body, exposing every muscle rippling down his back and into his low-slung pants. *What is wrong with me? No decent women would look at men this way.* She turned away.

In five days the sweet smelling lumber had been hammered into a stable and corral. Amelia and Dr. Stein climbed the steps to the barn-like room above the stable.

"We cut a hole in the roof for the stove pipe." Charlie spread his arms to show where the stove would be. "When do you think it'll arrive?"

Dr. Stein shrugged, "this week if it's available in Galveston. And if Captain Whipple gets the *Yacht* here on time. He keeps getting further behind on his schedule with cold fronts blowing in and running the ship aground every time he tries to cross Gallinipper Bar."

"I'm anxious to move Lou down here. We'll hope the stove arrives."

"If it doesn't, she can have your place on our parlor floor."

It was only two days before a stagecoach rumbled along the road toward the store. A determined-looking young woman, her hands gripping the reins, skillfully halted the horses with the stage doors positioned for passengers—if there had been any—to step right onto Stein Mercantile's front porch.

"This is Lou," Charlie beamed like a man showing off his prize.

Lou scrambled from the seat, her full skirt parting like trousers. She stood a head taller than Amelia and extended a hand gloved in soft leather. "Thank you for doing business with us. We can't wait to get this stage line going."

She moves like a woman who gets what she wants. I must take lessons. "Did Charlie say your name is Lou?"

"Daddy wanted a boy. He was going to be Louis, Jr. When I surprised him, Mother named me Louise. Daddy cut it to Lou. Been my name ever since."

Amelia laughed. "It's a perfect fit."

Dr. Stein gazed at the broad-shouldered girl whose chestnut-colored hair curled out from under a drooping felt hat. She grabbed his hand in both of hers. "Charlie told me all about you both."

"We'll help any way we can." Dr. Stein kept nodding, his eyes darting between the two young people as though he were trying to grasp the dynamics—Lou strode to the end of the porch, her gaze measuring the nearby stable and corral. Charlie was wiping the horses.

"Micah will help get the stove upstairs," Amelia said.

"No need for that. We'll get it all moved in before dark." She swung herself easily onto the driver's bench and eased the horses toward the stairs alongside the stable.

As soon as the horses were turned loose in the corral, Lou and Charlie began unloading, easily hauling a small wardrobe up the stairs. It was completely dark when they came for the stove. "We'll get it connected tomorrow."

"Do you have enough blankets?" Amelia held the lantern as they hoisted the stove up the stairs."

"Yes. And we have each other." Lou heaved the stove a little higher and backed in the door.

I already knew that. Amelia smiled, lowered the lantern and went back into the store.

Dr. Stein was out of breath when he came back from meeting with local merchants and representatives of the German Emigration Company, the group that was taking the place of the bankrupt Verein. "Did you see that Harrison & McCulloch Stagecoach go down the road? They've got four horses pulling that thing."

"I heard it rumble past, saw a cloud of dust blow across the front of the store."

"They're at Runge's warehouse dock. He says they'll make weekly runs to Gonzales and meet a stage to Houston. At New Braunfels, they connect with a stage to San Antonio and Austin. Can you believe we'll have access to all the major towns in Texas?"

"Will it stop here?"

"They won't dare skip us." Dr. Stein thrust out his chest and folded his arms. "The new company plans to land at our pier. They bought a third of Samuel White's remaining town lots. Part of the deal includes selling exclusively to settlers. No more property going to American speculators." Dr. Stein started toward the door and turned back. "What do you think of buying several lots when they survey the tent camp? More settlers would stay if they could rent a small house."

"I'd like to see houses in place of all those tents." Amelia looked toward the expanse where so many had struggled to survive. All the vegetation was gone, the gray soil was scarred from years of people living and dying on it. When it rained, the rancid dirt turned to mud. "It needs loving hands to plant gardens and flowers."

Chapter Nineteen

1848—The war is over...

Lou had acquired Frau Fischer's habit of jangling the bell before coming in the front door. Her hair was tied back in a tight black ribbon, but curls crawled out and hung along both sides of her face. "Since Harrison & McCulloch Stagecoach is already here, I intend to get acquainted with every person in this town. Let them know that Masters Stage Line is part of this community."

"When Dr. Stein finishes with his patients, he'll be glad to take you to meet the Runge brothers and that commission merchant that's building the new pier."

"No need. I'm not a bit shy. Thought I'd stroll down the street and introduce myself. I need to meet Mr. Clegg. Let him know we plan to have passengers staying at his hotel."

Amelia watched Lou tying her broad-brimmed bonnet over her restless curls as she strode confidently away. *She will know everyone in this town before the week is out. I wonder if she's that sure of herself with Charlie.*

In early February, when the four-horse Harrison & McCulloch Stagecoach pulled to a stop at the front door, Dr. Stein came downstairs. The driver leaped to the porch holding a stack of newspapers. "Morning, ma'am and sir. I'd like to make your acquaintance. See if you want the new *Lavaca Journal?* It'll be printed every week." When he grinned, his missing front teeth exposed yellowed tobacco gums. "Let you folks in Indian Point know what's happening with your Lavaca competition."

"Sounds like a good idea." Amelia reached for a bundle of papers, damp from the windy ride under the driver's seat.

Dr. Stein shaded his eyes as they watched the coach barrel toward town. "I hope Charlie and Lou can keep up with that big rig."

Amelia opened the stack of papers and called to Dr. Stein as he started up the stairs to his office. "Listen to this editorial. The *Lavaca Journal* is accusing Henry Huck and Captain Whipple of bias. It says they are blinded by personal financial gain. They're misrepresenting the facts of the commercial advantages of Indian Point over Lavaca."

"Nobody's going to accept talk against Henry Huck. We can't even count how many coffins he gave away or how much wood he donated when his men couldn't build caskets fast enough to keep up with the demand."

"They're trying to make the captain look bad rather than admit that Gallinipper is a maritime hazard. That will not sit well with the captain," Amelia said.

On the morning in late February when the oxcart driver delivering the *Texian Advocate* arrived yelling, "The war's over!" he was mobbed by the families surging out of the tents, following him to the store, demanding details.

Amelia heard the commotion and rushed to meet him on the porch.

"Tell us what it says," sounded in full chorus from the sea of haggard tear-stained faces gazing at Amelia.

I feel like the town crier. Thank the Lord this is good news. She grabbed the paper and read as loud as she could shout, "The Treaty of Guadalupe Hidalgo, which ended the war, was signed on February second. The men should be returning soon."

The roar was deafening. Frau Fischer, who had come on a run, her morning coat hanging loose below her heavy winter shawl, elbowed her way to the edge of the porch. She threw her arms around a heavy woman with spikes of black whiskers on her chin and teeth like kernels of corn. The two cried and beat each other on the back. Men began leaping on the porch and taking turns grabbing Amelia to dance her in circles.

Dr. Stein was caught in the melee and danced with men and women. When calm finally returned, the remainder of the day was spent with tears and speculation about how long it would be until their sons returned.

March brought springtime storms with welcomed heavy rain to fill the dwindling cisterns. Then, another cold front sent cutting winds across the bay. On one of those rare days when the sun drenched the coast in faded rays of welcome warmth, Captain Whipple arrived wearing one of his big smiles. Three passengers disembarked, and the crew rushed to unload luggage and the supplies ordered by Stein Mercantile.

Right on schedule, Charlie rolled in with his stage. Lou helped him greet the ship's passengers, and Charlie carried them to the Planter's House with assurances that their luggage would be loaded for departure first thing the next morning.

Captain Whipple came into the store to warm his hands over the stove and sip a cup of coffee.

Dr. Stein handed the *Lavaca Journal* to the captain. "We saved this editorial. Thought you'd want to be prepared for some hostility when you dock in Lavaca."

The captain shook his head and tossed the paper on the counter. "This is my last attempt to cross that bar. I've timed the trip to coincide with high tide. Regardless of what happens, I'm quitting when I get back to Galveston."

When Amelia gasped, the captain laughed. "I want out. This editorial is just the latest volley. Lavaca merchants are swearing I'm incompetent and out to ruin them. Morgan's son and son-in-law are running this end of the business from New Orleans. They don't know anything about Lavaca Bay. I'm buying a little ship of my own. I'll haul along the coast for good folks like you." He patted Amelia's shoulder. "This town's thriving. I want to be part of it." He rummaged in both coat pockets then pulled out a wrinkled pamphlet.

"This was published by Dr. Levi Jones, one of the founders of Galveston. He's explaining why he's bought land down the coast and plans to develop a port called LaSalle."

Dr. Stein examined the claims in the pamphlet and then handed it to Amelia. "I'm glad he sees great potential here. I wish he'd build in Indian Point instead of developing a new town just six miles down the coast."

Amelia stared at the drawing of a long pier extending into the bay and buildings along a wharf. *This store has become a gathering place for people who have become my regular customers. I've already built a business.* She tossed the crumpled paper on the counter, "I don't see anything much different from what we have right here."

They watched the *Yacht* ease away from the dock and sail toward Lavaca. Amelia was closing the store when Dr. Stein came downstairs and grabbed the binoculars. "Whipple's stuck again. I'm glad he's getting out of that Lavaca turmoil. It's going to get ugly as their merchants face the fact that we provide a better port."

It was two weeks before the *Yacht* returned without Captain Whipple. A young man in a freshly pressed captain's uniform hurried down the gangplank. "I'm Captain Anson Bolling. I'll be making this trip from Galveston every week. Morgan Lines tells me a stagecoach from Victoria will be here for my passengers."

"Masters Stage Line intends to make this a regular run." Amelia pointed toward the stable as Lou came down the pier and stretched out her hand to the captain.

"I don't have a passenger today, ma'am. We're trying to get this run organized so that passengers can depend on us."

"When fewer cold fronts blow in, we expect you'll have better luck," Lou said.

"It's not luck, ma'am. I expect no problem with Gallinipper in any weather."

"Today should be a good test," Lou said. "The tide's out. I'm sure you can feel that north wind."

"I'd hoped to get a cup of hot coffee and a smoke while the crew unloads."

Captain Bolling sipped his coffee and strolled about the store. He picked up both Meerschaum pipes. "These are beautiful. Where did you get them?"

"From some of the German immigrants."

"I can't imagine anyone in this tiny place owning something so elegantly carved. These are as lovely as anything in New Orleans."

"You'll discover, Captain, that people in Indian Point have traveled and lived all over the world. Much farther away than New Orleans."

"How much do you want for them? I'd like both."

"Two hundred."

"My goodness. Since I'm taking both, can you make me a deal?"

"That is a deal, Captain Bolling. They are hand-carved and quite valuable."

He withdrew a leather wallet engraved in gold with his initials. Will you accept notes from the Commercial and Agricultural Bank of S. M. Williams?"

"Of course. We have excellent relations with Mr. Samuel May Williams." *No need to say he owns the hotel when I worked as a chambermaid.* She held out her hand as the captain carefully counted out the payment in twenty-dollar bank notes.

"Do you have tobacco?"

"I do. It's one dollar a pouch."

After Captain Bolling started up the pier toward the *Yacht,* Micah came out of the storeroom cackling. "I hope he enjoys those fine pipes."

Amelia joined in the laughter. "Truth is, Micah, I rather enjoyed over-charging him. And I'm ugly enough to hope he finds Gallinipper Bar more of a challenge than he imagines." Amelia walked to the window and watched the *Yacht* ease out into the choppy waters of the bay.

When Dr. Stein returned near sunset Amelia was standing at the window. "It looks like the *Yacht*'s new captain is sitting atop Gallinipper."

The first of April copies of the *Lavaca Journal* arrived, and Amelia tapped on the ceiling for Dr. Stein to come downstairs. She pointed to the front-page story. "Captain Whipple's been vindicated. The *Yacht's* Captain Anson Bolling caused nine hundred in damages when he went aground on Gallinipper. After the repairs, they tried lightering. Too expensive."

Dr. Stein laughed, "Let's save the paper for the captain. He deserves to read this."

Chapter Twenty

We wait for the men to return...

Amelia watched Dr. Stein and the Masters walking up the road after a meeting of merchants and representatives of the German Emigration Company. Dr. Stein was grinning, obviously as excited as Lou and Charlie, who were swinging their clasped hands like two children.

Dr. Stein stepped on the porch, "With four piers extending into the bay, Indian Point is ready for a massive influx of business. The new government wharf is already unloading personnel and equipment for building army posts out west."

Charlie wrapped his arm around Lou's shoulder. "Getting to Victoria in one day has made Masters Stage Line the most popular on the coast."

Lou snuggled against Charlie. "The emigration company warned that upheavals all over Europe are driving more settlers to Texas. We need to be ready."

"Not another tent community." Amelia looked to Dr. Stein, shaking her head.

"The company assures us these people will come prepared to care for themselves. No more empty promises."

They all turned to stare as two huge freight wagons thundered past loaded with mounds of canvas bundles and huge crates.

"Who's moving in?" Lou started after the billowing clouds of dust. "Come on, Charlie. Let's go see what's happening?"

"Let us know what you discover," Amelia called.

Dr. Stein turned to go upstairs. Amelia touched his arm. "They're holding hands again."

"I noticed."

Why do I keep torturing both of us? She went into the store, letting the front door slam shut behind her.

Late that afternoon Lou rang the bell extra hard. "You won't believe who is moving in here. Mrs. Angelina Eberly's leaving Edward Clegg's hotel in Lavaca. She's opening the American Hotel right here on Main Street. That's one more loss for Lavaca."

Charlie added, "She plans to advertise private rooms for families. We've agreed to carry some of our passengers, especially families, to her hotel."

Amelia grabbed the broom and knocked on the ceiling for Dr. Stein to come downstairs.

"I can't wait for the captain to hear the news." Dr. Stein laughed, "That's one loss Lavaca can't blame on the good captain or on Henry Huck. I hope Whipple decides to stay in Mrs. Eberly's hotel in support of her leaving Lavaca."

Lou's face lit up in a mischievous grin, "Guess what else. She had a piano on that wagon. It was wrapped like the finest gift. She watched every move the men made as they set it in the meeting room."

"A piano? In Indian Point?" Dr. Stein kept staring into a space that only he could see. "I'll visit Mrs. Eberly tomorrow; maybe she'll let the Saengerbund practice with her piano."

Late one afternoon in mid-May, a steamboat whistle sounded way off toward Pass Cavallo. Several customers looked out the back windows. "It's large. Government steamers never come in this late."

Dr. Stein rushed down the stairs. "That's a transport. Could it be our boys?" All the customers hurried behind him down the dock toward the government pier.

Amelia watched from the store as the setting sun shone like a spotlight on the ship inching toward the government facility. Townspeople ran along the road calling to the ship, scrambling onto the pier.

The gangplank dropped, and cheers exploded as young men

sprinted off the ship into the arms of waiting families.

Amelia watched the melee until some of the men who were not from Indian Point began drifting along the dock and into the store. She waited on the soldiers, listening to their chatter and their plans to continue on to their homes, all the time watching for Dr. Stein to return. Finally, he came in the front door, his cheeks flushed with excitement. "It's a beautiful sight. Families are rejoicing."

"Was Hans on the ship?"

"Absolutely. He looks healthy. Frau Fischer's a mighty happy woman."

While Amelia helped the steady stream of soldiers coming into the store, Dr. Stein kept returning to the window. Finally, he called out, his voice breaking with emotion, "Here he comes."

Hans, in all his handsomeness—black hair combed rakishly over one eye and a massive chest bulging beneath medals—stepped in the door with Frau Fischer clinging to his right arm and Maria Christina clutching his left.

"Welcome home, Hans." When Amelia realized that neither woman would allow the young man a free hand, she rose on her toes, and kissed his cheek, which showed evidence of a heavy, late-day beard.

"Thank you, Frau Stein." He smiled at Dr. Stein. "I'm happy to see you, sir."

"We'll have to visit after you're settled. I'd like to hear all about it." Dr. Stein, seeing that a handshake was impossible, gripped Hans' shoulder.

Maria Christina stared dreamily at Hans. "I just finished cooking stew and a large white cake. May I bring it to your house for a celebration?"

"I haven't had cake in a long time," Hans mumbled.

"Will you join us?" Maria Christina looked at Amelia and Dr. Stein shaking her head NO obviously not wanting to include them in the celebration she was organizing at Frau Fischer's house.

Maria Christina has taken charge. "Let Hans get settled tonight. We'll visit later." Amelia noticed that Frau Fischer stood silently clinging to her son's arm.

By morning, townspeople and camp settlers had organized a victory parade. Every trumpet, violin, harmonica, and accordion had been brought out, polished, and tuned. The march started down at Powder Horn Bayou with some older children carrying an American flag, followed by rows of beaming soldiers and then the informal band. The procession trooped along Main Street to the thrilling sound of Beethoven's *York'scher March* and *Horse-Music*. Whistling made up for the lack of flutes. When the flag was raised on the pole on the new town square, men, women, and children saluted along with the proud soldiers.

Colonel Jack Hays, the regiment commander, praised Major Augustus Buchel for his leadership. Then Buchel made a brief speech praising his men for their bravery and valiant service to their new country. Henry Huck, the probate judge, was asked to add a few words.

Tears flowed without restraint, even among the young men who marched with such pride enjoying the shouts and hugs and words of praise. Local men had cleaned up the abandoned pavilion, and the women laid food out on freshly scrubbed tables.

Amelia was setting out pralines and cans of peaches, when Dr. Stein approached with a worried look on his face. "Frau Fischer sent word for me to come to her house. Hans wouldn't get out of bed this morning."

Amelia's heart sank. "I kept looking for him in the parade."

"I'll be back as soon as possible." Dr. Stein rushed off through the crowd.

Chapter Twenty-One

Big changes...

The postwar celebration continued throughout the day and into the evening. The arrival of each new keg of brandy and mustang grape wine from the Runge cool cellar fueled the volume and the discord of the singing. At first, the gunfire sounded like a few celebratory shots. Then, the air shook with thundering volleys so fierce that the candle on Amelia's table trembled and the smoke and caustic smell of gunpowder drifted in the windows. Amelia pulled the candle closer to her supply list and reluctantly added more barrels of black powder and lead.

Finally, the crowd began thinning, singing their way back to the tents or to their new homes in town. Amelia had crawled into bed when she saw the glow of Dr. Stein's lantern approaching the house.

He set the lantern on the floor and sighed as he sank to the foot of the bed. "I hope you'll agree with what I did tonight. I offered Hans a job in the store. I think he needs to get his mind off the war. Have a challenge, a reason to get moving." He began his usual preparations for bed, bending to unbuckle his boots.

Amelia sat up cross-legged in the bed, unable to see her husband's face in the light cast by the lantern. "Will he help me, or is he going to run the store?"

Dr. Stein blew out the lantern and began removing his trousers. "He's not ready to be in charge, but he'll be a help. You won't have to listen for a customer to ring the bell when you're in the garden or cooking supper. He knows about quality goods because that's the way he's been raised—only the finest."

She stared into the darkness, aware that he was stripping to his drawers. "We don't have many aristocrats in Indian Point."

"We're getting business people and professionals, especially the Americans. They'll want nice things—china, good fabrics, fashionable clothing."

"When's he starting?"

"Tomorrow. I think he needs to get busy immediately." He lay down and rolled toward the wall.

He's made the decision without me. I have a new employee or maybe a partner whom I hardly know. Hans is his friend and Maria Christina's future husband. And his mama's precious boy. She sat in the darkness listening to her husband's steady breathing. *He shuts me out of his life by sleeping like he doesn't have a care in this world.* She lay down and turned her back to him, painfully aware that it was an empty gesture unnoticed by the man in her bed.

Amelia entered the store and met Micah on his way to the barn with his milk pails.

"That son of Frau Fischer came knocking on the door about an hour ago. I told him you don't open until daylight."

"He's going to start working here."

"Funny thing. I watched him walk up the beach toward the tents. He was all dressed up like it was a funeral. Look, here he comes now —mighty fine dresser. Like his mama."

"Good morning, ma'am." Hans' smile was contagious, and Micah was correct about his dress. His coat fit close at his waist and bloused over his slender hips. He had tied a scarf, a cravat, at his neck and tucked it into his blouse. His boots were caked in wet shell.

"Welcome to the store. Micah said you were very early. I'm glad you're eager to start."

"Yes, ma'am, I appreciate you and Dr. Stein giving me a chance."

"We're the same age, Hans. Why don't you call me Amelia?"

"Sounds perfect, Amelia." He gazed about the store. "There's so much here. I like the colorful bonnets stretched across the wires. Everything's folded as neat as in the army. Is that decanter Waterford crystal?" He reached for a delicately cut piece that Amelia had traded with a family for supplies.

"Everything on that shelf came in as barter. I thought the decanter was especially fine."

"It's beautiful. The family must have hated parting with it."

"That's one of the hard parts of this job, paying people a fair price for their treasures. Ordering what customers want to buy is another challenge. I'll show you the list of what we need."

Hans grinned. "I'm glad the list's in German. I'm struggling to read English."

"When I'm in a hurry, I resort to German."

"I have a suggestion. Cigars. Almost all the men, except me, developed a taste for the dark, Cuban variety. They're everywhere in Mexico. Chewing tobacco, too."

"I've stocked pipes and chewing tobacco. We'll ask Captain Whipple to get cigars."

"Do you order everything from Galveston? Prices would be better from New York or even from New Orleans."

"I'd love to find business contacts beyond Galveston. We can make that one of our long-term plans. To begin the day, we need to sweep. I didn't get it done before the party last night."

Hans' eyebrows shot up in surprise. "I've never swept."

"I'll show you." Amelia demonstrated the whisking motion.

"Do you go back under those low counters?"

"Every day. When a customer comes in with white shell on his boots like you've done this morning, we sweep up as soon as he leaves."

Hans looked at the crusts of dew-dampened shell marking every step he had taken across the floor. "I hadn't noticed." He began awkwardly stabbing at his tracks with the broom.

Dr. Stein came downstairs wearing a broad smile. "How's it going this morning?"

Amelia pulled the bundle of *Texian Advocate*s from under the counter. "The papers came late yesterday."

Dr. Stein and Hans each picked up a copy. Hans struggled to read a few sentences and tossed the paper aside. "The United States is paying Mexico fifteen million dollars for land all the way to the Pacific. I feel like a thief. Mexico didn't have a chance. How many

died for all that land? I rushed to war simply to get away from here."
His eyes brimmed with tears, and he turned his back as two
customers came in the front door.

Amelia hurried to greet the customers. Dr. Stein led Hans out on
the wharf and around the building to the stairs.

In midmorning, Maria Christina tiptoed in the front door, slipped
a royal blue shawl from her hair and looked around. "Where's Hans?
Frau Fischer said he's working here."

*That girl is not wasting time. Hans is about to find himself
married.* "He's upstairs with Dr. Stein. He'll be back later."

Her shoulders sagged. "I was coming for flour. Hans enjoyed my
cake so much; I thought I'd bake another."

"Do you want to come back to buy flour when Hans is here?"
Amelia couldn't suppress her grin.

"Yes, I will." Maria Christina heaved a sigh. "No sense
pretending. You know what I'm doing."

Amelia didn't try to hide her laughter. "I wish you luck."

It was well after noon before Hans returned, looking
embarrassed. "I'm sorry to abandon you on my first day. Sometimes,
for no reason, I think I'm going to burst out crying like a baby." For
the remainder of the afternoon, he charmed the women customers
with his gallant greetings and the men customers with his boisterous
laughter.

Frau Fischer clanged the bell and entered the store, beaming
proudly, gazing at her handsome son. "I didn't send my new girl for
eggs. I keep forgetting her name's Eva." She smiled conspiratorially.
"Besides, I wanted an excuse to see how you're doing."

"Doing well, Mama. I'll tell you about it tonight."

"Maria Christina's invited herself again tonight. She's bringing
another cake."

Hans shrugged and reddened slightly. "Her cakes are good."

Frau Fischer pursed her lips. "Certainly better than those hard
things Eva slams together."

Frau Fischer had not been gone long before Maria Christina
appeared with a bowl for her flour purchase. Neither she nor Amelia

mentioned her previous visit. "I wanted to bring some brandy for the dinner, but Runge only sells it by the barrel." She looked through lowered lashes at Amelia. "Would you please keep brandy and wine for customers who only want a pitcher for a nice evening?"

"I've been thinking I should do that. Perhaps Hans wouldn't mind taking the cart down to Runge's and getting a barrel of each."

"I'll go with him." Maria Christina clutched Amelia's arm and squeezed a private thanks.

As evening approached, Amelia reminded Hans that he still had not swept the entire store. "I'm going to start supper. Lock up before you leave. Micah has his own key."

Soon after Amelia finished supper, Dr. Stein came home, grinned at her while dramatically scraping his feet on the front step. "I hear Hans' boots made a mess this morning."

"After he swept it up, he realized how much he'd tracked in."

"Do you really think he needs to sweep?"

"I sweep. At least once a day."

"But you know how." He began blowing at his soup.

She reached across the table and curled her fingers around his hand before his spoon reached his mouth. "I learned to sweep. Like Hans, I wasn't born knowing how."

"He's grown up not having to do household tasks."

"You want him to learn how to run the place? Sweeping's part of it."

"Why don't we hire Micah? Hans even suggested Eva. Frau Fischer doesn't need her all day."

Amelia tossed her spoon in her bowl and stood, knuckles on both hips. "Is that what you two talked about the entire morning? He came to work and spent half the day upstairs with you."

"I've never seen you like this. I thought hiring someone to sweep would help you both."

"It's interesting you didn't think of that until Hans arrived. Your peasant wife has been sweeping all along. When one of the gentry shows up, you're suddenly concerned."

Dr. Stein reached for her hand. "Come. Sit. You know I don't think you're a peasant."

"Then let me run the store. I'll have a talk with Hans tomorrow. Find out if he wants to work with me. Then you can decide which of us you prefer."

"No, Amelia. I want you to run the store." He ran his fingers through his hair. "Can't you see, I'm trying to help Hans adjust to life outside the army."

The next morning, Hans' boots were clean, and he was not wearing the scarf and fancy coat of the day before. "Since I still had the key after locking up, I wanted to get here early."

"Thanks for opening. We'll have to make a key for you."

Hans smoothed his hair over his eye and looked sideways at Amelia. "I swept before I left last night."

"Good. As I said, we'll do that at least once a day. More often if needed. And we aren't going to hire someone to do it for us."

Hans nodded, his face reddening as he looked out the window. "I shouldn't have mentioned that to Dr. Stein."

"That's between you and me. I reminded Dr. Stein that no one is born knowing how to sweep. We all must learn."

Hans grinned. "I got better at it before I finished."

"Let's decide how we're going to start selling the brandy and wine. I don't want to run a tavern."

"How about selling it by the pitcher for customers to take home?"

Families who had waited lethargically in the tents had come alive with the return of their sons. The boys, transformed by the war into men, took the family reins and quickly moved away from what they were all calling Old Town. Some headed inland; others decided that Indian Point offered the best future.

Dr. Stein stood for a long time watching the workmen for the German Emigration Company clearing the old campsite. "It's time to buy some lots and build small houses, create a decent place for newcomers to live until they get established."

Amelia leaned her head against his shoulder. "I was hoping you still wanted to make Old Town look new again."

"I also want to increase our income." He patted her back and walked over to the money drawer under the counter. "You, my dear, are the one bringing in the silver dollars. I'm proud of your business sense. You've made the store a community center, and that has brought in customers."

She hugged her arms around her waist, aching with the awareness of his walking away from her touch. "People in our village always claimed that Herr Klein was supposed to be our merchant because Jews have good business sense." *Perhaps that's what we have in common—our business sense.*

Dr. Stein raised one eyebrow and continued counting the silver dollars in the cash drawer.

Right on schedule, Captain Whipple returned in five days with their order and a Presbyterian minister and his wife from North Carolina, who planned to open a school for young women in Victoria.

Also on schedule, Masters Stage Line pulled in with two merchants from Victoria. Charlie loaded the minister and his wife into the stage with the merchants and carried them all to the American Hotel for the night.

Lou had already started hauling the preacher's household goods and luggage down the pier when Charlie returned to help her load the stagecoach for the early morning trip to Victoria.

Hans turned away from the window. "I love watching Lou and Charlie work together. They make it look like fun."

Amelia nodded, continued folding work shirts.

Dr. Stein finished breakfast and gathered his music folder and medical bag. "Hans is excited about Saengerbund practice tonight. I hope I don't get called to deliver a baby. Now that families are out of those tents, I'm expecting the number of births to really pick up." He started out the door and stopped. "Did Anna tell you she's expecting again? Reuss told me she's upset about it."

Amelia's heart sank. "No. She hasn't come to the store lately. Maybe she doesn't want me to know."

Amelia gathered baby August into her arms and sat on a bench at the table still cluttered with breakfast dishes. "You look so tired. Tell me what's wrong."

Anna sank to a chair, "I'm having another baby. I can't keep food on my stomach. August isn't even crawling, and I'm carrying another child."

Amelia pulled a wrinkled handkerchief out of her pocket and handed it to Anna. "Maybe Frau Fischer's Eva can help out."

"Rachel said nursing those two babies had kept her from getting pregnant. It didn't work for me."

"You're not over having this big boy." Amelia bounced August on her knee. "You needed more time to get your strength back."

"All I want is to lie down."

"Do it. I'm taking August with me. We're going to see if Eva will come for a while." She grinned, "Remember, Frau Fischer says Eva's cakes are hard as our cornbread in the pavilion."

Anna laughed in spite of the tears. "I'll not ask her to make cakes."

As they started out the door, August wrapped his arms around Amelia's neck and pressed his warm little belly against her breast. She had not walked far in the morning sunshine until his head drooped to her shoulder. Her lips nuzzled his fuzzy head that still had very little hair. She was sorry to reach Frau Fischer's house so quickly.

On hearing of Anna's news, Frau Fischer pulled the baby into her arms. "He will have to share too soon." Frau Fischer leaned her head into the kitchen, "Eva will be delighted to help, won't you, Eva?"

"Yes, ma'am. I'll get right over there." The lilt in Eva's voice sounded like it might be a treat to get away for a while.

"Before you leave, make us some tea. Amelia never comes to visit."

Chapter Twenty-Two

Dr. Stein is a maestro...

Dr. Stein hurried in the door, his hair and coat wet from the fog blanketing the coast. "I had to feel my way home. Even if I'd stumbled into the bay, this has been the best night I can remember in a long time. The men sounded wonderful. Their voices have matured into rich musical instruments. Mrs. Eberly's piano was the crème de la crème."

Amelia laughed, handed him a towel, and watched him rub vigorously at his head.

"We're holding a concert in two weeks. You'll love Hans' voice. He's a virtuoso. I can't believe his range. With his talent, I don't know why he's staying at Indian Point."

"Do you think he'll leave?"

"He insists he's happy here. Says having the Saengerbund every week is all he wants. That and seeing Stein Mercantile become the most sought-after shop on the coast."

"I guess we need to have a serious talk. Find out how he plans to make that happen."

"Don't let the talk of a twenty-six-year-old get under your skin."

"Hans and I are the same age."

He frowned, still clutching the towel in both hands. "That's hard to believe. You seem much older... I mean experienced." He kissed her forehead. "That's a compliment, my dear."

She laughed. "I'm going to remember. I'm not 'old'. I'm 'experienced'." *Sometimes I feel old when I see Hans' whole life stretched out in front of him. The store is my future.* She turned, began removing her dress, aware that her husband was not watching her prepare for bed.

The night of the concert Amelia carried August for Anna whose skin held an ashen pallor. Frau Fischer and Eva joined them for the walk to Mrs. Eberly's American Hotel. She had opened all the rooms on the first floor for the overflow crowd.

Dr. Stein surprised everyone when he sat down at the piano and began the program with a rousing version of *Die Muehle*. Even the new Americans in town who didn't know a word of the song quickly caught on to the rhythm and clapped with enthusiasm at the appropriate times.

Dr. Stein joined the men's voices in four-part harmony so robust that the applause thundered between each folksong. Anna reached for Amelia's hand and blinked back tears when they sang *Der Wanderer*.

After thanking everyone for coming and announcing that the Saengerbund planned monthly concerts, Dr. Stein took his seat at the piano and Hans stepped forward. As Dr. Stein's fingers tore across the keys, Hans's chest swelled, and a beautiful tenor voice filled the hall with Beethoven's *Adelaide*. The audience was transfixed. As the second movement was about to begin, the culmination of the lover joining with his Adelaide, Maria Christina rose from the front row. Her hair framed both cheeks in delicate curls; her dress, a sculpted taffeta, clung to her body. She cast a seductive glance at Hans, and her soaring soprano joined his tenor in the triumphal march in which the young lovers are united. The blending of voices ended and for an instant, there was not a sound. Then, lifted into one mass surge the crowd stood, bursting into applause and bellowing cheers that shook the building.

Maria Christina and Hans, both flushed with their achievement stood for a moment until she reached for his hand and the two bowed.

The sudden noise and jostling startled August, who lifted his voice in loud shrieks. Amelia clutched him against her, stroking his head, pushing her way through the crowd clamoring toward the two performers and the other members of the Saengerbund.

Outside, she walked up and down the street in front of the hotel softly singing *Wiegenlied* against his ear and stroking his head.

By the time Anna reached them, August had settled down and was beginning to drift into sleep. "I had no idea those two could sing like that," Anna said. "It was the most romantic thing I've witnessed since Joseph proposed to me."

"I can't wait to ask Dr. Stein if it was planned. I know she hasn't been practicing with them. Shouldn't we wait for Frau Fischer?"

Anna burst into laughter, "Absolutely not. She's the proud mama. She took her place between Hans and Maria Christina."

Amelia had given up and crawled into bed before Dr. Stein came home. "I'm awake, maestro," she called as he gently closed the front door. "Why didn't you tell me you could play so well?"

"I'm not formally trained. My mama was a gifted teacher. Against her wishes, I stopped serious practice when I went off to university."

"You should be bursting with pride. Tonight was the most exciting evening the town has ever known."

Dr. Stein sighed heavily, sat down on the side of the bed, and pulled off his boots. "It certainly is the biggest surprise the Saengerbund has ever had."

"You didn't know Maria Christina would sing?"

"Absolutely not. She must have been slipping around when we practiced. There's no other way she could have known." He blew out his lantern.

"What did Hans think of it?"

Dr. Stein stretched out on the bed, rubbing both hands through his hair. "I think his reaction was a lot like it's been about her cakes. He accepts the gift, but he's not eager to reciprocate."

"Poor Maria Christina. She's doing all she knows to get his attention. It's not working."

He grunted, "I think Hans is overwhelmed."

On the way to the store the next morning, Amelia met Micah carrying milk pails toward the barn. "No need to hurry. Mr. Hans is already sweeping. His smile's as big as a quarter moon."

"He was a big success last night," Amelia said.

"My woman cooks for Mrs. Eberly. She told me the crowd whooped and hollered for Mr. Hans and Missy Maria Christina."

"I didn't know you had a wife."

"She's not my wife. White sold her to Mr. Jordan. He does the lawyering for White's business. I have to buy her if I want to marry her."

The wind pierced through her summer dress, and she shivered, suddenly chilled by the notion of having to buy your wife. "How much does he want?"

"First, he asked one thousand. She, being with child, he upped it to twelve hundred. He says with that new one, he's building his stock."

"When will the baby come?"

"About cool weather, I suppose."

"I'm going to talk to Dr. Stein."

"Thank you, Missy. I'd be obliged if you do."

She listened to the forlorn sound of the milk pails rattling in the dark as he headed toward the barn. *Lord God, I don't know what trouble is.* She pulled her arms tight around her chest and walked toward the store.

Hans looked like he was dancing with the broom. "Good morning, Amelia."

"I agree with Micah. He said your smile's the size of a quarter moon. You were terrific last night. And so was your partner."

He rubbed the broom in circles like he was trying to scrub something off the floor. "That's the first time we've sung together."

"It was elegant."

He sucked in a breath. "She'll be wanting to continue."

Not knowing what else to say, Amelia busied herself heating water to warm the churn for Micah.

A flood of customers began arriving to purchase an item or two, eager to visit with Hans and talk about the concert. Hans kept glancing down the street until Maria Christina arrived with her usual burst of charm. Her dress cinched her waist, and her hair was twisted into a new fashion of buns and ribbons. As she walked toward him, he bent in serious conversation with one of the new American women who wanted to look at bonnets.

Maria Christina stationed herself at the door, greeting customers. In response to every comment about the marvelous duet, she coyly dropped her eyes and looked through lowered lashes at Hans, who avoided looking in her direction.

Each customer, most of whom were women, moved quickly from Maria Christina to the dashing young man quietly holding forth across the room near the accessories—shoes, bonnets, ribbons—a long way from the day-to-day necessities for running a household.

Mrs. Jordan, wife of the new lawyer and owner of Micah's woman, paid Maria Christina very warm compliments and then rushed toward Hans. "My husband has sent me to inquire about your boots. We were on the front row last night, and he admired them."

"We've ordered these elastic-sided boots from J. Sparkes-Hall of London. He's shoemaker to Queen Victoria." Hans pointed his toe and eased his trouser slightly above the top of his boot. "They slip on easily. They're perfect for men and women who love to walk."

Mrs. Jordan clapped her hands very softly. "I must have them. How soon do you expect a shipment?"

Hans raised his eyebrows and glanced toward Amelia. "Once they reach New Orleans, they'll be here in three days."

Amelia nodded, hoping she didn't look as pretentious as Hans.

"I'd love a pair also," Maria Christina moved close to Mrs. Jordan.

"We've ordered a few with cream satin tops for ladies' evening wear." Hans continued directing his comments to Mrs. Jordan.

Mrs. Jordan reached for Maria Christina's hand. "We'll both get a pair."

Maria Christina remained in the store the rest of the day looking at Hans, who continued busily about the store, engaging every woman except the one most eager for his attention.

As the sun began setting, Amelia completed her list of needed merchandise, a list that had grown remarkably long that day, thanks to Hans and Maria Christina being such good draws for business. She called to Hans, "I'm leaving the store for you to close."

"I was wondering if you'd like a cake for your supper tomorrow night?" Maria Christina stood at the front door as though she might be about to leave with Amelia.

"Mama has invited the Jordans and Mrs. Eberly to supper tomorrow night."

"That would be perfect. Eva makes such terrible cakes."

"Well. Yes. I'll tell Mama tonight that she need not worry about dessert."

"I'll deliver it late in the day. So it will be fresh."

"Would you like to join us? I mean, since you're making the cake." Hans' smile looked more like a grimace.

"Oh, my, I would love it." Maria Christina grabbed Amelia's hand and squeezed.

Dr. Stein had patients all day and did not get home until well after Amelia had prepared supper. "I hope babies decide not to come tonight and people stay well. I want to go to bed as soon as we eat."

"Did you know Micah has a woman?"

"Who is she?"

"Her name's Jessie." While she explained the situation, Dr. Stein stopped eating, slumped wearily, his elbows on the table holding his head.

"Micah asked me if he could buy one of those houses I'm building. He's saved $600 since he paid off his loan to me. Ironically he wants one of the houses that'll be on White's old property."

"Why on White's land?"

"He wants to live as a free man, owning property on the spot where he used to be a slave."

"Can we afford to help him?"

"We've got to help."

She laughed. "I wish you could have been in the store today. The silver dollars flowed because half the town came to see Hans. Maria Christina was an added treat. Everyone shopped. The Americans bought almost all our lovely bonnets, and the silk shawls that Hans thought we needed to stock."

"He understands the shopping habits of people with money."

"I'm listening to him."

Dr. Stein looked out the window toward the store. "There's still a candle lit in Micah's storeroom. I'll go have a talk with him."

"Let me come with you."

"Will you be embarrassed if Jessie's there?"

"I hope she is. If he loves her, he'll want her there every night."

He reached for his lantern. "I am aware of that, Amelia." He stepped outside without looking back.

At the front door of the store, Dr. Stein called to Micah.

"Yes, boss. I'm right here."

"Is it okay if Amelia and I come in?"

"Sure, boss. Let me get on my shirt."

Jessie's black eyes glowed in the candlelight, and her smile was that of a timid child. Dr. Stein brought two chairs in from the store for him and Amelia. When Micah and Jessie sat together on the narrow cot, Amelia realized that he was far younger than she had thought.

Dr. Stein began explaining their visit, and Jessie grew stone still, her hands folded in her lap, tears glistening on her cheeks.

"We want to see how we can help you buy Jessie's freedom and also afford to buy that little house," Dr. Stein said.

"I'll pay for both. I want Jessie, and I want us to have that house to raise our child."

"I think it can be arranged. Let's go tomorrow to see if we can make a deal to buy Jessie from Adrian Jordan."

"We got two new preachers. A Presbyterian and a Methodist. You suppose one of them would marry us?" Micah reached for Jessie's hand.

Dr. Stein slapped his hands on both knees, "We'll pay the preachers a visit after we talk to Jordan."

"I'll be ready soon as I finish churning."

"You bring the milk. I'll churn," Amelia said.

As they stood to leave, Jessie reached for Dr. Stein's hand. "Micah and I'll pay you back quick. I'm a good cook for Mrs. Eberly. I make good money for Master Jordan. When I'm free and keep my own, I'll pay you every dollar."

The next morning, when Amelia woke, the lantern was already glowing in the barn. She had barely unlocked the store when Micah appeared wearing a suit coat and a pair of too large trousers. "I was so worked up, I didn't sleep ten minutes. Figured I ought to get something done, so I went to milking."

"I'll go to churning," Amelia said.

The morning dragged and by the time Dr. Stein returned from Jordan's office, the store was filled with customers eager to see Hans. Dr. Stein stuck his head in the door. "It's done," he called to Amelia and then headed upstairs.

Amelia caught glimpses of Micah hauling manure from the White's old barn. He spent the rest of the day working on the construction of Dr. Stein's houses being built on the grounds of Old Town.

That night, Dr. Stein's smile lit his face as he stepped in the door. "I know you suffered with curiosity all day. I couldn't get away to talk to you."

She served his plate and sat down immediately.

"Jordan told me I was a fool. I think he was embarrassed to charge for the baby, but he overcame his qualms and decided twelve hundred was fair since he would be losing income from Jessie working for Mrs. Eberly."

"Did Huck sign the paper freeing her?"

"Yes, but Mrs. Eberly was not so happy with an employee rather than a slave. At first, she was going to reduce the pay. Unlike Jordan, she was too embarrassed to follow through."

"Did they get married?"

"Not until tomorrow morning. Mrs. Eberly wouldn't let Jessie off. Said she needed a cook for three meals."

"Did Jessie stay there?"

"Of course. She needs that job. Micah and I found the Methodist preacher at his house. He agreed to perform the ceremony at five in the morning. It'll be quick so Jessie can get breakfast cooked at the American Hotel."

"We've got to be there."

"Of course. We'll be their witnesses."

"I'll take off early and make them a cake. They'll enjoy it when they come in tomorrow night."

"Do you have any lanterns in the store? We need to give Jessie one when she walks home from Mrs. Eberly's."

"And plenty of oil to keep it going."

Jessie had wound a pink oleander blossom into fine braids across the top of her head, and she wore a dress of heavy sack material that was bleached to almost white. Micah's coat and pants were pressed smooth. A pink oleander was anchored in a pocket on his breast.

The Rev. Henry Bauer, who had come to Indian Point to establish the German Mission for the Methodist Episcopal Church, had slipped a coat over his nightshirt, and Mrs. Gladys Bauer was still wearing a nightcap when they opened the door to their tiny house. "You are right on time."

Dr. Stein pumped the preacher's hand. "We appreciate you performing the ceremony at this hour. Jessie has to be at work by half past five."

"I'm obliged." The reverend's rosy cheeks still held the nighttime stubble of whiskers.

"We're offering these ten silver dollars for your church mission," Dr. Stein said.

"How generous. Let's get these two young people properly married."

Henry Bauer moved quickly through the ceremony. When he invited Micah to kiss the bride, Micah pulled a thin band of gray metal from his pocket. "My mama gave it to me when I was sold away. I've kept it sewed inside every shirt." He placed it on Jessie's finger, then bent and kissed her hand.

Micah used the new lantern to walk Jessie to the American Hotel. Amelia and Dr. Stein started back toward the store.

"I was touched when he pulled out that ring," Dr. Stein blew his nose.

"Me, too." Amelia stepped in a wagon rut, and he reached for her arm as she stumbled, holding it securely against him as they picked their way along the road in the circle of lantern light.

Finally, he said, "Jordan said nobody's going to say anything about a few freedmen in town so long as they behave themselves."

"Why would anyone care?"

"Jordan says it's against the law to free slaves. With so few freedmen here, nobody pays it much attention. Then he asked me if I wanted to buy the whole lot. Free every damn slave in town. After what we just witnessed, I wish we could buy freedom for all of them."

She patted the hand still holding her arm, "Maybe, someday."

As empty as a feel when I see other couples who care for each other, I must remember that I'm married to a good man. She looked up in time to see him nod. They continued in silence, two shadows in the night, following a yellow light.

Chapter Twenty-Three

1848—Indian Point thrives...

The arrival of government transports had become a common event all during the summer, returning the last of the troops from the Mexican War and coffins bearing the dead. The soldiers were jubilant and thrilled to finally reach land after the voyage from Vera Cruz. Indian Point residents continued honoring the returning men— standing at solemn attention along the government pier as coffins came down the gangplank. They cheered the veterans who walked along the wharf and roamed into the store. Soldiers spread out over the town before they were loaded onto wagons for the trek to their homes.

In mid-summer, the captain of a transport announced from the deck of his ship that four large wood boxes held the bones of seventeen Texans who had been executed in the infamous Black Bean episode. The crowd listened in shocked silence as the captain explained, "Responding in 1843 to continued Mexican attacks on San Antonio, these brave men took part in the failed Mier Expedition. When they tried to escape their Mexican captors, General Santa Anna decreed that every tenth man would be shot. A pot of white beans held seventeen black beans and the men who drew the black beans were executed on the spot."

Hans stood beside Amelia on the wharf just below the government pier watching the military escort carry the boxes off the ship. "Before we sailed out of Vera Cruz, I heard rumors that a captain, who had drawn a white bean and escaped the firing squad, had led a group to the gravesite and exhumed the bones."

After the boxes were placed on wagons, members of the escort came into the store. Hans identified himself as a veteran of the war. "Where are you taking the remains?"

A young man as tall and tanned as Hans had been when he returned from Mexico, smiled proudly. "We're heading to LaGrange to bury them atop a 200-foot bluff overlooking the Colorado River. They'll be put to rest with the bones of men from the Dawson Expedition, who had gone to San Antonio in 1842 in response to another Mexican raid on the town. They were outmatched in a fight with Mexican cavalry and were left where they fell."

Hans stared at the soldier like he couldn't understand what he heard. Then, without a word, he turned and walked out the back door onto the wharf.

Amelia stayed busy helping the soldiers and the locals who hung around to visit and get the latest details on conditions in Mexico. Soon, Dr. Stein came downstairs. "I saw Hans walk to the end of the pier and just stand there. I thought you might need help with all this crowd."

For once, he's thinking of me before worrying about Hans. "I do. Would you restock what they're buying."

"I hear you're heading to LaGrange," Amelia said to no one in particular.

"No, ma'am. "My regiment's heading out west. We're going to build forts and chase Comanches. Soon as we get all the supplies off the transport, we'll be on our way."

Dr. Stein had hauled more barrels of pralines out of the storeroom and restocked shelves with chewing tobacco, pipes, and cigars. As the crowd dwindled, he stepped behind the counter. "I'll go talk to Hans."

Amelia watched them standing for a long time on the end of the pier. The afternoon sun made the bay sparkle, and the breeze whipped at their shirts. When they returned, Dr. Stein went around the side of the building and headed upstairs.

Hans stepped around the counter, leaned down and whispered, "Sorry, I left you to handle that bunch all alone. I don't know what's wrong with me. Sometimes I think I'm going to burst out screaming."

"What does Dr. Stein say?"

Hans shook his head and stared at the ceiling. "I don't know, but he helps." Hans grinned. "It's your turn to get out of here. I'll finish up and restock. And I'll sweep."

She scooped up the string of fresh trout and bundle of asparagus she'd traded for a pitcher of brandy. The last of the military wagons ground slowly past the store's porch. Most of the soldiers stared straight ahead, a few waved. The excitement of landing and the welcoming handshakes had come to an end; families had gone home to supper. *All the attention, events that seem so important for the moment don't last, and then they are left alone, looking for what comes next.* She nodded farewell to the solemn young men who had seen too much war.

Late that afternoon, heading to Anna's with a bowl of hot fish stew, Amelia scanned Old Town dotted with skeletons of new houses rising out of the scarred earth. Jessie's and Micah's new home sat near the White's barn that leaned like a tired old man toward a quickly diminishing pile of manure. She waved to Micah perched at the top of a ladder painting his house a clean white. Oleanders bursting with pink blossoms hugged the porch. Micah had awakened the White's abandoned garden with a blanket of lush squash vines. Green beans climbed a lattice arbor, and late tomato plants drooped with heavy red fruit.

She found Anna lying on the bed. "I hoped you'd come for a visit." August crawled around the room, pulled himself up to chatter against his mama's face, and tumbled back to the floor.

"If August can eat this really tender fish, I'd love to feed him."

"He's getting teeth. Since it's too late for nursing to do any good, I've stopped." Anna sat up wearily. "I'm hiring Eva's little sister a few hours each day. Clara's only twelve. She says Rachel's taught her to read and do numbers. That's all she needs. Frau Fischer insists on coming every day to train Eva. Gives her an excuse to see August."

"Frau Fischer's not been to the store lately."

"She's avoiding Maria Christina."

"Everyone's avoiding the poor girl."

"Frau Fischer's afraid she'll get Hans." Anna laughed. "From what some of my visitors tell me, she doesn't need to worry."

"Lots of men would be delighted if Maria Christina glanced in their direction. Too bad she's got her heart set on Hans."

August chomped his food, rubbed his hands in the bowl and then smeared it in the little bit of hair that was beginning to cover his head.

Amelia bathed him, enjoyed letting him splash water over the floor and all over her before she laid him in his crib. "I wish I could hold him while he sleeps, but I need to feed Dr. Stein."

Anna slipped her arms around Amelia. "You need a baby. You'll be a good mama."

I'm sick of pretending. I'm sick of looking like a happily married woman. The store is like my child, I constantly think of how I can make it grow and be healthy. It's become my greatest source of satisfaction. She hugged Anna and left quickly. Clouds hovered so low that the heavens offered not a single star. A faint light burned in Dr. Stein's office.

At home, she lit a candle, wrote a long letter to Papa and Helga, and finally dressed for bed. She was almost asleep when Dr. Stein slipped in the front door. "Fish is on the stove." She listened to him clattering with the pot and his plate. When he brought the candle into the bedroom, his eyes looked hollow with fatigue.

"I thought you'd be asleep." He sat on the bed to unclasp and remove his boots.

"Were you talking to Hans all this time?"

"He's doing better, I think. Some of the other men are having trouble settling down since the war. Lots of drinking going on." He blew out the candle and lay beside her, "Sure is hot."

I'm so glad dear Hans is doing better. I wonder if the doctor thinks I'm doing well? "Maybe it'll rain tonight." She listened to his breaths grow deeper.

It didn't rain that night, and it didn't rain for days into late August.

Heading toward the store, Amelia carried a basket she had just filled with eggs and Micah swung along with her pulling his cart of milk pails. Hans was already opening the front door of the store when a team of mules rattled toward them in the dark. Lou and Charlie pulled the wagon up to the porch. The rim of Lou's big bonnet was tied down over her curls; a heavy work shirt covered her dress and her booted foot kicked the brake. "We rented this wagon. I'm heading to Green Lake for water. Charlie's staying here to meet today's ships."

Amelia set her basket on the porch. "How about me hiring Micah to go with you in exchange for you bringing us some water?"

"If he's got time, it's a deal," Charlie jumped from the wagon. "I've tried telling her it's too dangerous to go alone."

Micah's eyes grew big at the prospect of extra money. Then he shook his head. "I don't know about leaving Jessie alone for a whole night. She was right next to her mama until she was sold to the White's. Then she slept next to Miss Sarah's bed."

"I'll tell her to come to our house."

"I get her from Mrs. Eberly's every night." Micah kept shaking his head.

"We'll get her home safely. You know how much we need that water."

Micah grinned. "Our cistern's almost empty. We been rationing it. Saving the dishwater to wash our feet." He blew out a long breath. "I'll go. I'll be thankful for you looking after my woman." Micah climbed onto the seat beside Lou.

As they pulled away, Hans whispered, "You notice she's doing the driving."

Charlie laughed, "I'm sure she'll drive every mile. She's not a gal to give over the reins to anybody."

Amelia shook her head, "It's twenty miles. Can they get back by tomorrow night?"

"It'll be late, but she'll get here. She knows we're low on water." Charlie followed them into the store and sat with Amelia while she churned the butter.

Amelia entered the kitchen through the back door of Mrs.

Eberly's American Hotel. Jessie was scrubbing an iron kettle as large as a washtub. A pot of boiling chickens covered two burners on a massive black stove. Jessie wiped sweat on her apron and frowned. "I'm praying you don't bring bad news?"

Amelia explained her mission, while Jessie's hand covered her mouth to stifle her laughter. "That man does love me. He thinks I'm a little black princess."

"He's worried about you." Amelia could not stop her own laughter.

"I've been roaming this country since before any Germans got here. Don't pay no attention to him. I can walk home alone and sleep sound as a house cat."

"If he hears I haven't kept my word, he won't go again. As long as this drought lasts, we'll need him to make these trips to Green Lake."

"I'm done about ten." Jessie rolled her eyes and went back to dishwashing.

Captain Whipple's ship arrived in mid-afternoon, followed very soon by the *Globe* and the *Portland,* two Morgan Line vessels that docked at empty piers down the coast. "The government's returning ships to their owners that had been leased for the war," Captain Whipple said. "More ships will increase competition for the Morgan Line, force them to reduce their high transport fees. Ought to save you some money."

"We're looking to cut the expense of shipping through Galveston, make connections for quality merchandise in New Orleans and Europe," Hans said.

"I know the Galveston merchants, but New Orleans is too big for me. You'll have to visit the shops that carry those specialty goods."

Hans nodded toward Amelia, "That's why Amelia should go to New Orleans, get to know those merchants,"

"Me? You're the one who knows what we need."

"I can't leave Mama. She's not feeling well."

"She hasn't been coming to the store." She did not add that she thought Frau Fischer had been avoiding Maria Christina.

"She's promised to see Dr. Stein today. I keep watching for her to go up to his office."

That night, Amelia and Jessie walked home under a full moon reflecting off the shell beach and the road, making the lantern unnecessary. "A lot of nights when I'm sitting on my front porch, I see you and Micah working by the light of the moon in your garden. You've turned your place into a real home."

"We want it ready when this baby gets here."

When they reached the Stein house, Amelia said, "Micah wants you to sleep on the floor at our house tonight."

"Thank you, Miss Amelia. I been sleeping in a bed for two months. I don't aim to go back to the floor."

"You'll come if you get scared?"

"I ain't scared of nothing or nobody. It's Micah who's scared."

Dr. Stein was eating the chicken she had left on the stove. "You're awfully late getting home."

"Frau Fischer's not well. When Hans got home, he found her in bed. Inconsolable. Came back to find out what's wrong."

"What *is* wrong?"

"Cancer of the breast. She was too embarrassed for me to look. I offered to call for you. She couldn't bring herself to disrobe. Finally, she let me touch her through her dress. I could feel a large tumor. Fluid is coming from her breast."

"Can you help her?"

"The treatment's too painful. Nitric acid will eat off the breast. It's a slow, agonizing process. We could try a mastectomy, but I'm hesitant to use ether at her age. Patients suffer horribly from all the procedures, and I don't think they live any longer."

"Did you tell her that?"

He shook his head. "I told Hans he'd have to be strong. It'll not be easy."

"Hans said he couldn't leave her. He wants me to go to New

Orleans to find suppliers for some of the better items we need to stock."

"That's a good idea," he stood very slowly. "Meantime, I'm going to bed. We'll have water tomorrow night. I hope to get a bath."

Is it his religion, or lack of religion that's built this crust around him? He's sensitive about the peasants and worries about them, but those close to him hardly distract him at all. He's thinking about a bath and getting to sleep.

Chapter Twenty-Four

"Gold in California!"

The headline spread like a brush fire, igniting excitement that raced through Indian Point. "Prospectors will be landing on Matagorda Bay, the most western terminus and the shortest route to the gold fields. The trail is safer; there are fewer mountains, hardly any snow." Amelia couldn't decide who was more excited, the merchants who stood to make a fortune or the prospectors who tumbled off ships by the hundreds from the East Coast and towns all along the Mississippi River.

Plans were put on hold for Amelia's shopping trip to New Orleans. They stayed busy selling the basics for travelers about to make the rugged trip out west. They shipped in lanterns, cooking pots for life along the trail, and boots—Chelseas for those planning to get rich quick. For the more practical, they stocked sturdy, waterproof footgear that could withstand miles of walking and years of searching for riches.

Charlie and Lou branched into the sale of mules and wagons, necessities for prospectors that believed it would be cheaper to haul their own supplies to California and for whole families that wanted to accompany their men to the wealth that lay ahead.

When Lou clanged the bell and strolled into the store in late October, Amelia noticed that her dress that had always flowed full and loose was fitting snugly against her middle.

"I don't know why we worried about competition from the Harrison & McCulloch Stage Line. We need their help. We can't keep up with the traffic moving through here. Morgan's shipping schedules have become so regular that travelers arriving by ship in the morning can be out of here before nightfall. We've got two drivers helping, and Charlie's looking for two more."

"Surely you're not going to start driving that Victoria route," Amelia said.

Lou kicked her boot-clad foot against the empty butter churn. "I guess you've noticed that I'm filling up this dress?"

"I wondered about that."

"We figure to get an heir for the Masters Stage Line about spring time."

Hans spread his arms, turning himself in dramatic circles. "With all these babies coming along, we don't need new settlers. The town's thriving with newborns."

"You could contribute to the population if you'd marry Maria Christina. She's the prettiest girl in this town. Make you some mighty handsome children." Lou stuck her chin out at Hans.

Hans rolled his eyes. "You're the hundredth person to say that."

"Well? When?"

Hans' face reddened to the shade of a turnip, turning his whiskers into a black shadow over his cheeks and around his chin. "I've got way too much on my mind to think of courting." He turned abruptly, went into the storeroom, and began lugging barrels of soap and candles out to the shelves.

"I think I hit a tender spot," Lou whispered.

This is not the time to focus on my own barrenness. I'm going to be happy for Lou and Charlie. Amelia was glad Lou rushed off to tend to the stables and she was glad Hans stayed busy in the storeroom until she could regain her composure. She decided not to mention it to Dr. Stein until she was sure she could discuss it without blaming him.

The hotels remained packed with travelers. When Jessie had a beautiful baby boy, Mrs. Eberly claimed to be so busy that she allowed Jesse only three days before reporting back to the kitchen with young Isaac strapped to her back. Amelia visited with a new baby gift of little blankets and a fancy christening dress that Hans insisted they stock since the town had two ministers and expected to get a Catholic priest. "Is it wise for you to return to work so quickly?"

Jessie pulled baby Isaac to her breast and laughed, "My mama carried me on her back to the field every day. I remember, even when I was a big girl, her warm back bending and stooping and rocking me to sleep. Thinking of it still makes my heart feel good."

The jangle of spurs and bawling of anxious cattle signaled the arrival of more livestock being driven into town for shipment to New Orleans. Amidst the dust from thundering hooves and the constant barnyard smell, the second issue of the November *Texian Advocate* arrived. "Look at this headline," a man shouted who had grabbed a paper from the oxcart driver delivering the news. "It says Col. Jack Hays has completed an expedition, proving for all doubters that the best Chihuahua trade route from the silver mines in northern Mexico stretches through West Texas to Matagorda Bay."

The crowd huddled close to hear Amelia read, "Investors from Boston and St. Louis are putting $12,000 and 800 wagons into the venture. They expect the Gulf route through Matagorda Bay will also increase the California traffic."

One of the grizzled old German immigrants who had chosen not to move inland leaned on the counter stroking his thinning beard, and spoke in broken English, "We had some hard times. But this is going to make us all rich. I'm buying my wife a bonnet and me a pitcher of brandy."

The Reuss's baby made its arrival in the chill of early December. Dr. Reuss hurried to call Amelia and Dr. Stein, but his behavior, this time, was that of a seasoned father. Anna delivered a tiny girl in record time.

"She's beautiful and as bald as her brother," Dr. Stein's voice boomed with excess enthusiasm.

Anna clutched Amelia's hand. "Is she healthy?"

"She's perfect, as delicate as her mama." Amelia tried not to show her concern. The baby's body was as shriveled as a little old man. Despite a weak hunger cry, she made no response to Anna's breast.

Although Dr. Reuss did not pace this time, he cradled Anna with all the gentleness he had shown when August was born. "I want to be the one to wash our baby girl..." His way of saying he and Anna needed to be alone.

Walking home, Amelia reached for Dr. Stein's hand. "She's dangerously small."

"I'm afraid so. I hope they let Anna recover before they have another child."

"You don't think the baby will live?"

"Not unless Anna's milk is awfully rich. She's so thin; I don't expect she can offer much to this baby."

Early the next morning Amelia found Anna propped up in bed urging the tiny mouth to suckle. "I've tried moistening my finger with my milk and dropping it on her tongue. Nothing arouses her interest."

Amelia held August who kept clutching her face in both his hands to keep her attention away from the baby sister. "Let me take August to the store with me until Clara gets here. I'll start saving cream for you every morning. It should build your strength."

Late in the afternoon, agonized screams for Dr. Stein came from a man running up the road with a child in his arms, so much blood smeared over both of them that it looked like they had been ripped wide open. Dr. Stein helped carry the child upstairs.

"Hans, you better come help," Dr. Stein called as he and the man struggled into the office.

Hans looked at Amelia, as if asking for permission.

"Of course. He needs you."

A crowd followed, claiming the blood had left a wide trail. "It's his arm," a woman said. "He fell from a ladder onto a saw horse. The bone's out of the flesh."

"It's more than any man ought to shoulder. Last month Herr Hamilton buried his wife and little girl. He and the boy moved from the tents into one of Vogel's new houses. Julius was helping his papa paint."

The child grew quiet. "Maybe he's fainted," whispered through the crowd lining the porch and leaning against walls and counters. When the sun moved to just a sliver across the bay, Amelia lit a lamp and stoked the stove. No one spoke. They listened to the clumping sound of Dr. Stein's feet. "He's still alive or they would have come down," The voice was loud enough for all to hear.

It had grown completely dark, and the north wind had started rattling the windows. Amelia was about to stoke the stove again, when Dr. Stein came down. His clothes were soaked in blood, and a red smear creased his cheek like a desperate hand had reached out to him. "The boy will be fine. I gave him ether. He'll sleep a while." Dr. Stein looked at Amelia. "I'm going to keep the boy and his papa here for the night. Will you bring me clean clothes and supper for Herr Hamilton?"

The crowd began to murmur and move off the porch. "I'm going to lock the store," Amelia said. "If you need anything, please get it now."

A few people bought canned peaches. Several borrowed pitchers to take home red wine or brandy.

Hans looked pale and exhausted when he came into the store as Amelia was following the last customer to the door. "I'm not much help. I'll go check on Mama."

The next morning Hans had the fire blazing in the stove and had finished sweeping. "I hope Joe's not disgusted with me."

"Joe?"

"I mean, Dr. Stein. He said university friends called him 'Joe.' It fits him, I think." Hans's face reddened.

"Why should he be unhappy with you?"

"I got sick last night. All that blood...." Hans went into the storeroom. The rest of the day he worked in silence, chatting very little.

It was almost closing time when Dr. Stein and Herr Hamilton

carried Julius on a cot to Lou's waiting wagon. Herr Hamilton extended both square hands to clutch Dr. Stein's and kept shaking. "Julius is all I got left. I'll pay as soon as I get back to my fishing boat."

"It was my pleasure to help Julius."

Gustav Hamilton climbed into the wagon and stroked his son's cheek. Lou eased the wagon forward.

"I'm going home." Dr. Stein's stubby whiskers emphasized the dark hollows around his eyes.

"I'll close the store," Hans said.

As they walked, wrapped against the blowing north wind, Dr. Stein said, "From now on, when I need help, I'll call you."

She listened in silence.

"Hans was worthless. We'd gotten the boy on the table where I could see how the bone protruded. I needed help holding the child, but Hans had turned whiter than a snowstorm. I told him to sit and put his head between his knees. He vomited on the floor."

Hans has fallen off his satin cushion. "What did you say to him?"

"I told him to clean it up. Then, I sent him out. I think he stayed in the outer office. When I came down to ask for supper, I found him huddled in a corner like a scared rabbit. He may have expected to be fired. Or shot."

On the eve of 1849, only the longtime residents followed the tiny casket on which Conrad Swartz had carved the image of a baby angel. The Old Town cemetery, which Anna had watched with so much sorrow, still bore a maze of crooked wood crosses. Dr. Reuss clasped August in one arm and almost carried Anna with the other. Even the preacher had few words of much comfort for yet another family placing its infant into a gaping hole.

Frau Fischer, wrapped in layers of shawls and a heavy woolen hood, cried softly as she stumbled between Eva and Hans. "I'm the next one," she whispered, bending to kiss the casket.

Dr. Stein returned from the February meeting of the town's businessmen. "What do you think of Indian Point getting a new name, one that sounds more like a city than a coastal village?"

Amelia lifted her head from her work on the supply list. "It never crossed my mind."

"Mrs. John Henry Brown suggested Indianola."

"Do we know her?"

"It's the new family from Victoria. Her husband is one of the partners in that new warehouse. He's a commission and forwarding agent and part owner with White in the Old Town tent site."

"Why Indianola?" Hans stopped in the middle of the store, his arm muscles bulging from the weight of a barrel of soap.

"We keep Indian and add *ola,* which is the Spanish word for wave," Dr. Stein explained. "All the business owners voted for it. They suggest we keep both names for a while to avoid confusion."

Amelia leaned on the counter. "We have people calling this place 'Carlshafen,' 'Old Town,' 'Indian Point,' and now we've added 'Indianola.' I'm not sure what address to use when I mail our supply orders."

The four horses pulling the Harrison & McCulloch stagecoach appeared to be coming into town at an extra fast clip. As the driver slowed his team, the bay winds picked up the dust his stagecoach had created, blowing it forward in choking billows all over his passengers. Amelia and Hans stepped out the front door as the driver bound quickly off the high seat and almost fell in the slippery shell dust settling on the porch.

"Sorry for this gritty mess, ma'am, sir. Thought you'd like the news. Lavaca just raised its docking fees, and Morgan Steamship Line is pulling out. Word is, the shipping business is moving down here. Setting up shop next to Powder Horn Bayou." The driver leapt back on the seat. The horses responded to his shout and a lively tap, jerking his passengers with a neck-snapping jolt.

"Joe will want to hear this." Hans took the stairs two-at-a-time.

Dr. Stein came downstairs. "Charles Morgan's son and son-in-law have been running the Morgan Line's shipping business from New Orleans to Matagorda Bay. But I bet old man Morgan's behind this move. I've heard he can be a tough man, doesn't put up with anyone raising his docking fees. Think I'll close the office and roam around town for a bit."

Charlie and Lou came to the store to hear the news when Dr. Stein returned late in the afternoon.

"Morgan's a shrewd old man. He's had people in here looking over our western shore. They've made soundings and charted the bay. When Lavaca stupidly raised its docking rates, Morgan knew right where he was moving. He plans to build a wharf into water deep enough to accommodate any ship that can make it through Pass Cavallo."

"Where will he put the wharf?" Charlie asked.

"On our side of Powder Horn Bayou. It'll set this place on fire." Dr. Stein pursed his lips and stood in silence for a moment. "You realize, the main part of town is going to be moving three miles down the coast to be near Morgan's pier?"

"Sounds like we need to be down there." Amelia slumped against the counter, rubbed at her arms.

"John Henry Brown, Samuel White, and several partners have bought land across the bayou. They're calling it 'Brown's Addition.' Thielepape, who laid out Indian Point, will survey Brown's property and the land on our side of the bayou. They plan for Indianola to have 834 blocks for buildings and sixty-four wharf lots."

Amelia looked around the sprawling store, stocked to the ceiling with merchandise. She leaned her shoulder against Hans', "Do you think we can shift all this to a new store?"

Hans gazed around the room like a man seeing a vision. "It's our chance to create a fine new mercantile business."

Progress on the town of Indianola, including the Brown's Addition across the bayou, moved so fast that Amelia was surprised by something new almost every day. A Frenchman named Casimir

Villeneuve and his rich young wife, Matilda, swooped into town and bought several lots on Main Street. Before all the streets were laid out, the Villeneuve's impressive Alhambra Hotel dominated the downtown.

All the hotels stayed full, including Mrs. Eberly's American Hotel that continued catering to families. Travelers from New Orleans and all over Texas claimed to have seen Casimir Villeneuve's newspaper ads boasting of a bar with every kind of liquor and "the largest kinds of Peninsular Oyster served up with every variety of style." Most people wanted to see his Billiard Room, and everyone bragged about the good food and drink.

Dr. Stein bought lots on Main that backed up to Water Street to give the new store access to the docks. He also bought a lot across the street from the future store. "I think we should live upstairs over my office. Patients have trouble getting up these stairs." He grinned at Amelia. "And I'm tired of carrying them up there."

Chapter Twenty-Five

1850 begins with expansion and tragedies...

The weather, like a fickle lover, teased with balmy spring-like temperatures that drove everyone out of doors into gardens. Construction began in a beehive of activity along both sides of Main, especially the buildings backing up to Water Street and the long docks. Then, in a petulant swing of only a few hours, icy, wind-driven rains turned the streets into soggy clumps of shell and mud, forcing wagons and workers to a complete stop.

Dr. Stein's new downtown office and their upstairs living quarters on Main Street fell under the same unpredictable schedule—intense activity interspersed with days of idleness. As the construction was getting underway, Dr. Stein had bent over the counter in the store showing Amelia the drawings that Vogel and the new architect had laid out for his two-room office to open on the wood walkway fronting all the buildings. His fingers traced the plans that showed window and door openings. "This cavernous room behind my offices will serve until we get a hospital. He pointed to a narrow walkway between the buildings that would offer access on the side and around at the rear of their quarters. "All the buildings on Main Street will have walkways between them that lead back entrances."

I'm supposed to be looking at plans for our new home, and I can't stop thinking about how close he's standing to me. I thought I was getting better, learning to ignore my urges. What's causing me to be like this? She studied the floor plan. "Is that a big kitchen and washroom forming an ell behind the building?"

"Yes, and these stairs on the back porch lead to our second-floor parlor, dining room, and two bedrooms."

Amelia stared at the space behind the building. "It looks like I'll have plenty of room for a garden."

"We'll have space for the henhouse, smokehouse, and privy back there with a site for a carriage house facing the alley. Vogel says there'll be plenty of room for an opening in the gate to let a carriage drive in."

"If we ever have a carriage."

"Don't be so grumpy. You know we'll get a carriage."

Amelia kept her voice low so the customers visiting with Hans would not hear. "I have no complaints about any of these plans except that I wasn't included in the design."

He stretched to his full height, shook his head and rolled his eyes. "Can't you settle for being happy with our prosperity? Can't you celebrate how our fortunes are improving?"

I want to be as excited about this move as Dr. Stein. I keep thinking of Anna staying in their Old Town house with her growing family. I will be moving into Indianola with my growing business. "Yes, I expect our fortunes will continue to improve." She folded the plans and handed them back to her husband.

In mid-January, the steady blasting of a ship's horn through a dense, cold fog brought a wave of local residents hurrying to meet the brig *Matagorda* sailing past the newer docks, heading directly to Stein Pier. As the gangplank was being secured, a frail boy of about eight jumped to the pier shouting for the doctor as he hobbled toward the store. "We got really bad frostbite."

Charlie, who had joined the crowd that rushed onto the pier, lifted the boy into his arms. Filthy rags fell loose exposing the child's swollen, black toes. Crewmen that had started stumbling down the gangplank before it was securely anchored looked as near death as the three men they carried on litters. Townspeople ran to relieve the litter-bearers. Others scooped their arms around those still walking but deformed by swollen, discolored noses and ears. Their toes protruding from dirty rags looked like chunks of coal and rotten turnips. The smell of decaying flesh moved with them.

Dr. Reuss materialized out of the crowd, helping Dr. Stein direct the mass of moving horror up the stairs to the office.

The men who were the least maimed lowered themselves to benches lining the outer office. The captain, a burly man with thin whiskers to his belt and wiry black hair that hung straight to his mid back, thanked every man who had helped get his crew up the stairs. "We've been twenty-one days coming from New York. We hit a god-awful blizzard, and the men have been suffering all this way. I remembered the doc when I was through here on the *Matagorda*'s maiden voyage two years back. We had 90,000 feet of white pine lumber for Henry Huck's yard. When we was unloading, one of the crew got a bad broke leg. Dr. Stein fixed him right up. I kept telling my boys to hold on; we'd find us a good doctor when we got here."

The crowd that had helped the men to the office promised to return with food, cots, blankets, and hot coffee. The room grew eerily quiet, all senses trained on the comments of the doctors in the inner office as they examined men who had infections in their damaged tissues. The dreaded words "gangrene" and "amputation," rang like a death knell throughout the two rooms. Amelia wanted to close the door separating the offices to muffle the sounds of suffering, but the open door and windows blew out some of the stench pervading the clothing, hair, and breath of every man.

Charlie sat on a bench with his arm around the boy he had carried upstairs. As Amelia set a pan of warm water for the boy's swollen, black toes, she heard him saying, "They could've thrown me over." His cheeks looked like red wax. "You think the doctors will cut off my toes?" He covered his eyes with fingers swollen with blisters.

How has a child this small survived? "Tell me your name," Amelia stroked his matted blonde hair that stank like the rest of him.

"Branson Forbes," came as a whisper.

Charlie nodded to Amelia. "I'm taking Branson to our tack room. This is no place for him. We have a cot down there for our stagecoach drivers. Lou and I'll take care of him."

As Charlie lifted Branson, the child roused from a half sleep, wrapped his arms around his benefactor's neck mumbling, "I'll work to pay my keep."

Charlie patted Branson's back. "You get well. Then, we'll talk about your keep."

All eyes of the ragged seamen followed Charlie carrying Branson out the door.

The captain's voice cut through the silence, "Hope he keeps the boy. We'll be charged with kidnapping if we take him back."

Not believing what she was hearing, Amelia said, "Wouldn't his family thank you for bringing him home?"

"His ma don't want him around her place of business, and his pa beats him senseless. They wouldn't hesitate to call the law on us. Maybe make a dollar out of the deal."

"What business does she have?"

A raspy voice behind her said, "A whorehouse. It's right handy there on the New York docks."

Amelia did not turn around, and the captain nodded like a churchgoer who agreed with the words from the altar.

The shout from Dr. Stein's office jolted all eyes toward the door. "No damn ether. Give me whisky."

"Get what he wants," Dr. Stein spoke so loudly that Micah and Hans both bolted downstairs for a keg of brandy.

Amelia and Hans moved among the men cutting away the dirty rags and soaking their hands and feet in warm water. Despite obvious pain when a few began experiencing the return of feelings in fingers and toes, no one made a sound. Instead, they rocked, clutched their arms around themselves for the only comfort they could find, their faces twisted in agony.

The howls coming from Dr. Stein's office as the doctors amputated a foot or a hand ripped like a blade of terror through the silence. Micah glided among the men with buckets of water, returning again and again with the Indianola residents' offerings of food and coffee. Every sound coming from the next room jerked the men to attention, every movement past the door an indication of what might come next.

When the doctors were done amputating the foot of the man who wanted whisky, Amelia watched Hans step into Dr. Stein's office, slip his arms around the semi-conscious man. "Let me move him, Joe."

Dr. Stein raised his head. For one instant the two men looked at each other before Dr. Stein said, "Good," and turned to the next patient.

The doctors worked all night. Hans and Micah shoved benches together in Dr. Stein's office to form makeshift beds for those too sick to be moved.

As the sun rose high on a new, cold day, several women took soiled rags and sheets home to their wash pots. Near noon, Maria Christina arrived with an enormous cake covered in sugar icing. She appeared to float about the outer office serving the astonished crew who could not stop staring at the woman whose sky-blue eyes matched the dress tucked tight against her waist.

Maria Christina could not keep her eyes off Hans.

Hans kept his eyes averted, bending over, trying to engage the distracted crewmen in conversation.

When all the cake was gone, and there was no reason for her to remain, Maria Christina looked through her thick brown lashes at Hans. "My mama is sending an invitation for you to come to supper tonight."

Hans looked first at Amelia and then at Dr. Stein, who had just stepped into the outer office. "I'm really needed here. Please send my regrets to Frau Vogel."

Maria Christina smiled sweetly and floated down the stairs, her dress billowing suggestively in the breeze.

"Are you crazy?" a crewman said. "I'd abandon my own mother for an invitation to her house. Hell, I'd shoot my mother for a chance to look under that skirt."

Hans pushed back his sleeves, clenched his fists, exposing bulging forearms. "If you want to stay here, you'll not say a word about any of our women."

"Sure. Didn't mean no disrespect," the seaman said.

By late afternoon, the men who lost only a few toes or fingers, including the captain who lost fingers on one hand, were bandaged and sent back to the ship with instructions to return at any sign of gangrene. Both doctors warned that even if gangrene didn't set in, fingers and toes could eventually fall off. It might take months to know the final results.

The captain was adamant, "I'll sail as soon as we build a new crew. My job's to get this vessel loaded and back to New York." He pointed a bandaged nub down the beach. "The Runge brothers have a warehouse full of pecans and the last of the cotton crop. If I want to keep my job, I'll be out of here in days. When we return, we'll pick up the men who couldn't make it."

Conrad Swartz built cots for six men to convert Dr. Stein's outer office into a hospital. The doctors took turns spending the night. Hans and other local men provided assistance for each doctor.

The first night that Dr. Stein came home, he looked little better than the patients he had been tending, and he smelled worse. Amelia poured a tub of water and was surprised that he did not hesitate to shed his stinking clothes and sink into the warm suds. He scrubbed himself vigorously and then kept his back turned as he accepted the towel she offered. She wondered if he had always been so thin. His backbone looked like a string of knots.

He sank onto the bed and whispered. "Did you notice? Hans has grown up?"

Of all things to remember. "Yes." She tucked the cover around her already sleeping husband.

In a little over a week the captain had assembled enough crew to load the cotton and pecans waiting in the Runge warehouse. Amelia and Hans listened to the shuffle upstairs of the men left behind as they moved to the back windows to watch the fast little brig sail away from the Runge pier and into the waves of the bay capping white with the arrival of another cold blow from the north.

"My heart breaks for those men upstairs," Amelia said.

Hans turned, masked his face in a smile as two customers entered the store's front door.

Hans and Amelia took turns reporting to each other their observations of the events unfolding next door at Charlie and Lou's stable. Unlike the sadness they felt for the men still hospitalized upstairs, Branson Forbes captured their attention. Lou reported that two more toes had fallen off in Branson's bed. "They were beyond rotten. They dropped off like neglected fruit falling unnoticed from a tree. He didn't know it happened until he woke up."

The redness in Branson's cheeks began fading and his fingertips dried to crusty nubs.

Lou and Branson spent most days together in the stable, feeding and tending the horses. Branson quickly mastered the crutches that

Conrad designed with a special grip for his damaged hand. At first, Lou stayed by Branson's side as he and his crutches approached the horses. It soon became obvious that boy and animals had an understanding. Branson learned to grab the horse's mane in his good hand and swing his leg over the animal's back. The instant he landed, he wrapped his arms around its neck and pressed his face into its mane.

When stages came in, Lou showed Branson how to unhitch the horses and rub them down. Hans and Amelia kept the window open so they could listen to him giggling at the horses rolling in the dirt. One morning Amelia went to the window and heard the soothing sound in Branson's voice. He had pulled his bench up to brush Red, Lou's favorite horse, for far longer than grooming required. *We missed an opportunity to make Branson our child.* She turned away from the window.

Dr. Stein returned from the February meeting of business owners wearing his wicked grin. "That group can be like a bunch of lady gossips. Before Mrs. Eberly arrived, word spread that the 1850 census shows she's the wealthiest individual property owner in the county with assets of $50,000."

Amelia gasped, "Did anyone mention it to her?"

"No one dared say a word. When she arrived, they launched immediately into explaining that five buildings and warehouses are being constructed for the government's quartermaster depot. Mrs. Eberly announced that Indianola's resident Quartermaster, Major Charlie P. J. O'Brien, and his family will stay at her hotel until their home is completed. Indianola will be the depot for military outposts on the western frontier."

"Major O'Brien will actually live in Indianola?" Hans was incredulous. "During the war, General Taylor came into the field to give Major O'Brien special thanks for his leadership at Buena Vista."

Dr. Stein turned to go upstairs and then stopped in the doorway. "As soon as Vogel finishes my office and our quarters, we should get that new store built. This town's booming."

Hans grinned, "It's time for Amelia to go to New Orleans, for the specialty items and household goods for the store's grand opening."

Dr. Stein nodded. "Give the weather time to improve before Amelia gets on one of those fancy new ships."

At least he's concerned for my safety. She watched him hurry out the door, his thoughts already far away from her.

The sound of Charlie's bugle—almost always off key—was Branson's warning to be ready to swing himself onto the bench beside Charlie for a ride to the Alhambra Hotel. As they pulled away, a government wagon sped past, its occupants waving and laughing at Charlie's stagecoach.

A passenger with dust caked in the creases around his eyes and powdering his hair yelled out Charlie's coach window, "Don't let them beat us. We've been racing that team for the last twenty miles."

Charlie's horses bolted into the dust roiling behind the government wagon.

"It was a tie," Branson shouted when the coach returned to the stable. He leapt down and began unhitching the wagon, glancing to make sure that Charlie was observing how well he was doing the task.

A cannon boom from the harbor split the air. "I almost forgot," Charlie laughed. "It's March second, Texas Independence Day."

Squinting into the morning sun, Amelia could see naked ship masts bobbing in the bay and along the piers unfurling brilliantly colored banners. A band started playing and people began cheering as they streamed out onto the piers.

"There's going to be a parade at nine o'clock," Charlie shouted above the noise. "It starts at the Planter's House and goes to Mrs. Eberly's hotel. Major O'Brien was in that government wagon. He made it back just in time. They grabbed him as soon as his wagon slowed down."

"That's how we had a tie," Branson put his arm around Charlie's waist in obvious pride at their accomplishment. "We caught up with his wagon just before it stopped."

"Branson wants to see all the excitement." Charlie patted the boy's shoulder. "You watch out. There're going to be a lot of wagons and some rowdy mules."

They watched Branson maneuver crablike on his crutches toward town.

Lou laid her hand on her belly. "I hope this one is as strong a character as Branson. That child has brought us so much pleasure."

Charlie wrapped his arm around Lou's shoulders. "We'd like to talk about buying your house when you move into town. It'd be easy to add a little room for Branson. We don't like him sleeping down in the tack room."

Dr. Stein nodded, reached to shake Charlie's hand, "That sounds like a good plan."

It would be so natural for Dr. Stein to slip his arm around me. She looked up into her husband's smiling face.

Late in the day Branson dragged back, excited to share every detail of the celebration, but so worn out from the effort to get about town that he slumped on the front porch and gobbled a chunk of Lou's fresh baked bread. "They had lots of prayers. Someone read the Texas Declaration of Independence. Major O'Brien made a speech and so did a lot of others. There was plenty of good music. Tonight they're having a big party at the Planter's House." He grinned wearily. "I don't think I could make it to a dance."

Chapter Twenty-Six

Another good-bye...

Branson kept sticking his head in the store's front door to let Amelia and Hans know of Charlie and Micah's progress moving Dr. Stein's office to the new building. Each time they loaded more furniture on Charlie's freight wagon, Branson spread himself across the top for the ride into town.

Amelia was captivated by the giddy boy. "I'm not sure he's much help, but he's having a wonderful time riding and watching the whole operation."

Late in the day Branson shouted, "Dr. Stein says you can come see it now.

Hans shooed Amelia out the door. "I'll close the store. I looked in last night on the way to Saengerbund practice. You're going to be impressed."

Branson was already scrambling into the wagon when Amelia climbed on the bench next to Micah. "We got the last of the sawdust out, and all the furniture moved. It's so big; you can hear your own voice coming back at you."

Branson crawled on his knees right behind the wagon bench. "Dr. Stein said, it's an echo."

Micah pulled the wagon even with the boardwalk that fronted all the businesses along Main Street. "I tell you it's mighty fine."

Branson tossed his crutches on the walk and scrambled to open the door, which had *Joseph Stein, Medical Doctor* painted across the glass.

Dr. Stein and Charlie were both soaked with sweat and grinning.

"All we need is a note on the door of my old office directing patients to this new location."

Amelia stood in the doorway gazing at the white walls, high ceiling, and windows overlooking the street. "Conrad did a masterful job blending all your furniture with the new benches and cabinets."

She roamed through the waiting room, Dr. Stein's examining room, and into the sprawling hospital room at the rear of the building. Cots were arranged for the men from the *Matagorda,* who were anxiously watching for its return. Windows across the back of the building provided a view for hospital patients beyond the porch to the flourishing raised garden that Amelia had worked every evening while the building was under construction.

Dr. Stein followed her, "When the kitchen stove arrives, we'll be able to move into our quarters."

"And we can buy your old house," Branson followed along, sitting on each bench and trying Dr. Stein's desk chair.

The clanging of the bell on the store's front porch announced the arrival of Frau Fischer carrying a bundle. "I guess you're surprised to see me instead of Eva. Hans keeps talking about your buying trip to New Orleans. I want you to have this shawl for the ship."

Amelia stared at the lush paisley in swirling shades of blue and gold. "It's so lovely."

"My husband ordered it from Kashmir just before he was killed. It's wonderful on a windy ship deck." She held the finely woven softness up to Amelia. "My goodness, it makes your eyes look so blue."

"It's too early for such a generous loan. I'm not sure when or even if I'm going."

"It's not a loan, my dear. It's a gift. I won't be going on ships ever again." She shrugged her shoulders and blinked back moisture in her eyes. "I want you to have it."

Amelia hugged the shawl against herself and bent to kiss Frau Fischer's cheek. "You're so generous. I'll feel grand in this."

"You look grand. And I'll miss you." She held out a bowl for butter. With a sly grin, she extended an even larger bowl for pralines.

"Eva can come for the rest." She tossed her coins on the counter and walked out.

She is pale as paste and moves like an old woman. Amelia walked onto the front porch, staring after Frau Fischer.

Amelia was dreaming of the incessant sound of hammers constructing their new home. She awoke when Dr. Stein opened the door to a sobbing Branson. "Can you come? Lou's awful bad off. She's not making any more sounds."

Dr. Stein stepped into his pants, and Amelia pulled a dress over her gown. They started toward the stable, and Dr. Stein stopped. "Give your crutches to Amelia. We'll go faster if you jump on my back."

In one quick leap, the boy mounted Dr. Stein and buried his face in his shoulder. "I know when they stop hollering, and the baby doesn't start crying, it's a bad sign."

"How do you know any such thing? You're just scaring yourself." Dr. Stein bounced Branson like he was trying to shake the worry out of the boy.

"The ladies at Ma's whorehouse had babies all the time. They died after they stopped yelling."

"Okay, boy. I'll see if I can help." Dr. Stein eased Branson to the ground at the foot of the stairs. "I'm sorry to leave you here. Amelia will let you how she's doing."

Branson nodded, slumped onto the bottom step, and covered his face with both hands.

"I should've called you right away. We wanted to deliver our baby ourselves." The candlelight made Charlie's face look like a mass of red welts.

Dr. Stein moved the trembling man out of his way and knelt by the bed.

"She kept saying she could do it. The baby's not coming. And she's stopped talking to me." Charlie knelt, stroking the sallow dampness on Lou's face.

Dr. Stein bent low over Lou. "I'll try turning the baby. It's head is in the wrong position, pushing against bone."

186

Lou's eyes were open but not seeing. Even the contractions brought no response. She was like a rag doll arched by an outside force. Dr. Stein's manipulations did not bring any sign of pain or response.

"The head is coming now, just one more thrust." Dr. Stein stood quickly, his bloody hands held a big, lifeless boy. He began forcefully massaging the tiny chest. He blew into the mouth and popped him on the rear. The child never drew a breath.

Charlie remained crumpled on the floor. He tugged at Lou pulled her into his arms and begged her to live. "Breathe, please breathe. Don't leave me, Lou."

She did not make a sound, slipping away while Charlie pleaded and rocked her.

Amelia stared at the young woman who had been so vigorous, so strong—someone who should have lots of babies.

Dr. Stein laid the baby on Lou's still breast, wiped his hands on a clump of rags, clutched Charlie's shoulder.

Amelia slipped out the door and went down to Branson.

"I know she's dead." Branson threw himself against Amelia and cried in deep wrenching sobs. "She's the best ma. Why would God let such a good woman die?"

"I don't have an answer, Branson. I wonder the same thing." Amelia rocked the boy until his crying slowed to gasping, hiccup whimpers.

"I've got to tell Red. He's been her favorite horse since she was a girl. He's going to really miss her."

"I'll go see if I can help Charlie get her body ready for burial."

Branson pushed into the stable, laid his crutches against the wood fence, and heaved himself on the back of Lou's handsome horse. Red stood perfectly still as Branson stretched his arms around the animal's neck. "God took her away, Red. Not even Dr. Stein could save her. You aren't going to be alone. I'll stay with you as long as Charlie wants me." Branson's words disappeared into tears as he nuzzled the horses' mane.

Charlie was still on his knees holding Lou's body. "I want to wash her and the baby. It's my last chance to touch her."

Dr. Stein pounded Charlie's shoulder. "We'll be next door when you're ready for us."

They closed the door just as the sun peeked above the flat prairie. Amelia stopped on the porch, unable to stop her tears. "Branson asked me why God would let such a good woman die. I'm wondering why God would destroy such a happy marriage? Why not take ours?"

Dr. Stein's mouth opened as if he couldn't draw his breath.

She continued looking up into his face until he shook his head. "I don't know, Amelia."

They both jerked as a blast of cold north wind hit them. The sudden chill made her tears dry like paste against her cheeks.

Dr. Stein went into the corral and lifted the sobbing child from the horse and held him in his arms. "We need to get your warm coat out of the tack room and take you home with us for a while."

Branson plastered himself against Dr. Stein's back for the walk back to their house. He sat perfectly still before his bowl of warm grits, holding his head, tears running off his chin and soaking the front of his shirt.

I can never take her place, but this child needs mothering. Amelia moved her bench next to his chair and drew him close.

Finally, he took a drink of hot coffee. "She was better than a ma."

Dr. Stein nodded, "She was a special woman. I'm glad we had her in our lives."

"You think Charlie will send me back when the *Matagorda* returns?"

"We won't send you back. Indianola's going to be your home," Dr. Stein reached for Branson's shoulder.

"What about Charlie? You think he'll keep me?"

"Charlie's got to grieve for a while." Dr. Stein stood, picked up his bag, ready to head into town to his new office.

"Then will he keep me? I'm not going back. I'll jump ship at the first port."

Dr. Stein set the bag down and knelt beside Branson, wrapping his long fingers around the boy's nubby hand. "I can't say what Charlie will do. But you'll have a home here with Amelia and me, no matter what."

He is calling us a family. She continued holding the trembling child. "We would love to have you as our son."

Branson nodded, "Thank you." When Dr. Stein closed the door,

Branson took a deep breath. "I better feed the horses. If you need a worker, I'll come help in the store."

"I would like your help when you're available."

The procession the next morning to Indianola's new cemetery with the body of Lou cradling their baby son inside one of Conrad's beautifully polished caskets was made even more bleak with the arrival of cold blowing rain.

After the brief graveside service, Dr. Stein hoisted Branson on his back as he and Amelia walked on each side of Charlie hunched forward into the cutting rain.

When they reached the stable, Charlie pulled Branson from Dr. Stein's back and slowly rocked the boy. "I've got to go tell Lou's parents. I'll be coming back in a couple of days. Can you take care of the horses that come in while I'm gone?"

Branson kept squeezing Charlie and beating him on the back. "I can. I'll take care of everything. You don't worry about nothing."

It took a long time for Amelia to help Charlie pack Lou's clothing. His hands, extra large for a small man, caressed every garment. He held up a blue gingham dress and looked at it for a long time. "She was wearing this the day I met her."

Micah helped load the wardrobe. "That was a wedding gift from her parents." Charlie looked at Amelia, his eyes swollen almost shut from crying. "Lou's parents wanted her to marry better than me." He snorted and turned away. "Now, I've got to admit to them that I didn't take care of her."

Amelia couldn't stop her tears. "I'm sure her parents changed their minds. You two had the best marriage I've ever seen."

Charlie threw his arms around Amelia, pounding her on the back. "I'm going to remember your words when I face Lou's parents."

His jaw clenching, Charlie slapped the reins across the backs of Lou's favorite team and headed to Victoria to tell her parents their only child was gone.

"Branson, come to the store to get warm when you finish your chores. Until Charlie gets back, you'll stay with us." Amelia watched the boy swing away on his crutches toward his beloved horses.

"My heart breaks for that man and that boy." Hans stood with Amelia watching Branson scramble onto one of the horses and then stretch his body along its neck, his face buried in its mane.

"The world feels upside down when a good marriage gets torn apart." *And one like ours keeps going.* Amelia headed back into the store where the stove had been allowed to grow cold.

Amelia asked Micah to move Branson's cot to their parlor. She left the store early to gather the few surviving greens from her garden, bake cornbread, and cook a pot of oyster stew. She knew Dr. Stein would eat with relish, but she wasn't sure what to expect from Branson, who had spent the entire afternoon at the stables.

"You won't be in New Orleans for very long, will you?" Branson dove into the supper with the vigor of a farm hand.

"I may be gone for two weeks, not much more. I won't leave until Charlie returns."

"Good. I like everybody close. You think I could still go to Miss Rachel's school? She told Lou I could start any time."

"Why don't we go see her tomorrow?"

"I can read. Miss Betty was teaching me. That's why Ma was sending me to live with Pa. She didn't want me to like whoring. I wasn't liking whoring. I was liking reading."

Dr. Stein had been eating in silence. "Did your pa want to get you away from the whorehouse?"

I will not let myself look shocked at such talk coming from a child. Amelia brought more cornbread to the table and buttered another piece for Branson.

"Not really. He likes having me to beat when he wakes up feeling awful after a long drinking spell. He's meaner than a wharf rat. I don't aim to live with him ever again. That's why I followed Captain Hopkins when he left Ma's place. He was so drunk; I figured he'd never notice me trailing him up that gangplank. The watchman thought I was helping the captain. Then, he forgot I never left the ship."

"So that's how you became a stowaway." Dr. Stein appeared as comfortable with the conversation as Branson.

"They all knew me. Ma's place is just a block from the docks. They all came in to see Ma's ladies. Sometimes they were so drunk they tossed me two bits when I was waiting on the front stoop."

Amelia began removing dishes from the table. "Don't you want a bath before you go to Miss Rachel's school in the morning?"

"That sounds like a first-rate idea," Branson grinned. "That's what Charlie always says when he agrees with Lou's plans."

Chapter Twenty-Seven

I am New Orleans bound...

By early April, the weather had calmed. Construction on the store was already moving along quickly, but the move into their quarters had been delayed as they waited for delivery of the kitchen stove.

Micah stuck his head in the store's front door, "Dr. Stein said for you to hurry along. Your fancy cook stove just got delivered."

Amelia waved to Hans, pulled off her apron, and started out the door with Micah hurrying along beside her. "Will you have time to help Charlie move us into our quarters?"

"You betcha. Me and Charlie been waiting for this day. He wants to get him and Branson in your place."

They stepped off the boardwalk fronting all the buildings on Main into the walkway that ran down the side of the buildings. A narrow covered porch opened into the kitchen. She had insisted that both the kitchen and the washroom extending in an L back from the main part of the house have lots of windows for good cross ventilation.

Dr. Stein stood in the kitchen grinning at Amelia and Micah. "It's mighty fancy, but it should make cooking a lot easier for you."

I must remember that he tries to think of me. She stared at the huge cast iron stove standing on curved six-inch legs. Its oven door and warming reservoir were patterned in raised curls and circles that would require regular scrubbing to keep out grease.

Dr. Stein bent toward her frowning, "Don't you like it?"

"I expected a plain black stove. Like the one in our cabin."

"Not in a house of this size," he spread his arms. "Look at all the space you have for a table. We can easily seat eight people in here. Save the dining room upstairs for larger groups."

"Sure is fine," Micah kept whispering as he followed them out onto the porch and gazed at the garden that Amelia had already staked for tomatoes and green beans.

"Come see where we'll need all the furniture," Dr. Stein said to Micah as they climbed the stairs off the back porch to the second level.

"This is a mighty fine veranda. Looks right down on your garden," Micah said.

A cool breeze blew down the center hall as Dr. Stein pointed to the empty rooms on its west side. "Amelia will have to order furniture for the parlor and dining room when she goes to New Orleans. Both bedrooms will be on the other side of the hall."

"My oh my, how about that gallery looking down on Main Street?" Micah clutched his felt hat against his chest as his eyes roamed to the high ceilings and rows of windows opening on all the outer walls. "Me and Charlie are going to have a big time moving your things into this fine place."

Micah's delight always cheers me. "Then, you'll need to help Charlie and Branson move into our old house."

"Yes, and first thing we got to pick up Branson's new desk. He's been telling me that he hopes you'll move soon so as he can get to doing his studies on his desk."

I wish we could move that child into our extra bedroom. If a day passes and he doesn't come by, I feel lost. "Dr. Stein and I have grown attached to that child."

Dr. Stein nodded, "He's the best thing that's happened around here."

Amelia paced the floor of Dr. Stein's new office, fanning herself with the pages from her latest order. "Hans says some of our calico isn't good quality. He says we need to start offering specialty items like top hats and parasols and a wider selection of ribbons, even corsets." She stopped and looked at Dr. Stein, who had been mixing his medicines with his back turned. "I'm not so sure about his wallpaper idea. He says it's popular east of the Mississippi. I don't know how we'll keep it on the walls in this humidity."

He turned suddenly, still holding a vial of powders, his face crinkling in a smile, "I agree with Hans. When the store's finished, we need to open with an impressive selection of merchandise. You've delayed your departure long enough. Have a good visit at the Tremont. Firm up your connections in Galveston. Then, discover how much more is available in New Orleans."

"Hans knows so much about what pleases the rich."

"He shouldn't leave Frau Fischer. She's sinking. You know how often he goes to check on her."

She sank into a chair, still clutching the list of supplies. "Hans says the same thing."

"He's right. You've been running the store. You know the merchandise, and you're already the contact person."

"I'd like to sail with Captain Whipple to Galveston. He can introduce me to some of the merchants. If Hans needs to be with his mama, I'm sure we can hire Maria Christina to fill in for me."

Dr. Stein's eyebrows arched. He ducked his head, but not before an angry scowl showed on his face. "She's always in the store."

Why does he disapprove of Maria Christina? "It will take a strong one to get Hans away from his mama."

"She's obviously determined."

After supper, Amelia began packing Frau von Ewald's lovely dresses and her slippers that she had saved for special occasions. Kneeling beside the little sea trunk, she ran her fingers over the delicately painted spring blossoms that Frau von Ewald must have feared she'd never see again in this harsh new land. Despite all the expense of building new quarters, the little trunk and the highly polished Biedermeier wardrobe offered the only color in the room. Sometimes the clusters of flowers made her long for the delight she used to feel with the coming of spring.

Dr. Stein prepared for bed. "You're the most capable woman I've ever known."

She sat back on her heels, looking into the warmth of his smile. *I wish you wanted me to stay at home.* "This is a really big trip."

"Not as big as your trip to Texas."

"This one's different. I'll be coming back. Sometimes I wonder how I could have left my family. I made that decision so much faster than I made this one." Amelia pulled the delicate softness of Frau von Ewald's dress to her face to hide tears.

"Are you sorry?" His voice was soft.

If it weren't for leaving Branson, I can imagine boarding that ship and sailing away. Amelia shook her head, choking back a sob.

On the morning of departure, Micah, as eager as if he were the one going to the far off lands of Galveston and New Orleans, hoisted her von Ewald trunk onto his shoulder and hurried to the Stein Pier.

At the door, she felt the pressure of Dr. Stein's hand on her shoulder. Turning, she pressed against him and felt the hollow in her belly as he eased her away to plant a quick kiss on her cheek. "I don't need to tell you not to let anyone intimidate you. You understand the value of goods."

"That's true." She said, and shaded her eyes as she stepped off the side porch into the glaring morning sun.

A slight breeze ruffled the bay. Waves sparkled, slapping gently against the piers stretching like raw cypress fingers toward waiting ships. Soldiers, horses, and freight wagons destined for duty chasing Indians at posts scattered along the edge of the western settlement were clattering off a ship anchored at the government pier. The mules snorted and pawed at the wood planking, trying to regain their land footing while drivers hitched the traces to the wagons and followed the slow procession toward the shell road. Soldiers ambled along the dock, forming a line into Stein Mercantile. They couldn't have been much younger than Amelia, but they seemed like eager children when they made their first onshore purchases. The pralines from New Orleans were a big hit. Just like Dr. Stein had said, razor strops and shaving mugs were popular items for boys who probably would not use them more than once a month.

Hans, framed in an open store window, the lock of wavy black hair combed across his brow, waved from behind the counter, grinning sideways as he took the money from eager customers.

Captain Whipple's crew helped freighters load bales of gama grass hay onto his steamship sitting at the end of the long Stein Pier. He met them at the top of the gangplank and directed Amelia to his cabin. Over her protests, he said, "There are no staterooms on this packet. Passengers usually stay below with the cargo."

"I can stay below."

"Absolutely not. You need to be rested when you get to Galveston."

"What about you, my captain?"

"I have a hammock that rocks me like a baby."

After vigorously shaking Captain Whipple's hand and saying three times how much he appreciated his watching over Amelia, Dr. Stein touched her shoulder, kissed her lightly on the forehead, and strode quickly down the gangplank.

He's such a commanding figure, towering above men and mules along the pier. No one would ever know that he isn't a happily married man. She watched him squeeze between the line of soldiers and disappear into the store.

Despite two brass-rimmed portholes, cigar smoke sucked the air from the tiny cabin. Amelia propped open the door, allowing the sea breeze to blow through as the last of the gama grass was loaded. She kept watching, wondering when Dr. Stein would leave the store and head back to his office.

Suddenly, Branson's blonde head bobbed between the line of soldiers. He shouted as he propelled himself in quick twisting motions along the pier, "Miss Rachel let me come to say good-bye."

Amelia rushed down the gangplank to meet him and pulled his sweating little body into her arms.

His breath came in gasps, "I was afraid you'd sail before I could convince her it was important."

"I'm so glad you made it. I wish you could go with me."

He looked up, his face a sweaty rose color. "Me too." He gulped air. "I just wanted to remind you not to stay gone too long." He shrugged, his brown eyes as big as walnuts. "I dreamed last night that you ran off."

Dear God, has this child been abandoned so often that he senses my urge to run away? "Don't you worry for a minute, I'll be coming back."

He sucked in a deep breath. "Good. I wanted to make sure. That dream sort of scared me." He turned and swung back to the dock where he stood and watched while the ship moved out into the bay.

I already miss this child. I must find ways to reassure him that he will not be abandoned again. She made one last big wave before his image blended with the crowd of soldiers on the dock.

Amelia was surprised to see how the Galveston Harbor had changed. The early morning sun glistened on rows of houses edged with oleanders bursting with pink and white blossoms. Very black men were still moving mounds of cotton bales just as they had been doing when she first arrived. New, two-story frame buildings loomed against the docks, and several men were perched in upper story windows fishing in the swirling water stirred by the approaching steamer. The ship eased against a white wood building with *Osterman Merchants* printed in bold black letters across the second floor; a massive door slid open, and black stevedores swarmed out like ants to secure the ship against the cavernous opening.

A handful of passengers, mostly soldiers returning from the war with packs on their backs, rushed down the gangplank and disappeared into the building.

The captain had instructed Amelia over breakfast to wait for him to complete his duties. "I'll introduce you to Mrs. Osterman. She's a sharp businesswoman, runs the place for her husband. She'll make sure you meet the merchants you need to know."

When they finally descended the gangplank, Captain Whipple led her into a dark cypress-walled room where a powerful looking woman in a plain black dress was telling workmen where to stack barrels and crates that had just come off the captain's ship. The captain beamed with pleasure as he clasped his hands behind his back and rocked onto his toes. "It's my pleasure to introduce my two good friends who are very capable businesswomen."

Mrs. Osterman's face brightened into a wide smile as she gripped Amelia's hand. "You're A. Stein? I had no idea you were a woman." Her dark hair, pulled back in a tight bun, made her huge head look like she didn't have a neck. Her chin rested on a white collar edging the top of a dress made of heavy black cotton.

Amelia felt her face reddening. "I signed the orders with my initial believing I'd get better service."

"Right you are, my dear. Keep it up. I'd do the same, but my husband got the business going before I took charge. I didn't have to open doors."

"She's here to shop for her store," Captain Whipple said.

"Good. Go up to the front and look around while the captain and I settle up."

Maybe I don't need to say I'm going on to New Orleans. Amelia stepped into the Osterman Store where bolts of colorful cloth were stacked to the high, wood-beamed ceiling. Bonnets swung from lines strung above counters holding gloves, shawls, shaving supplies, and notions—items not much different from what Stein Mercantile offered.

"You look a little disappointed. Pardon me if I'm too forward." Despite sandy hair curling at his temples and brown eyes that smiled with mischief, he was dressed like a gentleman with a loosely tied cravat tucked into his blouse and a coat that fit low on his waist making his shoulders look extra broad. He bowed slightly, like he was addressing a genteel lady.

"I expected to find..." Amelia shrugged. "I'm looking for quality goods for my store."

He lowered his voice to a whisper. "Not in Galveston. The prosperous in this town keep their wealth a secret. Instead, they dress their slaves in silks and brocades."

"I don't understand."

"The upper classes in Galveston have a backdoor approach to flaunting their position. They dress in very ordinary clothing, while encouraging their house servants to gad about town in finery, even allowing them to borrow their carriages on holidays."

"Really? I thought Americans were eager to have fine goods."

"They're a different breed here. I've been coming to Galveston for several years and have yet to figure out why."

Amelia turned slowly, eyeing the cone-shaped cubes of sugar wrapped in blue and purple paper dangling by strings from the ceiling, barrels of coffee, and sacks of tobacco. "We need sugar and tobacco..."

"New Orleans is where you'll find a source for better fabrics and accessories."

"He's the man who knows." Mrs. Osterman stepped into the store smiling broadly, her big arms extending down to tiny hands folded across a full middle securely cinched in a black apron. "Have you been introduced to Mr. Waters? Mr. Al Waters, this is A. Stein, who I've just discovered, is a lovely young woman."

"Smart move," Al Waters laughed, throwing his head back like a man perfectly at ease with himself. "I bet you gave A. Stein a better price than you would have given a lovely young woman." His eyes, crinkling at the corners, settled with a bemused gentleness on Amelia.

Mrs. Osterman burst into a deep laugh that gave her cheeks a rosy glow. "Al, you call my bluff every time."

"So, A. Stein, what is your name? It's obvious Mrs. Osterman isn't going to introduce us."

"I'm Amelia Stein. I'm glad to make your acquaintance Mr. Al Waters."

"If you'll call me Al, I'll call you Amelia instead of A."

"Sounds like everyone's acquainted." Captain Whipple strode toward Al Waters with his arms extended. "I thought you were going to Washington County. What're you doing in Galveston?" He and Al Waters shook hands vigorously.

"I'm headed to New Orleans. Unlike the Galveston residents, planters in Washington County want some finery in their homes and garments. I've opened stores in Independence and Brenham."

"Don't be fussy, Al. We're not ostentatious here." Mrs. Osterman smiled at Amelia. "You should have Al introduce you to his New Orleans brokers. If the Germans at Indianola want finery, he's the man to know."

"It's not the Germans. It's the new Americans who keep asking for more fashionable things like patterned fabrics, Indian muslin, and large-brimmed hats."

"I'm sailing tomorrow morning. You're welcome to make the trip. I'll be delighted to introduce you to folks like George Opdyke. His clothing store caters to southern planters. I'll be there a few days; then I'll be coming back."

"There you go. You'll be with the best in the business." Mrs. Osterman grinned. "And you'll not have to worry about traveling alone. We can vouch for him, can't we, Captain."

Captain Whipple slapped Al Waters on the back. "Absolutely. And he's an excellent New Orleans guide."

"May I give you two a lift to the Tremont? My carriage is waiting."

The driver heaved Amelia's trunk on top of the coach. Al Waters took her hand, smiled reassuringly as she stepped from the raised wooden porch into the small coach. Captain Whipple sat beside her, and Al Waters arranged himself on the seat facing them, carefully bending his knees to avoid pressing against her.

This is the same bumpy street I traveled with the von Ewald's. This day is the other bookend around the past four years. She watched the wood buildings slip past, allowing the two men to catch up on the news since they last met.

"Frau Stein, what a great surprise." Oscar Wilhite rushed to the hotel door. "And Mr. Waters, you've brought the good captain." He stopped, bowed slightly, "And where is the good doctor?"

Captain Whipple smiled, "Frau Stein's on a shopping trip for Dr. Stein's new mercantile store. She needs one of your safe, first floor rooms. I'd ask for one of those rooms that are not so pricey, but I'm staying on shipboard. I'll sail at first light tomorrow."

Al Waters leaned toward Oscar Wilhite and whispered loudly. "Don't tell them that I'm on the second floor. I'll look like a snob."

"No, sir. It will be our secret." Oscar Wilhite waved his arms to direct a bellman—still dressed as before in a gleaming white uniform —to carry Amelia's trunk down the hall.

"Will you join me for dinner tonight?" Al Waters bowed again, ever so slightly.

"Thank you. I worked here before I met my husband. I want to see if my friends are still here and eat with them."

"Really?" Oscar Wilhite raised both eyebrows. "Frau Stein, you know they eat in the kitchen?"

Amelia forced a smile. "I want to be with them for at least one meal."

"Well, of course. I'll have a bellman let them know to be expecting you in the kitchen."

"Let me surprise them."

"Well, of course, madam. Whatever you wish."

"I'll arrange passage for you if you're sure you want to make the New Orleans connections." Al Waters ignored Oscar Wilhite, standing awkwardly to one side as if he were offering them privacy.

"I think it's an excellent idea." She extended her hand. "Thank you, Al Waters, for offering your assistance."

Al Waters bent toward Amelia, cut his eyes knowingly in the direction of the preening hotel manager and barely suppressed a grin.

Chapter Twenty-Eight

A Reunion...

"Amelia, is it really you?" Harriet leaped from the bench, almost overturning her bowl of gumbo.

Frau Beatrice whirled from her position next to the stove and rushed with Mary Van Dunn into the group embrace. "What're you doing here? You look so pretty. You aren't coming back?"

Amelia settled at the table, explaining the reason for her trip.

"When Fannie finishes her work on Saturday night, she always comes to see us. Just like she planned, she's the head housekeeper at Mr. Samuel May Williams's big house."

After meeting four new chambermaids, Amelia said, "What happened to Angela? Where's Sarah?"

"Angela's uncle came to claim her. We're not sure she'll be more than a maid at his house, but she'll be with family." Harriet heaved a sigh, ran her fingers through her mass of dark curls. "Timid little Sarah ran off. They found her down by the docks trying to get on a ship to New York. Mr. Samuel May Williams sold her to a planter up the river."

"She'll have babies, so her master increases his stock." Mary Van Dunn spoke with her back turned, but her voice boomed through the steamy, hot kitchen.

The kitchen door burst open, "Lord, God, it's you!" Fannie screamed, rushing to embrace Amelia.

Amelia clung to the tiny black woman wearing a high-collared, green satin dress and feathered hat. "You are the finest looking woman."

"Yep. I'm a looker. I got me a good job. Mrs. Williams likes my work and me." Fannie spun around to fully demonstrate the effect of her costume. "Now tell us about you. How many children you have now? What're you doing here leaving them behind?"

Amelia laughed, grabbed both Harriet's and Fannie's hands and pulled them to the bench. "No children. I guess you'd call me a businesswoman."

"What business?" Fannie raised both eyebrows suspiciously.

Amelia explained about the store and her mission. Fannie kept eyeing her with a grim look on her face.

"Has that man made you happy?"

"Of course. He's a good man."

"I mean happy, girl. You know full well what I mean."

Amelia's throat tightened and before she could get control, tears burned hot. Harriet and Fannie shoved themselves tight against her.

"Yep. I knew something wasn't right. You don't come off like this without your man if he's making you happy. Let's get out of this hot dungeon." Fannie looked at Harriet. "We can sit on your bed."

Amelia nodded and blew a kiss at Mary Van Dunn standing stone-still in front of her stove, cursing men, a giant spoon clutched in her hand like she was ready to strike the first man who entered her domain.

The rush of cool dampness in the alley calmed Amelia before they entered the narrow, dingy chambermaid's quarters. "I'm sorry to act like such a baby. I'm settled down now."

"Settled? You tell me what's settled about that man?" Fannie tossed her feathery green hat aside and pulled Amelia down beside her on the bed.

"He's loved by everyone. He's a fine doctor."

"And? What about you, girl? Is he making you happy?"

"He's very good to me."

"Happy? You know about happy?'

Amelia looked at the black eyes staring intently at her in the dim candlelight.

"No. I don't know about happy."

Harriet snuggled up behind Amelia. "Can you live like that?"

Amelia nodded. "I'm doing it. I have a lot of satisfaction running the store. And there's a boy, a runaway who has filled the empty places in my heart. I'm already missing him, and the trip has just started."

"You're better off than when you were here, aren't you?" Harriet whispered like she didn't want the other chambermaids, who had gotten very still, to hear what she was asking.

"Life's much easier. I have lots of friends. Especially Anna. You would adore her precious little boy."

"Miss Anna's happy, then?" Fannie sucked in her breath making her little nostrils draw in like an aristocratic lady passing judgment on the situation.

"She's very content. Her baby boy calls me Tante."

"How long will you be here?" Fatigue lines showed in Harriet's creamy white face as she glanced across the room at the other four chambermaids who were settling into their beds.

"I'm leaving in the morning for New Orleans. In a few days, I'll return, and we'll visit more." Amelia kissed Harriet's cheek and squeezed her into a tight hug. "You look like you need to get to sleep. You've got lots of chamber pots waiting for you."

Harriet whispered, "A bad marriage might be a good tradeoff."

"I often remind myself of that." Amelia reached for both Harriett's work toughened hands. "You could come home with me. There's plenty of work in Indianola that's better than hauling chamber pots."

"Yes! Absolutely!" Fannie shouted. "You've got to go."

Harriet's shoulders dropped, and she bent forward like the breath had been kicked out of her. "Leave here?" She kept sucking in deep breaths. "I never imagined...."

Fannie grabbed both of Harriet's shoulders. "Imagine it. Right now. You got a chance, girl. Take it!"

"People need cooks and housekeepers." Amelia stroked Harriet's cheek, pushing one of her black curls away from her face.

"She can read and write, too. No use for that here when you're slopping chamber pots. I say you got to go, girl." Fannie's black eyes snapped, did not leave Harriet's face.

Harriet gulped air and began smiling. "I'll do it. It can't be any worse than this."

Fannie and Amelia squeezed her between them until she began to giggle. "Let go. I've got to think what I need to do."

"When I get back from New Orleans, we'll book passage together. You can stay with Dr. Stein and me until you get settled."

"Get yourself ready for better times." Fannie arranged her big hat carefully on her head, pulled the bow tight to one side of her face, and followed Amelia into the alley. "You have a room on the first floor?"

"Yes, Mr. Wilhite has me well protected."

When Amelia and Fannie reached the hotel lobby, Al Waters rose from the red horsehair sofa where Amelia and Dr. Stein had sat on the night he proposed. "I'm glad I caught you before you retired."

Amelia introduced Fannie, ignoring Oscar Wilhite and two other men in the lobby glaring at Fannie.

After a gracious bow, Al Waters said, "I secured passage for you. I have a carriage leaving at six in the morning."

"I'll see you when you return," Fannie said, her questioning eyes staring from under half-closed lids.

Amelia bent to get under the billowing hat and hugged Fannie. "I see what you're thinking," she whispered.

"Have a wonderful trip, you two." She glided like an elegant lady out the front door, ignoring the annoyed stares.

Al Waters, unlike the other men in the room, appeared not to notice that a white woman had just embraced a finely dressed slave. "I suppose we should retire. Will you join me for breakfast at five?"

"That sounds perfect." Amelia extended her hand.

Does my hand feel as cold as his? Amelia nodded *goodnight* to Oscar Wilhite and headed down the hall to her room.

Amelia made it a point to go to the privy, to leave as little work for the chambermaids as possible. She wished she could ask Harriet about Al Waters' habits in his fine upstairs room.

At breakfast, he was impeccably groomed and smiling broadly as he held her chair at the table.

This is the same table where Dr. Stein lifted my chair to seat me. She kept her smile to herself.

Al Waters wanted to know all about how she came to Texas, her work at the Tremont, and how she met Dr. Stein. "I've heard

Indianola's becoming an important port. I became friends with Henry Huck when he first landed in New Orleans. When he made return trips from Indian Point in the early days, he shared shocking stories about the Germans' treatment by the Adelsverein."

"You know everybody."

"It's my business. I'm a merchant. Actually, I'm a peddler. The only difference is that I don't carry my goods around in a wagon."

"Al, no one would ever call you a peddler."

"Amelia, you are most gracious."

Her stateroom was small, but the richly paneled walls and porcelain bowl and pitcher anchored in the polished wood grooves of a table made it feel luxurious. A curved oak board edged the bed just high enough to keep her from being storm-tossed onto the thick wool rug. A brass-rimmed porthole opened to a cloudless sky.

She pulled a brush from her trunk and stood before the large, gold-framed mirror brushing her hair back into braids haloed around her head. The soft rose color of her bonnet complimented her dress and made her cheeks glow.

Are my cheeks red from rushing to meet Al on the promenade deck? I'll walk leisurely, give my breathing time to settle down. She smiled at seeing him leaning on the ship rail, gazing out to sea.

He turned as she approached. "Come watch the dolphins chasing our ship." He pointed to the bowed backs of a half dozen creatures leaping wildly in the wake. "They're playing a game with the ship. They aren't racing; they're toying with us. Sort of flirting."

His hair doesn't tousle in the wind. Whatever he puts on it would be a best-seller in Indianola. "Why're you opening mercantile businesses in Washington County?"

"My brother and his wife have a large plantation there. He's not well, and I'm arranging my affairs so I can watch over him a bit."

"Is there a large town in Washington County?"

"Independence isn't large, but it's the wealthiest town in Texas. Baylor University, a coeducational college, has been there almost ten years. There's no finer spot in the state for an elegant mercantile business. Unlike the Galveston elite, the planters have no trouble wearing and using the finest available."

"And, you're going to see that they get what they want."

He leaned so close that she felt the warmth of his breath near her ear. "Absolutely. And I'll help you do the same for Indianola's elite."

She stood very still, not turning her head to look directly at him, but allowing him to see her smile. "I think I'm going to enjoy this buying trip."

"We need to get you out of the sun and wind. That pretty bonnet won't protect you. Let's go in the smoking room. We can watch the water, sip a mint julep, and avoid uncomfortable burns."

They settled at a tiny table in an alcove overlooking undulating waves of the Gulf of Mexico. Her mint julep was served in a silver cup with a sprig of mint floating on top. "Tell me what to expect in New Orleans?"

"Tobacco, molasses, coffee, sugar, and salt will have a better price if you order from New Orleans. Get it shipped directly to Indianola and avoid the markup in Galveston. I'll take you to my bank. You can establish a line of credit to make it easy to quickly move your orders."

"My business partner needed to make this trip. He knows much more about what the wealthy want to buy. His mama's illness kept him from coming."

"I'm glad he didn't come." Al grinned, then ducked his head. "What I meant to say is by the time I've shown you all the places offering New York and European imports, you'll know just as much as your partner."

The day passed quickly. Al shared stories of what to expect in the city and the places he wanted to show her. That evening, she hurriedly changed for dinner, glad that she had saved Frau von Ewald's dress that was such a faint blue that it looked like ice on a frozen lake. The Chelsea boots that Hans insisted she needed for New Orleans felt soft and cushiony on her feet. Smiling at her reflection, she did not see a peasant or a small town merchant. She saw a stylish young woman enjoying a steamboat trip.

Al waited just two doors away. "You look lovely." He offered his arm.

The unsteady rocking of the ship made it seem natural to hold fast to Al. The gentle swaying pushed them together as they made their way along the passage lined with full-length gold-framed mirrors.

"Tell me about your New Orleans family." Amelia broke the silence that made his nearness feel uncomfortable.

"There's no one left. I lost my wife and son in childbirth two years ago. Both my parents passed a decade before."

"No wonder you want to escape to Washington County."

"Actually, I don't want to leave New Orleans. I love the place. I grew up there. My father was born there. I'm trying to make the move tolerable by opening the businesses. I'll have an excuse to travel back and forth as often as possible." Al reached for the door of the dining saloon. She felt his hand touch her back as she stepped into the huge room with candles blazing in chandeliers reflecting in floor-to-ceiling mirrors along the walls.

When their waiter came for their order, Al grinned. "They have good Rhine wines that will suit your German tastes, but I recommend their champagne. It's as fine as any ship on the Cunard Line."

"Mrs. Osterman said I could trust your judgment." *What would she say about such a lavish evening?*

"Master Al? I can't believe my eyes." A handsome black man wearing a black suit, white shirt, black bow tie, and sparkling white gloves almost lifted Al off his chair.

The two men beat each other on the back and hugged with abandon.

"What're you doing here, Master Al?"

"I'm not your master, Antone. I'm just plain Al."

"I can't help it. Changing your name from master is like starting to call my mama, Sally. I can't do it."

"Well, try." Al turned to Amelia. "I want you to meet the best friend I ever had. We grew up together. Played and fought with each other every day until Antone decided to become a seaman."

"I'm glad to meet you, ma'am. This man's the finest. First thing he did when his papa passed was give me my freedom."

"Are you doing well?" Al motioned for Antone to sit at their table.

"I can't sit. I'm the second steward, in charge of all the waiters. If I sit, they quit work." Antone grinned, his teeth a brilliant white between very black lips. "I'll keep checking on you. Is your service good so far?"

"Absolutely," Al looked at Amelia for her nod of approval.

As Antone moved away, Amelia said, "He was your slave?"

"Yes. He was my father's carriage man, took care of the horses, drove my father to work and my mother on her errands. My family had several house servants. Our plantation up the River Road generally kept twenty to twenty-five slaves for the fields and around the house. When my father passed away, my bother Charles and I sold the plantation. Charles took the plantation slaves with him to Washington County. I kept the home in New Orleans."

"Do you still have slaves in New Orleans?" Amelia felt tension rising, disappointment turning to sadness.

"I freed them when I freed Antone." Al reached for Amelia's hand. "I see revulsion in your face, and I'm sorry. I hated the idea of enslaving people, but I was alone in my belief. I remedied the situation as soon as I had the authority."

"Being a slave-holder seems out of character for you."

"I grew up knowing about a slave revolt that occurred up the River Road, not far from our plantation. It happened in 1818, seven years before I was born, but it was whispered about. It gave me nightmares until I was almost grown."

Amelia leaned close. "What happened?"

"Almost 600 slaves revolted. The militia went after them. Those who were not killed in the fight were beheaded. Their heads were placed on stakes along the River Road. I imagined those heads staring at me as we rode to and from the plantation."

"Your brother still has slaves?"

Al nodded. "That's part of why I dread living up there. He doesn't mistreat his slaves." Al shrugged, "If you can say that owning humans is not mistreating them. He'll pass soon. I think I can convince his wife to free them and then hire them to work."

The sun had slipped behind them into the Gulf creating a warm, rose-colored glow across the lazily undulating waves.

Chapter Twenty-Nine

*Vendors balance baskets of brilliantly colored flowers
on their heads...*

After dinner, strolling the slightly swaying promenade deck, Amelia held to Al's steady arm, pleasuring in the warmth of his touch and the cool sea air against her face. Even as they leaned against the ship rail watching the rising moon paint its path across the water, she kept her arm tucked in his. Passengers strolled past like shadows without disturbing their silence. The moon rose high, lit the deck in its frosty white light.

"I suppose we should retire. We're alone out here."

Al squeezed her arm. "Let's make one more circle before we give up."

Papa would say, a married woman does not clutch the arm of a man who is not her husband. "I'd love it."

Lying in bed, staring sleeplessly at the stars dancing outside the porthole, Amelia held her arms against her breast hugging herself with the pleasure of the day.

"I've been hoping you'd join me on the deck." Al clasped her hand and tucked it under his arm. "Let's have a late breakfast and skip lunch. I want you to see some amusing tricks that professional gamblers who're operating on this Galveston to New Orleans run are about to play on a poor fellow."

"You think it's funny for a man to be cheated?"

"I've been there myself. First solo trip I made on a ship from New Orleans to Washington, I learned an expensive lesson. It's like a rite of passage."

"Did you lose a lot?"

"I was twelve. Lost one hundred dollars on my way to a Jesuit boys school. I did not admit the folly to my father until Christmas break when I returned home with only one change of clothing."

"You lost your clothing?"

"I learned merchandising. Sold the clothes off my back to pay my expenses."

When they were seated in the smoking room, Al leaned close and pointed out three men. "When I was having coffee this morning, I heard the tallest man arranging to meet that young fellow in here at ten. Watch the two other men standing over in the corner."

The tall man suggested a card game called Three-card Monte. He quickly laid down three cards and the other two men moved in, asking if they could join the game. The young fellow and the two newcomers were all betting on which card would turn up. At first, the young one picked the correct card, and he was clearly excited with his winnings. Then, his fortunes reversed, and he began to miss. The other two began winning, and the young man started wiping his face with his handkerchief, obviously distressed.

"Why don't you stop them? Tell him he's being cheated?"

"And get my throat cut tonight?" Al laughed. "Some things have to be learned, and often the lesson is expensive."

He's from a world I've never known. "Men can be so cruel to each other."

"Let's walk around the promenade deck. Come back for a mint julep, and you'll feel better." He was not trying to hide his mirth.

They stepped onto the deck, and he reached for her hand, tucked it into the crook of his arm. "This is another thing about men. We like to imagine we're taking care of the ladies. You obviously can balance just fine on your own, but I hope you'll indulge me."

I love this attention. She didn't try suppressing her laugh. "It's my pleasure."

"We'll arrive tomorrow about mid-morning. I'd like to show you my city before we start working. I conduct a pretty good tour, including a late lunch."

They spent the day exploring the ship, sharing their life stories. He talked about his years at the Georgetown Preparatory School north of Washington. His face showed its first sign of grief when he spoke of his wife and her death in childbirth. Amelia told him about Branson's worry that she might not return and how much she wished she and Dr. Stein had taken him in when he hobbled off that ship. And she told him about the store and her satisfaction with making it grow. After dinner and a full bottle of champagne, they returned to the promenade deck.

"I've enjoyed this trip."

"It's not over." Al squeezed her arm tighter against his chest. They stood at the railing, bathed in the brilliant light of another full moon.

I should break this silence; it feels too intimate. "We're the last people out here."

Al's hand clasped hers as they moved apart. "If you'll rise early, we'll watch the creatures come alive on the Mississippi Delta. It's a 100-mile trip from the Gulf to New Orleans."

"I'd like that."

She slept very little, the feel of his hand, her arm tucked against him kept her awake. She slipped out of her stateroom and found Al at the rail looking into the fading night sky.

"Have you been waiting long?"

"I couldn't sleep. Decided to come out here and watch the night life."

I want to slip my hand into the bend of his arm, but the ship's perfectly steady gliding over the smooth river surface. She whispered, "It's beautiful and primitive and goes forever toward the beginning light of the new day."

Al whispered, "It's mosquito-infested, alligator country that changes its plants and colors and smells every few miles." He reached for her hand, pulled it into the bend of his arm. His face close to hers, to direct her gaze to bumps at the edge of the water. "Those are alligator eyes spying on us for invading their territory."

Whispering feels so personal; I can barely breathe. She pointed to the pink spoonbills and snowy egrets wading along the bank under trees drooping moss that looked like shaggy old man whiskers. "They stalk the bayous behind Indianola." She jumped as the sudden cannon sound shattering the stillness as they watched birds rise in a black cloud above the forest. Then the red sun creased above the horizon and painted the flat land spread out ahead of the ship in a sea of deep blue.

"That's indigo. It goes for miles. Soon you'll see towering stalks of sugar cane. Closer to New Orleans, cotton fields form great long lines stretching over the bend of the earth."

Al kept swatting at the mosquitos. "I wish we could stay out here with this swamp life, but the mosquitoes will eat you alive. Let's watch from the saloon and take a long time to eat breakfast."

"Is the trip better in winter when the mosquitos aren't around?"

"The mosquitoes are the masters. They never leave." He brushed at her hair, let his hand slip along her cheek as he flicked away another mosquito.

At breakfast, Al looked steadily at her from across the table, "Tell me about your husband."

A hot surge of blood roasted her cheeks. "He's a good man, a wonderful doctor. To a person, he's loved in the community."

His eyes are such a dark brown and so intense that I should look away, but I can't. "He's been good to me."

"If you were my wife, I'd keep you next to me, night and day."

"I always thought husbands felt that way. Papa spent most every hour with Mama, or telling her all about what he had been doing when he came home."

"He doesn't keep you close?" Al's eyes never left her face.

"He loves me, Al." Then she whispered, "Like a sister." She turned her head toward the window in time to see a coiled snake slither into the river.

"I'll be damned."

"Al, I thought I recognized you." The man wearing a long double-breasted morning coat and striped trousers towered above their table, his face radiant with pleasure. "Who's this lovely lady?"

Al stood quickly, vigorously shaking Jerome DeHart's hand. He introduced Amelia as Frau Stein, a merchant who'd be visiting DeHart's bank to establish a line of credit.

"If Al recommends you, the credit's already set up. I'm sailing tonight for St. Louis. I'll leave word at the bank to get you settled with us." He slapped Al on the shoulder. "Don't stay so long in Texas. Life in the Quarter isn't the same without you."

Al grinned as Jerome DeHart kissed Amelia's fingers when she extended her hand. "He's an old-time Creole. You'll have to get used to their charm."

"I'm honored," she said. "Our German gentlemen aren't so gallant."

By the time DeHart disappeared across the saloon, ships began appearing on both sides of the river, which spread out like a broad lake. Warehouses loomed behind wide docks. Stacks of enormous tree trunks and huge sacks of grain formed islands with freight wagons winding between.

Al pointed to bales of cotton stacked as high as the warehouse roofs. It was being loaded to the top of steamboat smokestacks. "Looks like the factors are releasing the cotton. It's been stored in their warehouses since last fall, waiting on the price to go up."

"What's a factor?"

"A factor is a man who buys cotton, tobacco, or sugar directly from planters and that's the end of their deal. A commission merchant stores the goods in his warehouse for the planter and then sells it later. The planter pays the commission merchant a percentage of the sale for keeping the goods and for handling the sale for him. I'll introduce you to both while you are here."

Al did not let go of her arm even after he guided her to a spot at the railing between passengers who were shouting and waving to friends on the dock. To avoid looking at the dead fish and rotten garbage slapping against the ship as it maneuvered into place, she lifted her eyes toward the skyline at buildings of three and four stories.

"The rounded towers in the distance are St. Louis Cathedral. The Spanish built it in 1794. It's only a couple of blocks from my townhouse." He pointed to a dome rising on columns atop a roof. "That's the St. Charles Hotel where you'll be staying."

Al hailed an open carriage, which stopped immediately. The driver leaped to the wooden pier greeting Al like an old friend. Al lifted her up into the open carriage, settled in against her on the narrow leather seat. Beyond the dark warehouses, the streets, some covered in cobblestones and others laid with thick wood planks, came alive with color. Women with skin the shade of creamed coffee wore billowing dresses as colorful as flower gardens and sang out their wares in languid lyrics. "Rubyyy-red straw-ber-rees. Pret-ty pur-pully plums!" Their bodies flowed smoothly as they balanced on their heads trays or baskets overflowing with figs, carrots, and greens twisted in mounds, cones of brown sugar colored popcorn balls, and stacks of pralines. Fluttering among the throng, fanning themselves with sprays of palmettos, crossing and often standing firmly in the middle of the street, flower women wrapped their heads in brightly colored scarves that Al said were *tignons*. They balanced atop their headgear bouquets of violets cupped in tissue paper and baskets of dahlias, japonicas, and roses. Al signaled for the driver to stop for a kettle of brown sugar coffee and a bouquet proffered by women positioned to reach into passing carriages.

He handed the tiny cup and the violets to Amelia. "They only charge a picayune, such a little, less than a penny. We'll have to get you a supply for shopping along here." He pointed to markets, spread out under extended roofs where reds, yellows, and greens of vegetables painted brilliant portraits around darkened doorways. Buckets of fresh cut flowers formed tiers of color across the front of greenhouses, exuding a sweet aroma of jasmine and honeysuckle.

She sipped from the rich thimble-size coffee cup, soaking in the sounds of the city—the echo of hooves on the plank streets, the rattle of freight wagons, and the musical notes of soprano and alto voices chanting "horseradish roots, cream cheese, fresh gumbo filé, herbs, fresh herbs."

The carriage turned onto a broad cobblestone avenue, so wide that it could have accommodated several buildings across its girth. "This is Canal; at 171 feet, it's the widest street in the world." Al's voice held the pride of a native son. "It was supposed to carry a fifty-foot canal running all the way from the river to Lake Pontchartrain. We got this immense avenue instead. It divides the French Quarter, where I live, from the new town where the Americans settled."

Three and four-story buildings on both sides of the street displayed signs for dry goods, clothing, and general merchandise. Delicate cast iron columns supported broad porches on first and second floors, and ornate facades created a fanciful appearance for serious business houses.

Two blocks from Canal, the St. Charles Hotel, dominating the street of the same name, sprawled over an entire block. It looked like a government building with massive columns rising three stories to the circular domed roof that she had seen from the ship.

"This is where I'll be staying?" Amelia heard the wonder in her voice and knew she sounded like a German peasant.

"The St. Charles is known as the finest building in the South."

"My goodness, I'll hardly know how to act in such a massive place." She did not mention the dirty water running down the streets or the garbage that no one seemed interested in sweeping. *Indianola may be a tiny port of little renown, but the streets are kept clean.*

"I want to take you to the Garden District. Then, would you like to see my family townhouse?" Al's question sounded tentative, almost timid.

"I'd love to see your home." Amelia touched Al's arm and did not look away from his very serious eyes. *Papa, I can hear your disapproval. But it feels right to touch this man.*

Chapter Thirty

The heartbeat of the city...

They rode in silence out St. Charles Avenue next to the tracks that ran down the middle on which appeared a horse-drawn, box-shaped carriage carrying passengers hanging from rails along the sides and sprawled leisurely on its roof. "That's our public street car. I'll treat you to a ride if you like," Al had to shout over the rumbling sound of the vehicle and its merry passengers calling greetings to anyone who looked in their direction.

Live oaks, heavy with Spanish moss canopied the street. Hidden behind iron fences and palmetto thickets, gardens blazed in such profusion that the mingling of scents masked the stench of the open sewer running along the track in the middle of the street. The houses grew larger, circled by broad verandas supported by thick columns that rose two and three stories. "I've never seen so many enormous houses. Each one is as large as the von Ewald's."

"There're no gentry here. It's true that some think they're gentry."

Riding back into the city Al began to explain. "My grandfather moved the family into town in 1794, right after the last big fire in the Vieux Carré. Now that so many Americans have moved in, we call it the French Quarter. Property was cheap after the fire. He wanted my father to be born in New Orleans instead of on the plantation."

The streets grew narrow, edged with brick buildings, many covered in stucco hues of blues and yellows. Black shutters hung open at upper windows and curly iron railings framed balconies on upper floors.

The carriage pulled through a narrow wrought iron gate and down a brick passage hung with baskets of drooping ferns and cascading roses.

A woman as black as polished ebony stepped onto a narrow porch, her voice echoed between the buildings, "Come quick, Percy. Mister Al's home."

Al leaped from the carriage and hugged the woman who was a full head taller than he. "Violet, I've brought Frau Stein to see the house." He told the driver to wait and reached for Amelia's hand. "This is the woman who raised me. She whipped me when I needed it, and she hugged me every day."

Violet clutched Amelia's hand between her rough palms; her eyes rimmed red and watery. "I'm glad you've come with my boy. Look, here's my man, Percy." Violet stretched out her arm to tug at the crisp white sleeve of an equally black man.

"Good day, ma'am. We're glad to have you here." Percy bowed and then grinned at Al.

"Amelia's a merchant, a businesswoman from Texas. I'll be driving her to the St. Charles this afternoon."

"You got here just in time to tell us good-bye. We're going to see the grandbabies. Be gone about four days."

"I better get my coat." Percy slapped Al's shoulder. "You be good now, boy."

The two servants clasped hands as they walked up the drive to a door in a separate rear building.

"They live back there and take care of the house." He opened French doors into a high-ceilinged parlor with windows to the floor opening onto the busy street. The chairs were large and roomy and covered in soft sandy shades of plush materials. The tables held lamps strung with dangling blue teardrops of fine cut glass.

Al led her through a dining room where a chandelier hung over a polished table, and a sideboard boasted fresh flowers spread over silver trays. "I want to show you the kitchen where I spent many hours waiting for Violet to give me one of her cakes."

"She was a slave?" Amelia stopped to gaze at the huge kitchen with shiny copper pots stacked on rows of shelves and hung from the ceiling.

"That's how I grew up. I freed them when I could. They're like parents to me." He stood very still, his eyes holding her; not turning away or offering more explanation.

Someone shouted on the street. A horse clomped past. His lips were soft. His hands stroked her back. She pressed her body against him, clinging to him, melting into him.

The clang of a bell shook them apart. "Oh, god, I forgot the driver. I told him we'd be right out."

She trembled, no longer her former self. "Send him away. I don't want to leave."

"I'll get the trunks."

She turned, clutched the edge of a huge chopping block scrubbed to the color of sun-bleached sand. Tall windows stretched the length of the kitchen, a neighboring brick building beyond the driveway was hung with baskets of ferns. Al appeared in the doorway holding Frau von Ewald's flower garden trunk like an offering.

"I've never touched another man's wife."

She stood perfectly still and gazed across the room at the only man who had ever kissed her. "I'm a maiden, Al. I've slept in the same bed with Dr. Stein for over four years. And I'm still a maiden. I don't want to be a maiden any longer."

"My god, Amelia." He sat the trunk down and almost staggered as he rushed to her. "I've fought myself to keep from crushing you against me since that first day." He was lifting her and carrying her up the stairs.

His mouth moved over her neck and across her shoulders as he unfastened her dress. When it fell to the floor, she loosened her petticoats and felt the coolness of the room against her naked body. She could feel his hardness, and she wanted to touch him, to feel his hardness in her hand.

"I'll be gentle. I don't want to hurt you." He lifted her onto the bed, his hands caressing her, bringing her to a hunger to have him, to pull him into her, to feel him. Even as the hurt came, it drove her harder against him until her body pulled at him of its own accord.

When the quiet came, they clung to each other laughing softly.

"Did I hurt you?" He stroked her sweat soaked face.

"It was good, a long-awaited hurt. Thank you for my pleasure."

Al rolled over and pulled her on top of him. "I never thought about it being a gift. I offer it happily."

When they roused from sleep, Al poured a pitcher of water in the basin. "Let's see what Violet's cooked for my welcome home."

When she gathered her dress from the floor, Al pulled it away. "Wear my shirt. I want to look at your legs."

"My legs?"

"While we're at the bank and visiting all the merchants on Canal, I want to remember what's hidden under all those petticoats."

Amelia clutched his face in both hands. "I'll love knowing what you're thinking." She pulled his wrinkled shirt over her head and padded barefoot downstairs to the kitchen.

Violet had baked a long loaf of bread, stored cheese in a cupboard, and stacked strawberries, bananas, and grapes in a bowl. Al kindled a fire in the huge iron stove and heated a large pot of gumbo, which he claimed was Violet's specialty.

"Do you mind waiting until morning to begin all your business?" Al wrapped his arms around her and began kissing her neck. "I want to make more love to you."

"This is the way it is, isn't it? I've always imagined it must be special like this."

"Yes, it's special. It's what keeps the species eager to keep going."

That night, lying in the darkened room, the French doors opened to the screech of birds and the rustle of tall palms against the porch; Amelia whispered, "Now I understand why women are willing to suffer through childbirth. I even understand my dear friend Anna, who has lost a baby, and is expecting another far too soon. She and Dr. Reuss enjoy the love too much to give it up."

"I'm trying to pull away from you and not give you a child. Unless you stay with me, I don't want you to suffer with the consequences of my child."

"I'd love to have your child."

"He wouldn't demand a divorce?"

"Never. A divorce would destroy his position in town. He wanted a wife because it's expected. He'd be unhappy at first. But a child would add to his family image."

He pulled her onto his shoulder. "Stay with me. Don't go back."

She wrapped her leg over his body and squeezed him to her. "I want to stay more than anything I can imagine. But I can't abandon

Branson. If we had taken him as ours, I could go back and bring him here with me. But he belongs with Charlie. Now that Lou's dead, he needs me as much as I need him."

Al stroked her hair and rocked her against him. "I don't have an ounce of shame for taking you away from that man, but guilt would eat at me over that boy."

"And, I can't humiliate Dr. Stein. He trusts me to be his partner." She raised up in the dark. "When we met, I knew better than to encourage you, but I didn't want to stop. You've given me a chance to be a real woman."

He pulled her back against his chest, "For God's sake, Amelia. Why'd you ever think you weren't a real woman?"

"I wasn't wanted."

"I want you. And don't you dare thank me."

Chapter Thirty-One

Canal is the widest street in the world...

Amelia awoke to the raucous sound of birds calling and fluttering through the jungle of trees and vines canopying the rear courtyard. She slipped out of bed, wrapped in Al's shirt, and stepped between the layer of mosquito netting covering the French doors and onto the wide balcony swaddled in the forest of foliage. Movement below caused her to jump back into the shadows of the room. Violet was squatting over a washtub in the far corner of the courtyard.

Al grinned at her from the tangle of sheets. "You leaped back in here like you'd stepped on a hot coal."

"Violet's back; she's washing."

Al curled into a knot and held the sheet over his face to muffle his laughter. "I forgot to tell you. There're no grandbabies. Violet's begged me to bring someone home ever since Priscilla died. That was her way of letting me know she'd give us privacy."

She stared at the man convulsed in laughter. *Have I been a stupid dunce?* "You knew all along? You deliberately let me embarrass myself?"

He tossed off the sheet and bound naked across the bed to grab her. "Oh, no, my love. I'm sorry. I got busy making love, forgot those two old codgers were back there hoping you wouldn't leave." He pulled away, his eyes pleading, "Believe me, I wasn't laughing at you. I laughed at the absurdity of an old lady trying to match make." He cupped her face in his hands, "I was too stupid to realize you wouldn't understand about Violet."

I want to believe him. I want him to be who he seems to be. I don't want to be fooled again. She stroked his face with both palms. "You're a scoundrel, and you're scratchy."

"I'll shave right away."

"Not yet. I like feeling you. I've never felt whiskers."

"I've never felt a body that looked like pure white porcelain." Al began leading her to the bed. "I'll have a busy mind all day."

She pulled away. "I need to iron my dress. I left it in the trunk downstairs."

"I bet Violet ironed it long before daylight."

"Would she do that?"

"Of course. I told you she's cared for me all my life. If you're with me, she'll care for you. She probably ironed every dress in that trunk."

"She's even ironed my drawers," Amelia whispered and then gazed across the kitchen at a pan of fluffy square pastry and coffee on the warming burner. "I can't imagine living like this with people taking care of you like you're a child."

"You don't have to whisper. Violet won't come in. I know it's strange. They're a shadow family, always in the background, aware of everything." He picked up the pan of pastries. "These are beignets, her other treat. She always makes a fresh batch when I've been away. I'll pour you some Creole coffee." He stirred in molasses and warm cream. "If it's too strong, I'll cut it." His fingers slipped across her hand as she accepted the cup.

After the very rich and foreign breakfast, Al set their dishes on a tray and started toward the kitchen, "While you dress, I'll arrange a carriage. We could walk to the bank, but we'll need the carriage for the rest of the day."

Amelia was dressed by the time Al returned, out of breath and beaming with self-satisfaction. "I found Sampson, who drives the best carriage in the Quarter."

"You and Violet are treating me like royalty."

"Violet and I are mighty happy to have you here." He kissed her nose.

"I've been admiring your bed. I've never slept in anything so large or so lovely."

"It's a Mallard. See his trademark duck egg at the top of the headboard? The canopies on his beds are all half-testers. And they're big enough for a giant to sleep crosswise. I bought it after Priscilla, and the baby died. Our family bed held the births and deaths from the days of my grandfather. It was time to close the door."

"I'm sorry." Amelia pulled his hand to her lips.

He squeezed her fingers and turned away, "You'll find a good market in Indianola for Mallard furniture. He imports most of his pieces from New York and Paris. His store is just a few blocks away on Rue Royal."

"I'm sure Hans will want a bed like this for his mama."

"After Prudent Mallard's shop, we'll go to Francois Seignouret's. He's from Bordeaux, imports fine wine and makes some of the South's best lounges and armoires."

Al reached for a broad-brimmed hat as they stepped onto the carriageway.

She touched his pressed shirtfront, "You look like a country gentleman."

"I have to keep up appearances when I'm escorting a beautiful woman." He waved to Sampson, who wore a stovepipe hat, a tattered black suit, and greying white shirt. Jumping from the high seat of his carriage, Sampson bowed low, his arm swooping toward his fine vehicle and handsome horse.

"My head's spinning. This feels like a whirlwind."

"Beware, I'm trying to seduce you." Al clutched Amelia's waist and lifted her to the high carriage step. The seat was fine, soft leather, warm from the morning sun.

Al and Sampson exchanged an odd-sounding French. Sampson tipped his hat and snapped the reins, backing expertly into the narrow street.

"That's not French?"

"It's *Gombo*. We grew up in the Quarter speaking a local slang, probably a slave invention. I told Sampson to circle past Jackson Square so you can see St. Louis Cathedral. You saw its spires from our ship. It's being rebuilt so we can't go in to hear the organ."

Within two blocks, enormous paddle wheelers churned the water on the other side of a levee edging the Mississippi River. The ships glided past the handsome old cathedral wrapped in scaffolding and dominating Jackson Square.

Al pointed to a side-wheeler, its two red smokestacks swinging a bale of cotton in between. "That's the *Natchez*. You can spot her because she's the only one with red smokestacks. All the others are black."

Amelia smiled at a chimney sweep, dirty as those in Germany, but very black. Along with his rope and bundle of broom straws, he was swinging several bunches of palmettos. Men and women balanced baskets of strawberries and blackberries on their heads. Several women wearing wildly colored, flowing dresses swung their arms to a rhythm that only they could hear while carrying huge bundles of laundry on their heads. "Those women are *blanchisseuses,* washerwomen who do the laundry for every family in the Quarter except us. Violet refuses to let go of that chore."

A dreadful smell grew stronger as their carriage neared the French Market, a broad, low roof covering an arcade of open stalls. The building backed up to the river where little boats with square sails that Al called luggers, were being emptied of oranges and baskets of vegetables. Next to the street, feathers flew from the hands of black children plucking chickens. Women tossed the guts into the drain moving sluggishly along the street. Other women gutted fish and paid no notice to their feet stomping the entrails into the market's dirt floor. Stalls opened along the street. Vendors waved long, thin loaves of bread. A multitude of fruits and vegetables piled high on tables, and the aroma of coffee blended with a cacophony of languages.

"There's the U.S. Mint." Al pointed across the street to a looming red brick building garrisoned behind an iron enclosure. "It's the only place in the country that mints silver coins. Every other mint produces gold. Look at your coins and you'll see the letter O for Orleans. The new Liberty quarters and the seated Liberty half dollars have an O right under the eagle."

She fished in Frau von Ewald's little needlepoint chatelaine for some coins and was surprised to see that all the silver pieces bore the letter O. "It's amazing that the Mexican gold and silver headed for that building comes through Indianola. Hundreds of freight wagons and Mexican *carretas* pass along the road in front of our store."

Amelia felt for Al's hand. "When it gets here, you'll know I saw it pass my store."

"I don't want to think about that." He looked away.

She held fast to his hand tucked under the edge of her skirt. The carriage turned on Rue Royal, and Al lifted her hand to his lips. "*La Banqu de l'Etat de la Louisiane,* is a couple of blocks away."

The carriage neared a stucco-covered brick building like so many in the Quarter. It pulled under a balcony with a wrought iron railing prominently displaying '*LSB,*' which Al explained was a Creole style monogram for Louisiana State Bank. The carriageway opened into a spacious courtyard edged with pink azaleas and a full magnolia heavy with bowl-sized blossoms. Wide double doors opened into the bank lobby infused with warmth from brilliant colored glass in the domed ceiling.

The staff rushed forward, greeting Al in French and welcoming Amelia in German. Jerome DeHart, true to his word, had left papers providing Frau Amelia Stein, a partner in Stein Mercantile of Indianola, Texas, an extensive line of credit.

"I'm breathless," Amanda murmured as they were whisked back to their waiting carriage. "You have amazing connections."

Ignoring the proffered hands of two doormen, Al clutched Amelia's waist and lifted her up to the carriage, whispering, "It's been too long since I touched you." He directed Sampson to deliver them to *Magasin de Meubles,* one block down Rue Royal. "Mallard is a Frenchman, and his name isn't pronounced like the green-headed duck. The accent is on the last syllable even as he capitalizes on the mallard egg on his pieces."

"Al, you rascal. I've been missing you." A rosy-cheeked little man with receding hair, colored almost the shade of his maroon satin vest, burst through wide front doors. "And who is this lovely creature?"

With Al's introduction, Amelia extended her hand and received Prudent Mallard's firm kiss. "Welcome, Frau Stein, to my curiosity depot. Come and explore."

The sprawling interior was a showcase of rosewood dressing tables, mahogany chairs, and the great half-tester beds. Gathered white satin and soft rose velvet filled the half-testers, and each one displayed the famous mallard egg nestled in various designs of petals and flowers. Porcelain, silverware, glassware, rich textiles, and paintings were displayed as though they had been placed in a luxurious home.

Amelia ordered a rosewood half-tester and one in mahogany with a matching armoire, confident that Hans would be the first customer. Al's subtle nod assured her that she had made good selections when it was time to move on.

A long archway opened off the street, and Sampson maneuvered into a courtyard paved with wide sandstones and circled by French doors. Curving stairways disappeared past ferns and hanging baskets into second and third floors. Francois Seignouret, while not so flamboyant as Mallard, was delighted to see Al and shook his hand vigorously. He, too, kissed Amelia's hand and led them immediately to his *entresol*, a half-story above the main floor where he stored wine imported from his home in Bordeaux. "Share a glass with me, Frau Stein, and you cannot resist ordering a few cases for your Indianola shop."

They followed him to the third floor where he poured their wine. He moved to a huge organ and played the German love song, *Du, Du Leigst Mir Im Herzen*, while they sipped the mellowed sweetness. Al moved his arm around Amelia's waist.

"I'm delighted you selected that beautiful piece," Amelia said.

"It seemed appropriate for two young people who honored me with a visit." He led them to the balcony edged with ironwork and the letter *S* hammered prominently into a fan-shaped screen at its center. "You see my trademark? All my designs bear this *S*, sometimes in places you least expect."

Amelia ordered a dozen cases of Seignouret's Bordeaux and then was enthralled by the delicate tables and tiny upholstered chairs, so different from Conrad Swartz' heavy pine and walnut furniture. She ordered a few pieces with Seignouret's assurance that she would be writing for more very soon.

On the way to the St. Charles for lunch, they passed an organ grinder whose knees peeked from his pant legs. His elbows made faded white spots in his coat sleeves. Oblivious to his attire, or perhaps because of it, he cranked steadily at his instrument while loudly quoting Shakespeare. His monkey bounced expectantly, tin cup in hand, between those who had stopped to watch the spectacle and pedestrians trying to maneuver through the crowd. The sudden screech of "ICE CRRrreeeam!" next to the carriage made Amelia jump. A large black woman balancing a freezer on her head walked alongside the carriage, crying her wares.

"It's so warm here. Where do you get ice?"

"It's shipped in from Maine." Al seemed distracted, oblivious to the hubbub. He leaned close to Amelia. "There's a slave auction at the St. Charles every day at noon. It's held in the bar near the dining room."

Al tried without success to maneuver them through the throng pushing forward to stare at people who were all shades of black and brown. Each slave was herded onto permanent boxes situated at each end of the bar to offer buyers easier inspection. Most of the men had been dressed in black top hats and evening clothes complete with black ties and dingy white shirts. The women, some of whom were beautiful and slender, others who were full-breasted and rounded like huge balloons, wore brightly colored *tignons* tied into elaborate turbans. The colors highlighted the creamy smoothness of coffee milk-colored skin and the shining ebony of faces set with knowing eyes.

Eyes like Fannie's that have seen more than any white person can imagine. She clung tightly to Al's arm as the auctioneer rattled the numbers in such a staccato rhythm it was impossible to know who made a purchase or how much they paid. Some of the very attractive teased with nods and curtsies. Others stood in sullen silence.

One strapping young man in the line kept clutching a woman with one hand and a boy of about three with the other. He was talking hard and fast to a potential buyer. "You'll never find a better field hand than me. My woman's good in the field and she can cook. This here boy's little, but he can pick up scraps of cotton faster than a field mouse."

Al pulled at Amelia's arm. "That poor bastard's too eager. He's never going to keep his family together." She looked back in time to see the planter move away from the desperate man trying to sell himself and his family as a single unit.

The dining room walls, circled with bold round columns, soared as high as a second floor. Gold leaf edged mirrors filled the spaces between each column. The tables dazzled with white cloths, sweet-smelling flowers, and glasses sparkling under the lights of massive chandeliers suspended from the ceiling.

Al reached for Amelia's hand as soon as they were seated. "I wanted to show off this amazing hotel. A slave auction is not the way to do it."

"It's heartbreaking. I've heard rumors that some people in Indianola want to get more planters into town by offering slave auctions. Look at all the people visiting, laughing. It's as if nothing significant is going on right outside this room."

"It's part of every day here." Al clutched her hand until she relaxed.

"I read about slavery before immigrating. It's not so real in a book."

The waiter, as black as coal dust, wore an equally black jacket over a shirt so white it made his skin glow. "Our *crawfish étouffée* is especially good today, sir."

"I'd love to try it. Our cook at the Tremont claimed to make the world's best."

Al whispered, "Let's eat a lot so we can stay in tonight. I want you all to myself."

"I was about to make the same suggestion."

They stepped onto an arcaded sidewalk where women hawked bundles of flowers whose aroma masked the sewer smell along Canal. Merchants fronting the most fashionable street in the city touted everything from black wigs to top hats and corsets just as Hans had said. They strolled under a colonnade connecting twelve, four-story mercantile buildings opening into shops on the first and second floors. The owners welcomed Al and courted Amelia with discount prices for their best merchandise from fine fabrics and laces to parasols.

Al placed her arm securely under his and guided her across the wide expanse of Canal. A large open area, handsomely designed for gaslights and trees, ran between two broad carriage lanes. He explained that the middle of the street, called the "neutral zone," separated the Creole section of the city from the American zone. Amelia noticed that the mix of cultures swarmed on both sides of the street.

They approached two large show windows anchoring double doors that Al said housed the mercantile cathedral of D.H. Holmes, the "merchant prince." Gold leaf gaslight chandeliers reflected in ornately framed French mirrors. Elegantly gowned young women, whom Al said Holmes encouraged to come to the store as a meeting place, purchased the latest fashions from Paris and London. Fine leather gloves, cashmere shawls, hats and bonnets, more exquisite than any Amelia had ever seen, lay invitingly on open counters and inside lovely glass-topped cabinets.

Remembering to breathe deeply to keep the tremble out of her voice, Amelia selected a few items at each shop for shipment to Indianola. Al's introductions to the owners—all his friends—resulted in Amelia having a list of merchants eager to accept future orders.

Staring toward the endless line of storefronts crowding both sides of Canal, Amelia pulled Al against her. "I must stop this madness before I fall apart. Will you take me home with you?"

"Yes, thank God." Al waved his arm as a carriage pulled to the walkway. A gentleman alighted, tipped his top hat, and rushed off down the street.

Al lifted her into the carriage that had a bonnet-shaped covering and wrapped his arm around her. "Every time you charmed another merchant and set up a good wholesale deal, I was proud of you. But each deal pulled you farther away."

Amelia closed her eyes, "I've been telling myself that I'm not leaving, that the purchases are for our store, that we're partners. Then, reality makes me almost double over with grief."

He tucked her against his shoulder whispering, "I want you, Amelia, but I can't torment you with begging."

Chapter Thirty-Two

I hate to leave New Orleans...

Amelia could not hold back tears that had been hovering near the surface all afternoon. She buried her face against Al's chest, feeling the strength of his hand under her bonnet as the carriage bounced through the streets. Vendors hawked their wares. Wagons squeaked past, and people shouted and laughed, calling out to each other.

Al whispered, "We're home, precious."

As soon as they entered the house, he lifted her into his arms, his lips against her cheek and carried her up the stairs. Lying together on the bed, she felt his tears against her cheek as he rocked her, unbraiding her hair and stroking her back.

"I want to remember how you feel through your clothes. I want to remember every minute." Al's voice was husky against her breast. "I want to remember how you look as I undress you, how white your body is as I unbutton your clothes."

When he had fully undressed her, she held his face in her hands. "I want to undress you. I want to touch you and remember how you feel." She felt the softness of his cravat that had twisted loose from his collar, the coarseness of his coat and the dampness of his sweat-soaked shirt. His trousers bulged under the broad front flap, and his hands eagerly helped her unfasten all the buttons.

They fell amid the twisted pieces of clothing and shoved themselves together in eager grasping hunger. "I can't pull away," Al gasped as she clung to him, wrapping her legs around him, holding him inside herself with all her strength.

Spent and sweating, they lay clasped together. "I don't want to

let go." Amelia kept her legs curled tightly around Al's body.
"You kept squeezing me. I couldn't pull away from you in time."
"I didn't want you to. I wanted all of you."
"If you have my baby? If he sends you away? Will you come to
me?" Al reached for his wadded shirt and wiped the sweat from her
back and shoulders.
"He'll accept our baby. It'll give him a family without him
having to touch me."
"Damn, Amelia. I don't want that man raising my baby." Al
rolled her over on her back and stared down at her in the dim light.
She ran her fingers through his hair that lay in short, wet curls
against his face. "It hasn't happened, my love. I doubt I'll be so
fortunate."
Al swung off the bed and rummaged for his trousers. "I've got to
get up, or I'm going to start begging you to stay. Let's go downstairs
and find something for supper."
Amelia wore his wrinkled shirt as they sat at the oak table in one
end of the kitchen, sipped a bottle of Seignouret's fine Bordeaux, ate
strawberries, and slathered butter on slices of Violet's bread.
"Tomorrow, I'll take you to some factors who deal directly with
planters. You'll get a better price on rice and tobacco. Then, you can
compare it with what Mrs. Osterman offers. Once they know there's
competition, prices get lowered. The commission merchants will
have cornmeal, flour, and bacon. They'll offer better prices than you
get in Galveston."
"New Orleans's so different. Our store carries everything. Silk
stockings, garters, and cravats are displayed near barrels of molasses
and loaves of sugar dangling from the ceiling."
"It's the same in Independence and Brenham. When you get
some competition, you can specialize. Sounds like old Hans will be
happier with clothing and furniture. Let another store handle all the
everyday merchandise."
Amelia laughed. "Absolutely. Hans is quite a dandy."
"Like me?" Al pushed his uncombed hair out of his face and
leaned to kiss Amelia's neck."
"Never. Hans doesn't like women. At least, not women his age."

The factors' offices proved to be crowded rooms tucked into corners of sprawling warehouses. Men, some in top hats and others in shirtsleeves pouring over ledgers at chest-high tables were, to a person, glad to see Al and perplexed at seeing a woman. Al's explanation of Amelia's business eased most of the awkward tension. She ordered barrels of corn and oats, and let it be known that she was comparing their prices for sugar and molasses.

The commission merchant, busily moving wagons of ice packed deep in layers of sawdust, made it clear that Indianola was too small to provide enough profit for the added freight expense. She had much more success with orders of cornmeal, bacon, and flour. Her orders would be shipped before she left for Indianola.

They left the carriage and walked among the street markets, allowing Amelia to spend some of the *picayunes* jangling in her chatelaine. She bought a dozen picayunes, twelve-inch-tall wood dolls with jointed arms and legs. Their smooth heads and all their features, as well as their clothing, were painted in bold colors. She stuffed her purchases in a broadcloth bag that Al swung in one hand. He insisted that Amelia keep her arm securely tucked into the fold of his other arm. They munched on oranges, figs, and French bread. The evening grew cool, and gaslights gave the streets a party atmosphere—laughter became louder, couples strolled closer together, and single men abandoned their brisk business walk.

Light rain forced them into a carriage for the ride to Antoine Alciatore's Restaurant located in a *pension*, a boarding house that Antoine and his wife ran on Rue Saint Louis across from the slave mart.

As with all the other places in the Quarter, Antoine and his wife greeted Al with great affection and insisted that Amelia did not have to enter by the door reserved for women. Several patrons at the bar recognized Al and came over to clasp him in affectionate embraces.

Seated at a table away from the bar, Amelia felt Al's knee push against hers. He ordered Antoine's famous pressed duck. A waiter brought the roasted bird to the table, removed the legs and slices of breast, then using a silver press, he crushed the juices and marrow from the bird. He blended the mixture with a cognac sauce, which he poured over the saved breast and legs and topped the dish with shaved truffles.

Amelia leaned close to Al. "I thought I might faint when he crushed that duck. I admit it's absolutely delicious."

"Let's not rush. But I can't wait to get you home."

The night passed too quickly, even as Amelia lay awake feeling Al's soft breath against her cheek and relishing the touch of his hand against her back. The rattle of a passing carriage on the brick street or the shout of a drunk roused Al just enough for him to press her closer and nibble sleepy kisses against her ear. She wanted to remember every touch, carry the memory with her. *I am not going to think about the end of this.* She pulled the sheet up to her face to absorb her tears.

Branson hobbled into the store. She tried to reach him to tell him she was there, but he moved out on the pier. She followed him, straining to catch him, unable to move her body, trying to call out to him. No sounds would come from her mouth. She awoke with a start; sweat matted her hair against her face, her eyes ached from dried tears.

Light began outlining features of the room, the massive wardrobe with a mirrored door reflected the growing dawn. A delicate chair with curved legs sat before a writing table. The mosquito net, anchored with wide brocade trim, billowed only slightly. Birds, squawking louder than a yard full of roosters, caused Al to open his eyes and smile. "You've been awake? Why didn't you wake me so I could comfort you?"

"I wanted to feel you against me. I love the way you respond to me even in your sleep."

"Come on, my woman. Let's have one last bath in my big tub." He pulled her to him and began making vigorous love as she clutched him with all her strength.

Standing in the cool darkness of the washroom drying each other, Amelia could see Violet in the far corner of the yard bent over a wash pot stirring laundry with a long stick. "She knows we're leaving tonight, doesn't she?"

"Be prepared. She always cries on my last day. Since I was a kid going off to school in Maryland, she thought she'd die before I returned. Now, she very well could."

"Does she know I'm not coming back with you?"

"She doesn't need to know."

Violet hugged them both and cried copious tears. Percy beat Al on the back several times and then clutched him in a tight embrace. "You take care of yourselves," his voice so husky that it was hard to understand him.

Al swung into the carriage, his eyes red-rimmed. "You shouldn't see a grown man cry over leaving two old black servants. If they didn't take my leaving so hard, I could get away without imagining they'll be gone the next time I return."

Amelia pulled his hand to her lips. "They're imagining the same thing."

Al sucked in his breath. "Today, I'll introduce you to merchants you need to know for linens, curtains, and rugs. We'll also spend time at Leon Godchaux's. He specializes in French and American clothing. His store is the largest in New Orleans."

"Hans will be delighted."

"I'll take you for an early dinner at the St. Louis Hotel. A slave auction is held in its rotunda at lunchtime. We'll wait until it's all cleared out."

"You don't have to protect me from seeing the reality that's so much a part of this place."

Al leaned over, nuzzled inside her bonnet. "I wish I could hide it all."

Sprawled next to the street of the same name, the St. Louis Hotel's white facade rose four stories boasting balconies edged with black iron railings. Al led her through the almost empty rotunda, famous for daily auctions of fine art, elegant furniture, and slaves. His heels clicked on the marble floor, and he caressed her hand that gripped his arm. Late afternoon rays of light streamed through the domed ceiling falling on the stone auction block spread between two marble columns. In preparation for the dinner crowd, black women scrubbed the rotunda, a thorough cleansing to rid evidence of the midday sales.

Gaslights in the dining room cast a sparkling glow on crystal and gleaming silver—reminiscent of the St. Charles. Waiters, dressed in evening attire, seated them in an alcove that offered a view of a sprawling courtyard, a cloistered, peaceful scene of blooming plants and lush green foliage.

Al ordered mirlitons, a kind of squash she had never seen that was stuffed with spicy shrimp. Despite a long day and no lunch, they nibbled at the hotel's famous dish. He leaned close, "I wanted this to be a special meal, but it feels more like a funeral wake."

They rode pressed against each other in silence. Gaslights grew brighter, casting shadows in doorways and reflecting a rosy glow against brick buildings hugging the street. Ships loomed ahead—silent mountains of light, floating cathedrals—easing along the river in both directions. The thrust of paddlewheels and din of motors grew into clashing sounds of activity as their carriage wound between barrels and black-ribbed crates stacked in islands along the dock.

The city lights receded. The river lengthened behind them like an empty black slate. Flashes of lightning lit the horizon, so far away that its cannon boom of thunder took a long time to arrive. The breeze began to whip through her hair. She pulled Frau Fischer's cape tighter around herself, finding little comfort in its luxurious softness.

"Let's watch the storm from the porthole in our stateroom so I can kiss you every time there's a clap of thunder." Al nuzzled against her ear as they moved almost as one body toward their private place.

The ship tossed in the worsening storm. Clutching the brass rail edging the wall under the porthole, she remembered the terrifying trip through Pass Cavallo when Dr. Stein had stood so rigidly beside her, unable to pull her to him.

I'm clinging to a man who wants me, who stirs the woman in me that's been hidden for so long. Am I mad to give it up? I can't forget how much Branson needs me, and I need him. I can't forget that Dr. Stein trusts me. Am I selfish to take so much love from Al and walk away? She clutched Al's hand against her lips as they turned away from the porthole.

They made love as the storm tossed them about the bed, blew cold air into the open porthole, and howled like a grieving lover. As they lay spent, chilled by the wind-dampened sweat, Amelia said, "I'll never again be in a storm without remembering this night with you."

"I'm not forgetting a single minute since the time I laid eyes on you in Osterman's Mercantile Store."

"Were you attracted to me? I mean other than wanting to help me in New Orleans?"

Al broke into a spasm of laughter. "My darling Amelia, I'm not in the habit of taking strange women on trips. You're the most alive woman I've ever met. I wanted you the minute I saw you."

She laughed, clutching him in a tight hug. "I confess to being attracted to your attention. It felt so good. I kept wanting more." She shook him with all the force she could muster. "And I got it, didn't I?"

Al smothered her again with kisses to her eyes and nose. He rolled her over and kissed the back of her neck and her shoulders. "I'm going to keep on like this until I have to stop."

Just before she drifted off to sleep, she said, "I'm not afraid of this storm. I don't care what it does to this old ship as long as you're holding me."

Chapter Thirty-Three

Harriet sails to Indianola...

Morning fog lay on Galveston like a shroud, made the dock slippery with mud, and created a cloying closeness that held the smell of dead fish.

A wagon pulled up beside barrels the slaves were unloading from their ship. Mrs. Osterman, holding a black umbrella, sat straight as a poker next to the black driver. "Hello, you two. Did you come in on this ship?"

"The pretense begins already," Al sent the carriage with their trunks on to the Tremont.

"Let me count my delivery. Then you can walk with me back to my store. I want to hear what you bought. I might beat some of the New Orleans' prices. Shipping rates are a lot lower from Galveston."

Mrs. Osterman checked off her order in a leather-bound ledger and then tucked her arm through Al's, and the three of them made their way carefully through the slush to the raised walkway along The Strand. After a friendly visit over a cup of weak coffee, Mrs. Osterman had reduced her prices on oats and corn. She offered a better price than the New Orleans factors on sugar and molasses from plantations along the Brazos River.

Al kept shaking his head and looking at Amelia as their carriage wheels splattered through standing slush on the way to the Tremont. "You are terrific. All it takes is a little competition to get decent prices. Mrs. Osterman admired your charming way of getting her prices down."

Oscar Wilhite hustled, elbows out and head held high, to provide Amelia a room at the end of the first-floor hall. Then, almost wringing his hands, he apologized profusely for having to place Al on the first floor. "We're simply stuffed full, Mr. Waters. Spring is such a busy time. Then all the rain slowed several departures. I'll be able to move you upstairs tomorrow."

Al shook his head. "I'm very happy on the first floor. If we can make the connections, Frau Stein will leave tomorrow for Indianola, and I'll be off to Washington County."

Harriet grabbed Amelia. "We didn't think you were ever coming back. Fannie's come every night looking for you. Do you still want me to go with you?"

"Of course. Al Waters will help us get our bookings."

"I haven't told Mr. Wilhite. I was afraid you might stay gone."

Harriet changed into a soft calico dress of blues and grays and carried a thick cloth bag bulging with coins. "I bought this dress for the trip. All the money I've made in five years sits in this bag. I can pay my keep until I find work."

Al played the role of helpful gentleman, smiled kindly, offering his hand to Harriet as they climbed into the carriage for the trip to the docks to book their passage. The *Portland*, a Morgan Line vessel coming from New Orleans, would dock the next morning only long enough to take on Indianola passengers.

When they returned to the hotel, Al arranged to meet Amelia for dinner and then walked down the street toward the Tremont's bar.

With ticket in hand, Harriet announced her departure as soon as they stepped in the hotel lobby.

Oscar Wilhite clutched weakly at his breast. "Well, I never expected that. You're our only experienced girl."

"The job's not hard to learn, sir. It's just nasty."

He whirled away, and over his shoulder he said, "I won't have your pay until morning."

Harriet's black eyes snapped. "Good. Then, I'll stay in my quarters tonight."

Fannie swept in the front door clutching a blue umbrella that perfectly matched a rustling taffeta dress. "You came back. We were hoping you had better sense." She looked around conspiratorially. "Did Harriet tell Wilhite to go to hell?"

"I did not. I'm too much of a lady. How do you like my dress?" Harriet turned with just as much grace as Fannie always exhibited.

Fannie wriggled her shoulders. "For a white girl, it's very nice. Can we go to Amelia's room for the latest?"

As soon as Amelia closed the door, Fannie tossed her umbrella on the bed and loosened the ribbon around her neck allowing her hat to drop down her back. "What happened? You look exhausted. Is that good?"

"It's been the best time of my life. And yes, I'm very tired."

"Lack of sleep?" Fannie's eyebrow arched suspiciously.

"Yes."

"Good. So why're you going back to Indianola?"

Amelia crumpled into the only chair in the room. "I can't give you an answer that will make sense to you. I know that I must return."

"My God, white women are the dumbest creatures. You had the best time of your life, and you're giving it up?"

"Stop, Fannie. Can't you see Amelia's miserable? She doesn't need to be tormented." Harriet laid her cheek against Amelia's. "We love you."

Fannie carefully anchored her hat. "I've got to get back to the house. Mrs. Williams's having a party tonight, and I'm serving. Very fine event." She looked at Harriet. "I'm depending on you to let me know how Amelia's doing. Right now, she don't look so good."

Amelia reached to hug the little slave woman. "I love you, Fannie."

"I know you do, and I love you and Harriet." Fannie hugged them both and as she turned Amelia could see the redness in her black eyes.

Al rose from a table in the dining room. His hand stroked Amelia's arm as he seated her on the side of the table instead of across from him. "I want our knees to touch."

"Have you waited long?"

"Nope. I've been consuming all I can find in the bar. May I order a bottle of their really good champagne?"

"I want to stay awake tonight. I'll have a glass of white wine."

"I won't sleep. I promise."

When they left the dining room, he pointed down the hall. "My room is two doors from yours. I'll come as soon as the place settles down."

Amelia asked for a kettle of warm water for a bath. As she brushed her wet hair, she heard the soft tap. Al stepped inside the room before she could get to the door. His hair was still wet, and he smelled like a barbershop. He grabbed her, held her until they lost their balance and tumbled on her bed.

The night flew past, despite their determination to savor every second, talking of all they had done and avoiding talk about the future. Finally, like a wake that offered the last time with a loved one, the future that provided no time together, had to be faced. "Promise you'll come to me or write if you need me. I'll come for you. Don't imagine for a minute that I'll forget." Al stroked her face, kissed her tears. "I'm going to remember how salty you taste."

Right before dawn, he kissed her for the last time before he slipped into the hall. She watched him close the door to his room.

They ordered breakfast, but neither of them could eat. When Harriet peeked in from the kitchen, they both nodded and headed to their separate rooms. The bellman carried Amelia's trunk to the carriage. Al's trunk sat on the porch to be loaded into a carriage scheduled for the steamer that would take him up the Brazos River to the town of Washington.

Their carriage was a small, enclosed coach that felt as cold as a block of ice. Harriet sat across from Amelia and gazed intently out the window as though she could not get enough of the dingy frame buildings lining the street. Al slipped his hand inside Frau Fischer's

MYRA HARGRAVE MCILVAIN

shawl and stroked Amelia's hand that refused to stop trembling.

Before the driver opened the door, Harriet bound from the coach, "I'll see you in our stateroom."

The ship whistled its last warning. She reached for his hand, held it far longer that would be expected of a business associate. "Goodbye, my love."

Al's face blazed like a man burned by a desert sun. "My love, my love..."

The horn blew again. Amelia rushed up the gangplank as the crew unleashed it. The black water swirled foam against the pilings, and the steamer inched away from the dock.

Al did not move. His arms hung by his sides. As the ship sailed past vessels anchored against the dock, he followed, never taking his eyes off Amelia.

She clutched the polished railing and walked toward the rear of the ship. *I can jump, swim toward him and he will come to meet me, hold me to him in the swirling waters of Galveston harbor.*

Then he reached the end of the docks and waited motionless. She strained to see above the spray of the paddlewheel, ignored the dampness that drenched her hair and penetrated her clothing.

242

Chapter Thirty-Four

Returning to a new store...

"Madam, the captain sends his concern. We're well into the Gulf. He fears you'll be chilled from all this spray."

Amelia turned, smiled at the young black man. "Thank the captain for me. I'll go to my stateroom now."

Harriet jumped from the bed, "You're soaked. You need to get warm and get some sleep."

Amelia nodded, allowing Harriet to undress her and pull her nightgown over her head.

Harriet's cool hand stroked Amelia's cheek. "They rang the supper bell. It would help you to eat."

Amelia looked around the crowded stateroom. "I'm sorry to make your first day of freedom so dreary. Have you waited for me all this time?"

"No. I've walked the promenade deck and met some friendly people. I feel like a princess."

Amelia pulled on Frau von Ewald's ice blue dress that Violet had ironed so beautifully, and the two women made their way to the saloon for dinner.

I will pull myself together, offer Harriet a semblance of friendship on her first voyage. I am behaving like someone died. Amelia asked for a table by a window on the Gulf side of the ship. "I'm glad you explored the ship today. What did you think of it?"

Harriet's pink lips spread into a broad smile. "I love you, Amelia. I'm perfectly comfortable managing for myself." She squeezed Amelia's hand. "You don't need to entertain me."

My eyes feel like sand has collected under the lids. Tears don't wash away the grit. She looked out the window to keep tears from starting again. "Thanks for not scolding me."

"I'll make a deal. I won't share my past, and I won't ask about yours. Let's be present day friends."

"You're a woman of wisdom. Some wounds don't need probing."

"I've heard that when passengers clear the deck late at night, stars spread a sparkling blanket over all the world. I want to see that. Why don't you go to bed? I'll be very quiet when I come in."

Pass Cavallo opened its arms and offered an easy passage into Matagorda Bay. Amelia stood on the promenade deck with Harriet and all the other eager passengers, allowing the evening breeze to dry the tears that erupted with the return of another memory—the streak of moonlight dancing on the water, even the smoothness of the polished railing she had leaned against as he tucked her hand into the fold of his arm.

Indianola danced like a mirage on the far shore. Lights glowed in low-slung buildings. Piers sprawling into the bay sparkled with lanterns. Ships lined both sides of the piers, creating more lights, reflecting in the bay's rippling waves. *It's a different world from the bare landscape covered with dirty white tents and wooden lean-tos that first greeted me. And I am a different woman.*

The ship eased up to the end of the Morgan Line pier, which ran farther into the bay than any of the others. The bump as it connected brought her home once again. Her heart fluttered in a surge of anticipation when she read **Stein Mercantile** painted across the second floor of a stark white building at the foot of the pier.

Carriages formed a long line waiting for passengers. Masters Stage Line's new driver stood by four frisky horses. Freight wagons waited to take on cargo after the passengers moved out of the way.

Amelia took Harriet's arm, directing her past the maze of waiting vehicles. "They'll deliver our trunks to Dr. Stein's office. Let's walk through the store. I want you to meet Hans. I'm eager to see how much he has moved into our new building."

Harriet walked like someone in a dream. "I can't believe how clean it is. It doesn't even smell."

"We have plenty of bad odors. But things get washed around here." She realized she was smiling. It was going to be a pleasure introducing Harriet to a life better than chamber pots.

Amelia caught her breath when a wagon moved out of the way and opened a view of lights glowing brightly in the store. The shipment from Mallard's curiosity depot had arrived, and Hans had already mounted wall sconces that used reflectors to enhance the lard-fueled light shining through each chimney. He was bent over a wood crate when Amelia and Harriet stepped through the wide back door opening onto the wharf.

"Amelia! Thank God, you're home." Hans came forward with both arms extended. "I've never missed anyone so much. And I'm not the only one. Branson has been here every day, after school and again before bedtime." He whirled away, "How do you like it? Have I created a first class shop?" His arms spread out, and he turned with as much grace as Fannie had ever shown.

"You've transformed it," Amelia was so filled with wonder at the beauty of the store that she could barely speak.

Finally, she introduced Harriet, who gazed wide-eyed at her surroundings. She shook Hans' hand and then eased slowly around the massive room with its oak beam ceiling and broad open windows.

One side of the store housed merchandise for daily life, including barrels of coffee, flour, lard, and cornmeal that had already arrived from New Orleans. On the opposite side of the store, wide double doors opened off the street into the fancy shop of dry goods, including only one Mallard bed. Hans had arranged linens, gloves, slippers, top hats, and an endless assortment of unnecessary but lovely items with just as much casual elegance as any shop on Canal Street.

"Your gift for decoration is immense," Amelia said. "You've done wonders."

Hans clutched both hands in prayer fashion and bowed his head. "Your wonderful selections made it easy. I bought the other Mallard bed and armoire for Mama. It's way too crowded in her bedroom, but she's in heaven."

"Is Dr. Stein in his office? I want him to meet Harriet."

"He just left. Anna is about to lose another baby."

The words stabbed at her belly. "I feared as much. And I'm not even with her."

"Go! Now! I'll look after Harriet. Anna depends on you." He grabbed at her arm. "Tell Charlie you're back. Branson will be in bed, but he'll want to know when he wakes in the morning."

"Please go, Amelia. Tell Anna I'll come to see her tomorrow. I'll enjoy Hans' tour of the store." Harriet was as charmed by Hans as were all the women in town.

She pulled Frau Fischer's shawl about her shoulders. *I must stop this aching desire for Al, for the feel of my arm tucked in his, for his warmth in this chilly breeze.* She walked quickly, focusing on the sound of her Chelsea boots crunching the shell road, trying not to look at the darkened houses where couples were wrapped together in their beds.

A candle glowed in their old house. She tapped lightly on the door and heard Charlie moving about. He burst into a wide grin when he opened the door. "You're a welcome sight. Branson has worn me out worrying about you. I'm going to wake him so he'll sleep better."

"Tell him I'll be looking for him after school tomorrow."

Charlie shook his head. "He'll probably run by before school. He's been going to your house every morning since you left."

"I'd love that," She clutched her fists against her chest to ease the guilt over even imagining that she could not come home to this child.

The Reusses had chosen to add rooms instead of moving out of Old Town. The doctors' lanterns lit the bedroom, silhouetting both men against the mosquito netting covering the window.

Anna roused to the sound of Amelia's voice. "You're here. You've come in time."

Both doctors looked at Amelia and shook their heads.

Anna clutched a tiny, barely formed baby girl to her breast and kept murmuring a German lullaby, gently shaking the still form. She looked at Amelia through black sunken eyes. "Joseph says no more babies."

Dr. Reuss knelt beside the bed, cradling Anna's head in his big hands. "I've told her she's too precious. I can't chance losing her."

"Precious." The word forced a sob as Amelia bent to kiss Anna's cheek. Dr. Reuss was a blur through her tears. "Thank you for loving her."

Dr. Stein touched her arm. "Why don't you come back tomorrow? After Anna's had some rest."

She nodded, unable to stop the rush of tears.

Dr. Stein lifted his lantern, took her arm, and guided her out the door and down the path toward the road. "You're much too tired to help Anna tonight. Tomorrow you'll feel better."

She stumbled blindly along the road with Dr. Stein gently holding her arm, as he would have done for any distraught patient.

By the time they reached the arched entryway on the walk that led between the buildings to their side porch, the wind had dried her tears, and she remembered to tell him about Harriet staying with them.

"Did you have a good trip?"

"Very good."

"Hans is so happy with everything that's arrived. Did you see how well he's managed the move?"

"He's very creative. You were smart to hire him."

Harriet stepped onto the back porch when they reached the top of the stairs. "I'm happy to meet you, Dr. Stein. Your house and your store are beautiful."

Amelia burst into fresh tears, "Anna lost her baby girl."

Harriet and Dr. Stein led her to bed.

Chapter Thirty-Five

A new home, a new life....

Amelia awoke in the dark, cold to the bone. Rain beat against the porch, not quite reaching the windows, but sending a blanket of icy wind across the room. Dr. Stein lay beside her, undisturbed, his breath coming in a long easy rhythm. She pulled quilts from the wardrobe. Harriet had politely closed the door between the rooms, which cut off the usual cross ventilation, but the breeze from the parlor and center hall, spread a chill over the upstairs. She laid a cover on the foot of Harriet's bed and heard her mumbled thanks as she scooted under the quilt.

Curling under the cover's heavy warmth, she counted the hours, wondering if Al's little river steamer had been able to get through the debris in the Brazos River after all the rain. He could even be in a Washington hotel by now.

My body hurts like something has been torn out of me. Is this going to be my punishment? I wish I'd told Al that I was willing to go to hell to have that time with him. She pulled her pillow tight against her, trying to find comfort.

The grinding crunch of wagon and carreta wheels and the low chatter of drivers, floated through the windows before light framed the rooftops across the street. Hans had warned that in the past week hundreds of Chihuahua trade freighters had started camping overnight out beyond Old Town. They were scrambling each morning to be first in line to unload and then fill their wagons for a return trip.

Living in downtown means getting used to the noise and dust and the smell of animal dung. She slipped out of bed, dressed quietly, and went down to the kitchen to start the fire in her handsome iron stove. It quickly heated the large kitchen, which confirmed how right she had been to insist on windows lining all the walls. To reduce the summer heat from the west, she had ordered shutters from a sash company in Galveston. The long table and matching benches that Conrad had polished so beautifully fit perfectly in front of the new pie safe. She would miss meals at the little table that she had given Dr. Stein for their first Christmas. She'd kept one of the chairs in the kitchen so Dr. Stein wouldn't have to fold his long body onto a bench and placed the other chair and little table below the windows in their bedroom—a good place for her to keep records for the store, for Dr. Stein's office, and for their businesses and rent properties.

Her spirits lifted on seeing Harriet's excited smile as she bound into the kitchen. "You look rested and happy."

"I feel badly for Anna, but I couldn't be happier being here." She scurried about helping with breakfast and insisting on serving Dr. Stein like a man dining at the Tremont House.

She heard Branson's footsteps pounding along the front walk and between the buildings. She flung open the door and scooped the sweating boy into her arms before he could knock.

"I didn't think you would ever get back," he gasped. "I been checking here every morning," he grinned at Dr. Stein.

"Yes, he hasn't missed a day." Dr. Stein leaned back in his chair, smiling, "We're both glad you're back."

Amelia introduced Harriet and invited him to stay for breakfast, but he shook his head. "Miss Rachel doesn't like me to be late. I'll come by the store after school." He tore out the door and disappeared quickly around the corner.

Freight wagons clogged the road on the way to Old Town. Harriet was almost skipping. Her bonnet fell down her back; the breeze tousled her black curls. Her gaze moved from buildings to wagons, and back to Amelia. "I can't believe I'm actually here. I never expected to see you or Anna again."

Amelia had just pointed out their little house when Charlie

stepped on the narrow porch. "Branson tore out the door to see you this morning without breakfast." All the time he spoke, his eyes were on Harriet, "Who's the lovely lady?"

After Amelia made introductions and explained Harriet's new situation, Charlie began grinning, "Are you interested in staying nights with a boy of eight when I'm on a stage run? Since the Steins are no longer next door, I've been looking for someone to watch after my boy Branson."

This is an answer to prayer. "He reads like a whiz, and he knows all about caring for the horses."

"Let me know when you need me." Harriet didn't ask any questions until they were out of earshot. Before they reached the Reuss' house, she knew all about the handsome Charlie Masters and Branson.

The tiny casket sat next to Anna's bed. Despite her face being the color of clabber, Anna let out a scream of sheer delight on seeing Harriet. "I thought I'd never again lay eyes on your beautiful face." She held out her arms and enfolded Harriet.

Dr. Reuss rose from the side of the bed, holding onto August, who had been squirming, trying to climb on his mama. As soon as he saw Amelia, he shouted "Tante" and leaped from his papa's arms to grab Amelia.

"I have a picayune doll for you. It's painted just like you with blonde hair and blue eyes and a yellow suit." Amelia pulled the little wooden doll from her pocket.

August was off and running to show his doll to Clara, who was washing breakfast dishes.

Joseph Reuss lifted the little body from its casket and Anna kissed the shriveled face before she turned away and sank back on the bed.

The sun glistened on the polished wood coffin the two doctors carried between them. Amelia and Harriet walked just behind, clutching hands. Harriet gasped as they walked past the new houses in the former tent community and the expanse of mounded graves and crooked crosses spread before them. "I never dreamed you had lost so many."

Two workmen stood off to one side away from the freshly opened grave next to the iron cross for the Reuss's baby boy so recently buried. Dr. Reuss stood perfectly still gazing at the two gravesites. Finally, he nodded to the men to take the casket and turned away. "Let's get back to Anna. I don't want to leave her alone."

As they walked away, they were followed by the thumping sound of dirt falling on the little wood coffin.

Just as Amelia had hoped, when they returned from the cemetery, Dr. Reuss offered Harriet a job. "Anna needs complete rest. Clara does a fine job, but it's too much work for a girl so young."

"I'll be up soon," Anna insisted. "You can look for permanent work while I get stronger."

Harriet tossed her bonnet on a nearby chair and asked Clara for the soiled sheets. She enticed August to follow her to the yard where she began building a fire under the big black wash pot.

Dr. Reuss watched Harriet taking charge. "She's exactly what Anna needs." He knelt, cupped Anna's face and kissed her cheeks, nose, and forehead, whispering his love again and again.

Amelia pulled her fist into the ache that cut her middle and walked into the kitchen. *If I touch the hot stove, I'll feel a different pain.*

Hans had thrown open all the store windows to welcome the slight breeze. The rain left humidity thick enough to touch as the air warmed. Amelia helped uncrate supplies from New Orleans and was delighted to see that Mrs. Osterman had already shipped barrels of oats, corn, molasses, and cones of sugar. A steady stream of customers kept Hans and Amelia busy until late afternoon.

Branson swung himself through the front door, books tied in a strap around his neck. "You sure got a lot of stuff for the store."

Amelia rushed toward him wanting to hug him again, but he

stood near the door, grinning at her. Suddenly he leaned his crutches against the counter and lunged for her. He buried his face in her breast and almost crushed her mumbling, "You were gone an awful long time."

She stroked his tousled head and felt her heart would break.

He went through the litany of each day's happenings, including what Rachel was having him do for homework and how he had helped Hans get moved into the store. By the time he slung his books back around his neck and headed home, she knew she belonged here.

She was about to go home to start supper when Frau Fischer arrived. She looked frail and leaned heavily on her cane. "You're a magnificent shopper." She kissed Amelia on both cheeks. "I adore my bed and armoire. I've come to look at all the treasures." She moved about the store, exclaiming over each item. She filled a bowl with pralines, then sat behind the counter to regain her breath. Finally, she rose very slowly and disappeared between wagons waiting for admission to the wharves.

"I won't have her much longer." Hans wiped at his eyes with a freshly ironed handkerchief. "I asked Joe if I could rent the upstairs over the store after she's gone. I hate that little house. I'm only staying to watch after Mama.

Late that afternoon, Amelia was checking her new garden, picking a few early tomatoes and beans for supper when Maria Christina rounded the side of the house. Her eyes were red-rimmed, and she covered her nose with a wrinkled, lace-edged handkerchief.

Amelia reached to hug the distraught girl. "Don't let me get mud on that lovely yellow dress."

"I don't care if it gets dirty. I really don't care about anything." She knelt beside Amelia in the damp earth and began picking beans. "Did you have a good trip?"

"Yes. I love New Orleans."

"Hans is so excited over all the beautiful things you sent back. I bought some of the ribbons and two of those gorgeous bonnets."

"I'm sure you'll be beautiful."

"I'm going to Mobile. My cousins have invited me for a long

visit."

"You sound like you don't want to go."

"I've given up. I can't make Hans notice me. We had another Saengerfest while you were gone. It was fabulous. I sang beautifully, but Hans wouldn't respond. Even Papa noticed." She blew her nose hard into her handkerchief. "Papa says he'll buy me a whole new wardrobe if I'll leave town for a while." Fresh tears streaked her cheeks. "Do you think I should forget Hans?"

Amelia took Maria Christina's muddy hands into hers. "I think you should find a man who'll love you madly. You don't want someone who doesn't respond. I can tell you that having a man who loves you with his whole being is wonderful."

She threw her arms around Amelia. "I knew you'd be the one to talk to. You have such a wonderful marriage."

"I'd love for you to find real joy."

Maria Christina stood, ignoring the muddy knee impressions on her dress. "I may not even tell Hans I'm leaving."

They had started breakfast when Charlie banged on the side door. "Sorry to bust in this way. I've got to make a run for a sick driver who came in late last night. I'm hoping Harriet will come visit with Branson before he goes to school. I'd like him to be comfortable with her spending the night."

"Of course," Harriet smiled at Amelia and Dr. Stein. "I'll be right along."

After Harriet rushed out the door, Dr. Stein raised both eyebrows. "She's mighty eager."

Amelia stood to clear the table, "I'm not sure her enthusiasm is only interest in a job."

Amelia spent the day unpacking New Orleans shipping crates. Each item brought another crushing memory—the Johann Heinrich Keller soap they used in Al's big tub, mosquito net curtains like those covering the French doors in his bedroom. She wanted to caress the fly-front trousers, the shirts, and the colorful cravats.

Hans got breathless with excitement. "You selected the very best and latest fashion." He stretched out one of the new mosquito net curtains. "Imagine adding fabric on the edge of the netting. Keeps it from looking like military equipment."

I wonder if I look as guilty as I feel? Maybe Hans senses the truth and is too polite to tell me that I must have had help selecting all these beautiful things.

In mid-May, a ship arrived with a load of German immigrants and a bulging mailbag with a fat letter from Helga and Papa. His news was always about the parish, the crops, and his garden. Helga started with news of the children, their improving studies and command of English. Then, she wrote that Papa was slowing, had not worked in his garden, leaving it mostly to Helga and Max. She ended with big letters. *We're having* **another baby. Sometime in September.**

She left Hans to close the store and dodged between wagons and animals to get across to the walkway leading to the back of their building. She held the letter against her cheek, remembering Helga and Papa watching her ride away with the von Ewalds. She had never allowed herself to imagine not seeing them again, or to think of how they must have felt as she waved from the departing carriage. *Dear Papa, forgive me. You knew I was gone forever, and I broke your heart.*

Chapter Thirty-Six

I am going to have a baby...

Over the next few weeks, Harriet blossomed. If she wasn't busy working for Anna, she was helping Branson with horses or staying with him while Charlie was on a San Antonio trip. One morning, before leaving for Anna's, she asked Dr. Stein if he had a basic book about medicine that Branson could borrow. "He's outgrown all the books at Rachel's school. He wants to know about illnesses, especially what made his fingers and toes die after getting so cold." Harriet followed Dr. Stein into his office and thanked him for *Observations on the Preservation of Health in Infancy, Youth, Manhood, and Age.*

"I doubt Branson will find anything in that book about frostbite. Tell him to come see me with questions. When he finishes this book, I'll loan him another."

"I'll drop if off this morning." Harriet hurried up the street, the book tucked under her arm.

Dr. Stein shook his head. "Wouldn't it be something to see the son of a whore become a doctor?"

"You think a whore's child can't be smart?"

"It's not that he can't be smart. It's the influences."

"Did you forget, it was one of his mama's whores who taught him to read?" Amelia stood. "Apparently she did a pretty good job."

"I don't mean to be insulting."

"Well, you are." She left the kitchen, allowed the back door to slam. She pumped water from the cistern, carried it to the black cast iron wash pot in the center of the backyard. She touched her stomach and bent to light the kindling. *I should have had a flow before now. If I have Al's baby, will he call me a whore?*

By the end of June, Harriet spent evenings with Branson, even when Charlie was home. He walked her home long after Branson had gone to bed, even after Dr. Stein returned from his house calls, which was usually after Amelia went to bed.

Amelia had started clearing the supper dishes, and Dr. Stein was about to make house calls when Harriet, Charlie, and Branson stepped on the side porch. "Is it convenient for us to come calling?" Charlie was holding Harriet's hand.

"What a surprise." Amelia opened the door and called to Dr. Stein. "I'll pour some tea. We can visit upstairs in the parlor."

All three visitors sat awkwardly on the new blue damask sofa from Francois Seignouret's shop.

I must remember to get Branson to help me find Seignouret's hidden S on the sofa. "You're our first parlor guests." Amelia set the tray and tea service—porcelain pieces she had taken in on trade—on a table and lit the candle in the table lamp. Dr. Stein brought the candle in from their bedroom.

Despite a breeze blowing through the open window, Charlie was sweating and refused the tea. "I know Harriet's not in your hire, but you brought her to Indianola. It seems appropriate that I ask you for permission to marry her." His hand fumbled for Harriet's. He also reached, as if for reassurance, for Branson's hand.

"We wanted to come like a family to ask you." Branson was the most composed of the three.

"That's wonderful," Amelia wanted to shout.

Dr. Stein stood. "This calls for more than tea. Amelia brought some fine Bordeaux wine from New Orleans. I'll open a bottle."

Branson trailed Dr. Stein to the kitchen and helped carry the glasses upstairs by stuffing them in his pockets. He was the first to offer a toast. "After Lou died, I thought I'd never have a ma. Harriet's going to be a good one. She's learning about horses."

"I have a good teacher." Harriet put her arm around Branson.

"I wish Fannie were here. I'll write her tonight." Amelia was trying not to cry.

Plans for Harriet's and Charlie's wedding turned Anna into a chattering girl. "I love seeing those two holding hands. Charlie's been so lonely. And Branson needs a mama. When I was in Galveston, I worried about Harriet. Fannie let it slip that Harriet had come to Galveston believing she was to marry someone Fannie called 'a damned man.' When she arrived, he tried to sell her like a white slave. Fannie slapped her hand over her mouth and never uttered another word."

They held the wedding on a Sunday afternoon in the Stein's parlor. Henry Bauer, the Methodist preacher, performed the ceremony. He and his wife joked that they were glad it wasn't one of those five-in-the-morning affairs like they had for Micah and Jessie. Hans and Dr. Stein carried Frau Fischer up the stairs. She cried throughout the brief ceremony and kissed Harriet several times before they helped her back down the stairs. Rachel and Conrad brought a raft of children—their two and all four of the Deutz clan. Jessie and Micah brought Isaac and a huge basket of garden vegetables for a wedding gift. Anna and Dr. Reuss beamed like newlyweds as they corralled the squirming August.

When Dr. Stein opened a bottle of Bordeaux to offer a toast to the couple, the good reverend and his wife decided it was time to go home.

Branson said he wanted to toast the couple. He held his glass of wine high like he had seen it done before. "I was never good at praying, but I've been practicing on Charlie and Harriet." He grinned. "It worked."

I wish Dr. Stein and I had scooped up Branson when he hobbled off that ship. Amelia held her glass high.

By August, Indianolans were in a stew about the new town of LaSalle. Dr. Levi Jones had surveyed a 5,000-acre tract about three miles down the coast. Wealthy Galveston men had invested heavily because Jones had been one of the organizers of the Galveston City Company that had developed that great port.

Dr. Jones had built a long wharf into the bay to a depth of ten feet. Then, he planned a gala event at the end of August to launch his new city. It was to be held at Casimir and Matilda Villeneuve's elegant Alhambra House. Dignitaries from Austin, San Antonio, Galveston, and New Orleans swarmed into Indianola for the festivities. The gentlemen, including Drs. Stein and Reuss enjoyed an afternoon event in the Alhambra House saloon. Dr. Stein reported that they dined on turtle soup when he came home to dress for the evening's gala.

He offered to help Amelia as she struggled to fasten the ice-blue gown that had belonged to Frau von Ewald. When she tried sucking in her breath for him to close the dress, he said, "You've thickened at your waist."

"I'll let the seams out." Amelia slipped out of the dress and wearing only her undergarments, pulled her sewing box over to the little table.

"I'll wait downstairs."

At least I am no longer yearning for his attention and feeling such pain when he avoids seeing me without clothing. The seams were ample, and it didn't take long to release the strain on her middle.

The grand ball and all the talk about LaSalle becoming a major port encouraged several businessmen to move to the new town, including one of the largest forwarding and commission firms in Indianola. The biggest shock came when Mrs. Eberly succumbed to the promotion and leased a building in LaSalle for a new hotel.

Micah delivered the news of Mrs. Eberly's move when he arrived with the last payment on their house. "I told Jessie when we paid off our loan to Dr. Stein—she don't need to go to that hotel before daylight ever day of this world. We're getting us another little one. Jessie's going to have her hands full chasing after Isaac and caring for a baby."

"Mrs. Eberly's going to miss Jessie. She's the best cook in this town."

"Yes, sir, they'll all miss her. But me and the children will be awful glad to have her home." Micah grinned, "Come by and see the extra room we're adding on our house."

Amelia made a late afternoon visit to check on Anna, whose cheeks were finally regaining some color. Anna smiled conspiratorially at Amelia. "You're looking very healthy and plumping up more than I've ever seen. Are you feeling well?"

Amelia checked to make sure they were alone, that Harriet and Clara were otherwise occupied. "I haven't told Dr. Stein."

Anna squealed and grabbed Amelia. "I knew it. I won't tell a soul. It's perfect timing. You'll get your baby soon after Helga has hers."

"I haven't written the family."

"Let me know when you tell so I can shout it to everyone."

It's not necessary for Anna to know who fathered this baby. Amelia headed to Micah's and Jessie's to see the addition on their house. It sparkled white, the neatest of all the homes in Old Town. The new room was almost complete, and it smelled of fresh sawed lumber. Jessie, still carrying Isaac on her back, was beginning to bulge with a new baby.

"Please have tea with me." Jessie loosened Isaac from her back, and he scampered around the room, hanging first on Jessie's leg and then inching timidly toward Amelia. She extended one of the picayune dolls that had milk chocolate skin and blue trousers and shirt. Accepting the doll, he crawled on her lap allowing her to hug him.

"You'll have one soon, won't you?" Jessie grinned.

"Why, yes. I hadn't realized it showed." Amelia automatically touched her belly.

"It does, and you look wonderful."

Tonight, I must face Dr. Stein with the truth. I pray for calm. Walking home she took deep breaths to quiet the building tension. She would talk to him as soon as he came in for supper. Between house calls and Saengerbund, he stayed gone most evenings until after she went to bed.

While she prepared supper, she kept glancing at the door leading to Dr. Stein's office, a slight nausea making the sauerkraut smell extra pungent. Then the door opened, and his body filled the frame. Her breath came in shallow gasps. She tried to suck in courage. "I need to talk to you."

A slight, questioning smile tinged his lips. He sat down at the table, placed his fork on his plate and nodded for her to sit down.

"I'm going to have a baby. It should be here in January." The words spilled out in a whisper.

He did not blink. He looked steadily at her for several seconds. Then he began slowly shaking his head. "I've not wanted to believe what I was seeing. I've shamed myself for thinking that could be why your clothing looks so different."

"It's my body, Dr. Stein. It's my body that looks different."

He winced like she had slapped him. "I kept telling myself that you'd never break our marriage vows."

"What marriage? You can't even speak of my body. You just referred to my clothes. Our marriage is for show, a protection for your image."

His eyes flashed anger, and his upper lip trembled. "You've betrayed my trust, Amelia. I trusted you to be faithful."

"And I trusted you to love me in all the ways a man loves his wife. You betrayed me. In almost five years, you've never touched me in an intimate way. That's betrayal."

"Are you going to walk away from our marriage? Are you going to go to your..." His mouth twisted like he needed to spit, "your lover?"

"I had the company of a man for almost two weeks, knowing all the time that I would return to you."

"You planned it? You're not even saying you lost control? Or that he took advantage of you?" His neck lengthened as if he were pulling backward, away from her.

She forced herself to look into his black, piercing eyes. "I used him selfishly to find out that I was desirable, a live woman who had feelings, who attracted a man."

"Having an affair with a stranger told you all that?" He kept his voice low and steady as steel.

She breathed hard, stared in disbelief at his calm. "Coming back to you was the hardest thing I've ever done. I came back because of you and Branson—"

He lifted his palm like a shield, "Don't bring that child into this mess."

I will not fall apart. "I could not do something to shame you in this town."

"Shame me? My God, Amelia, you could not have found a more cruel way to shame me." His eyes stared at her belly like it housed the devil.

"No one will know it's not yours." She was spent. Her strength, her resolve had vanished. She remained still, watching his face contort, tears brim, redden his eyes.

Both hands raked wildly through his hair. He stood with such force that his chair clattered backward to the floor. He walked like weights anchored each foot, allowing the door to slam shut behind him.

She sat motionless, watching the wisp of steam disappear from the bowl of sauerkraut and sausage. She held the bulge of her belly and imagined the life that was growing there. Finally, she cleared away the dishes, set the sauerkraut on the warming plate at the back of the stove and climbed the stairs. Nothing in the house had changed. The breeze still blew down the center hall. She lit the candle on the little table in their bedroom. Hans was putting out the lights in the store. The snort of mules and rattle of the traces, the low hum of voices in the street, and the occasional whistle of a ship had become commonplace.

The candle flickered and burned out. Unfastening her dress, she let it fall to the floor. Chilled, she pulled a gown from the wardrobe, and crawled in bed. The breeze stirred against her cheek, tickled at her hair. She heard Dr. Stein's feet on the stairs. He closed the door between the bedrooms and let his boots drop. His bulk made the narrow bed in the other room squeak as he lay down.

Chapter Thirty-Seven

A cocoon cushions me and my baby...

The days and the nights came, the breezes blew, and the rain fell. Life went on with little notice of the changes. Dr. Stein purchased a large bed and wardrobe from Conrad Swartz and moved into the back room. Amelia worked in the store, cooked meals, and tended the business ledgers.

She walked to Conrad's shop, surprised to see that it had grown quite large with several men bent over hand tools, carving into beautiful pieces of wood. Conrad still looked like a boy, not a prosperous furniture maker. He continued the habit of peeking from under a swath of sandy hair. "I can make you a fine rocking chair out of walnut from New Braunfels."

"Walnut sounds wonderful. How do you make the rocker?"

"My papa traveled to Austria to learn from Michael Thonet. He steamed wood to bend it. That's what Papa taught me."

A few weeks later, when Conrad walked in the store's front door with a beautifully crafted rocking chair, the customers gathered round to admire. Ducking his head like he had no idea that people would be interested in his rockers, he quickly accepted two orders. Amelia left the chair in the store for the rest of the day, and several more customers decided to visit Conrad's shop.

Hans laughed every time someone rocked for a while and then headed to Conrad's. "He may appear to be the shyest man in town, but he knew what he was doing when he delivered the chair to the store instead of taking it to your quarters."

"He'll have a big business in rocking chairs." Amelia ran her fingers along the wood so finely finished that it felt soft. A perfect place to snuggle with my baby. That night, Dr. Stein agreed that the rocker was beautiful. He carried it up to her bedroom and left for Saengerbund practice. Amelia rocked in the darkness, arms around her belly, singing *Wiengenlied*, the cradle song her mama sang to her and to Helga's babies.

Unlike Fannie, who would have figured the expected date, and pinned Amelia down for a definite answer, Harriet never mentioned the New Orleans trip. She accepted Amelia's life just as it appeared to everyone in Indianola.

It was not lost on the Indianolans that LaSalle's wharf was attracting large ships with cargos of up to 78,000 feet of lumber. Amelia had spent the day listening to the worries of customers who were imagining the end of their port city. That night, Dr. Stein came to supper with questions. "Are we collecting our rents on time? When will the loan to Runge's bank be paid? Are you really getting profits for all those expensive beds and tables from New Orleans? Shouldn't you stick with Conrad Swartz furniture, support his business?"

"Why don't you look at the ledgers?" she said after each question. "The income's right there. You'll be reassured."

"I've got to see some patients tonight before Saengerbund meets." He quickly finished his supper and stood. "I've heard so much negative talk today. I needed to hear from you that we aren't going broke. All my patients think LaSalle will destroy us."

I betrayed you, and you still trust me to manage your money. A cold wave of sadness chilled her. She watched him bend to gather his medical bag and the leather case holding Saengerbund music. Their life was a business arrangement. He didn't know the pleasure of touching, of delighting in the physical presence of another human being. She closed her eyes, warming herself with the memory that she carried inside her, shutting out the clatter of the side door and the thump of his feet across the porch.

Al, I wish you could feel our baby move.

Within a week, Amelia was awakened by a fierce wind slamming shut all the doors and ripping shingles off the buildings across the street. She and Dr. Stein stood at the front windows listening to the roaring of the wind and the sound of splintering wood. Through flashes of lightning, she could see the masts of ships anchored at the far end of the piers dancing wildly above the rooftops across the street.

Al and I made love all night during a storm like this. I wish I could tell him I'm remembering. She slipped back under the quilts, tucking the memory to herself.

Before dawn, the wind lay down, and the port came alive with merchants and townspeople milling in the streets, checking the damage. The store's interior came through unscathed, but roof damage left the upstairs a soaked mess.

In mid-morning, Dr. Stein came in the store, mud and gravel to his knees. "The *Palmetto* is sitting on the beach where our pier used to be. She was anchored out in the bay with the lighter *Jerry Smith* and a Guadalupe River steamer lashed to her. Both smaller vessels broke loose, and the *Palmetto* was driven right across our pier. She barely missed our old store."

"Can we replace the pier?"

"The pilings laid up on the beach are riddled with shipworm holes. New wharves have copper sheathing on the pilings to keep the worms from boring into the submerged wood. It's the same thing they put on ship hulls to protect them." He paced along the aisles rubbing the stubble he had not shaved off that morning. Finally, he stopped and looked directly at her, "Captain Whipple's been talking about building a downtown dock. I think we should invest with him instead of going to the expense of rebuilding. Old Town's not going to thrive like this area."

I think he's asking for my opinion. "He's talked about settling here, hiring out his ship to another captain. Maybe we can encourage him by offering a partnership."

A week later, a man rushed into the store. "Did you see that gang of gentlemen getting off that government ship? I counted 105, all wearing black suits with silk vests and top hats."

The customers rushed to the back windows to look. "That's the Boundary Commission," a young man's voice rose above the chatter. Everyone in the store gave him their attention. "I'm Andrew Frazier. I opened my law office here this week. I've been expecting them to land at Indianola. They're heading to El Paso to meet with Mexican officials."

"And why's that?" The man who had rushed in the store with the announcement placed both hands on his hips, glared at the lawyer who had captured all the attention.

"They'll survey and mark the boundary between the two countries. The commission was formed by the 1848 Treaty of Guadalupe Hidalgo that ended the Mexican War. It's taken all this time for Texas to give up some of its land in exchange for ten million dollars."

Several men muttered, shuffling their feet and looking sideways at Andrew Frazier. One man finally tilted his head back and called out to no one in particular, "So, Texas is giving up land? Didn't we win the war? Why're we being cut short?"

Andrew Frazier grinned like he was delivering a big secret. "Because Texas is flat broke. We need to pay off the debts we accumulated while we were a republic."

Hans introduced himself and shook hands with Andrew Frazier. "Who are all these men with the commission?"

Andrew Frazier raised his voice to be heard by the crowd that kept milling around glancing at him. "They're astronomers, mineralogists, naturalists, surveyors—people needed to get the boundary marked. They'll be waiting for equipment to arrive."

Hans visited a while with Andrew Frazier. After the crowd thinned out and Mr. Frazier left, Hans whispered. "If they're here for a few days, we should get some good business."

The next morning Amelia got an early preview of how keenly aware Indianola's business leaders were of the Boundary Commission's significance when Micah showed up with the milk, carrying Isaac strapped to his back.

"I'm toting Isaac while my missus takes on a job for Mrs. Eberly." Micah started laughing. "The town folks plan a big blowout for those boundary fellows. When they couldn't find a place to feed the whole bunch, Mr. John Henry Brown up and emptied his entire warehouse."

"That's the biggest building in town," Amelia said.

"You know the best part? Mrs. Eberly sent for Jessie. She's paying her good money to be the cook. The ladies say it's going to be a first-class welcome. They intend for every person to sit down at a table to eat. They say it's not a dinner or a banquet. It's a supper," Micah cackled. "They think saying it's a supper sounds more like Texans."

It's a joy to view the world through Micah's lens. "I expect it'll be fancy."

Micah was right. It was a fancy affair. Amelia felt lovely when Dr. Stein complimented her dress. She had purchased pale green silk damask in New Orleans and sewed it with front tucks, planning for its use after the baby's birth.

To Jessie's credit the turtle soup, fried fish, oysters, and crabs were delicious. Military leaders, judges, and everyone of any importance attended. The toasts and the cheers for the commissioners continued until midnight, including a hearty toast to the heroes of San Jacinto. The hostesses—Mrs. Angelina Eberly and several Indianola women—were toasted and hailed as "Angels of Heaven inhabiting Earth." By the time Mrs. Eberly received her personal toast, the liquor and the generosity were flowing freely. She was named "one of the early mothers of Texas."

Chapter Thirty-Eight

My baby grows, and the port grows...

In the months that Amelia's baby grew, stretching her middle, fluttering at first like tiny bird wings and then kicking and shoving a foot across her belly, Indianola was also growing in amazing ways. The traffic in 49ers—determined to get rich in California—increased dramatically. Traveling from the East, huge numbers discovered how much easier it was to reach California by sailing into Indianola instead of trekking across the Central Plains or taking the long trip around Cape Horn or across the disease-infested jungles of Central America. The admission of California as a state in early September proved a further catalyst for get-rich-quickers to head west.

Expansion of the holding pens for livestock along Powder Horn Bayou made room for cattle being driven into town from out west. The beasts waiting to be shipped to New Orleans kept the night air alive with the sound of bawling and the smell of manure.

By October, the inland demand for lumber had increased until seven ships were running regular trips from Mobile and Pensacola carrying cypress and juniper shingles and yellow pine lumber.

The year ended with a week-long visit and good news from representatives of the shipping tycoon Charles Morgan. Hans rushed into the store. "Morgan Lines is placing two new steamers that will run between New Orleans and Matagorda Bay. They'll have luxurious staterooms and public saloons. They'll be in here five days a week."

I felt the baby jump at the mention of New Orleans. Or was it me realizing how easy it would be to return? Her gaze fell on the ships lining the piers.

In mid-January, a ship from Bremen arrived with a huge sack of mail. The letter in Helga's bold hand began with ANNA, A HEALTHY GIRL. In her excitement to share the good news with Anna Reuss, Amelia left Hans visiting with the newly arrived Germans crowding into the store.

Anna threw her arms around Amelia. "I hope she named her baby after me."

I don't need to spoil Anna's dream by saying our grossmutter's name was Anna. "Let me read the rest of the letter. Maybe she says."

In just a few lines, the happy news was forgotten. Amelia pressed the letter to her face. "Papa has fallen. Hermie found him in the garden. He's confused, keeps calling for Mama." Amelia leaned her head on Anna's shoulder. "This is when I'm sorry I left home. I could be with him at the end. I could help Helga with the new baby and our sick Papa."

"I miss my home too. But I wouldn't have Joseph and August if I'd stayed. And look at you. You've got a wonderful husband and a baby coming. From the looks of you, it'll be here any day."

"The baby's gotten very still. I think he's getting ready for his trip into the world."

"Listen to you. You think it's a boy?"

"I'm sure it is."

"Have you decided on a name? Surely not another Joseph," Anna laughed. "We have so many."

"Albert. I'll call him Albert Anton." *He's a combination of our names and of us.*

Starting home, she wrapped herself in her shawl, covering her face to escape the blowing dust stirred by passing freight wagons. She was glad Dr. Stein planned to eat his supper at Mrs. Eberly's hotel before Saengerbund practice. The dogged loneliness was not for Dr. Stein, but persistent longing for Al to be with her when his baby was born.

She stepped on the wooden walkway along the front of their building. Hans was locking the store's front door. He waved and shouted above the din of wagons and snorting mules that he was going to Saengerbund.

The house was dark and cold. The fire in the kitchen stove had gone out. The windows were closed against the steady wind, but her body ached from the penetrating dampness. The effort to climb the stairs increased with each step. She decided to crawl into bed and warm herself before lighting a candle. As she warmed, the ache began centering as a cramp in her abdomen. The aching developed a steady pattern, stirring the realization that her baby was coming. Wrapped in the quilt from the bed, she gathered rags and extra sheets she had stored in the wardrobe. She expected Dr. Stein to return long before he was needed, but she moved her sewing basket next to the bed to easily reach the scissors and thread.

The windows rattled, and the wind howled a mournful, lonely sound. She crawled back into bed, tried to relax, to let her body perform as was intended. The pains grew steadily stronger. She listened to the noise in the street trying to estimate the hour. The freighters didn't usually come into town after dark, staying at the campsite, waiting to be first at the docks before dawn. There were a few shouts and some laughter—noises of men coming out of one of the saloons.

Her water broke, soaking the bed. The pains came harder and closer together. She dried herself and padded the bed with the rags. She wrapped in the quilt from the bed and tugged open a window. The gust of cold drove her into a hard contraction. As it eased, she felt fluid run down her legs. "Please get a doctor." *Did I call loud enough to be heard?* She couldn't see anyone in the street. After another hard contraction drove more fluid onto the floor, she thought she yelled very loud for a doctor.

"Will do, lady." A man's voice echoed. Or did she imagine it? It didn't matter now. She would deliver this baby herself. "Al, I can do it. I can birth our baby."

The bed was wet, and she was surprised that its coolness felt good. The contractions came with increasing force. She wondered if she yelled. If Anna were here, she knew she wouldn't yell. Anna would hold her hand and wipe the sweat. The pain took over, and her body heaved with a force like it came from another being. Finally, he was there; her hand touched his head just as another agonizing surge pushed him onto the bed. Raising herself, she tried to see him in the dark. The cord felt short. She needed to tie it off. Running her hand along his chest, she felt the cord in a lump, a big lump at his neck. The scream may have come from somewhere on the street. It was so loud. She gritted her teeth to hold the scissors steady as she snipped at the bundle cutting off the life of her baby. "I'm hurrying, Albert. I'm going to take care of you. Breathe, son. Please breathe for me."

The yellow light of the lantern glared in her face. "Amelia, I'm here. Give me the scissors. I'll do it."

"Please hurry. He's not breathing."

Dr. Reuss laid the boy on her chest. "I'm sorry, Amelia. I'm so sorry."

"Albert, wake up. Please cry for me." Amelia clutched the wet baby, rubbing his back, patting him.

"Let me take him," Dr. Reuss said. "I'm sorry, Amelia."

"I've got to hold him. He's warm. I want to keep him warm."

Dr. Reuss went into Dr. Stein's bedroom, returned with a quilt and wrapped Amelia and the baby in its dry warmth. "I sent word to Anna and Harriet. They'll stay with you until Joe comes in."

Amelia stroked Albert's body until all the fluids dried on both of them.

Anna's voice trembled as she knelt beside Amelia, "Where's Joe?" Her hand, still cold from the winter, felt good on Amelia's hot cheek.

Dr. Reuss whispered, "Saengerbund."

"Saengerbund? At this hour…"

Harriet laid her cheek against Albert's head, matted with dried fluids. "He's beautiful, Amelia. He's a fine boy."

Anna and Harriet murmured loving sounds as they gently cleaned Amelia and Albert without moving the baby away. When all the warmth left his little body, when all the fluids that had joined them together were washed away, Amelia wrapped Albert in his own blanket, and folded her body around him.

"I see you've finally gotten home." It was Harriet's voice, dagger sharp. "Amelia delivered her baby alone. He's dead."

Dr. Stein bent over and touched her forehead. "I'm sorry you've been through this alone."

Dr. Stein did not say as Dr. Reuss had done that he wanted to be alone with his wife and son. Instead, he paced the hall, his feet thumping loudly.

Anna and Harriet sat quietly with Amelia as she cradled Albert against her.

When it grew light, she called to her husband, "Will you ask Conrad to make him a casket? I want to bury him in the new cemetery."

When he returned with a casket saying that Conrad had one already made, he did not offer to take the baby. She handed Albert to Harriet, who placed him in the cotton-lined pine coffin.

"I want to go to the burial."

"It's too soon for you to walk that far," Dr. Stein said.

"I don't care if it's too soon."

Amelia sat in the rocker looking at Albert. *He could be asleep, fists curled tight. Such fine blond hair and fat little cheeks. His mouth looks ready to nurse. My breasts ache to provide milk for my son.*

Dr. Stein and Harriet each took one of Amelia's arms. Hans and Eva held Frau Fischer between them. Branson hobbled beside Charlie. Anna held to Dr. Reuss, her face twisting in pain. Rachel and Conrad Swartz were circled by a cluster of their children and those in Rachel's class. Micah came alone. Jessie stayed home with Isaac and their month-old son they had named Jacob.

The only sound was the swish of feet, brushing through the low scrub that clung to the prairie. Crosses, many of iron and decorated with baby lambs and clusters of roses reminded Amelia of the cemetery next to Papa's church. The place where her mama rested and Papa would soon join her.

The grave had been dug. It was deep and only long enough to fit Albert's casket.

Rev. Bauer walked with them to the cemetery. "What is the child's name?"

"Albert Anton Stein," Amelia said, ignoring the sharp intake of Dr. Stein's breath as he heard the child's name for the first time.

The preacher said some words that drifted away on the wind. A quartet of Saengerbund members sang a heart-wrenching graveside song, a custom from home for the dead child of one of the members of the singing group. The first few shovels of dirt made a clumping sound against the little wood coffin. Then, men worked in silence as the deep hole swallowed all evidence of Albert Anton Stein.

Dr. Stein continued gripping Amelia on one side, and Harriet held her tightly on the other. Walking back home, rain came in torrents, pounding on their umbrellas, squishing mud over their boots, and making the alley behind the buildings a trail of slush.

Amelia sank into her bed, looked at Harriet's face, strained ashen white. "You know this is my punishment?"

"I don't believe that. Remember the joy this baby brought you." She tucked the quilts tightly around Amelia.

Chapter Thirty-Nine

Life moves on...

Rain beat in thundering torrents on the roof and came in driving sheets across the porch. Amelia curled in a knot under a mound of quilts, holding her empty belly.

Harriet's cool fingers stroked her cheek. "You aren't alone, Amelia. The house is full of people who love you."

Amelia nodded. "I'll be up soon. I need to let all of it pass away. Every part of it is gone now."

"You have memories. Don't get rid of the things that warm your heart."

Harriet knows and cradles me. That's enough. She clutched Harriet's hand, kissing the rough fingers that smelled like a horse stable.

The kitchen was warm with food spread over the long wood table. Dr. Stein moved among friends, a somber figure, accepting their hugs. He pulled a chair up to the table for Amelia. She turned away to be embraced by Frau Fischer, leaning heavily against her cane. She clung to Amelia saying, "I would have taken his place."

"I know you would, but we need to keep you for a while."

Branson stood awkwardly between Charlie and Harriet. "Dr. Stein loaned me another book. It's about babies being born."

Amelia touched Branson's cheek. "Captain Whipple should return soon. He has shelves of books you'll enjoy."

"You like my new book satchel?" Branson extended his arms out from his crutch and turned slowly, modeling a red broadcloth vest with wide pockets on each side of the front and a pocket extending low across the back that Branson demonstrated he could reach. "Harriet made it. I can carry all kinds of things." Branson pulled the book about babies from the front pocket.

"Harriet's a good designer."

Branson grinned and leaned his head against Harriet's shoulder.

Dr. Stein stood beside the empty chair until Amelia sat down. He motioned for Anna to sit on the bench beside Amelia.

Anna reached for Amelia's hand and whispered. "If you need to talk..." the sob came with such force that Dr. Reuss rushed from across the room, lifted her into his arms.

"We'll come back later." He wrapped a shawl around his wife, folded her into the protective circle of his arm, and led her out the door.

Did she see that it's different for me? That we don't have the same kind of marriages? She watched Anna stumbling out the door.

In early March, Charlie bounded through the store's front door wearing a broad smile. "I jumped into a big contract with the U.S. government—the mail route from here to San Antonio."

"What about passengers?"

"You may not like that part. We'll have coaches here to meet every Morgan Line ship. Move them out of here as soon as they're unloaded. The hotels and saloons are complaining, saying we're cutting into their business—they want passengers to stay overnight." Charlie shrugged like a kid who might be in trouble and couldn't come up with a good excuse. "I'm hoping you aren't too unhappy."

"We have enough business. We don't depend on the travelers who browse through the store."

Charlie shuffled his feet, stuffed hands in his pockets. "My biggest worry is Harriet and Branson. Until we can afford to hire more drivers, I'll be gone a week on every run. Sure would appreciate you watching out for them. Harriet doesn't know many people." Charlie grinned, "Of course, Branson knows everybody."

"I watch for him to come by the store after school every day." *He eases the ache that comes in waves and makes me want to fold into a knot.*

By late April, spring dressed the entire town in color. Downtown buildings displayed baskets of flowers on porches, both upstairs and along the street. The days passed in a flurry of steady business that helped fog the memory of those same spring days the previous year. At night, lying in bed, watching stars blanketing the sky above the rooftops across the street, all those things she had said she wanted to remember, came back with painful clarity.

Al, are you remembering my legs holding you tight against me? I'm remembering the way you reached inside my bonnet to caress me. I hear you call me 'precious'. Sleep became the elusive drug that dangled just out of reach.

Branson asked to help Amelia with the inventory, claiming that he needed to work on numbers. "I've been spending all my time reading. Miss Rachel says I should practice multiplication and regular old adding." He could barely concentrate on the task at hand for chattering about the latest book he'd borrowed from Captain Whipple. "Oliver Twist was about my age when he got sent out of the baby farm where he lived after his ma died borning him. I burned up a whole candle last night reading." He patted the bulk of the book in his satchel vest pocket.

The ship horn on the government pier caught their attention. Huge crates were being hustled down the gangplank and loaded on freight wagons forming a line that stretched back to Water Street.

Branson hobbled out to meet a man in a military uniform coming down the pier toward the store. "Hey, Mister, what're you unloading?"

"We've got astronomical equipment and a mighty important man on our ship. He's Lt. Col. James D. Graham, chief astronomer and head of the Scientific Corps."

"He knows about stars?" Branson's voice held hushed respect.

"You bet. He uses the stars to figure boundaries between countries."

"What countries?" Branson tucked in his chin, eyeing the army man with a tinge of suspicion.

"He figured the boundary between Texas and the United States when Texas was still a republic. He also ran the boundary between the state of Maine and New Brunswick. Last year he re-surveyed the Mason and Dixon Line."

"What's that?

"It's the line dividing the states of Pennsylvania, Maryland, and Delaware. For some reason it had to be corrected. Lieutenant Colonel Graham was the man to do it."

"What's he doing here?"

"Haven't you heard about the Boundary Commission? They're drawing the official line between the United States and Mexico. Lieutenant Colonel Graham is the new astronomer for the commission."

Amelia noticed John Henry Brown, the very influential new resident who was involved in a multitude of local businesses, standing in the shade of the building listening to Branson's questions.

"Young man, I'm here to meet the gentleman you've been asking about."

"Really?" Branson turned around and wiggled his eyebrows at Amelia.

"Would you like to meet Lieutenant Colonel Graham?"

"You bet, Mister. My name's Branson Forbes." In a quick move, Branson slapped his right crutch into his left hand and balancing on that single support, extended his hand.

"I'm John Henry Brown. Aren't you the boy off the *Matagorda*? You're living with Charlie Masters?"

"Yes, sir. We operate the Masters Stage Line and the new U.S. Mail service to San Antonio."

"Here comes the man you want to meet." John Henry Brown took long strides up the pier.

Branson slapped his crutches under both arms and took off at a fierce pace to stay beside him.

Amelia thought she might burst with pride watching Branson

shake hands and swing along beside the two men.

"I'm curious to know Indianola's latitude," the astronomer was saying. "How about meeting tonight. It should be clear. I'll take some measurements."

"My wife's extending an invitation to dinner. Afterward perhaps?"

"Splendid." The officer looked at Branson. "Young man, would you like to meet me about eight tonight at the Brown's home? You could be an observer."

"Yes, sir. Yes, sir. I'll be there."

"We'll see you at eight," John Henry Brown guided the important man to his waiting carriage at the end of the pier.

"Did you hear that? Can you believe I'll get to watch him take measurements?"

"How lucky you are." She clasped her hands around his cheeks.

"I really got a good life after I got frostbit." He grinned at Amelia. "Wish Ma and Pa could see me now."

"They'd be proud."

"Look what's coming off that other government ship. Horses. There must be a million." The pier rumbled with the thunder of hooves being led, four abreast, by cavalrymen.

"Where're you going?" Branson shouted above the din at the man leading the first group of horses.

"We're delivering 2,000 horses to troops out west. You want to come with us?" The cavalryman laughed and mounted his horse for a few quick turns on the wharf before man and horse, leaped into the street.

"Lou could do a lot more with a horse than that fellow." Branson stared after the rider who was making his horse strut, stirring up shell dust.

"She was a wonderful lady."

"I miss her every day. Harriet's a good woman. But..." Branson's lip puckered. He turned away. "I gotta go."

That night, Amelia was working on their business ledger when she heard Branson calling from the street. "Do you want to know where we are?"

"Absolutely," she called. "I'll meet you in the kitchen."

Branson was at the door before she got downstairs, his breath coming in gasps, sweat making his face glow in the candlelight. "At thirty feet behind Mr. Brown's house, the latitude is 28 degrees, 33 minutes, and 19 seconds north."

"What does that mean?" She poured him a cup of water and reached in the pie safe for a bowl of pralines.

"It's how far we are from the equator." He gulped the water and then clutched the candy between dirty fingers. "I could show you if we had a map."

"Why don't we ask Captain Whipple where to get a map for you?"

"Really? A map for me? Wait until I tell Charlie and Harriet." He stopped suddenly. "I was supposed to go right home after the measurements."

Chapter Forty

We survived a storm...

Every afternoon for a week, Branson had come to the store looking for Captain Whipple. When the captain landed and heard that Branson wanted to see one of his maps the fatigue lifted from his face, and he rushed back to his ship for a map.

Amelia's throat swelled with fullness at the sheer pleasure of the child when she saw him swinging along the pier with the captain who was carrying the map rolled under his arm. "He's got one," Branson shouted as they came through the back door. "It's a Cruchley Map of the World."

The captain spread it on the counter and Branson hovered—as reverent as an altar boy—his eyes moving slowly over the greens of the oceans and the soft shades of continents. "The whole world is spread out. And there're the latitude numbers along the side."

The captain used a broom straw to point to every place Branson could name, beginning with New York City and then New Orleans.

Customers crowded around, drawn to the eager boy who did not lift his head until Charlie came in the front door looking for him.

Hans stood on the store's front porch beside Amelia and Captain Whipple, watching Branson swing along toward home with Charlie, who was carefully carrying the map. "What would we do without that boy to brighten every dark corner of our lives?"

I would run away except for him. Amelia reached for the door. "He's like glue holding us all together."

Summer began earlier than usual. Heat and humidity combined forces to drive everyone under the nearest shade except for the dust and sweat-soaked freighters. Their wagons continued clogging the street, and tempers flared as some of them tried to push ahead in the endless lines. The bay lay as still as soup just before it reaches the boiling point. In late June, Matagorda Bay began to boil.

Hans had stepped onto the dock to enjoy the breeze that swept through the store like a welcome gust from a giant fan. Amelia hurried to the door when she heard him slamming shutters across the back of the store.

"Look at that cloud. A solid wall of black is coming from the Gulf." Hans's perfectly combed hair blew in wisps across his face and his clothes flapped against his body. He rolled empty barrels they had set out for rainwater into the store. "These things will be instruments of destruction when that wind hits."

While they fastened shutters and brought in benches along the front of the store, several families arrived, including Frau Fischer, who leaned heavily on Eva. "This is the safest place for a storm that big and black." Frau Fischer settled on a stool behind the counter, her eyes never leaving Hans as he and Amelia shoved display tables around and stacked merchandise out of the way to make room for the increasing number of people flocking into the safety of the store.

Amelia looked out the front door through sheets of rain. "Dr. Stein's closed the shutters on his office windows and in our quarters. Looks like he won't try to get over here in this storm." Light that had spilled through seams around the doors and shutters disappeared as the sky turned the afternoon to night.

Hans hurried to light all the sconces circling the big room. Tin lamps had to be lowered on pulleys from the high ceiling. The wind came in increasingly heavy gusts slamming debris against the back wall. The building trembled, driving the refugees into a huddled cluster toward the center of the room.

Hans kept spirits high, moving through the crowd, chatting casually with the women, laughing boisterously with the men about the mess that would await them when the storm passed.

A ripping sound on the roof sent everyone to the floor, hovering between the long lines of tables—the safest place if the ceiling caved in. Hans raised his voice over the roar of the storm. "I'm putting out all the lamps. We don't want a fire."

Men rushed to help extinguish the lard-fueled lights. The blackness, so intense it sucked the breath out of the room, caused a hush that felt like everyone had disappeared. Children huddled against parents and listened with the same intensity as the adults.

"We could tell ghost stories." The voice that sounded like Hans', brought a murmur of laughter.

Water seeped and then came in rivulets under the back door, spreading across the floor, forcing everyone onto tables and counters stacked with merchandise. The rain sounded like a waterfall washing down the back walls. Children settled down and slept. Adults comforted themselves with the low, assuring sounds of their own voices, guessing on the damage—not their homes—to rival LaSalle and Lavaca.

Hans moved to the table beside his mama who clung to him in silence.

Why do Charlie and Harriet need to be so independent? Why didn't they bring Branson in here? Amelia waded in water over the tops of her shoes to the counter near the front door, listening for anyone who might be looking for shelter.

Morning arrived, still and crisp. The sun dazzled a scene of destruction. Crowds poured into the street. Buildings that backed up to the wharf, including Stein Mercantile, suffered extensive damage. Stein's roof was ripped up like a giant had tilted it open to peek inside. Water stood ankle deep in all the upstairs rooms and poured through the ceiling into the store. The wharf lay under mounds of boards that had been ripped from piers and slammed against buildings lining the waterfront.

Amelia's heart raced when Branson and Charlie hurried in the front door. She rushed toward them and Branson threw his arms around her. "We wanted to come see if you were hurt. You got a lot more flooding than we did in Old Town."

Charlie looked over the top of Branson's head. "We should have brought Branson in here. He's not slept a wink all night worrying about you."

Amelia stroked Branson's cheek. "I didn't sleep a wink worrying about you."

Branson pulled away, gazed around the store. "You got a mess. We had a ship break loose, shattered one of the old piers and sank. Lots of small boats are knocked to pieces on the beach." He stopped and looked over his shoulder at Charlie. Miss Rachel isn't having school today. Why don't I stay here and help Amelia and Hans?"

Charlie grinned. "I think we can spare you. Come home before supper."

Most of the people who spent the night in the store had rushed home to check on damage. Some returned, joyous over escaping destruction and spent the rest of the day helping dry out the upstairs and sweep water from the first floor. Branson worked all day carrying buckets of water that leaked through the ceiling by hanging the bail of each bucket on the special grip carved into his crutches and wobbling to wash off the back of the store and the mud-caked dock.

Branson was reluctantly heading home for supper when Dr. Stein returned from treating some minor injuries. "Did many people get hurt last night?"

"A few got hit by debris and had some broken bones."

"That's why Charlie and Harriet wouldn't let me come check on you. They said I'd get hit by flying stuff."

Dr. Stein stroked Branson's tousled hair. "I'm glad you listened to them."

Dr. Stein began helping Hans sort through the water-soaked merchandise.

He laughs with Hans and jokes about the expensive clothing that was used for mattresses, so different from the man I've been living with. She moved a bucket under another leak coming through the ceiling.

Amelia and Hans worked into the night inventorying what

needed to be replaced. "I think we should have a big sale," he said. "Reduce prices on damaged goods."

While Hans cordoned off most of the store for the sale, Amelia worked on orders from all her contacts in Galveston and New Orleans. Dr. Stein treated some minor injuries in his office and left to deliver a baby in Old Town.

When the stagecoach from Lavaca arrived the next day, the driver delivered a package of newspapers. "Good thing they got the paper printed before the storm hit. Lavaca was hurt bad. The docks are ripped apart. A huge warehouse on the waterfront is almost destroyed. Homes suffered serious wind damage."

A ship captain came into the store, walked around shaking his head at the wet stacks of clothing and dangling cones of sugar that were partially melted by water running in rivulets through the ceiling. "I docked early this morning at LaSalle. The railroad track running the length of its long pier was ripped up and thrown clear into the bay. LaSalle didn't escape this time."

Dr. Stein had followed Henry Huck and his crew around the store while they assessed what had to be repaired. "They'll replace the roof before it rains again. The upstairs has to be gutted. New floor up there and new ceiling in the store." He grinned, ran his long fingers through his hair. "Otherwise, the building's in good shape."

At noon on the third day after the storm, Amelia leaned wearily against the counter they had moved to the front porch. "Hans, you're a merchandising genius. Look at this crowd. They're snatching clothing and fabric. Most of it's still wet and even stained."

"That's because we cut the price. They think they can clean it up and use it." He grinned at Amelia. "And they can."

The sale on the front porch continued for over a week while they slowly cleared out the store to make room for repairs.

A couple of weeks later, Branson was visiting, inspecting the repair work on the store, when a ship docked at the Morgan pier with Indianola's first load of ice. He raced back to report on the shipment. "We can have ice cream. And water can be cold. Are you going to sell ice in the store?"

"If we can get walls built thick enough and plenty of sawdust to keep it from melting."

"You'll have lots of business. When they taste those cool drinks, they'll be here for ice every day."

"Did you have ice cream often in New York?"

"The whores loved it. Those from the South liked ice in their tea with sugar. I liked it too. But not as much as ice cream."

Amelia ordered ice picks and a few zinc-lined boxes to test the interest in keeping ice at home. They sold out immediately to locals and to California-bound travelers who had heard ice had to be shipped to California from Russia. They didn't want to wait when they got rich for the arrival of an ice box. She also ordered hand-cranked ice cream makers like those she had seen in New Orleans. They didn't stay on the shelf for long.

The August 7, 1851 issue of the *Texian Advocate* made quite a stir among the gathered crowd. Casimir Villeneuve, known for his flamboyant French style and penchant for advertising, had sent a huge block of ice bundled in sawdust to the Victoria paper. The editors wrote a long, wordy story about sharing it with their "neighbors and the boys, who had a glorification over it."

The laughter was long and loud. There also was a certain amount of pride. After all, Indianola had ice.

Amelia awoke to pounding on the door downstairs. She found Eva in the kitchen, wringing her hands and crying. "It's Frau Fischer."

Dr. Stein took her arm and rushed out the door without looking at Amelia.

His message is clear. I'm not part of his friendship with Hans and his mama. She dressed quickly and hurried along the dark street toward Frau Fischer's. Candles burned in all the rooms. Dr. Stein's lantern glowed in Frau Fischer's bedroom. The old lady, a white night cap halfway off her graying hair, was dead, propped up in her half-tester Mallard bed. Her fingers, burdened with rings that sparkled in the candle and lantern light, were folded like she was in the midst of her evening prayers. Hans was sobbing in Dr. Stein's arms.

"She went easy, Hans. Look at her face. Not a frown. It could have been so bad. Her heart must have quit."

He's stroking Hans' hair, and caressing his shoulders like he's a child. She turned away when Dr. Stein led Hans into the parlor and closed the door.

She sat at the kitchen table with Eva, who kept twisting her handkerchief and repeating, "She was fine last night. I tell you, she was fine. Ate a good supper. Not a lot. She never ate a lot. I tell you, that boy let out a yell. Sounded like a wolf howling. Scared me something awful. He's gonna have a time without his mama."

When Eva was ready to help Amelia prepare Frau Fischer's body, they selected one of her blue morning dresses in layers of soft muslin. Bending to remove Frau Fischer's dressing gown, Amelia was struck by a smell so foul she had to breathe through her mouth.

"It's her breast." Eva grabbed a rag and scooped the soiled dressing from Frau Fischer's chest. "She changed those rags several times a day. I never saw the breast, but I buried those rags as fast as I could."

Amelia stared at the mass of purple lumps that had oozed thick yellow pus across Frau Fischer's chest. "Did Hans know how bad she was?"

"Goodness, no. She was very modest. Very clean. Scrubbed herself with lye soap every time she changed the dressings."

"I didn't dream she was so thin. This must have been horribly painful."

"She never said a word. I could see the pain in her eyes. She was a hard woman sometimes. Other times she was good to me, like a sister."

"She was far stronger than I realized." Amelia gently washed the stink from Frau Fischer's chest.

At daylight, Amelia went to Conrad's and selected the most beautiful walnut casket in his shop. Conrad had carved lilies into the lid and lined the wood with soft blue velvet. When she returned, Dr. Stein and Hans were still closed in the parlor.

"Conrad will deliver the casket later this morning."

The repairs on the store were almost complete, and some of the new merchandise had arrived. Amelia spent the day unpacking and waiting on customers. Several patients stopped at the office looking for Dr. Stein. They left when they read the note that she had placed on the office door. Others came to the store to find out what had happened to call the doctor away for a whole day.

Anna and Harriet took charge of accepting food and arranging for the service to be held the next day at the new Presbyterian Church building. Amelia didn't hear Dr. Stein return that night. When she rose at daylight, he was already in his office.

She reached the church just as Hans and Dr. Stein entered the front door. Hans' hair was perfectly combed in the usual way over one brow, and his dark brown suit looked like the fashions Amelia had seen in New Orleans. His face was ashen, and he leaned like an old man on Dr. Stein.

The church was so packed that people stood outside. Hans had won the heart of the town with his beautiful voice and his charming ways with all the customers at Stein Mercantile. The days when people laughed about Frau Fischer's precious son were long forgotten.

Just as Hans had said, he did not continue living in his mama's house. He moved within days to the spacious, newly rebuilt rooms above the store. The half-tester Mallard bed and armoire fit perfectly under the high ceiling in the upstairs bedroom. He rented his mama's house and employed Eva to live in one of the store's back rooms that she entered from stairs on the outside of the building. She may have been near Hans's age, but she cooked, cleaned, and pampered him just like she was his mama. Hans adjusted better to the loss of Frau Fischer than Eva. He complained that every plate she sat before him brought fresh tears.

He ordered chairs and lounges for his parlor and furniture for his dining room from Francios Seignouret. He and Amelia and Branson had fun searching for Seignouret's trademark *S* on each piece. He also ordered a case of the Bordeaux wine. Amelia thought he would soon begin entertaining in his handsome bachelor's quarters, but if he did, she did not know about it. She and Dr. Stein dined with him often and decided that Eva had indeed learned to cook. Even her cakes were light and fluffy.

Soon after Hans settled upstairs, Amelia received a long letter from Maria Christina, telling about her wedding that was planned for early spring. "It's going to be such a big affair that Mama has already moved to Mobile to get it organized."

Hans wanted to hear the letter. "It sounds like she'll have all kinds of attendants. A wedding dress from New York should be spectacular. Don't you wish you could go?"

"It would be a lot of fun," Amelia laughed.

"It would really make me jealous if you went without me." Hans shook his head and hurried to the front of the store to wait on a customer.

Hans is showing more interest in the wedding than he ever showed in Maria Christina. Amelia set about writing Maria Christina a long letter. She decided not to mention Hans until Maria Christina asked about him.

Chapter Forty-One

Decisions...

Stein Mercantile was more crowded than usual on the bright January morning in 1852. The *Indianola Bulletin* had published the port's first newspaper. John Henry Brown, editor, wrote that his weekly publication would be "more strictly commercial, agricultural, and miscellaneous than political," a fitting philosophy for a port bent on cooperation for the financial benefit of all.

The new publication added a second day of the week for residents to gather at Stein Mercantile for a dose of news and a chance to argue about what was happening in their world.

Near the second anniversary of Amelia and Al's meeting, a letter arrived addressed to A. Stein, the return read A. Waters. The envelope of a rich, heavy paper, was not thick. It could not have held more than two pages. Clutching it against her chest, she darted between wagons, ignoring teamsters who pulled hard on their mules to let her pass.

Her breath came in gulps as she mounted the stairs, rushing up the hall to her bedroom, and crumpling into her rocking chair. The words began, *Precious, a day has not passed without you in my mind and tugging at my heart. You should get this near our second-year mark. I've wondered if you are raising my child, if it is a girl or a boy. I know the child is beautiful because he belongs to you. I pray your life is content.*

My brother passed a year ago. His wife has struggled to manage the large interests. She has asked me if I would consider marrying her to give her stability and help manage her affairs.

I want you, Amelia. I am writing in early March. I hope to hear from you by the end of June telling me to come for you. If I do not hear, if I finally must accept that I cannot have you, I will marry Samantha the first of August.

Please let me come for you. I will live anywhere and do anything that will make you happy. Even if I do not hear, I will hold you forever in my heart.

She pulled the pages against her belly, clutching at the raw core of pain cutting at her middle.

"Amelia, what's wrong with you?" Dr. Stein loomed like a tower in the doorway, his face a mask of horror. "You were almost run over stumbling across the street. As soon as my patient left, I started up here. You howled like a wild animal." In one bound he was across the room bending over her, pulling the pages from her fist.

She wanted to protest, to hold Al's words for her own. Her body would not respond. It had grown limp.

He slumped on the bed, the pages teetering like fragile bones on his fingertips. "Is this it?"

Amelia raised her head to look at the sag of his body. "Would you care?"

His mouth fell open, and his head sagged backward. "I know I've not been what you wanted. You made it clear when you deliberately took a lover." He hunched forward, his darkly circled eyes, pleading. "I wanted to be a normal man, have a family. I can't do it. Will you ever forgive me?"

She bent to pick up Al's letter that Dr. Stein had let flutter to the floor. "I suppose we both need forgiving."

"I'll try to look like a good husband."

"I never cared how you looked. I wanted a real marriage." She wanted to scream the words at him, but her breath barely carried her words. She folded the letter, held it between her palms like sacred writ.

The days passed. She heard Dr. Stein speaking to her, even touching her shoulder in the way he had done in the beginning, but he no longer stirred her desire. Only Branson's visits roused her from the stupor that fogged her days. She carried Al's letter in her pocket, pressing against her. She spent evenings in her rocker, reading his words, holding the thickness of the pages against her face. It would be easy to write, tell him to meet her in New Orleans. Board a ship and sail away. Then, her thoughts returned to what she would leave behind: Branson bursting into the store to share the details in his latest book or report on one of their sick horses. His daily presence became almost more than she could bear, filling her with love and tormenting her with the prospect of leaving him. He wobbled around the store, so at home, so comfortable with the customers. He knew he belonged. It was his second home. Dr. Stein would pretend he didn't know what had happened. He would be pitied for having a wife that would leave him. And she would be scorned for pretending to be the dependable town-crier, the reader of the news. Harriet would be the only one who understood, and she would remain silent. It was Branson who mattered for he would never understand why she left him. Finally, she knew what she had to do. Branson had become too much a part of her life, too much the child she always wanted.

She would not torment Al with more expressions of her love. Receiving her letter would lift his hopes, and her words would crush him once again. She knelt before Frau von Ewald's beautiful trunk and tucked Al's letter under the christening dress she had bought for Albert and young Otto's stiff little pony, *Galopp*. Then, she lay down beside the trunk and let the hardness of the floor press into her until sleep finally brought relief.

One morning in early June, Hans was late coming down to the store. He had been managing for himself or eating with the Steins or other friends for a week because Eva and Clara had saved enough money to take Masters Stage Line to New Braunfels to visit their parents. They would not return for two months. Amelia had opened the store, served several customers, and was greeting the usual crowd who came for the reading of the news. With two newspapers coming every week, each with a different focus on matters of importance, Stein Mercantile hosted twice-weekly newspaper readings and discussions.

She had already started reading about the upcoming vote to determine if Indianola would become the new Calhoun County seat of government when she noticed Hans had come downstairs and moved slowly into the store. His face was flushed. After the discussion ended, while people were milling around the store, he came to her, "I'm not feeling well. I'm going to see if Joe has something for my throat and my head."

Amelia patted his shoulder and felt the heat through his shirt. "When you get back, go upstairs and rest for the day."

She was so busy, she did not see him return from Dr. Stein's office.

She closed the store late and met Dr. Stein as she crossed the street. "I'm checking on Hans. I sent him to bed."

Amelia boiled vegetables and mashed potatoes. When Dr. Stein did not return, she left the food warming and went upstairs to work on the books. Hans' bedroom windows were dark. Dr. Stein's house calls lasted until well after Amelia fell asleep.

The next morning, Dr. Stein hurried through his breakfast. "This is the worst time for Eva to be off visiting her family. Until Hans feels better, will you take him part of our supper? I'll take some bread and butter over this morning. Will you chop some ice?"

The days spread into five weeks with Dr. Stein becoming more concerned each day. "I've bled him and given him quinine and mustard plasters, but nothing's relieving the fever or the headaches."

Anna and Harriet took food to him, and customers brought gifts of food and flowers. Each day, when Amelia went up to his apartment, she found him more listless and unresponsive. He grew so thin his cheekbones became pronounced, and his fingers looked like claws.

"His cough is deep and strained." Dr. Stein paced the floor, his boots clumping as loudly as the thunder, which was bringing much-needed rain. Dr. Stein became more agitated waiting for Amelia to finish preparing potato soup for supper. "I'm going on. Eat without me."

"It'll be done soon. Hans loves this soup."

"He's not eating. Besides, he has plenty of soup that Anna brought him for lunch." Dr. Stein picked up his bag, ignored his slicker hanging on a hook by the door, grabbed Amelia's store key, and let the screen slam shut behind him.

She ladled some of the steaming potato soup into a crock, covered it, and slipped into Dr. Stein's huge slicker. Starting out the side door, she stuffed the large ring of keys to all their buildings into the slicker pocket.

She stepped off the porch and was startled at the pellets of ice cutting her face, an eerie twist of nature for early July that made her shudder. The walkway felt slick. Rows of day lilies along the wood fence were bowing under the force of the hail. Making her way down the steps into the muddy crunch of the shell street, she could see a faint glow from the upstairs window over the store.

She set the crock on the bench stretching under the store windows and sorted the keys to all of Dr. Stein's buildings. Each key was tied with a different colored piece of heavy twine. In the darkness, she fumbled with three of the cold pieces of metal before the fourth yielded easy entry.

She made her way between the narrow cases of threads and Hans's favorite silk scarves and fine leather gloves to the stairway shrouded in darkness at the rear of the store. Inching her way to the top, she heard the deep, guttural groan that was part cough and part gasp for air.

"I'm with you, my precious." Dr. Stein's voice trembled. He lay on the bed, holding in his arms the twisting skeleton that had been Hans.

She stood, a marble statue, holding her breath as the scene unfolded. Dr. Stein lifted Hans, kissing the white, shrunken face, stroking his mass of dark hair. "My precious, my precious."

The heat of the pot against her belly roused her from her frozen state. "Here's your supper." She set the pot on a table, cluttered with vials of medicines. In a dreamlike stupor, she turned to leave.

"Amelia? I didn't hear you come in."

"I'm not staying."

"Wait. Amelia."

"No."

She felt her way down the stairs, bumping the wall. Store aisles grabbed at her, keeping her from running. Bile ran hot in her mouth, making her gag as she flung open the front door, vomit spewing down her front and onto the porch. The night air slapped cold against her face. Her body inside the slicker rattled like it was having a chill. She waded through the darkness and slush of the street, clutched the fence to the side door and went through the motions, the prescribed routine—wiped her feet, left muddy shoes at the door, hung the slicker next to the ring of keys, and slipped her feet into the warmth of knitted house shoes.

Her rocker's open arms held her as she stared blindly into the black night.

Chapter Forty-Two

The pieces will never fit together again...

Sharp light of the rain-washed morning filled the bedroom where Amelia sat in her rocker wrapped in the woolen blanket Frau Fischer had crocheted with such loving care. In mid-summer, when humidity made each breath feel damp, she felt cold as a dead body.

Wagons crunched through the slush, drying it to rutted dust. Boots scraped along the wooden sidewalks and patients rapped on Dr. Stein's door. Greetings muffled by the shouts of teamsters and the rhythm of Spanish chatter among the carreta drivers were no different from any other day, yet it had become foreign. She sucked in her breath like a drowning victim gasping for air. The dullness from having sat awake all night pulled at her eyelids.

Dr. Stein's boots shuffled on the back stairs. "Amelia? Are you up here?" His voice sounded high-pitched, the sound of a stranger. He stood in the doorway, his face ashen, his hair a mass of tangles like a wild thing.

"Precious. You called him Precious."

"You heard?"

"Yes."

He crumpled to his knees, tears streaming down his face. "He's gone. My precious is gone."

She sat perfectly still in her rocking chair staring at the bowed figure.

His long fingers covered his eyes. He sobbed like a child and rocked. "I'm sorry I've done this to you. I'm sorry you had to know what an abomination I am." He raised his head, staring at her.

"Amelia, I could not help myself. I could not help it."

"You let me think you couldn't make love. You shamed me for finding love when all the time you were doing that with Hans. Having—whatever you had—with a man I thought you were helping. You let me think you were the good doctor watching over Hans. You used our marriage to hide your secret."

Dr. Stein shook his head. "Amelia, I've loved you. I still love you. But Hans was different."

"You've loved me like a sister. Your maiden sister."

He cried with such painful force that she knew he needed her comfort, needed her to fold him in a tight embrace, hold him while the pain tore through him. She did not move from her chair.

"Who's preparing his body?"

"I did. I want to take him to the cemetery today."

She stood, anger shaking her with a trembling urge to beat him, to made him bleed. "I didn't go to Al when he wrote because I thought it would shame you in this town." She stopped, stared down at the man rocking in torment. "That's not the truth. The real reason I didn't go was because I couldn't bear to leave Branson. He has become the child you refused to give me. My God, Dr. Stein, if this town knew what you were doing with Hans..." She walked past him, felt his tug at her skirt. "I can't stand to touch you."

She heard deep gut-ripping sobs as she went down the stairs.

Anna arrived soon after Amelia started the fire in the stove. She grabbed Amelia in a tight embrace. "Let's make coffee and sit in your parlor."

"Let's stay here in the kitchen." *I hear my words. Another curtain drawn between me and my best friend. Am I protecting Anna from knowing or Dr. Stein from being exposed?*

Food began arriving along with condolences for the charming young man who offered such friendly service and quality merchandise. And special concern was extended to dear Dr. Stein, who had taken in the boy after the death of his mama.

By afternoon the heat had returned, the bay lay still, and no air stirred anywhere. She found Dr. Stein across the street with the pastor and a large gathering of townspeople in Hans' apartment. The death odor had been washed away and Hans, despite his sunken cheekbones and pallid color, looked handsome in his black suit and tie.

Your secret will be buried with you. Did Dr. Stein complain to you about my broken marriage vows? Did he assure you that my baby wasn't his? That you did not need to be threatened by me? Is that why you were so kind to me? She bolted from the room before she reached in the coffin and grabbed the dead body, before she threw the corpse at Dr. Stein. She pushed past people coming up the stairs, offering condolences, patting her shoulder.

They can think what they wish of me. She crossed the street, made it back upstairs to her rocking chair.

She walked to the cemetery beside Dr. Stein, who looked like a dead man, staring vacantly at the beautifully polished walnut casket. Hans was buried next to Frau Fischer.

Did she ever imagine what her son was doing with Dr. Stein? Amelia's eyes moved to where the sun cast a warm sheen on the lamb nestled in the arms of the iron cross over baby Albert's grave. *Albert will always be my darling. He will never break my heart.*

The large crowd of mourners began drifting away. *In a few days, Al will marry Samantha. Another marriage of convenience, an empty place where people go when there is nowhere else to turn.* She leaned against Anna and Harriet, who each slipped an arm around her as they walked back to town. They were like her sisters, her only family in this place.

The hours and then the days passed as the routine moved Amelia and Dr. Stein silently through their parallel lives. At night, she lay in bed watching stars blanket the sky, wondering if Al was staring at the same heavens. Other times, when she could not stop imagining him making love with Samantha, she focused on the sounds of Dr. Stein thrashing in his bed, pacing the floor, and then going downstairs. His footsteps clunked on the wooden walkway below the windows until they disappeared into the darkness toward Old Town.

Early one evening, they were about to begin supper when a well-dressed man, top hat under his arm, appeared at their door. "Forgive my intrusion. My name is Andrew Frazier. I am Hans Fischer's lawyer. I've been in New Orleans and returned this afternoon to discover that my client passed in my absence."

Amelia opened the door. "I remember meeting you when the Boundary Commission came through town."

He smiled. "Yes, that's when I met Hans. We became friends."

Dr. Stein shook the lawyer's hand and waited.

"I have Mr. Fischer's will. You, Dr. Stein, are the sole beneficiary except for a generous gift to his housekeeper, Eva."

What's he saying about Hans? "We'll give you Eva's address in New Braunfels. She's decided not to come back to Indianola."

Dr. Stein hunched forward, jaw sagging, fingers raking through his hair. "I never expected Hans would leave anything to me."

"Well, he did, Sir. And it's sizable. He has sold most of his holdings in the old country. A few transactions are still pending. Shall we go over that now?"

This is business. It isn't personal. "Why don't you go up to the parlor. I'll bring some coffee." She pointed Mr. Frazier toward the stairs. Dr. Stein walked in a daze, clutched the stair rail, pulling himself as if his weight was almost too much. His feet clumped along the upstairs hall.

When she carried the tray into the parlor, Dr. Stein appeared near tears. "Do you mind staying? You handle our affairs. I can't absorb this by myself."

Andrew Frazier placed his top hat carefully on the sofa next to him. Opening the folder of papers, arranging the sheets precisely with the edges straight as razors, he began his recital. "Mr. Fischer managed his mother's holdings. When she passed, it all came to him. He invested in many local enterprises and in banks in New Orleans and New York."

When Mr. Frazier had finished his business and given instructions for their next legal steps, she ushered him downstairs. Dr. Stein remained slumped on one of the little parlor chairs, staring at the floor.

Mr. Frazier smiled and bowed slightly. "I hope I haven't upset Dr. Stein. I've never had anyone be so reluctant to inherit a fortune."

"Surprised. I think Dr. Stein was just too surprised to take it all in."

"Well, good evening, madam."

He had not moved from the chair when she returned. He looked up, his face a sickly white. "Thank you, Amelia, for not walking out on me. You could have so easily told the whole town about me. Let them know about my hidden life. Told them what a monster I have become."

She sat on the sofa, her knees almost touching his. "I don't know what you are. I don't understand any of it. I do know that you are not a monster."

"I don't want Hans' money, Amelia. I loved him; I couldn't help loving him. Taking his money makes me feel filthy. Help me think of what we can do with it."

She reached for his arm, the first time she had touched him since before Hans died. It felt hard and thin under his black coat. "Why don't you go to bed? We don't need to make decisions tonight."

The next morning, Amelia rose before light, left hot cereal on the stove for Dr. Stein, and crossed the street. For the first time since the funeral, she climbed the stairs to Hans' apartment. The store lantern cast a yellow glow into the shadows. The rooms were a miniature version of a house as lavish as the von Ewald's. Every lamp, chair, and table was placed at a precise angle to complement its shape or color. Paintings, tiny porcelain figures, all blended into a picture of wealth. The last room, the bedroom, looked like Prudent Mallard's "curiosity depot."

When Hans had begun receiving shipments from New Orleans, and as far away as New York, she'd imagined that he was preparing his apartment to welcome some of the ladies who were so attracted to him. Now, standing in the room with his Mallard half-tester piled high with pillows and a royal blue satin covering, she realized he created it to welcome Dr. Stein. Her hand touched the walnut post at the foot of the bed and gripped its smoothness.

They were together here. Turning, she clutched the wall as she stumbled toward the door and down the stairs.

Harriet came to the store late in the afternoon. She waited until there was a lull in customers. "I need to talk to you. I've put it off as long as I can."

That lovely face is a picture of sorrow. Amelia caught her breath, fear gripping her heart.

"Charlie and I think Branson needs more opportunities for an education than he's getting.

Amelia began nodding, her throat getting tight.

"Rachel's smart and runs a good school, but Branson's already beyond what she can offer."

Branson's not mine. He's not mine. She kept nodding, waiting for Harriet to go on.

"Charlie's in San Antonio more and more for this new mail contract. He's met some priests in the Society of Mary who are opening a school for boys the end of August. They've tentatively accepted Branson."

This isn't happening. God, don't take that child away. She tried to control her face, tried to smile, and nod approval.

"We think he needs to remain with us *and* have the educational opportunity." Harriet began speaking quickly as if she wanted to hurry, get finished. "So, Charlie's rented a house, and we're moving the middle of August." She reached for Amelia's hands, "Sit down; you're pale as a sheet." She pulled Amelia to a chair behind the counter and knelt beside her. "Remember, we've got Troy coaches running constantly between here and San Antonio. There's no reason that Branson and I can't return often to see you."

I've got to breathe, suck in air. She forced a smile, pulled her hands into her gnawing middle. "I know it's best for Branson. He needs more challenges than we can provide."

"We talked to him about it last night. He's excited." Harriet pulled Amelia's hands away from her middle. "He wanted me to tell you before he comes in after school. He's worried about leaving you."

Amelia nodded, her throat so full she couldn't speak. She was relieved when Harriet finally stopped trying to make her feel better by sharing all the details of the school and of their move and hurried up the street toward the stables.

By the time Branson burst through the front door that afternoon, Amelia had made up her mind to greet him with the biggest smile she could manage. "I hear you have a wonderful opportunity."

Branson stopped, a question on his face for a moment and then he burst into a big grin. "I'll be learning Latin. It's a religious school, but I won't have to be a priest."

"Priests are well-educated. They can teach you more than you can imagine."

"The whores used to talk about how strict they are. Kick you out if you don't behave." He shrugged. "Miss Rachel said I wouldn't have trouble with that. She's awful glad for me."

Amelia reached for his boney shoulder, "We're all proud of you. You have a whole town who knows you'll be a good student."

"I can write to you. Practice my spelling. Maybe I can work in a San Antonio store to keep improving my arithmetic."

"Your adding and subtracting has improved so quickly. I know you will move right on to algebra. And the history you'll learn—"

"I want to learn about Germany, so I'll know about where you grew up."

I don't know how much longer I can pretend that my narrow little world isn't coming to an end. She grabbed him into a tight hug, smelling the stable odor that clung to him like a second skin. "I can't wait to know about all the things you'll be learning."

Branson had been patting her back, his head pressed against her breast. When she released him, he shoved at a tear with the back of his hand, smearing his dirty cheek. "I'll write you all the stuff I know, so you'll learn it too."

You'll do no such thing. You'll go on with your life like a normal boy with school, new friends, and a host of opportunities. She tousled his stiff, straw-like hair. "Why don't you help me empty some crates, and get some merchandise on the shelves before we close the store?"

She left supper on the stove and went upstairs to sink into the arms of her rocker. *This is my punishment, Papa. I deliberately broke my marriage vows. And I'm still not sorry.* She listened to Dr. Stein clattering around in the kitchen. He was coming home far earlier than he had for several years. After Hans died, she realized the late-night house calls her husband had been making were to see his lover. He used those times he claimed to be counseling Hans and comforting him after Frau Fischer died to hide what they were doing. And no one ever suspected because he was a happily married man.

He leaned in the bedroom door, "Goodnight."

"Did you hear that Charlie and Harriet are moving to San Antonio to get Branson in a new school?"

He eased like a shadow into the room, sat down hard on her bed. "That can't be true. Why would they do that to you?"

"They're thinking of Branson, not me. He needs far more than we can offer."

His shoulders sagged, and he stared at her. "You love that child," His face twisted in pain. "He's the only reason you've stayed here."

"It's too late now," her voice caught. "Al's married his brother's wife."

"So, you're not leaving?"

"Are you worried about your reputation?"

His head dropped into his hands, his elbows sinking to his knees, "I don't want to lose you, Amelia. I still love you. I never stopped loving you." He lifted his head, his eyes black circles of grief. "I've hurt you in the worst way a man can hurt a woman. I can't change the way I am. My own parents would be horrified if they knew what they had raised—a Jewish man who loves another man..." He stood slowly and started out the door.

"I know how I want to spend some of Hans' money."

He stopped and turned to look at her.

"I want a family. I want Helga and the children to come and give me a family. The von Ewalds will never let them stay on the manse property after Papa passes. They've let Papa stay out of respect for all his years pastoring for them and for the village. When he's gone, they'll want to find another pastor."

He nodded. "That's a good idea."

She continued, "Max can run the store. He'll get along very well with Hans' customers. He's a likable man, a terrific entertainer. Helga will need to have an income. I want to build a boarding house for Helga to operate. We need one on the road out toward Old Town, on our property that fronts the beach."

He leaned against the door frame as though he needed support. "What about Max's drinking? We'll need someone to be in the store if he gets drunk."

Ignoring him, she went on, "We'll need someone in the store from now on. I'll be getting the boarding house ready. I won't be working in the store every day."

He nodded. "Things will get better. I promise to make things better."

Chapter Forty-Three

Preparations for your arrival...

Branson shoved open the front door, a grin plastered across his face. "Look who's come to see the lighthouse get turned on." Three-year-old Isaac was swinging on Jessie's skirt, grinning shyly at Amelia. Jessie's arms were filled with the sleeping baby Jacob.

"Branson insisted we come early to get a good spot on the wharf."

Amelia picked up Isaac, whose compact little body required quite a lift. "It was a long, hot walk for Isaac's short legs." Balancing him on her hip, she chipped a piece of ice for him to suck, then set him down to roam the aisles. She handed Jessie a glass of cool tea.

Jessie shook her head as Branson hurried out the back door to save their place on the dock. "Micah will be along soon. He's helping Harriet hitch horses for a late stage coach headed to Victoria. She sent Branson to see the lighthouse start flashing. He's talked of nothing else for days."

Well before dark, people began crowding all along the waterfront. Amelia closed the store and scooped Isaac into her arms. "Let's find Branson."

Branson shouted as they approached, "Can you believe we can see that light all the way from Matagorda Island? The lighthouse is seventy-nine feet tall. Painted in red, white, and black stripes." He closed his eyes. "I wish I could see that thing."

Amelia was glad the evening would be clear. The whole town had been anticipating this night for several months. The light would be visible for sixteen miles. Its prefabricated cast iron parts had been delivered several months before and left on the island at Pass Cavallo until a similar lighthouse could be constructed on Bolivar Point across from Galveston.

"Let Isaac sit on my shoulders. He can see better from up here." Branson turned his back, waiting for Amelia to set the little boy firmly on his shoulders. The child grabbed a clump of Branson's blonde hair in each black fist and held on, his fat legs circling Branson's neck.

Jessie moved to one side of Branson and Amelia to the other. Isaac gazed about squealing with delight. "Get up, get up horsey."

"See how he loves it." Branson bounced his shoulders. "Jessie always walks with us. She thinks I'll drop him, but I never do."

At dusk, the blast of light lit the sky, forming a wide white streak that disappeared immediately. The entire harbor exploded in a roar. Branson, and then Isaac, yelled with the crowd. The baby Jacob jerked awake and then settled down as his mama nuzzled his cheek and ear, whispering something that he could not have heard over the explosions of gunfire and long blasts from steamer whistles. In ninety seconds the flash came again, prompting another round of celebration. Isaac kicked his feet, bucking on Branson's back. "Go, Branson. Go, Branson."

After the lighthouse flashes continued for a while on ninety-second intervals, the shouting faded, and people began drifting away from the docks. As they started back down the pier, Isaac kept gripping Branson's hair and looking back, squealing with each blink of the light.

"He liked it, didn't he?" Branson grinned. "I knew he'd like the lights and all the noise."

Micah appeared out of the crowd, and Isaac began reaching for his father. "We got the team ready. Harriet said for you to come home. You've got chores before bedtime."

Branson turned around and stood very still, watching the steady blast of light. "Someday, I'm coming back from San Antonio and taking a ship out to see that lighthouse."

Amelia watched them walking toward Old Town. Isaac's head bobbed sleepily on Micah's shoulder. The top of Jessie's red plaid scarf was swallowed in the crowd. Branson carried the lantern Dr. Stein gave Micah and Jessie when they married. It made a wobbly swinging motion in rhythm with Branson's crutches.

My life is going to be empty without Branson shining his light in the dark corners. She turned back to the store, welcomed the stragglers who wanted to shop for a while longer before returning home.

They had planned a hurried breakfast, but Amelia could only drink a little coffee. Dr. Stein moved his food around on his plate and finally settled on coffee. The day had arrived for Charlie to move Harriet and Branson to San Antonio.

Dr. Stein stood, mumbling, "Let's get this over with."

Amelia finished loading the basket of fried chicken, loaves of bread, and Branson's favorite, pralines.

Dr. Stein's lantern made a yellow circle of light guiding them away from tidal water still puddling the road. Oncoming freight wagons and ox-drawn carretas, positioning themselves in line to unload at the wharves, gave Amelia and Dr. Stein a wide berth.

Micah and Charlie had mounded furniture and trunks on one of Charlie's huge freight wagons. Harriet was stuffing last-minute items in spaces between the furniture. Branson was everywhere, a beehive of energy with no place to light.

Harriet clutched Amelia's hands. "Remember, this is not goodbye."

Dr. Stein held the lantern high, so that Branson could rummage through Amelia's food basket. "You're doing the right thing. But we'll miss you, especially Branson."

"He'll eat every one of those pralines before we get beyond Old Town," Harriet said.

"Hey Branson, would you like to ride Old Bessie?" Charlie grinned at Harriet. "That'll keep him out of the pralines for awhile."

"Really?" Branson started toward the mules and then turned abruptly, threw his arms around Amelia's waist. *No matter how good the intentions, it will be a long time before I hold this child.* She clutched him against her. Too soon, he reached for Dr. Stein, letting his crutches drop as he pulled them both into his arms. "Next time I come back, I'll probably be too big to ride on Dr. Stein's back."

"I hope you don't wait that long," Dr. Stein stroked Branson's head.

Branson whirled away, handed his crutches to Charlie. In one quick motion, he grabbed the mule's mane and threw his wiry body onto the animal's broad back.

"I'll bring them back often." Charlie lifted Harriet onto the plank seat and scrambled up beside her.

Charlie slapped the reins—Branson waved like he was at the head of a parade—the wagon creaked slowly forward.

Isaac ran down the path from their house shouting, "Bye, Branson."

Branson turned on the mule's back and with his nubby hand, blew kisses to Isaac. Isaac and Jessie stopped and began blowing kisses to Branson.

Micah shoved hands deep into his pockets, his shoulders sagging. "Sure hate to see those folks leave. Old Town won't be the same. I best be getting the milking done. Don't make no sense to stop going about your business. It only feels like somebody died."

"You're right, Micah. I guess we'll be getting on with our business." Dr. Stein took Amelia's arm.

Amelia's voice broke, "Branson is the closest we'll ever come to having a child of our own."

"And, we've lost him." Dr. Stein fished out one of the cloths he usually carried in his medical bag and blew his nose. Then he reached for Amelia's hand, and they walked in silence back into town.

He's touching me. He needs the comfort of human contact as much as I do. She did not try to hide the tears that washed her face.

The weeks passed, and Amelia continued to look up, expecting Branson to burst in the store's front door lugging one of Dr. Stein's medical books or eagerly recounting the latest story he had read.

The Matagorda Island Lighthouse had stirred a lot of interest, but nothing fueled civic pride like the overwhelming vote to move the Calhoun County seat from Lavaca to Indianola. The *Texian Advocate* editor had visited both towns in the spring and had written glowingly: "All evidence of petty bickering, if that ever existed, has passed away." It may have passed, but there remained plenty of boasting about getting the county seat away from their neighbor up the bay.

When Amelia read to the store crowd from the October 23, 1852, *Texian Advocate* that Indianola had grown faster in the past nine months than any town the editor had ever seen, the gathering erupted with a recital of all the events proving that the editor was a well-informed gentleman.

A man with his top hat under his arm and a cane with a gold head clutched in the other hand spoke in a thick French accent. "I met Monsieur Villeneuve and his lovely wife in Paris. Their description of this city and its rapid growth persuaded me to come all this way to design for them the most luxurious hotel in the West."

"Is that a fact? They had to go all the way to Paris, France, when we've got Carl Vogel right here at home?" The comment came from a man whose teeth stuck out so far that he looked like he was grinning except that his crossed arms dispelled any thought that he felt friendly. All eyes turned toward the foreigner.

"Right you are," the Frenchman shouted. "It's masterful advertising. Hiring an outsider makes the Casimir House all the more intriguing. I predict every one of you will be pleased to discover a fully appointed bar and completely furnished game rooms."

The buck-toothed man was not giving up. "I doubt any of us will be using that fancy place. Just where is the monsieur putting it?" The sneer in his voice was not lost on the grinning crowd.

The Frenchman started toward the door. "Watch for construction on Main Street. It will be situated to accommodate first class steamers from New Orleans."

"Seems to me that new wharf will do a lot more for this town than a fancy hotel." A young man Amelia had never seen spoke above the mumbling that followed the Frenchman. "It's sixteen feet wide and 1,500 feet long. A warehouse is going to be built out on the T-head. Five ships will be able to dock at the same time."

All eyes switched to the other newcomer who seemed perfectly comfortable being the focus of their curiosity.

"Did you come in with the outfit that's building the wharf?"

"Last week. I've been staying on the T-head. Sort of a night watchman."

"What else do you do?" A man put down his copy of the paper and eyed the stranger.

"For now, I'm operating the floating pile driver." The man grinned. "Come out tomorrow and watch how it's done. We're driving palmetto log piles into the bay floor."

A couple of men muttered about all the fancy equipment, and the group began drifting away, except for the new wharf worker who had wandered over to dry goods on the opposite side of the store. "You must have good contacts in New Orleans." He pointed to a display of top hats and stick pins next to cravats in patterns and bold shades of reds and blues.

On closer inspection, the man didn't look like a laborer. His boots, as fine as Hans', were polished to a sheen, and his trousers were a good fit, not the coarse, loose muslin of most dock workers.

"You're familiar with New Orleans merchants?" Amelia extended her hand and introduced herself.

He bowed graciously, "Cedrick Franz, from Oldenburg four years past. I hired on for this wharf project in New Orleans. Truthfully, I heard from some travelers that Stein Mercantile in Indianola might be needing a man who knows how to run a store."

"That's why you came all this way?"

"Afraid so, madam. New Orleans is a thriving, dirty place. I knew a German town would be thriving and clean. Is it true you might be looking for some help?"

"Tell me about your experience." Amelia motioned Cedrick Franz toward the counter and chipped ice for some tea."

"I grew up in my papa's haberdashery. He stocked the usual sewing items and fine fabrics. The economy's been bad, crop failures, and unemployment. His business is suffering. He begged me to make a fresh start where there's no conscription. The dream, of course, is that I'll get rich in Texas and send for my papa and my brother." Cedrick Franz grinned like a man willing to indulge their fantasies.

"This is the place for hard workers to do well."

He held out work-scarred hands. "These went from soft, Jewish merchant hands to calluses. I'll work hard if you'll have me."

Does he know Dr. Stein is Jewish? "Did you work in New

Orleans shops?"

"George Opdyke built a fine tailor shop on Canal. Just as I thought things were going well, Opdyke moved to New York and opened a mercantile store. Last I heard, he was getting rich."

"I bought trousers in his tailor shop. He must have moved soon after."

Cedrick Franz leaned close, gazing at Amelia. "How did you know about Opdyke?"

"Al Waters, a New Orleans merchant."

"My God. You know Al?" Cedrick Franz grabbed Amelia's hand. "You know he's gone off to some place here in Texas?"

"Yes." Amelia wanted to shake Cedrick Franz, to empty him of everything he knew about Al. "He was a helpful guide."

"My God, yes. He knows New Orleans inside out. You were lucky to meet him. Your merchandise shows his excellent taste."

"Would you like to give Stein Mercantile a try? We could see how we like each other."

"I would love it. When may I start?"

"As soon as you can leave that pile driving job on the wharf."

"How about tomorrow? I'll tell them first thing in the morning."

The following afternoon, Dr. Stein came in the store to meet the new man. He approached Cedrick Franz, who was bent over unpacking a new order of work clothes. "Welcome to Indianola and to Stein Mercantile."

Cedrick Franz shook Dr. Stein's hand for a long time. "I feel fortunate to have found you. When I saw this fabric and furniture. I knew it was the place for me."

"Amelia made a wonderful buying trip. Found good contacts."

"Al Waters was a lucky connection. He knows New Orleans merchants."

Dr. Stein leaned forward. "Are you speaking of Albert, Albert Waters?"

"Everyone calls him Al."

Dr. Stein ran his hand through his hair and turned away. "I'll let you unpack."

Amelia watched his awkward movement, his long arms bumping one counter after another until he reached the door.

Dr. Stein's exit was not lost on Cedrick Franz. His smile held an unasked question. "I better get busy if I'm going to get all these orders unpacked."

Amelia worked late tracking the inventory and showing Cedrick how she completed her orders. When she got home, Dr. Stein was not in his office. She heated sausage and went upstairs to work for a while. Quite late, she heard him rummaging around in his bedroom, then his boots dropped, and she knew he was crawling into bed.

In November, Helga's letter arrived. Papa had died in late August and lay at peace beside Mama. Helga and Max were grateful to receive the money for passage to Texas. The von Ewalds were allowing them a few extra days to vacate the property. Max was looking forward to a job in Dr. Stein's mercantile store. Helga wasn't sure how to operate a boarding house. She thought it must be like cooking and cleaning for a large family. The children were hardly able to contain themselves over the prospect of seeing their *tante*, Amelia. They were all speaking English. Even Anna was saying as many English words as German.

I rode away in the von Ewald's carriage without considering what Papa already knew—it was forever. She had rushed home from the store to read the letter. She sat in her rocker, clutching the pages to her breast. At first, she cried for her papa and then her tears were for all the losses.

Cedrick was as good with the customers as Hans had been. He was handsome in a raw kind of swaggering way, charming the women with his intense way of looking at them. Just like the first time he spoke up in the store, he had no trouble drawing attention to himself and making customers feel he was an authority. Men liked his easy manner and hint of coarseness left over from his work on the docks. Amelia liked how quickly he learned the merchandise, freeing her to work on Helga's boarding house.

Dr. Stein hired a local ship builder who drove corner posts six feet into the ground and fastened them together with metal crosspieces to make it one of the strongest houses in town. The first floor was almost higher than Amelia's head, and the framing to the second floor spiraled upward.

Micah hauled boards to the property and helped her stake out a garden behind the future boarding house. She intended for it to be thriving when they arrived.

The road in front served as the route to Victoria and beyond. A few houses had been built nearby, and the alley ran far enough behind the house to offer plenty of space for a hen house, smokehouse, and privy. The lot across the alley would be large enough for a milk cow.

Chapter Forty-Four

The Phoenix rises from the ashes...

Amelia leaned against her shovel, watching Anna approach with a jar of lemonade and plate of cookies.

Since the night Albert was born, she hasn't mentioned how alike our marriages are. And she has drifted slowly away like a feather on a calm sea. She dusted off a pile of lumber for a place to sit. "You know the perfect time to come with refreshments."

"When Joseph came home for lunch, he told me you were here working like a farmhand."

Our backgrounds are so different. Anna was raised in wealth. If it weren't for Papa being a pastor, we would have been peasants. "She smiled at Anna in her fresh morning dress and soft slippers. I'm eager to have a home ready for Helga."

"I need something to keep me busy. I'm still missing August. I should be happy since he's loving Rachel's school." Anna ducked her head. "I guess it's time to let you know; we're having another baby."

"That's wonderful. I noticed you were filling up your dresses. I thought you were getting round in the middle like I've been doing." Amelia tugged at her snug waist.

Anna laughed. "I thought maybe you were keeping a secret."

How I wish I could share my real secret. "I'm spreading out because I'm not working in the store. Cedrick knows about running a store, and he's learning the inventory quickly."

"Did you hear that Clara decided not to stay in New Braunfels? She's already started working for me."

"I'm glad she's back. You'll be needing her when this baby

comes."

"You didn't have someone after you lost Albert. You went back to work almost immediately. I feel like a weakling to ask for help."

"I wasn't being strong. I felt so lost that I didn't care if I hurt myself or even if I didn't get over the birth."

"Are you okay now?" Anna reached for Amelia's muddy hand.

She nodded, closed her eyes, and felt the sun warming her face. "My family coming is the best medicine."

Dr. Stein came in the store, stomping his feet to warm himself from the first icy blast from the north. "I ran into Captain Whipple. The pier's complete in time for winter shipping. I asked him to supper." He called to Cedrick, "why don't you join us? We'd like you to meet the captain."

"I'd be happy to come." He grinned at Amelia, who was already scooping flour to use for biscuits and picking up two bottles of Bordeaux.

She had offered Cedrick the little room that had been Eva's, concerned that its small cast iron stove was designed for heating more than cooking.

She fried a platter of chicken and made gravy using milk the way Harriet had shown her. The men ate and drank with gusto.

Leaning back and patting his belly, Captain Whipple said. "The fancy French food at Casimir House is good, but I've missed the home cooking at Mrs. Eberly's." He looked suddenly serious. "When Mrs. Eberly moved across the bayou to Brown's Addition, I decided not to follow. The hardest part of living at the Casimir House is being served by their slaves. Now that they've added a slave auction on the front porch every Wednesday and Saturday, I may be the first boarder at the Stein House when your sister gets here."

Dr. Stein poured more wine in all their glasses. "The Americans have convinced a lot of the businessmen that a slave auction will bring planters from up the Guadalupe and the Colorado rivers. Everyone wants that plantation business."

Captain Whipple raised his glass, "We need laborers on the docks. If we could get some of those slaves freed, we'd have a good work force. Here's to folks freeing their slaves."

"If shipping people got together, they could buy the slaves, free them, and then hire them on the docks." Cedrick sipped his wine. "I sound like my papa when I say that when I get rich, I'll do just that." He grinned sheepishly, "Papa's a big dreamer."

Dr. Stein stared at the faces around the table. "Why can't we do that? Amelia and I have a little money we don't need." He looked at Amelia, waiting for her response.

"I saw a slave auction in New Orleans. It was a terrible thing to watch."

"You have to be careful," Captain Whipple said. "You could buy one or two and a few weeks later buy one or two more. If you dominate the market, slaveholders, especially the planters, will turn on you in an instant. They're sensitive about protecting their valuable property."

"Are you really thinking of buying slaves and releasing them?" Cedrick looked first at Dr. Stein and then at Amelia.

"Let's try it." Dr. Stein's face brightened. "Maybe it's the Bordeaux, but I feel better than I've felt in a long time."

Before the evening was over, they had worked out a strategy for all three men to rotate the purchases to keep from drawing attention to themselves.

"Since, I'm staying in town to manage our new dock, I can help the men get places to live and understand how to survive as freedmen. Staying out of trouble is the first big test. This town's not looking to recapture slaves, but the law would allow them to be sold back into slavery to pay off a criminal offense."

"People wouldn't actually do that, would they?" Amelia was shaking her head.

"They do it in Galveston."

Amelia's heart sank, remembering that Fannie felt safer being a slave of Samuel May Williams than being free. And yet, being a Williams' slave and trying to run away had gotten poor Sarah sold to a planter.

"We'll need to get some houses built on our property out toward Powder Horn Lake." Dr. Stein looked at Amelia again and again for agreement.

"What about families? What about women? All three men turned to look at her. "I saw whole slave families in New Orleans."

"So far, they've auctioned farm laborers, strong men who could work the docks." Captain Whipple smiled, "We need women who can work in the homes, do sewing. If a family comes along, we don't want to let them be split up."

"I'd hire a seamstress or someone to clean Dr. Stein's office and our quarters."

"We'll do that. Look for help for Amelia," Cedrick lifted his glass and they all joined in another toast.

The auctions didn't work out as Amelia had imagined. All the slaves were strong young farm hands, and there were no women. Each time they skipped one of the auctions to keep from rousing suspicions, Dr. Stein came home and paced the floor worrying about what would happen to the men who were sold off to a planter up the river. Each time they had the same argument. He would say, "We can afford to free every slave that's coming through here."

And she would say, "No, we can't. Listen to the captain. He understands the American attitude toward slaves. This careful approach is working. Men are being freed, and we're not getting a fight going with the slaveholders."

In mid-December, Dr. Stein came home with another suggestion. "Cedrick plans to send for his papa and brother when he gets rich." Dr. Stein rubbed at his jaw and looked away from Amelia. In a low voice, he said, "I have to admit that Cedrick's better than Hans with the customers. Cedrick is more like ordinary people. Why don't we give him a Christmas bonus? Pay for his family to immigrate?"

Amelia looked at her husband's sagging shoulders and wondered what it would take to lift his burden? She'd hoped that the slave auctions would do that, but she often saw the faraway look in his eyes and the slump of his body.

Is he grieving for Hans like I've ached for Al? Amelia reached to pat his shoulder and drew her hand back as he turned toward the stairs.

"Why don't you tell Cedrick tomorrow that we want to bring his family to Indianola?"

He turned, his face breaking into a smile. "You're willing? It'll be expensive."

I feel no passion for this awkward, lonely man. He's hurt himself as much as he's hurt me. She shrugged. "We said we wanted to do good things with Hans' money."

"From what Cedrick says, they'll make good employees. Without you in the store, we can use experienced people."

The following day, Dr. Stein came to the store in the late afternoon as he and Amelia had planned. He paced the floor until Cedrick finished with his customer. "We have some good news."

"How many did you buy today?" Cedrick kept his voice low.

"It's not slaves. It's something we want to offer you."

Cedrick tilted his head, looking first at one and then the other. "You've aroused my curiosity."

Dr. Stein explained their wish to bring Cedrick's family to Indianola. Cedrick stared for a few seconds and then slumped against the counter shaking his head. "I think I'm dreaming. You'll pay for Papa and Ludwig to come all this way?"

"We need experienced employees in the store," Amelia said.

"We'll forward enough for them to close your papa's business and settle his debts."

"Please excuse me. I'm going to cry."

Amelia and Dr. Stein each laid a hand on Cedrick's shoulders and stood quietly while the young man sobbed.

Lifting his head, loudly blowing his nose, he said, "I'll write them tonight." He burst into laughter, "Before you change your minds."

"It's a firm deal." Dr. Stein reached around Cedrick's shoulder, squeezing him under his arm.

How many times did he hug Hans in that way? Amelia turned away, "I'm going to start supper."

The boarding house rose like a giant white beacon on the coast about a mile from Old Town. Conrad Swartz was as eager as Amelia to have the best and most spacious cupboards in the kitchen. He and his men built sturdy tables and benches for the dining room and strong, practical beds for all the rooms. Amelia had ordered an over-sized iron stove as the first item on her list. Bowls, pitchers, and chamber pots for each room arrived quickly from New Orleans. The pots and the dishes arrived in dribbles. She had insisted that the washroom be oversize to accommodate both laundry and washing of people. Mosquito netting with fabric sewed around the edges came in from stores in New Orleans.

Dr. Stein kept reminding her that Helga would need something to do when she arrived. "Cooking, cleaning, and running a boarding house will keep her busy," Amelia said and continued making preparations. She bought chickens and laying hens and hired Micah to salt beef and pork for the smokehouse.

All the time Amelia worked on the house, Cedrick worked on Hans's upstairs apartment. Soon after Hans died, they had moved his furniture to the store and sold almost all of it to wealthy Americans. Conrad's men built sturdy beds, tables, and chairs that turned the rooms into a comfortable home for Cedrick and his family.

Chapter Forty-Five

Together again...

Dr. Stein was not smiling when he came to the store following the February businessmen's meeting. "I've always been a skeptic. Believed if things start to feel like they're going just right, I better watch out. This is one of those times I should have been checking my backside."

Amelia poured a cup of coffee and motioned him toward the back of the store.

"We're getting some serious competition. An Irishman named D.H. Regan is moving his dry goods business across the street from the store, next door to my office. Men who know him say he's a strong merchant, caters to everyday kind of clothing, no frilly top hats or laces."

"I was told in New Orleans that when Indianola gets large enough, our store won't need to carry everything. Competition will push us to become a specialty stop. Do you suppose Indianola's grown that much?"

Dr. Stein looked away, stared out the window.

Please don't ask me who in New Orleans gave me that advice. She waited for his response.

Finally, his eyes returned to her, "That's not all. A German merchant who has had a store for several years in Columbia up on the Brazos River is opening a place here. He handles basic household items, orders good German-made farm tools and clothing. He's got connections with the planters up the Brazos. He'll undercut us on sugar, tobacco, and molasses." He called to Cedrick whose customer had just left the store.

Cedrick studied the floor as he listened to Dr. Stein's worries, and then he grinned. "You've got a tremendous following. A few customers will try the other stores, but the majority will keep coming right back here. They know you, and they trust you."

"We'll find out soon enough. They should both move in before the month's out."

"I figure it's a sign of Indianola's growth. You can't expect one store to meet the needs of a population that's growing as fast as this place." He swelled out his chest like a high-born nobleman, "Besides, we may decide to make Stein Mercantile a shop catering to Indianola's growing class that seeks the finer things."

Dr. Stein slapped Cedrick on the back. "You're good medicine."

Why do I notice him slapping Cedrick's back? She turned quickly and went to the front of the store to greet a customer.

Dr. Stein had walked out to the Stein Boarding House every few days during the construction. When the last of the furniture had been placed and the sign—**Stein House Room and Board**—hung over the long row of stairs leading up to the broad porch, he walked through the house with Amelia, inspecting every corner—the wraparound porch on both floors with doors and windows into every room, shutters on the west side to filter the afternoon sun, several beds in each room to accommodate families, and the stove large enough for preparing big meals. "You've thought of every detail. This is the finest boarding house in Indianola. It will be a good investment."

"I know they'll love it."

Dr. Stein paced along the hall, rubbing his palms together, "What do you think of charging sixteen dollars a month for one person in the two front rooms opposite the parlor? They're the best in the house. The upstairs rooms should go for fifteen."

He's ever the businessman, always thinking how to make a little more money. She stuffed her hands into her apron pockets and smiled at her preoccupied husband, "Thank you for making it possible."

"Hans' generosity's making a lot of good things happen. He knew we wouldn't waste his money."

She settled on one of the long wood benches in the parlor, closed her eyes, and felt the breeze off the bay blowing strands of hair loose from the single braid hanging down her back. "I've been worrying about some of my quick decisions. I know Helga can run this boarding house. She's smart, efficient, and tough, but I'm not so sure about Max managing the store. He's a lot of fun—until he's drunk."

Dr. Stein sprawled on the end of the bench, his legs splayed out and his head propped against the white, wood wall. "You've worked too hard to see the store fall apart."

She sat up straight. "I don't mean to make Max sound like a bad character. You'll like him. He's as rowdy as Cedrick." She grinned. "And women like him too. He's a brilliant musician. He'll be a tremendous asset to the Saengerbund." She exhaled, blowing a breath of resignation. "Do you think if we paid Cedrick well enough, he'd be willing to partner with Max, take on more than just being an employee?"

Dr. Stein plopped both feet on the wood floor and raised himself from the bench. "Let's go see how he feels about it."

This marriage is not what I wanted. It's not what Dr. Stein wanted. It's a business partnership that's working. She followed her husband out the front door.

Dr. Stein waited only long enough for Cedrick's customer to leave. "When Amelia's family arrives, are you interested in sharing managing duties with Max?"

Cedrick grabbed Dr. Stein's hand and stared up at him like a man in a trance. "Manager? I never expected to be a manager. I hoped that someday you'd let me buy in." He looked sideways at Amelia. "One day you're going to be ready for younger blood to take over."

My blood's only five years older than yours. Amelia looked at the men still clutching hands. She turned to leave, "I'm going to let you two figure out the details."

Helga's letter had said they would arrive about mid-April. Amelia spent the warming spring days working in both gardens and cleaning their quarters—tasks that she no longer had to squeeze in after a long day at the store. *When my family arrives, I won't need*

the store to fill that empty place in me, to keep me distracted from gnawing loneliness.

Cedrick drew large crowds with his reading each week of both papers. His looked perfectly comfortable—basking in the arguments —over boundaries the legislature drew for the newly incorporated city of Indianola. And he jumped eagerly into discussions of the election of a mayor and alderman and the appointment of a tax assessor-collector and city marshal.

I love the solitude of our gallery overlooking the downtown, yet removed from all the chatter. She focused her binoculars over the rooftops across the street and out into the bay to see what flags were flying on approaching ships.

The morning was clear, not a cloud marred the sky. The white sails rose like pointed sticks on the horizon. She returned again and again to the gallery with her binoculars. When the German packet took shape and headed straight for Captain Whipple's pier, she darted between freight wagons clogging the street and dodged prancing horses. Her boots thumped against the wooden pier as she hurried between waiting stagecoaches and ignored the snort of mules lined up next to two New Orleans bound ships.

Dock workers Dr. Stein had recently freed were hauling bales of gamma grass onto the first ship. At the end of the pier, they were heaving barrels onto their backs and toting them up the gangplank to a steamer. They sang a low, mumbling song in rhythm with their steps, reminding her of the foggy morning she had arrived in Galveston with the von Ewalds and had her first encounter with the slave dockworkers singing their mournful tune. She wondered if the sound comforted them, made it easier to keep moving as the heat intensified and the wood barrels bore into their bare flesh. Were they like Micah, so happy to be free that they found work a vehicle for satisfaction? She didn't know them. The men had very quietly made the purchases and negotiated the papers to set them free. Her only involvement had been ordering sufficient clothing and household supplies to get them established in the houses Dr. Stein was having built along Powder Horn Bayou. Two of the freedmen had opted to start a pig farm instead of working on the docks.

She had arranged her trips out to the boarding house at a time of day to avoid passing the slave auctions on the front porch of the Casimir House. The beautiful white building with its colonnaded front added a grandeur and prestige to Main Street. The richly polished woods in the game rooms and the handsome bar were the envy of all the hotels in town. Only the presence of a slave staff and the twice-weekly auctions stained an otherwise impressive business.

Passengers always lined the rails of incoming ships, but they looked different on immigrant vessels. The women wrapped their heads in wool shawls, and despite the heat, they stayed modestly covered. The men wore heavy, loose-fitting coats. By the time they were allowed to come down the gangplank, many were lathered in sweat and near fainting. They waved and called to shore, but were never as free with their shouts and greetings as travelers from New Orleans or other American ports.

Then, she spotted them—Helga pointing, directing the children's eyes toward the dock. They were no longer little ones, except for Anna. Helga was holding the blonde girl, pointing to her *tante* Amelia.

Trying not to bump the gentleman in the top hat standing next to her, Amelia jumped and waved her arms until the children picked her out of the crowd. The circle had closed. The family she wanted had arrived. Not the dreamed of family, but the real one.

The ship eased toward the dock until the thump and sliding sound of contact brought the vessel to a halt. Ropes arched toward dockworkers whose powerful black arms fastened the thick coils to pilings. The gangplank made a clumping sound as it slid against the dock. The faces became real and beautiful. Amelia moved forward, opening her arms to welcome her family.

ABOUT THE AUTHOR

Myra Hargrave McIlvain is a sixth generation Texan and a storyteller who began her career writing a family humor column while she raised her two children. After the nest emptied, her background in Texas history led to Austin where she wrote Texas historical markers that line the highways, designate historic homes, and chronicle the lives of cemetery residents.

McIlvain's love of a good story prompted her to write six nonfiction books about famous and infamous Texas sites and characters. Her most recent, Texas Tales, Stories that Shaped a Landscape and a People, is a collection of 113 of her favorite Texas history blog posts.

After several years offering Texas seminars, Myra and her husband began taking her classes on one-day historic trips that led to a worldwide tour business. When she retired, McIlvain lectured for the continuing education program at the University of Texas and other venues across the state. She published her first historical fiction in 2012 and is currently working on her fifth, *The Reluctant Bride*.

Whether she is telling stories in her books, her blogs, or her lectures, Myra McIlvain views history as the story of a people, and the people she knows best have made Texas home.